THE GOSPEL

ACCORDING TO

JESUS CHRIST

SHENENDEHOWA PUBLIC LIBRARY
47 CLIFTON COUNTRY ROAD
CLIFTON PARK, NEW YORK 12065

JOSÉ SARAMAGO

THE GOSPEL
ACCORDING TO
JESUS CHRIST

TRANSLATED FROM THE PORTUGUESE
BY GIOVANNI PONTIERO

Harcourt Brace & Company

NEW YORK   SAN DIEGO   LONDON

98948

FOR   PILAR

© José Saramago e Editorial Caminho SA, Lisboa—1991
English translation copyright © 1994 by Harcourt Brace & Company

All rights reserved. No part of this publication
may be reproduced or transmitted in any form or by any means,
electronic or mechanical, including photocopy, recording, or any
information storage and retrieval system, without
permission in writing from the publisher.

Requests for permission to make copies
of any part of the work should be mailed to:
Permissions Department, Harcourt Brace & Company,
6277 Sea Harbor Drive, Orlando, Florida 32887-6777.

This translation of *O Evangelho segundo Jesus Cristo* has been made possible,
in part, by a grant from the Instituto da Biblioteca Nacional e do Livro.

Library of Congress Cataloging-in-Publication Data
Saramago, José.
[Evangelho segundo Jesus Cristo. English]
The Gospel according to Jesus Christ/José Saramago;
translated from the Portuguese by Giovanni Pontiero.—1st ed.
p.   cm.
ISBN 0-15-136700-0
I. Pontiero, Giovanni.
PQ9281.A66E913   1994
869′.3—dc20   93-37595

Designed by Trina Stahl
Printed in the United States of America
First U.S. edition
A B C D E

FORASMUCH AS MANY HAVE TAKEN IN HAND TO SET FORTH IN ORDER a declaration of those things which are most surely believed among us, even as they delivered them unto us, which from the beginning were eyewitnesses, and ministers of the word; it seemed good to me also, having had perfect understanding of all things from the very first, to write unto thee in order, most excellent Theophilus, that thou mightest know the certainty of those things, wherein thou hast been instructed.

Luke 1.1–4

Quod scripsi, scripsi.
What I have written, I have written.

Pontius Pilate

THE SUN APPEARS IN ONE OF THE UPPER CORNERS OF THE
rectangle, on the left of anyone looking at the picture.
Representing the sun is a man's head that sends out rays
of brilliant light and sinuous flames, like a wavering com-
pass in search of the right direction, and this head has a
tearful face, contorted by spasms of pain that refuse to abate.
The gaping mouth sends up a cry we shall never hear, for
none of these things is real, what we are contemplating is
mere paper and ink, and nothing more. Beneath the sun
we see a naked man tied to a tree trunk with a cloth around
his loins to cover those parts we call private, and his feet
are resting on a piece of wood set crosswise, to give him
support and to prevent his feet from slipping, they are held
by two nails driven deep into the wood. Judging from the
anguished expression on the man's face and from his eyes,
which are raised to heaven, this must be the Good Thief.
His ringlets are another reassuring sign, for it is well known
that this is how angels and archangels wear their hair, and
so it would appear that the repentant criminal is already
ascending to the world of heavenly beings. Impossible to

1

say whether the trunk is still a tree that has been arbitrarily turned into an instrument of torture while continuing to draw nourishment from the soil through its roots, inasmuch as the lower part of the picture is covered by a man with a long beard. Richly attired in loose, flowing robes, he is looking upward but not toward heaven. This solemn posture and sad countenance must belong to Joseph of Arimathaea, because the only other person who comes to mind, Simon of Cyrene, after being forced to help the condemned man carry his cross, as was the practice when these executions took place, went about his own affairs, thinking more of a business transaction that called for an urgent decision than of the sufferings of a miserable wretch about to be crucified. Joseph of Arimathaea is that affluent and good-hearted man who donated a grave for the burial of the greatest criminal of all, but this act of generosity will be to no avail when the time comes to consider his beatification, let alone canonization. All he has on his head is the turban he always wears outdoors, unlike the woman in the foreground of the picture, whose hair hangs all the way down her back as she leans forward, enhanced by the supreme glory of a halo, in her case one edged with the finest embroidery. The kneeling woman must be Mary, because, as we know, all the women gathered here have that name, with one exception, she who is also called Magdalene. Anyone viewing this picture who knows the facts of life will swear immediately that this is the woman called Magdalene, for only someone with her disreputable past would have dared appear at such a solemn occasion wearing a low-cut dress with a close-fitting bodice to emphasize her ample bosom, which inevitably draws the lewd stares of passing men and puts their souls at grave risk of being dragged to perdition. Yet the expression on her face is one of contrition, and her wilting body conveys nothing other than her sorrowing soul, which we cannot ignore, even if it is hidden by tempting flesh, for this woman could

2

be completely naked, had the artist so chosen to portray her, and still she would deserve our respect and veneration. Mary Magdalene, if that is her name, is holding to her lips the hand of another woman, who has collapsed to the ground as if bereft of strength or mortally wounded. Her name is also Mary, second in order of appearance but undoubtedly the most important Mary of all, if the central position she occupies in the lower part of the picture has any significance. Apart from her grieving expression and limp hands, nothing can be seen of her body, covered as it is by the copious folds of her mantle and by a tunic tied at the waist with a coarsely woven cord. She is older than the other Mary, which is reason enough, although not the only reason, why her halo should be more elaborate, at least that is what one would conclude in the absence of more precise information about the privileges of rank and seniority observed at that time. Considering, however, the enormous influence of this iconography, only an inhabitant of another planet, where no such drama has ever been enacted, could fail to know that this anguished woman is the widow of a carpenter named Joseph and the mother of numerous sons and daughters, although only one of her children was decreed by fate, or whoever governs fate, to achieve a little renown during his life and a great deal more after his death. Reclining on her left side, Mary, the mother of Jesus, rests her forearm on the hip of another woman, also kneeling and also named Mary, who might well be the real Mary Magdalene although we can neither see nor imagine the neckline of her tunic. Like the first woman in this trinity, she lets her long tresses hang loose down her back, but to all appearances they are fair, unless it is only by chance that the pen strokes are more delicate here, leaving empty spaces between the locks and thus allowing the engraver to lighten the tone. We are not trying to prove that Mary Magdalene was in fact blond, but simply point to the popular belief that women with blond hair, whether it be natural or dyed, are the most effective instruments of sin. Mary Magdalene, who, as everyone knows, was as wicked a woman as ever lived, must have been blond if we accept the opinion held, for better or worse, by half of mankind. It is not, however, because this third Mary has skin and hair fairer than the first that we suggest, despite the damning evidence of the first's exposed bosom, that the third is the Magdalene. What confirms her identity is that this third Mary, as she distractedly supports the limp arm of the mother of Jesus, is looking upward, and her enraptured gaze ascends with such power that it appears to elevate her entire being, it is a light that outshines the halo already encircling her head, a light that overpowers every thought and emotion. Only a woman who has loved as much as we believe Mary Magdalene loved could possibly have such an expression, it is she and no other, and thus we rule out the woman standing beside her. This is the fourth Mary, her hands half raised in a gesture of piety and her expression vague, she is accompanied on this side of the engraving by a youth barely adolescent, his knee bent languidly while with an affected and theatrical right hand he presents the four women playing out the poignant drama in the foreground. This is John, who looks so youthful, his hair in ringlets and his lips trembling. Like Joseph of Arimathaea, he also blocks some of the picture, his body concealing the foot of the tree on the other side, where no birds nest. All we see at the top is a second naked man hoisted into the air and bound and nailed to the wood like the first thief, but this one has smooth hair and his eyes are lowered, perhaps still capable of seeing the ground below. His thin face arouses our compassion, unlike the third thief on the other side, who even in the final throes of torment defiantly shows his face, which was not always so pale, for thieving gave him a good living. Thin and smooth haired, the second man bows to the earth that will devour him, this pathetic creature condemned to both death and

4

hell must be the Bad Thief, an honest man when all is said and done, who, free of divine and human laws, did not pretend to believe that sudden repentance suffices to redeem a whole life of evil. Above him, also weeping and wailing like the sun in front, the moon can be seen in the guise of a woman with the most incongruous ring in one ear, an unprecedented liberty no artist or poet is likely to repeat. Both sun and moon illuminate the earth in equal measure, but the ambience of light is circular and shadowless, causing everything on the distant horizon to stand out clearly, turrets and walls, a drawbridge across a moat whose water glistens, Gothic arches, and, on the crest of the farthest hill, the motionless sails of a windmill. Somewhat closer, in this deceptive perspective, four horsemen in armor and helmets, bearing lances, proudly parade their horses with admirable dexterity, but they appear to have come to the end of their display and are making farewell gestures to an invisible audience. The same impression of closing festivities is given by that foot soldier who is on the point of going off, carrying something in his right hand that could be a cloth, perhaps even a mantle or tunic, while two more soldiers look annoyed, frustrated, as if they had lost at gambling, although from afar it is difficult to tell what is in their minute faces. Hovering over these common soldiers and the walled city are four angels, two of them portrayed full length. They weep and mourn, with the exception of the angel who solemnly holds a goblet to the crucified man's right side in order to collect the last drop of blood from a lance wound. In this place known as Golgotha, many have met the same cruel fate and many others will follow them, but this naked man, nailed by hands and feet to a cross, the son of Joseph and Mary, named Jesus, is the only one whom posterity will remember and honor by inscribing his initials in capitals. So this is he whom Joseph of Arimathaea and Mary Magdalene are gazing upon, this is he who causes the sun and moon to weep and who only a moment ago praised the Good Thief and despised the Bad Thief, failing to understand that there is no difference between them, or, if there is a difference, it lies in something else, for good and evil do not exist in themselves, each being merely the absence of the other. Shining above his head with a thousand rays brighter than those of the sun and moon put together is a placard in Roman letters proclaiming him king of the Jews, surrounded by a wounding crown of thorns like that worn, without their even knowing and with no visible sign of blood, by all who are not allowed to be sovereigns of their own bodies. Jesus, unlike the two thieves, has nowhere to rest his feet, the entire weight of his body would be supported by his hands nailed to the wood had he not life enough left in him to hold himself erect over his bent legs, but that life is nearing its end as the blood continues to flow from the abovementioned wound. Between the two wedges that keep the cross upright and that have also been driven into the dark ground, making a gaping wound there as irremediable as any human grave, we see a skull, also a shinbone and a shoulder blade, but what concerns us is the skull, for this is what Golgotha means, skull. No one knows who put these human remains here or for what purpose, perhaps it was simply a sly reminder to these poor wretches about what awaits them before they turn at last to earth, dust, and nothingness. But there are some who claim that this is Adam's skull, risen from the deep murk of ancient geological strata and, because it can not now return there, eternally condemned to behold its only possible paradise which is forever lost. Farther back, in the same field where the horsemen execute one last maneuver, a man is walking away but looking back in this direction. In his left hand he carries a bucket, and in his right a staff. At the tip of the staff there ought to be a sponge, not easy to see from here, and the bucket, one can safely bet, contains water with vinegar. One day, and forever after, this man will be much maligned, accused of having given Jesus vinegar out of spite and contempt when he asked for water, but the truth is that he offered him vinegar and water because at that time it was one of the best ways of quenching thirst. The man walks away, does not wait for the end, he did all he could to relieve the mortal thirst of the three condemned men, making no distinction between Jesus and the thieves, because these are things of this earth, which will persist on this earth, and from them will be written the only possible history.

NIGHT IS FAR FROM OVER. HANGING FROM A NAIL NEAR THE door, an oil lamp is burning, but its flickering flame, like a small, luminous almond, barely impinges on the darkness, which fills the house from top to bottom and penetrates the farthest corners, where the shadows are so dense that they appear to form a solid mass. Joseph awoke with a fright, as if someone had roughly shaken him by the shoulder, but he must have been dreaming, because he lives alone in this house with his wife, who has not so much as stirred and is fast asleep. Not only is it unusual for him to wake in the middle of the night, but he rarely opens his eyes before daybreak, when the gray, cold morning light begins to filter through the chink in the door. How often he has thought of repairing the door, what could be easier for a carpenter than to cover the chink with a piece of wood left over from some job, but he is now so accustomed to seeing that vertical strip of light when he opens his eyes in the morning that he has reached the absurd conclusion that without it he would be trapped forever in the shadows of sleep, in the darkness of his own body and the

8

darkness of the world. The chink in the door is as much a part of the house as the walls and ceiling, as the oven and earthen floor. In a whisper, to avoid disturbing his wife, who was still asleep, he recited words of thanksgiving, words he said each morning upon returning from the mysterious land of dreams, Thanks be to You, Almighty God, King of the Universe, who has mercifully restored my soul to life. Perhaps because he had not fully regained the power of all five senses, five unless at that time people were not yet aware there were five or, conversely, had more and were about to lose those that would serve little purpose nowadays, Joseph watched his body from a distance while it slowly was occupied by a soul making its gradual return, like trickling waters as they wend their way in rivulets and streams before penetrating the earth to feed sap into stems and leaves. Looking at Mary as she lay beside him, Joseph began to realize just how laborious this return to wakefulness could be, and a disturbing thought came to him, that this wife of his, fast asleep, was really a body without a soul, for no soul is present in a body while it sleeps, otherwise there would be no sense in our thanking God each morning for having restored our souls as we awaken. Then a voice within him asked, What thing or person inside us dreams what we dream, and then he wondered, Are dreams perhaps the soul's memories of the body, and this seemed a reasonable explanation. Mary stirred, could her soul have been near at hand, already here in the house, but she did not awaken, no doubt in the midst of some troubled dream, and after heaving a deep sigh like a broken sob she drew closer to her husband, with a sensuousness she would never have dared indulge while awake. Joseph pulled the thick, rough blanket over his shoulders and snuggled up close to Mary. He could feel her warmth, perfumed like a linen chest filled with dried herbs, gradually penetrate the fibers of his tunic and merge with the heat of his own body. Then slowly he closed his eyes, stopped thinking, and, oblivious to his soul, sank back into a deep sleep.

When he woke again, the cock was crowing. A dim, grayish light seeped through the chink in the door. Having patiently waited for the shadows of night to disperse, time was preparing the way for yet another day to reach the world. Because we no longer live in that fabulous age when the sun, to whom we owe so much, was so generous that it halted its journey over Gibeon in order to give Joshua ample time to overcome the five kings besieging the city. Joseph sat up on his mat, drew back the sheet, and at that moment the cock crowed a second time, reminding him that there was another prayer of thanksgiving to be said. Praise be to You, O Lord, our God, King of the Universe, who gave the cock the intelligence to distinguish between night and day, prayed Joseph, and the cock crowed for a third time. Usually, at the first sign of daybreak all the cocks in the neighborhood would crow to one another, but today they remained silent, as if their night had not yet ended or was just beginning. Joseph looked at his wife's face, puzzled by her deep slumber, since normally the slightest noise awakened her, as if she were a bird. Some mysterious power appeared to be hovering over Mary, pressing her down without completely immobilizing her, for even in the shadows her body could be seen to tremble gently, like water rippling in the breeze. Could she be ill, he wondered, but he was distracted from this worrying thought by a sudden urge to urinate, and this, too, was unusual. He rarely felt the need to relieve himself at this early hour or with such urgency. Slipping quietly from under the sheet to avoid waking his wife, for it is written that a man should do everything possible to maintain his self-respect, he cautiously opened the creaking door and went out into the yard. At that hour of the morning everything was gray as ash. Joseph headed for the low shed where he tethered his donkey, and there he relieved himself, listening with dreamy satisfaction to the explosive sound of his urine as it spurted onto the hay scattered on the ground. The donkey turned its head, two huge eyes shining in the dark, then gave its furry ears a vigorous shake before sticking its nose back into the manger, foraging for leftovers with thick, sensuous lips. Joseph fetched the large pitcher used for washing, tipped it sideways, and let the water pour over his hands, then, drying them on his tunic, he praised God who in His infinite wisdom had endowed mankind with the essential orifices and vessels to live, for if any one of them should fail to close or open as required, the result would be death. Looking up at the sky, Joseph was overwhelmed. The sun is slow to appear, in the sky there is not even a hint of dawn's crimson, no shade of rose or cherry, nothing except clouds to be seen from where he stands, one vast roof of low clouds like tiny flattened balls of wool, all identical and the same shade of violet, which deepens and glows on the side where the sun breaks through, then across the sky is increasingly dark until it merges with what remains of the night on the other side. Joseph had never seen such a sky, although old men often spoke of portents in the skies that attested to the power of God, rainbows that covered half the celestial vault, towering ladders that connected heaven and earth, providential showers of manna, but never of this mysterious color, which might just as easily signify the beginning of the world as the end, this roof floating above the earth, made up of thousands of tiny clouds that almost touch one another and reach in all directions like the stones of a wasteland. Terror-stricken, he thought the world was ending and he was the only witness of God's final judgment, the only one. Silence reigns in heaven and on earth, no sounds can be heard from the nearby houses, not so much as a human voice, a child crying, a prayer or curse, a gust of wind, the bleat of a goat or the bark of a dog. Why are the cocks not crowing, he muttered to himself, and repeated the

11

question anxiously, as if the cocks, crowing might be the last hope of salvation. Then the sky began to change. Pink tinges and streaks gradually, almost imperceptibly crept into the violet on the belly of the clouds, until finally it turned red, then was gone, and without warning the sky exploded into light, many shafts of gold that pierced clouds no longer small but now formidable, enormous barges that hoisted blazing sails and plied a sky that had at last been liberated. Joseph's fear subsided, his eyes widened in astonishment and wonder, and with good reason, for he alone was witnessing this spectacle. In a loud voice he praised the Lord of all creation for the eternal majesty of the heavens, whose ineffable splendors leave men struggling with simple words of gratitude, Thanks be to You, O Lord, for this and for that and for that. As he spoke, the tumult of life, whether summoned by his voice or rushing through a door that had carelessly been left open, invaded the space previously occupied by silence, leaving it scarcely any room, a patch here and there, such as those tiny marshes that the murmuring forests engulf and hide from view. The sun rose and spread its light, a vision of unbearable beauty, two enormous hands sending into flight a shimmering bird of paradise that opened its great tail with a thousand iridescent eyes, causing a nameless bird nearby to burst into song. A gust of wind hit Joseph in the face, caught his beard and tunic, eddied around him like a tiny whirlwind moving across a desert, unless he was imagining things and this was nothing more than the blood rushing to his head, a shiver going up his spine like a tongue of fire and stirring a quite different urge.

Moving as if inside a swirling column of air, Joseph went into the house and shut the door behind him. He paused for a moment, waiting for his eyes to become accustomed to the dark. The lamp cast scarcely any light. Wide awake, Mary lay on her back, listening, staring into space, as if waiting. Joseph quietly approached and slowly drew back the sheet. She averted her eyes, began to lift the hem of her tunic, and no sooner had she pulled it to her navel than he was on top of her, his own tunic hitched to his waist. Mary's legs now were open, perhaps they had opened by themselves as she dreamed and she did not close them out of this sudden lassitude, or else from the premonition of a married woman who knows her duty. God, who is omnipresent, was there but, pure spirit that He is, was unable to see how Joseph's flesh touched Mary's, how his flesh penetrated her flesh as had been ordained, and perhaps He was not even there when the holy seed of Joseph poured into the holy womb of Mary, both holy, being the fountain and chalice of life. For in truth, there are things God Himself does not understand, even though He created them. Out in the yard, God could hear neither the gasp that escaped Joseph's lips as he came nor the low moan Mary was unable to suppress. Joseph rested on his wife's body no more than a minute, and perhaps less. Pulling down her tunic and drawing up the sheet, she covered her face with her arm. Joseph stood in the middle of the room, raised his hands, and, looking up at the ceiling, gave the most heartfelt thanksgiving of all, which is reserved for men, I thank You, Almighty God, King of the Universe, for not having made me a woman. By then, God must have already abandoned the yard, for the walls did not shake or cave in, nor did the ground part. All that could be heard was Mary saying, in that submissive voice one expects from women, Thanks be to You, O Lord, for having made me according to Your will. Now, there is no difference between these words and those spoken to the angel Gabriel, for clearly anyone who could say, Behold the handmaiden of the Lord, do with me as You will, might just as easily have said, instead, this prayer. Then the wife of the carpenter Joseph got up from her mat, rolled it up together with that of her husband, and folded the sheet they shared in common.

13

Joseph and Mary lived in a village called Nazareth, a place of little importance and with few inhabitants, in the region of Galilee. Their house was no different from the others, a lopsided cube made of bricks and clay and as poor as poor could be. No striking examples of imaginative architecture to be found here. To save on material, the house had been built into a hillside, which formed the rear wall and allowed easy access to the flat roof, which also served as a terrace. Joseph, as we know, was a carpenter by trade and fairly capable, although he had neither the skill nor the talent for jobs that required fine workmanship. This criticism should not be taken too seriously, for one needs time to gain experience and acquire skills, and we must not forget that Joseph is barely in his twenties and lives in a place with few resources and even fewer opportunities. Nor should a man be measured simply on the basis of his professional ability. For all his youth, this Joseph is one of the most honest and pious men of Nazareth, assiduous in attending the synagogue and prompt in carrying out his duties, and while he may not be endowed with any special powers of eloquence, he can argue and make astute observations, especially when given a chance to use some apt image or metaphor related to his work, carpentry. He does not possess, however, what one might call a creative imagination, and during his brief life will never come up with a memorable parable to be handed down to posterity, let alone one of those brilliant conceits so clearly expressed that there is nothing more to say yet so obscure and ambiguous that they intrigue scholars for years to come.

As for Mary's talents, these are even less apparent, but no more than we might expect of a sixteen-year-old girl who, although married, is still a baby, as it were, for even in those days people used such expressions. Notwithstanding her frail appearance, she works as hard as all the other women, carding, spinning, and weaving cloth, baking the family bread each morning, fetching water from the well and then carrying it up the steep slope, a large pitcher balanced on her head and another on her hip. In the late afternoon she sets off through the byways and fields of the Lord, gathering wood and cutting stubble and filling an extra basket with cow's dung and the thistles and briers that thrive on the upper slopes of Nazareth, the best thing God could ever have devised for lighting a fire or braiding a crown. It would have been easier to load everything onto a donkey's back, but Joseph needs the beast to carry his lumber. Mary goes barefoot to the well, goes barefoot into the fields, in clothes that are forever getting soiled and torn and that constantly need washing and mending, because new clothes are reserved for her husband, women like Mary making do with very little. When she attends the synagogue, she enters by the side door, as the law requires of women, and even if she finds thirty other women there, or all the women of Nazareth, or even the entire female population of Galilee, they must wait until at least ten men arrive for the service, in which the women will participate only passively. Unlike Joseph her husband, Mary is neither upright nor pious, but she is not to blame for this, the blame lies with the language she speaks if not with the men who invented it, because that language has no feminine form for the words upright and pious.

Now one fine day, four weeks after that unforgettable morning when the clouds in the sky turned a mysterious violet, Joseph happened to be at home. The sun was about to set and he was sitting on the floor, eating his food with his fingers, as was then the custom, while Mary stood waiting for him to finish before having her own supper. Neither spoke, for he had nothing to say and she was unable to express what was on her mind. Suddenly a beggar appeared at the gate outside, a rare occurrence in this village, where people were so poor, a fact unlikely to have escaped the begging fraternity, which had a nose for places where there were pickings, and that was certainly not the case here. Nevertheless Mary ladled into a bowl a good portion of the lentils with chopped onions and mashed chickpeas set aside for her own supper, and took it out to the beggar, who sat on the ground. She did not need her husband's spoken permission, he merely nodded, for as everyone knows those were times when words were few and a simple thumbs down or up was enough to condemn a man to death or save him, as in the arenas of ancient Rome. The sunset, although quite different, was spectacular, too, with its myriad wisps of cloud scattered through the sky, rose-colored, mother-of-pearl, salmon-pink, cherry, adjectives used here on earth so that we may understand one another, for none of these colors, as far as we know, have names in heaven. The beggar must have gone without food for three days to have scraped and licked his bowl clean so quickly, and back he comes to return the bowl and express his gratitude. Mary, opening the door, finds him standing there, but somehow he looks broader and taller than before. So it must be true that there is a great difference between going hungry and just having eaten, for this man's face and eyes are glowing, his tattered clothes flap in a strange wind, blurring her vision so that his rags take on the appearance of rich raiment, a sight that must be seen to be believed. Mary put out her hands to receive the earthenware bowl, which, through some extraordinary optical illusion, perhaps due to the light of the sky, was transformed into a vessel of the purest gold. And, as the bowl passed from his hands into hers, the beggar said in resonant tones, because even the poor man's voice had changed, May the Lord bless you, good woman, and give you all the children your husband desires, and may He also protect you from my sad fate, for, alas, I have nowhere to rest my head in this wretched world. Mary held the bowl in cupped hands, one chalice held by another, as if waiting for the beggar to fill it, which is what he did. Without warning he bent down and gathered a handful of earth and, raising his arm, allowed it to trickle through his fingers while reciting in a low voice, Earth to earth, ashes to ashes, dust to dust, nothing begins without coming to an end, every beginning comes from an ending. Mary was puzzled and asked him, What does that mean, but the beggar simply replied, Good woman, you have a child in your womb and that is man's only destiny, to begin and end, to end and begin. How do you know I'm with child. Even before the belly swells, a child can be seen shining through its mother's eyes. If that is true, then my husband would already have seen his child in my eyes. Perhaps he does not look at you when you look at him. Who are you who knows so much without hearing it from my own lips. I am an angel, but tell no one.

Then his shining robe turned back to rags, he shriveled as if licked by fire, and this wondrous transformation took place just in time, thanks be to God, for no sooner had the beggar quietly disappeared than Joseph emerged in the doorway, his suspicions aroused by whispering voices and

17

Mary's absence. What else did the beggar want, he asked, and Mary, at a loss for words, could only repeat, From earth to earth, from ashes to ashes, from dust to dust, nothing begins without coming to an end, nothing ends without having a beginning. Was that what he said. Yes, and he also said that a father's child shines through its mother's eyes. Look at me. I am looking. I can see a light in your eyes, said Joseph, and Mary told him, It must be your child. As the evening sky changed from blue to the somber shades of night, the bowl began to glow with a radiance that changed Mary's face, and her eyes seemed to belong to a much older woman. Are you pregnant, Joseph finally asked her. Yes, I am, replied Mary. Why didn't you tell me sooner. I meant to tell you today, I was waiting for you to finish eating. And then the beggar turned up. That's right. What else did he have to say, for he certainly took his time. That the Lord should give me all the children you wished for. What do you have in that bowl to make it shine so. Nothing but earth. Soil is black, clay green, and sand white, of these three sand alone shines in the day, but it is night. Forgive me, I am only a woman and cannot explain these things. You say he took some earth from the ground and dropped it into the bowl, at the same time uttering the words, Earth to earth. Yes, those very words.

Joseph went to open the gate, looked right and left. No sign of him, he's vanished, he told her, and feeling reassured, Mary returned to the house, for the beggar, if he really was an angel, could only be seen if he wished. She set the bowl down on the stone slab of the hearth, took a live coal from the fire and lit the oil lamp, blowing until she raised a tiny flame. Puzzled, Joseph came inside, tried to hide his suspicions, moved with the solemnity of a patriarch, which looked odd in someone so young. Furtively he examined the bowl filled with luminous earth, his expression ironic and skeptical, but if he was trying to as-

18

sert superiority, he was wasting his time, for Mary's eyes were lowered and her thoughts elsewhere. Using a small stick, Joseph poked at the earth, fascinated as he watched it darken when disturbed, only to regain its brilliance, light sparkling in all directions over the dull surface. There's a mystery here I can't fathom, either the beggar brought this earth with him and you thought he gathered it here, or there is some magic at work, for who ever saw shining earth in Nazareth. Mary remained silent. She was eating what was left of her lentils with bread dipped in oil. As she broke bread, she observed the holy law by giving thanks in the humble tone befitting a woman, Praise be to You, Adonai, Lord God and King of the Universe, who brings forth bread from the earth. She continued eating in silence while Joseph mused at length, as if interpreting a verse from the Torah in the synagogue or a phrase from the prophets, the words Mary had spoken, words he himself spoke when breaking bread, and he tried to imagine what grain might grow out of luminous earth, what bread it would produce, and what light we would carry within us if we ate such bread. Are you sure the beggar took it from the ground, he asked Mary a second time, and Mary answered, Yes, I'm sure. Perhaps it was shining all the time. No, it wasn't shining on the ground. This should have allayed the fears of any husband, but Joseph believed, like all men at that time and in that place, that the truly wise man is on his guard against the wiles and deceptions of women. To converse little with them and pay them even less heed must be the motto of a prudent husband mindful of the advice of Rabbi Josephat ben Yochanan, for at the hour of death each man must give account of any idle conversations he has held with his wife. Joseph asked himself whether this conversation with Mary was necessary, and having decided that it was, given the unusual nature of what had happened, he swore to himself that he would never forget the holy words of the rabbi, his namesake,

19

for Josephat is the same as Joseph, rather than suffer remorse at the hour of death, which, God willing, will be
peaceful. Then he asked himself whether he should tell the
elders of the synagogue about this curious affair of the
mysterious beggar and the luminous earth, and decided he
should, to ease his conscience and keep the peace in his
own home.

Mary finished eating. She took the bowls outside to
wash them, but not the bowl used by the beggar. There
are now two lights in the house, that of the oil lamp struggling valiantly against the darkness of night, and the aura
from the bowl, flickering yet constant, like a sun that is
slow in appearing. Seated on the floor, Mary waits for her
husband to resume the conversation, but Joseph has nothing more to say to her, he is mentally rehearsing the speech
he will make tomorrow before the council of elders. How
frustrating it is, not to know precisely what transpired between his wife and the beggar, not to know what else they
might have said to each other, but he decides to question
her no further. He might as well believe the story she has
now told him twice, because if she is lying, he will never
know, while she will know and almost certainly be laughing at him, her mantle covering her face, just as Eve laughed
at Adam, but behind his back, for in those days people did
not wear mantles. One thought led to another, and Joseph
soon convinced himself that the beggar had been sent by
Satan. The great tempter, aware that times had changed
and that people were now more cautious, was offering not
one of nature's fruits but the promise of a different, luminous soil, counting once more on the credulity and weakness of women. Joseph's mind is in turmoil, but he is pleased
with himself and the conclusion he has reached. Unaware
of her husband's tortuous thoughts about Satan's intrigue,
Mary is troubled by a strange feeling of emptiness now
that she has told him of her pregnancy. Not an inner emptiness, to be sure, for she knows perfectly well that her

20

womb, and in the strict sense of the word, is full, but an outer emptiness, as if the world has receded and become remote. She recalls, but as if evoking another life, that after supper and before unrolling the mats for the night she always had some task in hand to fill the hours, but now she feels no inclination whatever to rise from where she sits gazing at the light that glows back at her over the rim of the bowl, gazing and awaiting the birth of her child. If truth be told, her thoughts are not that clear, for thought, when all is said and done, as others and we ourselves have observed before, is like a great ball of thread coiled around itself, loose in places, taut in others, inside our head. It is impossible to know its full extent, one would have to unwind and then measure it, but however hard one tries or pretends to try, this cannot be done without assistance. One day, someone will come and tell us where to cut the cord that ties man to his navel and thought to its origin.

The following morning, after a restless night in which he was constantly disturbed by the same nightmare, where he saw himself falling time and time again inside an enormous upturned bowl as if under a starry sky, Joseph went to the synagogue to seek the advice of the elders. His story was extraordinary, though more extraordinary than he knew because, as we know, he had not been told the whole story. Were it not for the high esteem in which he was held by the old men of Nazareth, he would have had to go home with his tail between his legs and the reproachful words of Ecclesiasticus in his ears, To trust a man hastily shows a shallow mind. And he, poor fellow, would not have had the presence of mind to reply with words from the same Ecclesiasticus, regarding the dream that had haunted him all night, What you see in a dream is but a reflection, a face in a mirror. When he finished telling his story, the elders looked at one another and then at Joseph, and the oldest man there, translating the silent mistrust of the council into a direct question, asked, Is this the truth you have

21

spoken, whereupon the carpenter replied, The truth, the whole truth, as God is my witness. The elders then debated among themselves while Joseph waited at a discreet distance, until finally they summoned him and said that they would send three envoys to question Mary herself about this mysterious event in order to discover the identity of the beggar whom no one else had seen, by learning what he looked like, the exact words he used, and if anyone could remember seeing him beg for alms in Nazareth or provide any information about the stranger. Joseph was pleased because, although he would never admit it, he did not want to confront his wife alone. Her habit in recent days of keeping her eyes lowered was beginning to disconcert him. There was modesty in it, but also, unmistakably, something provocative, as in the look of a woman who knows more than she is prepared to disclose or wants others to notice. Verily I say unto you, the treachery of women knows no limits, especially when they feign innocence.

And so the envoys depart, Joseph leading the way, and they are Abiathar, Dothan, and Zacchaeus, names recorded here to forestall any suspicion of historical inaccuracy in the minds of those who have acquired their version of the story from other sources, a version perhaps more in accordance with tradition but not necessarily more factual. The names having been revealed and the existence of the men who used them established, there can be no remaining doubts. The unusual sight of three elders moving in solemn procession through the streets, their robes and beards caught by the breeze, soon drew the local urchins, who gathered around them and began aping their walk as children will, jeering and shouting and chasing after the envoys all the way from the synagogue to the house of Joseph, who was much put out by this boisterous parade. Attracted by the noise, women began to appear in the doorways of the neighboring houses and, sensing something amiss, they sent their children to find out what such a del-

egation was doing at Mary's door. To no avail, because
only the elders were allowed to enter. The door was firmly
closed behind them, and no woman of Nazareth, however
inquisitive, learned or knows to this day what took place
in the house of Joseph, the carpenter. Forced to invent
something to satisfy the hunger of their curiosity, they accused the beggar, whom they had never set eyes on, of
being a common thief. A great injustice, because the angel,
if angel is what he was, did not steal the food he ate, and
even delivered a holy prophecy in exchange. While the two
senior elders interrogated Mary, the third, the youngest,
Zacchaeus, went around the immediate vicinity gathering
any details people could remember about a beggar who
answered the description given by the carpenter's wife, but
none of the neighbors could help, No, sir, no beggar passed
this way yesterday, and if he did, he didn't knock at my
door, it must have been a thief passing through, who when
he found someone at home pretended to be a beggar and
then left in a hurry, the oldest trick in the book.

Zacchaeus arrived back at Joseph's house with nothing
to report about the beggar just as Mary was repeating for
the fourth time the facts we already know. She stood as if
guilty of a crime, the bowl set on the ground, and inside
it, constant as a throbbing heart, the strange earth. Joseph
sat on one side, and the elders sat in front like a tribunal
of judges. Dothan, the second of the three, said, It's not
that we don't believe your story, but you're the only person who spoke to this man, if he was a man, all your
husband knows is that he heard his voice, and now Zacchaeus here tells me that none of your neighbors saw
him. As God is my witness, I swear I am telling the truth.
The truth, perhaps, but is it the whole truth. I shall drink
the water of the Lord and He will prove my innocence.
The trial of bitter water is for women suspected of infidelity, but you couldn't have been unfaithful to your husband
because he didn't give you enough time. Falsehood is said

23

to be the same as infidelity. That's another kind of infidelity. My words are as true as the rest of me. Then Abiathar, the oldest of the three, told her, We shall question you no further, the Lord will reward you sevenfold for the truth you have spoken or punish you sevenfold if you have deceived us. He fell silent, then turned to Zacchaeus and Dothan and asked them, What shall we do with this bright earth, which prudence demands should not remain here, for it might be one of Satan's tricks. Dothan said, Let this earth return whence it came, let it return to its former darkness. Zacchaeus said, We know not who the beggar is, or why he chose to be seen by Mary alone, or the meaning of the earth that shines in the bowl. Dothan proposed, Let us take it into the desert and scatter it there, far from the eyes of men, that the wind may disperse it and the rain erase it. Zacchaeus said, If this earth is some divine gift, then it must not be removed, if on the other hand it forebodes evil, then let those to whom it was given bear the consequences. Abiathar asked, What do you suggest then, and Zacchaeus replied, That the bowl be buried here and covered up so that there is no contact with the natural earth, for a gift from God, even when buried, is never lost, whereas the power of evil is much diminished if hidden from sight. Abiathar asked, What do you say, Dothan, to which the latter replied, I agree with Zacchaeus, let us do as he says. Abiathar told Mary, Withdraw so that we may proceed. Where shall I go, she asked him, whereupon Joseph, agitated, said, If we are to bury the bowl, let it be somewhere away from the house, for I will never rest with a light buried underneath me. Abiathar reassured him, That can be done, then he told Mary, You remain here. The men went out into the yard, Zacchaeus carrying the bowl. The sound of a spade could soon be heard digging as Joseph briskly set to work, and a few minutes later Mary recognized the voice of Abiathar, You can stop now, the hole is deep enough. Mary peered through the chink in the door, watched her husband cover the bowl with a curved potsherd then lower it into the hole as deep as his arm was long. He rose, grabbed his spade, filled the hole, and stamped the ground down firmly with his feet.

The men remained in the yard, conversing among themselves and gazing at the patch of fresh earth, as if they had just buried a treasure and were trying to memorize the spot. But this was not the topic of conversation, because suddenly Zacchaeus could be heard saying aloud, in a tone of playful reproach, Now then, Joseph, what kind of carpenter are you, when you can't even make a bed for your pregnant wife. The others laughed, and Joseph joined them rather than lose face by showing his annoyance. Mary saw them walk to the gate, and now, seated on the stone slab of the hearth, she was looking around the room, wondering where they could put a bed if Joseph decided to make one. She tried not to think about the earthenware bowl or the luminous earth or whether the beggar was really an angel or only some practical joker. If a woman is promised a bed for her house, she must start thinking about the best place to put it.

Between the months of Tammuz and Ab, when grapes were gathered in the vineyards and the figs began ripening amid the dark green vine leaves, certain events took place. Some were normal and commonplace, such as a man and woman coming together in the flesh, and after a while she tells him, I am carrying your child, others quite extraordinary, such as an annunciation entrusted to a passing beggar whose only crime seems to have been that peculiar phenomenon of the bright earth, which is now safe from prying eyes thanks to Joseph's mistrust and the prudence of the elders. The dog days are fast approaching, the fields are bare, nothing but stubble and parched soil. During the oppressive hours of the day Nazareth is a village submerged in silence and solitude. Only when night descends and the stars appear can one sense the presence of a landscape or hear the music of the heavenly planets as they glide past one another. After supper Joseph sat out in the yard, to the right of the door, to get some air. How he loved to feel the fresh evening breeze on his face and beard. Mary joined him, squatting on the ground like her husband but on the other side of the door, and there they remained in silence, listening to the sounds coming from the neighboring houses, the bustle of domestic life, which they, too, would experience once they had children. May God send us a boy, Joseph had prayed throughout the day, and Mary, too, kept thinking, Let it be a boy, dear God, but she had other reasons for wanting a boy. Her belly was slow in growing bigger, weeks and months would pass before her condition became visible, and since, out of modesty and discretion, she saw little of her neighbors, there would be general surprise when she turned into a balloon overnight. Perhaps the real reason for her secretiveness was her fear that someone might connect her pregnancy with the appearance of the mysterious beggar. Such thoughts may strike us as absurd, but in moments of weariness when her mind began to stray, Mary could not help wondering how all this had come about and who was the real father of this child she carried in her womb. As everyone knows, when women are pregnant, they are given to strange cravings and flights of fancy, some of them worse than those of Mary, which we shall not betray lest we tarnish the reputation of this mother-to-be.

Time passed, the weeks dragged, the month of Elul hot as a furnace, with the scorching winds from the southern deserts stifling the atmosphere, a season when dates and figs turn to trickling honey, and the month of Tishri bringing the first rains of autumn to moisten the soil in time for tilling and sowing, and the following month of Heshvan, when olives are gathered and the days finally turn cool. Unable to make anything grand, Joseph decided to make a simple bed where Mary might at last find rest for her swollen and cumbersome body. Heavy rains fell during the last days of Kislev and throughout most of Tebet, forcing him to interrupt his work in the yard. He took advantage of the dry spells to assemble the larger pieces of wood, but usually he had to work indoors in poor light,

27

and there he planed and polished the unfinished frame, covering the floor all around him with shavings and sawdust, which Mary would sweep up later and dispose of in the yard.

In the month of Shebat the almond trees blossomed. In the month of Adar, the feast of Purim had already been celebrated when Roman soldiers appeared in Nazareth, a familiar sight throughout Galilee. Detachments went from village to city and from city to village, while others were dispatched into the country in Herod's kingdom, to inform the people that by order of Caesar Augustus every family domiciled in the provinces governed by the consul Publius Sulpicius Quirinus must participate in a census, which like all the others would bring the records up to date on those who had not yet paid their taxes to Rome. Without exception, every family had to register in their place of birth. Most of the people who gathered in the square to hear the proclamation did not mind the imperial edict, for as natives of Nazareth, settled for generations, they intended to register there. But some families had come from other parts of the kingdom, from Gaulinitis or Samaria, from Judaea, Peraea, or Idumaea, from here and there, from far and wide, and these began making preparations for the long journey, complaining bitterly about the perversity and greed of Rome and asking what would become of their crops, since it was almost time to harvest the flax and barley. And those who had large families, with babes in arms and elderly parents and grandparents, unless they had transportation of their own, wondered from whom they could borrow donkeys, or hire them at a reasonable price, and if there was a long and arduous journey ahead, ample supplies of food would be required, and water bags if they had to cross the desert, and mats and mantles for sleeping, and cooking utensils, and extra clothing, because the cold wet season was not yet over and they might have to spend nights out in the open.

28

Joseph learned about the edict only after the soldiers left to carry their glad tidings elsewhere. His next-door neighbor, Ananias, suddenly appeared in a great fluster to tell him what had happened. Fortunately for Ananias, he could register in Nazareth, nor would he be celebrating Passover in Jerusalem this year, because of the harvest, so he was spared both journeys. Ananias came to warn his neighbor, but warned him with such a smug expression, as if bearing good news. Alas, even the best of men can be two-faced, and we do not know this Ananias well enough to decide whether his is a momentary lapse from grace or if he has fallen under the influence of one of Satan's wicked angels with spare time on its hands. Joseph, hammering away at a plank of wood, at first did not hear Ananias calling him from the gate. Mary, whose ears were keener, heard a voice call, Joseph, but it was her husband who was being summoned, and who was she to tug at his sleeve and ask, Are you deaf, can't you hear someone calling you from the gate. Ananias called out even louder, the hammering stopped, and Joseph went to see what his neighbor wanted. Ananias was invited in and, after the customary greetings, inquired in the voice of one who seeks reassurance, Where are you from, Joseph, and, surprised, Joseph told him, I'm from Bethlehem of Judaea. Isn't that near Jerusalem. Yes, quite near. And are you going there to celebrate the Passover, asked Ananias, and Joseph replied, No, I've decided not to go this year, because my wife is expecting our child any day now. Oh, is that so. But why do you ask. Whereupon Ananias raised his arms to heaven and wailed mournfully, Poor Joseph, the trouble that awaits you, the aggravation, all this work to be done here and you're expected to put down your tools and travel all that way, so help me God, who sees and assists all things. Without asking the reason for this sudden outburst, Joseph echoed his neighbor's pious sentiment, May God help me as well, to which Ananias, without lowering his voice, replied, Yes, with God all things are possible, He knows and sees all things, both in heaven and on earth, praise be to Him, but, forgive the irreverence, I'm not sure He can do much to help you this time, because you're in the hands of Caesar. What are you trying to tell me. Only that soldiers have been here to proclaim that before the month of Nisan ends, all the families of Israel must go and register in their place of birth, which in your case, dear Joseph, means quite a journey.

Before Joseph had time to react, Shua, the wife of Ananias, appeared, and going straight to Mary, who was standing in the doorway, she began commiserating in the same mournful voice, Poor child, and so delicate, what is to become of you, about to give birth any day now and forced to make the journey to who knows where. To Bethlehem of Judaea, Shua's husband informed her. Good heavens, all that way, Shua exclaimed, and in all sincerity, for once on a pilgrimage to Jerusalem she had gone to nearby Bethlehem to pray at Rachel's tomb. Mary waited for her husband to speak first. Joseph, furious that this news should come to Mary not quietly and with measured words from his own lips but blurted tactlessly by hysterical neighbors, said in a solemn voice, It's true that God doesn't always choose to wield the powers exercised by Caesar, but God has powers denied Caesar. He paused, as if to savor the profundity of what he had just said, before announcing, We shall celebrate the Passover here in Nazareth and then go to Bethlehem, and God willing shall be back in time for Mary to give birth at home, unless He decides that the child be born in the land of our ancestors. It might even be born on the road, murmured Shua, but Joseph overheard her and was quick to remind her, Many a child of Israel has been born on the road, and our child will be just one more. Ananias and his wife could only agree with the wisdom of these words. They had come to sympathize with their hapless neighbors, and to enjoy their own solicitude, only to find themselves rebuffed. But then Mary invited Shua inside to ask her advice about some wool she had to card, and Joseph, wishing to make amends for his harsh words, said to Ananias, Good neighbor, could I ask you to look after my house while I'm away, for we shall be gone for at least a month, counting the time the journey takes, then the seven days of seclusion, and more if by some misfortune the child should be a girl. Ananias promised his neighbor that he would look after the property as if it were his own, and suddenly it occurred to him to ask Joseph, Would you honor me by celebrating the Passover with my family and friends since neither you nor your wife has any relatives here in Nazareth, not after the death of Mary's parents, who were so old when she was born that people still ask themselves how Joachim could possibly have given Anne a daughter. Come now, Ananias, said Joseph, rebuking him playfully, have you forgotten how Abraham muttered into his beard in disbelief when the Lord told him He would give him offspring, and if Almighty God allowed a hundred-year-old man and a wife of ninety to conceive a child, why should my in-laws, Joachim and Anne, who were not as old as Abraham and Sarah, not do the same. Those were other times, Ananias replied, when God was ever present and manifest not just in His works. Well versed in matters of doctrine, Joseph retorted, God is time itself, neighbor Ananias, for God time is indivisible. Ananias was left speechless, for this was not the moment to bring up the old argument about the powers, whether consubstantial or delegated, of God and Caesar. Joseph, despite his demonstration of practical theology, had not forgotten Ananias's sudden invitation to celebrate the Passover with him and his family. He did not wish, however, to accept too quickly, because as everyone knows it is a sign of good breeding to receive favors without being too effusive, otherwise the granter will think we were simply waiting to be asked. So Joseph bided his time before

31

finally thanking Ananias for his thoughtfulness. The women reemerged from the house, Shua saying to Mary, You're an expert at carding, my girl, and Mary blushed on hearing herself praised in front of Joseph.

One pleasant memory Mary would cherish of this auspicious Passover was not having to help with the cooking or serve the men at table. The other women agreed she should be spared these chores in her condition. Don't tire yourself out, they warned her, or you'll do yourself some mischief, and they should know, because most of them were mothers with young children. All she had to do was attend to her husband, who was sitting on the floor with the other men. Bending over with some difficulty, she filled his glass and replenished his plate with unleavened bread, stewed lamb, bitter herbs, and biscuits made of ground dried locusts, a delicacy much appreciated by Ananias, for these biscuits were a family tradition. Several guests declined, doing their best to conceal their disgust and painfully aware that they were unworthy of the edifying example of those prophets in the desert who, making a virtue of necessity, ate locusts as if they were manna. As supper drew to an end, poor Mary sat apart, sweat running down her face, her great belly resting on her haunches, and she scarcely listened to the laughter, banter, stories, and continual reading from the Scriptures, feeling she might depart this world at any moment, her life hanging by the thread of one last, pure, unspoken thought. All she knew was that she was thinking without knowing what she was thinking or why she was thinking. She awoke with a start. In her dream she had seen the beggar's face loom from a great darkness, then his huge body in rags. The angel, if indeed he was an angel, had crept into her sleep unannounced, when he was furthest from her thoughts, and gazed at her intently. She sensed curiosity, but perhaps she was mistaken, he came and went so quickly, and Mary's heart now fluttered like that of a little bird. Difficult to say whether she had been startled or someone had whispered something embarrassing in her ear. The men and boys still sat on the floor while the women, hot and harried, rushed back and forth offering them more helpings, but the men were full now, and their conversation became more animated as the wine began to take effect.

Without anyone's noticing, Mary got to her feet. Night had fallen. There was no moon in the clear sky, only the twinkling stars, which sent out a kind of echo, a muffled, barely audible hum which Joseph's wife could feel on her skin and in her bones, impossible to explain, like a furtive voluptuous shiver that lingers. She crossed the yard and looked out. She could see no one. The gate was closed, but there was a vibration in the air, as if someone had just run or flown past, leaving only a fleeting sign that would leave others baffled.

THREE DAYS LATER, AFTER PROMISING HIS CUSTOMERS THAT their jobs would be completed on his return and after making his farewells in the synagogue and entrusting the care of his house and the worldly possessions therein to his neighbor, Ananias, Joseph the carpenter set out with his wife from Nazareth and headed for Bethlehem, where they would register as Rome decreed. If the news had not yet reached heaven, because of some delay in communication or a problem with simultaneous translation, the Lord God must have been surprised to see the landscape of Israel so altered, with hordes of people traveling in all directions, when normally during the first few days after Passover people moved centrifugally, as it were, beginning their return journey from that earthly sun known as Jerusalem. Force of habit, however fallible, and divine perspicacity, the latter absolute, will undoubtedly assist Him to recognize, even from on high, that these are pilgrims slowly making their way back to their towns and villages, but what about this bewildering maze, as those obeying the profane order of Caesar travel at random across more familiar routes. Unless Caesar Augustus is unwittingly complying with the will of God, if it is true that in His divine wisdom He has ordained that Joseph and Mary should go to Bethlehem at this time. Our speculation, arbitrary and irrelevant as it may appear at first, should not be dismissed lightly, for it helps us disprove those commentators who would have us picture Joseph and Mary crossing the inhospitable desert all alone, without so much as a friendly face in sight, trusting solely in God's mercy and the protection of His angels. For no sooner does the couple reach the outskirts of Nazareth than it becomes clear that they will not be on their own. Joseph and Mary meet two large families, a veritable clan of some twenty members, including adults, grandparents, and small children. It is true that these are not all traveling to Bethlehem, one of the families is only going half the distance and will stay in a village near Ramah, the other will head south as far as Beersheba, but even if they should separate before reaching Bethlehem, because there is always the possibility that some will travel faster, the couple will join other travelers on the road, and meet those going in the opposite direction, on their way to register in Nazareth. The men walk ahead in one group, accompanied by all the boys who have reached thirteen, while the women, girls, and grandmothers of every age straggle behind, accompanied by the boys under thirteen. When they set off, the men in solemn chorus recited prayers suited to the occasion, while the women merely mumbled the words, for it is pointless raising your voice if no one is likely to listen, even though they ask for nothing and are grateful for everything.

Among the women only Mary is in an advanced state of pregnancy, and such is the strain on her that, had providence not endowed donkeys with infinite patience and stamina to match, she would long since have given up and begged the others to abandon her at the roadside to await her hour, which we know is near, but who can say when or where, for this is not a race given to making bets or predictions about when or where Joseph's son will be born, and what a sensible religion to have prohibited gambling. Until that hour comes and for as long as this anxious waiting lasts, the pregnant woman will rely less on the distracted attentions of Joseph, who is lost in conversation with the other men, than on the reliable support of the donkey, who must be wondering, if beasts of burden are sensitive to such things, why the whip has not been much in use and why it is allowed to go at its own easy pace, the pace of its species. The women often lag behind, forcing the men, who are far ahead of them, to call a halt until the women get closer but not too close. The men prefer to give the impression that they have only paused for a rest because, although it is true that everyone may use the road, where cocks crow hens must not squawk, at most they may cackle when they lay an egg, for such are the laws of nature that govern the world in which we live. And so Mary journeys on, swaying with the gentle rhythm of her mount, a queen among women, for she alone is permitted to ride, while the other donkeys carry pack loads. To make things easier, she takes the three infants in the party onto her lap in turn, giving their mothers some relief and at the same time preparing herself for motherhood.

On the first day, they soon tired and covered only a short distance. Their legs were unaccustomed to walking for hours on end, we must not forget the number of old people and small children making this journey. The former, after a long life, have spent all their energy and can no longer pretend otherwise, the latter have not yet learned how to conserve their growing strength and wear themselves out after a brief spurt of wild activity, as if life were coming to an end and had to be enjoyed to the full while it lasted. On reaching a large village called Isreel, they stopped at the local caravansary, which they found in a state of chaos and uproar because of the heavy traffic. To

tell the truth, there was more uproar than chaos here, because as one's eyes and ears adjusted, some order emerged
from that multitude of people and animals within four walls,
like a disturbed anthill trying to find its bearings and re-
group. Despite the overcrowding, the three families had
the good fortune to find shelter under an archway, where
the men could huddle together on one side and the women
on the other as darkness fell and all in the caravansary,
people and animals, settled down for the night. But first
the women had to prepare food and fill the water skins at
the well, and the men had to unload the donkeys and water
them after the camels finished drinking. For in two great
gulps a camel can empty a trough, which must be refilled
again and again to slake its thirst. After watering and feeding the donkeys, the travelers finally sat down to eat, the
men first, of course. How often we need to remind ourselves that Eve was created after Adam and taken from his
rib. Will we ever learn that certain things can be understood only if we take the trouble to trace them to their
origins.

The men had eaten and were back in their own corner,
the women were finishing off the leftovers, when Simeon,
one of the most senior of the elders, who lived in Bethlehem but was obliged to register in Ramah, took advantage
of the authority conferred by age and the wisdom believed
to come thereof by asking Joseph what he would do if
Mary, although Simeon did not mention her by name,
should still be waiting to give birth when the last day of
the census passed. The question was clearly academic, if
such a word is apt for the time and place, insofar as only
the census officials, skilled in the finer points of Roman
law, would know how to deal with a pregnant woman
who turned up for registration and said, We've come to
register, no one having any idea whether she carried a boy
or a girl, not to mention the possibility of twins. Exem-
plary Jew as he was, the carpenter would never have dreamt

37

of pointing out with simple Western logic that it was not up to those who obeyed laws to defend the defects in them, and if Rome was incapable of foreseeing certain difficulties, then she was ill served by her legislators and her interpreters of Holy Scripture. Faced with this thorny problem, then, Joseph thought long and hard, searching in his mind for a subtle argument that would convince those gathered around the bonfire of his skill in debate. After much reflection, the carpenter raised his eyes from the flickering flames and told them, If by the last day of the census my child has not yet been born, this will be a sign from God that He does not wish the Romans to know of the child's existence. Simeon replied, Such presumption, to claim to know what God does or does not wish. Joseph asked, Does God not see my ways and count all my steps. These words, which we can find in the Book of Job, implied, within the context of this discussion, that before all present or absent Joseph was protesting his humility and submission to the Lord, a sentiment wholly opposed to the diabolic presumption of which Simeon accused him when Joseph had tried to probe the inscrutable will of God. This is how the elder must have interpreted his answer, for he fell silent, waiting for Joseph to continue. The days of each man's birth and death, said Joseph, have been put under seal and guarded by angels ever since the world began, and only the Lord can break those seals, first the one and then the other, although often together, with His right and left hand, and there are times when He is so slow in breaking the seal of death that He seems almost to have forgotten the existence of certain living souls. Joseph paused for breath, then, smiling mischievously, told Simeon, Let us hope this conversation does not remind the Lord of your existence. Those present laughed into their beards, for the carpenter was not showing the respect due to an old man. Simeon, tugging nervously at his sleeve, made no attempt to hide his anger as he told Joseph, Perhaps the Lord was hasty in breaking the seal of your birth and you were born before your time, if this is how you treat your elders, who have seen more of life than you have and gained more wisdom. Whereupon Joseph replied, Listen, Simeon, you asked me what I would do if my child was not born by the last day of the census, and I couldn't answer, I'm not familiar with Roman law, and I suspect neither are you. No, I am not. Then I said. I know what you said, you don't need to repeat it. It was you who started it, accusing me of presuming to know God's will, so forgive me if I hurt your pride, but you were the first to cause offense, and as my elder and better you ought to set an example. There was a murmur of approval around the fire. The carpenter Joseph had clearly won the argument, and the others waited to see how Simeon would respond. Lacking in spirit and imagination, he peevishly said, All you had to do was answer my question respectfully, and Joseph replied, Had I given you the answer you wanted, the foolishness of your question would have been evident to all, therefore you must admit, however much it rankles, that I showed the greater respect by providing you with an opportunity to debate a thing we'd all like to know, namely, whether the Lord would ever choose to conceal His people from the eyes of the enemy. Now you speak about God's people as if they were your unborn child. Don't put words in my mouth, Simeon, words I haven't spoken and will never speak, listen instead to what should be understood in one sense and not in another. Simeon made no attempt to reply to this, he got to his feet and took himself off to a corner along with the other men of his household, who felt obliged to accompany him because of ties of blood and kinship, although they were disappointed in the patriarch's poor showing in this verbal exchange.

The silence that followed the murmurings and whisperings of travelers settling down for the night was broken now and then by muffled conversations in the caravansary, by a shrill cry, the panting and snorting of animals, and the occasional awful bellow of a camel in heat. Then the party from Nazareth, all discord forgotten, could be heard muttering in unison the last and longest of the prayers of thanksgiving offered to the Lord at the end of the day, Praise be to You, O God, King of the Universe, who shuts our eyes without robbing them of light. Grant, O Lord, that we may sleep in peace and awaken tomorrow to a happy and tranquil life, help us to obey Your commandments. Lead us not into temptation and deliver us from evil. Lead us along the path of virtue and protect us from bad dreams, wicked thoughts, and mortal sickness. Spare us visions of death. Within minutes, the more just if not the more weary members of the party were fast asleep, some of them snoring unspiritually. And soon the others joined them, most with nothing more than their tunics to cover them, for only the elderly and the very young, both delicate in their own way, enjoyed the warmth and protection of a coarse blanket or threadbare mantle. Deprived of wood, the fire began to die, only a few weak flames continuing to flicker. Under the archway, the party from Nazareth slept soundly. Everyone except Mary. Unable to stretch out because of her belly, which could have been harboring a giant, she lay against some saddlebags in an effort to rest her aching back. Like the others, she had listened to Joseph arguing with old Simeon, and rejoiced in her husband's victory, as befits any wife no matter how harmless or unimportant the conflict. But she could no longer remember what the argument was about, her recollection of it already submerged in the throbbing of her body, which came and went like the tide of the sea, which she had never seen but had heard others describe, the restless ebb and flow as her child stirred in her womb. The strangest sensation, as if that living creature inside her were trying to hoist her onto its shoulders. Only Mary lay with her eyes open, shining in the shadows, still shining after the last flame had died away. No cause for wonder, for this happens to all mothers, and the wife of the carpenter Joseph was no exception, after the angel appeared to her disguised as a beggar.

Even in the caravansary there were cocks to greet the morning, but the travelers, merchants, drovers, and cameleers had to make an early start and begin preparing, before dawn, for the next leg of their journey. They loaded the animals with baggage and merchandise and made even more noise than on the previous evening. Once they have departed, the caravansary will settle down to a few hours of peace and quiet, like a brown lizard stretched out in the sun. The only remaining guests are those who have decided to rest all day, but by evening another group of travelers will start arriving, some more bedraggled than others but all of them weary, not that this has any effect on their vocal cords, because the moment they arrive, they start shouting their heads off as if possessed by a thousand demons. Back on the road, the party from Nazareth has grown bigger, ten people have joined them, so anyone who imagines this place to be deserted is much mistaken, especially when the feast of Passover and the census coincide.

No one needed to tell Joseph to make his peace with old Simeon, not because he was in the wrong but because he had been taught to respect his elders, especially those who were paying the price for long life by losing both their brains and their influence over a younger generation. So Joseph went up to him and said, I've come to apologize for my insolence last night, I didn't mean to be disrespectful but you know what human nature is, one word leads to another, tempers are lost, and caution is thrown to the winds. Without raising his eyes, Simeon heard him out in silence, then finally spoke, You are forgiven. Hoping his friendly overture would win more from the stubborn old man, Joseph remained at his side for a fair stretch of the road. But Simeon, eyes fixed on the dust at his feet,

41

continued to ignore him, until Joseph in exasperation decided to give up. At that very moment, seemingly roused from his thoughts, the old man placed a hand on Joseph's shoulder and said, Wait. Surprised, Joseph turned, and Simeon stopped and repeated, Wait. The others walked on, leaving the two men standing in the middle of the road, a no-man's-land between the group of men ahead and the group of women behind, which was gradually approaching. Above the women's heads, Mary could be seen swaying with the rhythm of the donkey.

They had left the valley of Isreel. Skirting great rocks, the road curved awkwardly up the first slope before penetrating the mountains of Samaria to the east, then along arid ridges before descending on the other side to the Jordan, where the burning plain stretched southward and the desert of Judaea fired and scorched the ancient scars of a land promised to the chosen few but forever uncertain to whom it should surrender. Wait, said Simeon, and the carpenter obeyed, suddenly uneasy. The women were drawing nearer. Then the old man clutched Joseph by the sleeve, and he confided, When I lay down to rest last night I had a vision. A vision. Yes, a vision, but no ordinary vision, for I could see the hidden meaning of words you yourself spoke, that if your child was still not born by the last day of the census, it would be because the Lord did not wish the Romans to learn of its existence and add its name to their list. Yes, that is what I said, but what did you see. I didn't see anything but suddenly felt that it would be better if the Romans did not learn of your child's existence, that no one should be told of it, and that if the child must be born into this world, at least let it live without torment or glory, like those men up there in front and those women bringing up the rear, let it be as anonymous as the rest of us until the hour of death and forever after. Humble carpenter as I am from Nazareth, what fate could my child possibly hope for other than the one you have just described. Alas, you are not the only one to dispose of your child's life. True, everything is in the hands of the Lord and He knows best. And so say I. But tell me about my child, what have you discovered. Nothing beyond the words you yourself uttered and which took on for me another meaning, as if on seeing an egg I could sense the chick inside. God wills what He creates and has created what He willed, my child is in His hands and there is nothing I can do. That is indeed true, but these are days when God still shares the child with its mother. But should it turn out to be a son, it will belong to me and to God. Or to God alone. All of us belong to God. Not quite all of us, some are divided between God and Satan. How can one tell. If the law had not silenced women forever, perhaps they could reveal what we need to know, for it was woman who invented the first sin from which all the rest came. What do we need to know. Which part of woman's nature is demonic and which divine and what kind of humanity they have. I don't understand, I thought you were referring to my child. No, I was not referring to your child, I was talking about women, who generate beings such as ourselves and who may be responsible, perhaps unknowingly, for this duality in our nature, which is base and yet so noble, virtuous and yet so wicked, tranquil and yet so troubled, meek and yet so rebellious.

Joseph looked back. Mary was advancing on her donkey, a young boy in front of her and astride the saddle like a grown-up, and for a second Joseph thought he was seeing his own son and seeing Mary for the first time, at the head of this group of women. Simeon's strange words still filled his ears, but he found it hard to believe that any woman could wield so much power, especially this unassuming wife of his, who had never shown any sign of being different from other women. Turning to look at the road ahead, he suddenly remembered the episode of the beggar and the luminous earth. He began to tremble, his hair stood on end, he got goose flesh, and when he turned back to take another look at Mary, he saw, saw clearly, a tall stranger walking by her side, so tall that the man was head and shoulders above the women, this had to be the beggar whom he had missed seeing last time. Joseph looked again, and there he was, a sinister presence among those women that defied explanation. Joseph was about to ask Simeon to look, to make sure he was not imagining things, but the old man had moved on, having spoken his mind, and was now rejoining his companions to resume his position as head of his clan, a role he cannot hope to play much longer. Deprived of a witness, the carpenter looked again in his wife's direction. This time the beggar was gone.

HEADING SOUTH, THEY CROSSED THE WHOLE OF SAMARIA
at great speed, with one eye on the road and the other
nervously scanning their surroundings. They expected some
act of hostility, of hatred, from the people living in these
parts, descendants of the ancient Assyrians, renowned for
their wicked deeds and heretical beliefs, who settled here
during the reign of Shalmaneser, king of Nineveh, after
the expulsion and dispersion of the twelve tribes. More
pagan than Jewish, these people barely acknowledge the
five books of Moses as sacred law, and they dare to suggest that the place chosen by God for His temple was not
Jerusalem but Mount Gerizim, which lies within their domain. The expedition from Galilee traveled at a brisk pace
but could not avoid spending two nights in the open in
this enemy territory, with guards and patrols for fear of
ambush. The treachery of the villains knew no bounds,
and they were capable of refusing water even to someone
of pure Hebrew stock who might be dying of thirst. Such
was the anxiety of the travelers during this stretch of the
journey that, contrary to custom, the men divided into two

45

groups, one in front of the women and children and one behind, to protect them from taunts and insults, or worse. The inhabitants of Samaria, however, must have been going through a peaceful phase, because apart from resentful looks and snide remarks the party from Galilee met with no aggression, no gang of robbers descended from the nearby hills and attacked them with stones.

Shortly before reaching Ramah, those who believed with greatest fervor or who possessed a keener sense of smell swore they were inhaling the sanctified odor of Jerusalem. Here old Simeon and his companions went their separate way, for, as we mentioned earlier, they had to register in a village in this region. Giving profuse thanks to God there in the middle of the road, the travelers made their farewells. The married women filled Mary's head with a thousand and one pieces of advice, the fruits of their experience. Then they parted, some descending into the valley, where they would soon rest after four days on foot, the others making for Ramah, where they would seek shelter in a caravansary, for it would soon be dusk. At Jerusalem, the group that set out from Nazareth will also separate, most of them heading for Beersheba, which they should reach in two days, while the carpenter and his wife will go to nearby Bethlehem. Amid the confusion of embraces and farewells, Joseph called Simeon aside and, with all humility, asked him if he could remember anything more about his vision. I've already told you, it wasn't a vision. Whatever it was, I must know the destiny that awaits my child. If you don't even know your own destiny as you stand here before me asking questions, how can you expect to know the destiny of an unborn child. The eyes of the soul see further, and since yours have been opened by the Lord to certain manifestations reserved for the chosen, I thought you might have seen something where I see only darkness. You may never live to learn your son's destiny, you may, who knows, meet your own fate very shortly, but no more

46

questions, please, stop all this probing and live for the present. And with these words Simeon placed his right hand on Joseph's head, murmured a blessing no one could hear, and rejoined his relatives and friends, who were waiting for him. In single file they made their way down a winding path to the valley, where Simeon's village nestled at the foot of the opposite slope, the houses almost merging with the boulders that stuck out of the ground like bones. Much later, Joseph would learn that the old man died before he could register.

After spending two nights under the stars, exposed to the cold on the barren plain, with no camp fire, for that might betray their presence, the expedition from Nazareth decided to take refuge once more under the archways of a caravansary. The women helped Mary dismount from the donkey, reassuring her, Come, it'll soon be over, and the poor girl whispered back, I know, I can't have long to wait now, and what clearer proof than that great swollen belly. They made her as comfortable as possible in a quiet corner and set about preparing supper, for it was growing late and the travelers planned to eat together. That night there was no conversation, no prayers or stories around the fire, as if the proximity of Jerusalem demanded respectful silence, each man searching his heart and asking, Who is this person who resembles me yet whom I fail to recognize. This is not what they actually said, for people do not start talking to themselves like that, nor was this even in their conscious thoughts, but there can be no doubt that as we sit staring into the flames of a camp fire, our silence can be expressed only with words like these, which say everything. From where he sat, Joseph could see Mary in profile against the light of the fire. Its reddish reflection softly lit one side of her face, tracing her features in chiaroscuro, and he began to realize, with surprise, that Mary was an attractive woman, if one could say this of a person with such a childlike expression. Of course her body was swollen now, yet he could see the agile, graceful figure she would soon regain once their child was born. Without warning, as if his flesh was rebelling after all these months of enforced chastity, a wave of desire surged through his blood and left him dizzy. Mary called out in pain, but he did not go to her assistance. As if someone had doused him with cold water, the sudden memory of the man who two days ago had walked beside his wife dampened Joseph's ardor. The image of that beggar had been haunting both of them ever since Mary discovered she was pregnant, for Joseph did not doubt that the stranger had been in her thoughts throughout the nine months. He could not bring himself to ask his wife what kind of man he was or where he went when he suddenly left. The last thing he wanted was to hear her say in bewilderment, A man, what man. And were Joseph to insist, no doubt Mary would ask the other women to testify, Did any of you see a man in our group, and they would deny seeing him and shake their heads at any such suggestion, and one of them might even answer in jest, Any man who hangs around women all the time is after only one thing. But Joseph would not believe Mary's surprise and that she had not seen the beggar, whether it was man or ghost. I saw him with my own eyes as he walked beside you, he would insist, but Mary, not faltering, would say, As is written in holy law, a wife must obey her husband, so if you insist you saw a beggar walking beside me, I will not contradict you, but believe me I didn't see him. It was the same beggar. But how can you tell, if you didn't see him the first time he appeared. It could only have been him. Much more likely to have been some traveler who was walking so slowly that we all overtook him, first the men, then the women, and he was probably alongside our group when you chanced to look back. Ah, so you admit he was there. Not at all, I'm simply trying as a dutiful wife to find some explanation that will satisfy you. Drowsy, Joseph watches Mary through half-closed eyes in the hope that he will find the truth in her face, but her face is now cast in shadow like the waning moon, her profile a vague outline in the light of the dying embers. Joseph nods, overcome by the effort of trying to understand, taking with him, as he falls asleep, the absurd idea that the beggar might be the image of his own son emerging from the future to tell him, This is what I'll look like one day, but you won't live to see it. Joseph slept with a resigned smile on his lips, a sad smile. He thought he heard Mary saying, God forbid that this beggar has nowhere to rest his head. For verily I say unto you that many things in this world could be known before it is too late, if husbands and wives would only confide in each other as husbands and wives.

Early next morning, most of the travelers who had spent the night in the caravansary left for Jerusalem, but those on foot stayed together, so that Joseph, without losing sight of his countrymen who were heading for Beersheba, accompanied his wife this time, walking alongside her as he had seen the beggar walk, or whatever he was. Joseph is convinced now that God bestowed a favor by allowing him to see his own son even before he is born, a son not wrapped in swaddling clothes, a tiny, unformed creature, smelly and bawling, but a fully grown man, taller than his father and most of the males of his race. Joseph is pleased to be taking his son's place, he is at once father and child, and this feeling is so strong that his real child, the unborn infant inside his mother's womb and heading for Jerusalem, suddenly becomes unimportant.

Jerusalem, Jerusalem, the pilgrims call out devoutly as the city comes into sight, rising before them like an apparition on the crest of the hill beyond the valley, a truly celestial city, the center of the universe. Sparkling in all directions under the midday sun, it is a crystal crown which will turn to purest gold at sunset and ivory in moonlight. Jerusalem, O Jerusalem. The Temple appears at that very

49

moment, as if set there by God, and the sudden breeze that caresses the faces, hair, and clothes of the travelers could be a divine gesture, for, looking carefully at the clouds in the sky, we see a huge hand withdrawing, its fingers soiled with clay, its palm marked with the lines of life and death of every man and creature in this world, but the time has also come for us to trace the lines of life and death of God Himself. Trembling with emotion, the travelers raise their arms to heaven and raise their voices in thanksgiving, no longer in chorus, but each one lost in ecstasy, the more sober of them scarcely moving but looking up and praying with great fervor, as if they were being allowed to speak to God on equal terms. The road leads downward, and when the travelers descend into the valley and climb the next slope, which takes them to the city gates, the Temple will tower higher and higher, also the dreaded Antonia fortress, where even at this distance one can make out the shadowy forms of the Roman soldiers who stand watch on the terraces, and see the gleam of their weapons. The group from Nazareth must say good-bye here, for Mary is exhausted and would never survive the bumpy ride downhill at this fast pace, which accelerates to a headlong rush once the city walls loom into view.

And so Joseph and Mary find themselves alone on the road, she trying to recover her strength, he impatient at the delay, now that they are so close to their destination. The sun beats down on the silent travelers. A muffled cry escapes Mary's lips. Worried, Joseph asks her, Is the pain getting worse, and she can barely say, Yes. Then an expression of disbelief creeps into her face, as though she has encountered something beyond her understanding. She certainly felt the pain in her body, but it seemed to belong to someone else. To whom, then. To the child inside her. How can she feel pain that belongs to another, and yet it could be hers, like an echo that by some strange trick of acoustics is louder than the sound that produced it. Joseph cautiously asks, Is the pain still bad, and Mary does not know how to answer. She would be lying if she said no, yet yes is not true either, so she decides to say nothing, the pain is there, she can feel it, but it is so remote that she has the impression she is watching her child suffer in her womb without being able to go to its assistance. No order has been given, Joseph has not used his whip, yet the donkey begins the steep slope leading to Jerusalem, as if looking forward to a full manger and a long rest. It does not know that there is still some way to go before reaching Bethlehem, and that, once there, things will not be so easy. Julius Caesar, for example, proclaims, Veni, vidi, vici, at the height of his glory, only to be assassinated by his own son, whose sole excuse was that he was adopted. Conflicts between fathers and sons, the inheritance of guilt, the disinheritance of kith and kin, and the sacrifice of innocents go far back in time and promise to continue in the future.

As they entered the city gates, Mary could no longer hold back her cries, now as heartrending as if a lance had pierced her. But only Joseph could hear them, such was the noise coming from the crowd, somewhat less from the animals, although between them they created a din reminiscent of a marketplace. Joseph decided, You're in no condition to go any farther, let's find an inn nearby, tomorrow I'll go on to Bethlehem alone and explain that you're giving birth, you can always register later if it's really necessary, because I know nothing about Roman law, and who can tell, perhaps only the head of the family needs to register, especially in our situation. Mary reassured him, The pain has gone, and she was telling the truth, the stabbing that caused her to cry out had become a mild throbbing, uncomfortable but bearable, rather like wearing a hairshirt. Joseph was relieved. To search for lodging in Jerusalem, with its maze of narrow streets, was a daunting task, especially now, his wife in the throes of childbirth and he as terrified as the next man at the thought of the

51

responsibility, although he would never admit it. He thought to himself that once they reached Bethlehem, which was not much bigger than Nazareth, things would be easier, because people are friendlier in smaller communities. It doesn't matter whether Mary is no longer in pain or simply putting a brave face on things, they are on their way and will soon be in Bethlehem. The donkey receives a slap on its hindquarters, which is not so much a spur to go faster amid all this traffic and indescribable confusion as an affectionate gesture expressing Joseph's relief. Merchants cram the narrow streets, people of every race and tongue jostle one another, but the streets clear almost miraculously whenever a patrol of Roman soldiers or a procession of camels appears, the crowds disperse like the parting waters of the Red Sea. At a steady pace, the couple from Nazareth and their donkey gradually emerge from the seething bazaar full of ignorant, insensitive people, to whom there would be no point saying, See that man over there, that's Joseph, and the woman who looks as if she is about to give birth any minute is Mary, they're on their way to register in Bethlehem. If our kind attempt to identify them goes unnoticed, it is simply because we live in a world where Josephs and Marys of every age and condition abound and can be found at every turn. This is not the only couple called Joseph and Mary expecting a baby, who knows, perhaps two infants of the same sex, preferably male, will be born at the same hour and only a road or a field of corn between them. The destinies that await these infants, however, will be different, even if we name both of them Yeshua, which is the same as Jesus. And lest we are accused of anticipating events by naming an unborn child, the fault lies with the carpenter, who some time ago made up his mind that this is the name he will give his first son.

Leaving by the southern gate, the travelers take the road to Bethlehem, glad that they will soon reach their destination and be able at long last to rest from their tiring journey. Mary's troubles, of course, are not over, for she, and she alone, still has to endure the trial of childbirth, and who knows where or when. According to Holy Scripture, Bethlehem is the location of David's house, the line from which Joseph claims descent, but with the passing of time his relatives have all died, or the carpenter has lost all contact, an unpromising situation which leads us to believe, even before we get there, that the couple will have a problem finding a place. Arriving in Bethlehem, Joseph cannot knock on the first door he comes to and say, I'd like my child to be born here, and expect to be greeted with a welcoming smile from the mistress of the house, Come in, come in, Master Joseph, the water is boiling, the mat laid out on the floor, the swaddling clothes are ready, make yourself at home. Things might have been so in a golden age, when the wolf, rather than eat the lamb, would feed on wild herbs. But this is the age of iron, cruel and unfeeling. The time for miracles has either passed or not come yet, besides, miracles, genuine miracles, whatever people say, are not such a good idea, if it means destroying the very order of things in order to improve them. Joseph is not eager to confront the problems that await him, but he considers how much worse it would be if his child was born by the roadside, and so he forces the donkey, poor beast, to go faster. Only the donkey knows how weary it feels, all God cares about are humans, and not all humans, because some of them live like donkeys or worse, and God makes no effort to help them. One of his fellow travelers told Joseph that there was a caravansary in Bethlehem, a stroke of luck that seems to be the answer to his problem. But even a humble carpenter would find it embarrassing to see his pregnant wife exposed to the morbid curiosity and wagging tongues of drovers and cameleers, and some of those fellows are as brutish as the beasts they handle, and their behavior is much more contemptible, for as men they possess the divine gift of speech, which animals are denied. Joseph finally decides to seek the advice and guidance of the elders of the synagogue, and wonders why he did not think of this sooner. Somewhat relieved, he is about to ask Mary if the pain is still there, but changes his mind and says nothing, we mustn't forget that this whole process, from the moment of impregnation to the moment of birth, is unclean, that vile female organ, vortex and abyss, the seat of all the world's evil, an inner labyrinth of blood, discharges, gushing water, revolting afterbirth, dear God, how can You permit Your beloved children to be born in such impurity. How much better for You and us had You created them from transparent light, yesterday, today, and tomorrow, the beginning, middle, and end alike for everyone, without discrimination between aristocrats and commoners, kings and carpenters. So Joseph asks only, and with seeming indifference, as if preoccupied with more important matters, How do you feel. The question is timely, for Mary now notices something different about the pain she is experiencing, about the pain, rather, that now is experiencing her.

They had been walking for more than an hour, and Bethlehem could not be far. To their surprise, they found the road from Jerusalem deserted, with Bethlehem so close to the city one might expect to see continuous movement of people and animals. At the point where the road forked, one road to Beersheba, the other to Bethlehem, the world appeared to contract and fold over on itself. If you were to visualize the world as a person, it would be like watching a man cover his eyes with his mantle and listen to the travelers' footsteps, just as we listen to the song of birds among the branches, and that indeed is how we must appear to the birds hidden in the trees.

To the right stands the tomb of Rachel, the bride for whom Jacob waited fourteen years. After seven years' service, he was wedded to Leah and had to wait another seven years before being allowed to marry his beloved, who would die in Bethlehem giving birth to a son that Jacob named Benjamin, which means son of my right hand, but Rachel, as she lay dying, rightly called him Benoni, which means child of my sorrow, God forbid that this should be an omen. Houses now begin to appear, mud-colored like those of Nazareth, but here in Bethlehem the color of mud is paler, a mixture of yellow and gray. Mary is near collapse, her body slumping farther forward over the saddlebags with each passing moment. Joseph has come to her aid, and she puts one arm around his shoulder to steady herself. What a pity there is no one here to witness this touching scene, which is all too rare. And so they enter Bethlehem.

Despite Mary's condition, Joseph inquired if there was a caravansary nearby, thinking they might rest until the following morning. Mary was in great pain but still showed no sign of being ready to give birth. But when, on the other side of the village, they reached the caravansary, which was squalid and rowdy, part bazaar and part stable, there was not a quiet corner to be found, even though it was still early and most of the drovers and cameleers would only start arriving later. The couple turned back. Joseph left Mary beneath the shade of a fig tree in a tiny square and went off to consult the elders. There was no one in the synagogue apart from a caretaker, who called out to an urchin playing nearby and told him to accompany the stranger to one of the elders, who might be able to help. Fortune, who protects the innocent whenever she remembers them, decreed that in this latest quest Joseph should pass through the square where he had left his wife, and just in time to save her from the deadly shade of the fig tree, which was slowly killing her, an unforgivable mistake, as fig trees abound in this land and they both should have known better. So, like condemned souls, they set off once more in search of the elder, but he had left for the countryside and was not expected home for some time.

On hearing this, the carpenter summoned his courage and called out, Is there anyone here who for the love of Almighty God will offer shelter to my dear wife, who is about to give birth. All he asked was a quiet corner, they had brought their own mats. And could anyone tell him where to find a midwife in the village who could assist with the birth. Poor Joseph blushed to hear himself blurt out these private worries and concerns. The female slave standing in the doorway went back inside to report to her mistress, and reappeared after a while to tell them that they could not stay there and must look for shelter elsewhere. Since there was little chance of finding a place in the village, her mistress suggested they take refuge in one of the many caves in the nearby slopes. And what about a midwife, asked Joseph, whereupon the slave replied that if her mistress agreed and he wished, she herself could help, for she had been in service all her life and had assisted at many a birth. These are cruel times indeed, when a pregnant woman comes knocking at our door and we deny her shelter in a corner of the yard and send her off to give birth in a cave, like the bears and wolves. Something pricked our conscience, however, and, getting up from where we were sitting, we went to the door to see for ourselves this husband and wife who so desperately needed a roof over their heads. The sadness in that poor girl's face was enough to arouse our maternal instinct, so we patiently explained why we could not possibly take them in, the house was already crowded with sons and daughters, grandchildren, in-laws. As you can see, there simply isn't any room here, but our slave will take you to a cave we use as a stable. There are no animals there at present, and you should be able to make yourselves comfortable. The young couple were most grateful for our generous offer, and we withdrew, feeling we had done our best and that our conscience was clear.

With all this coming and going, walking and resting, inquiring and pleading, the deep blue sky has lost its color and the sun will soon disappear behind that mountain. The slave, Salome, for that is her name, leads the way. She carries some hot coals to make a fire, an earthenware pot to heat water, and salt to rub down the newborn infant as a precaution against infection. And since Mary has brought cloths and Joseph has a knife in his pack to cut the umbilical cord, unless Salome prefers to use her teeth, everything is ready for the birth. A stable, when all is said and done, is as good as a house, and anyone who has slept in a manger knows that it is almost as good as a cradle. And the donkey is not likely to notice any difference, for straw is the same in heaven as on earth. They reached the cave when the hovering twilight was still shedding gold on the hills. If their progress was slow, it was not because of the distance but because now that Mary had a place to rest, she could at last abandon herself to her suffering. She pleaded with them to slow down, for whenever the donkey lost its footing on a stone, she suffered agonizing pain. The waning light outside did not penetrate the darkness of the cave, but with a handful of straw, the live coals, much puffing and blowing, and some dry kindling, the slave soon had a fire blazing as bright as any dawn. Then she lit the oil lamp that was suspended from a rock jutting from the wall, and after helping Mary lie down, she went to fetch water from the nearby wells of Solomon. On returning, she found Joseph distracted with worry, but we must not be too hard on him, for a man is not expected to be able to cope in such a crisis, at most he can hold his wife's hand and hope that everything will be all right. Mary, however, is alone. The world would crumble if a Jewish man in those days attempted any such comforting gesture. The female slave came in, whispered a few words of encouragement, then knelt between Mary's legs, for a woman's legs should be kept apart whenever something goes in or comes out. Salome has lost count of the number of children she has helped bring into the world, and poor Mary's suffering is

57

no different from that of any other woman, for as God warned Eve after she sinned, I will greatly multiply your suffering and your conception, in sorrow you will bring forth children, and after centuries of sorrow and suffering God is not yet appeased and the agony goes on. Joseph is no longer present, not even at the entrance to the cave, he has fled rather than listen to Mary's cries, but the cries follow him, as if the very earth were screaming. The noise is such that three shepherds who were passing with their flocks approached Joseph and asked, What's going on, the earth seems to be screaming, and he told them, My wife is giving birth in that cave. They asked, You're a stranger to these parts, aren't you. Yes, we've come from Nazareth, in Galilee, to register, and no sooner did we arrive than my wife started feeling worse and now she's in labor. The fading light made it difficult to see the faces of the four men, and soon their features would completely disappear, but their voices could still be heard. Have you any food, one of the shepherds said. A little, replied Joseph, and the same voice told him, Once the child is born, let me know, and I'll bring you some sheep's milk, and then a second voice said, And I'll give you cheese. Then a long silence, and the third shepherd spoke. In a voice that seemed to come from the bowels of the earth he said, I'll bring you bread.

The son of Joseph and Mary was born, like any other child, covered with his mother's blood, dripping with mucus, and suffering in silence. He cried because they made him cry, and he will cry for this one and only reason. Wrapped in swaddling clothes, he lies in the manger with the donkey standing nearby but unlikely to bite him because the animal is tethered and cannot move far. Salome is outside burying the afterbirth when Joseph approaches. She waits until he has gone into the cave, lingering there to inhale the cool night and feeling as exhausted as if she herself had just given birth, but this is something she can only imagine, never having had children of her own.

Three men come down the slope. They are the shepherds. They enter the cave together. Mary is reclining, and her eyes are closed. Seated on a stone, Joseph rests his arm on the edge of the manger and appears to be watching over his son. The first shepherd steps forward and says, Here's the milk from my sheep, which I drew with my own hands. Opening her eyes, Mary smiles. The second shepherd steps forward and says in his turn, I myself churned the milk that made this cheese. Mary nods and smiles again. Then the third shepherd, whose massive frame seems to fill the cave, steps forward and, without so much as glancing at the newborn infant's parents, says, I kneaded this bread with my own hands and baked it in the fire that burns beneath the earth. No sooner had he spoken than Mary recognized him.

Since the world began, for every person who is born another dies. The person now close to death is King Herod, who in addition to all imaginable evils suffers from a horrible itch, which has almost driven him insane. He feels as if hundreds of thousands of ants are gnawing incessantly at his body with their tiny savage jaws. Having tried, to no avail, all the balsams known to man, remedies from Egypt and India, the royal physicians scratched their heads, or, to be more precise, were in grave danger of losing their heads, as they frantically tried ablutions and household potions, mixing with water or oil any and all herbs and powders reputed to do some good, however contrary their effect. The king, foaming at the mouth like a mad dog, beside himself with pain and fury, threatens to have them all crucified unless they can relieve his afflictions, which go beyond the unbearable burning in his skin and the convulsions that leave him exhausted and writhing on the floor, his eyes bulging from their sockets as the ants continue to multiply and gnaw beneath his robes. Worst of all is the gangrene that has set in during the last few days, and this

60

mysterious affliction has started tongues wagging in the palace, as worms begin to ravage the genital organs of the royal person and truly devour him alive. Herod's screams echo through the halls and corridors of the palace, the eunuchs attending him are kept awake day and night, the slaves of lower rank flee in terror when they hear him approach. Dragging his body, which stinks of rot despite the perfumes sprinkled lavishly over his robes and rubbed into his dyed hair, Herod is being kept alive only by his own wrath. Carried around in a litter, accompanied by doctors and armed guards, he scours the palace from one end to another in search of traitors, whom he imagines to be lurking everywhere, an obsession he has had for some time. Without any warning he will suddenly point a finger, perhaps at the chief eunuch, accusing him of wielding too much influence, or at some stubborn Pharisee who has criticized those who disobey the law when they should be the first to respect it, there is no need to name names, and that finger was also pointed at his sons Alexander and Aristobulus, who were imprisoned and hastily sentenced to death by a tribunal of nobles convened for the purpose, what choice did the poor king have when in his delirium he saw those wicked sons advancing upon him with bared swords, when in the most terrifying nightmare of all he beheld in a mirror his own severed head. He has escaped that terrible end and can now quietly contemplate the corpses of those who a moment before were heirs to the throne, his own sons found guilty of conspiracy, misconduct, and arrogance and strangled to death.

From the murk of his troubled mind comes another nightmare to disturb the sporadic moments of sleep into which he falls from sheer exhaustion. The prophet Micah comes to haunt him, that prophet who lived at the time of Isaiah and witnessed the terrible wars that the Assyrians waged in Samaria and Judaea. Micah appears before him, denouncing the rich and powerful as befits a prophet, especially in this accursed age. Covered with the dust of battle and wearing a bloodstained tunic, Micah storms into his dream in a deafening blast from some other world. With hands of lightning he pushes open enormous bronze gates and gives solemn warning, The Lord will come down from His holy temple and tread upon the high places of the earth. Then he threatens, Woe to them that devise iniquity and work evil upon their beds, when the morning is light they practice it because it is in the power of their hand. And he denounces those who covet fields and take them by violence, and who take houses, oppressing a man and his house, even a man and his heritage. After repeating these words night after night, Micah, as if responding to a signal, vanishes into thin air. What causes Herod to wake up in a cold sweat is not so much the terror of those prophetic cries as the agonizing thought that this nightly visitor withdraws just as he is about to reveal something more. The prophet raises his hand and parts his lips, only to disappear, leaving the king filled with foreboding. Now, as everyone knows, Herod is not likely to be intimidated by threats when he does not feel the slightest remorse for all the deaths he ordered. For this is the man who had the brother of Mariamne, whom he loved more than any other woman, burned alive, the man who ordered her grandfather strangled and finally Mariamne herself, when he accused her of adultery. It is true that he later suffered a bit of madness and called for Mariamne as if she were still alive, but he recovered from it and discovered that his mother-in-law was hatching a plot, and not for the first time, to remove him from power. Instantly this viper was dispatched to the pantheon of the family into which Herod had married, with unfortunate consequences for all concerned, because the king's three sons became heirs to the throne, Alexander and Aristobulus, whose sad end we have already mentioned, and Antipater, who soon will meet a similar fate. But we must not forget, since there is more to life than tragedy and misfortune, that Herod had no fewer than ten comely wives to pamper him and arouse his lust, although by now they could do little for him and he even less for them. Therefore the nightly apparition of an irate prophet intent on haunting the powerful king of Judaea and Samaria, Peraea and Idumaea, Galilee and Gaulanitis, Trachanitis, Auranitis, and Batanaea, would make little impression were it not for that sudden interruption of the dream that leaves him in suspense, awaiting some new threat, but what threat, and how and when.

Meanwhile, in Bethlehem, on the doorstep of Herod's palace, as it were, Joseph and his family continued to live in the cave. They did not expect to stay there long, so there was little point in looking for a house, especially at a time when accommodations were scarce and the profitable practice of renting rooms had not yet been invented. On the eighth day Joseph took his firstborn to the synagogue to be circumcised. Using a knife made of flint, with admirable skill the priest cut the wailing child's foreskin, and the fate of that foreskin is in itself worthy of a novel, from the moment it was cut, a loop of pale skin with scarcely any bleeding, to its glorious sanctification during the papacy of Paschal I, who reigned in the ninth century of Christianity. Anyone wishing to see that foreskin today need only visit the parish church of Calcata near Viterbo in Italy, where it is preserved in a reliquary for the spiritual benefit of the faithful and the amusement of curious atheists. Joseph announced that his son should be called Jesus, and this was the name inscribed in God's register after it was added to the civil register of Caesar. Far from being resigned to this outrage inflicted on his person without any appreciable spiritual benefit in return, the infant howled all the way back to the cave, where its mother, needless to say, was anxiously waiting, this being her first child. Poor little thing, poor little thing, she said soothingly, and opening her tunic, she began to nurse the child, first on

63

the left breast, perhaps because that was closer to her heart. Jesus, although still unaware of his name, for no more than a babe in arms, gave a deep sigh of contentment the moment he felt the gentle pressure of Mary's breast against his cheek and the moist warmth of her skin on his. As the sweet taste of his mother's milk filled his mouth, the pain and indignity of the circumcision became remote, dissipated into a formless pleasure that surfaced and went on surfacing, as if arrested at the threshold and not allowed to define itself completely. On growing up, he will forget these first sensations and find it difficult to believe he ever experienced them, which happens to all of us, wherever we may have been born and whatever our destiny. But Joseph, if we had the courage to ask him about this, and God forbid that we should commit any such indiscretion, would tell us that a father's cares are more to the point, since he now faces the problem of feeding an extra mouth, an expression no less true or apt simply because a child is fed at its mother's breast. Indeed, Joseph has reason to be worried. How are they to live until they return to Nazareth. Mary is weak and in no condition to make the long journey, and besides, she must wait until she is no longer unclean and remain in the blood of her purification for the thirty-three days following her child's circumcision. The little money they brought from Nazareth has nearly all been spent, and Joseph cannot work as a carpenter here without tools or the means to buy wood. Life at that time was hard for the poor and God could not be expected to provide for everyone. From within the cave came a sudden whimper, which soon stopped, a sign that Mary had changed the little Jesus to her right breast, but that short frustration was enough to renew the pain where the child was circumcised. Having sucked to his satisfaction, Jesus will fall asleep in his mother's arms and barely open his eyes when she settles him gently in the manger as if entrusting him to an affectionate and faithful nurse. Joseph, seated at the en-

64

trance to the cave, is still trying to decide what to do. He knows that there is no work for him here in Bethlehem, not even as an apprentice, for when he made inquiries, the answer was always the same. If I need any help I'll send for you, empty promises that do not fill a man's belly, although this race has been living off promises since it came into being.

Time and time again one has seen, even in people not particularly given to reflection, that the best way of finding a solution is to let one's thoughts drift until the right moment comes to pounce, like a tiger taking its prey by surprise. And so the false promises of the master carpenters of Bethlehem led Joseph to think about God's true promises, then about the Temple of Jerusalem, still under construction, where there must be demand for laborers, not only bricklayers and stonemasons but also carpenters even if only to square joists and plane boards, basic tasks that are well within Joseph's capabilities. The only drawback, assuming they give him a job, is the time it takes to reach the site, a good hour and a half's walk at a brisk pace, because it is uphill all the way and there is no patron saint of hill climbers to extend a helping hand, unless Joseph rides there, but that would mean finding a safe place to leave his donkey. This may be God's chosen land, but there are still plenty of rogues around if we are to believe the dire warnings of the prophet Micah. Joseph was pondering this when Mary emerged from the cave after feeding her child and settling him down to sleep. How is Jesus, his father asked, conscious of how foolish the question sounded but unable to suppress his pride as the father of a son who already had a name. The child is fine, replied Mary, for whom the name was of no importance. She would have been just as happy to call him my child for the rest of her life, were it not for the fact that she would bear more children, and to refer to them all simply as my child would create as much confusion as in the Tower of

Babel. Joseph said, allowing the words to come out as if he was thinking aloud, which is one way of not showing too much confidence, I must earn a living while we are here, yet there is no suitable work in Bethlehem. Mary said nothing, nor was she expected to speak, she was only there to listen, and her husband had already made an enormous concession by taking her into his confidence. Joseph looked at the sun, trying to decide whether there was enough time for him to go and come back. He went into the cave to fetch his mantle and pack and, on reappearing, told Mary, I'm off, trusting in God to find work for this honest artisan in His tabernacle should He deem him worthy of such an honor. Joseph threw his mantle over his left shoulder, adjusted his pack, and went off without another word.

Truly all is not gloom. Although work on the Temple was making good progress, laborers were still being hired, especially if they accepted low wages. Joseph had no difficulty passing the simple test given by the head carpenter, which should make us reflect whether our earlier disparaging comments about Joseph's professional skills might not have been unjustified. This latest recruit for the Temple site went off giving profuse thanks to God. Along the way he stopped some travelers and asked them to join him in praising the Lord, and they cheerfully obliged, for these people see one man's joy as something to be shared by all. We refer, of course, to people of humble condition. When Joseph reached the spot where Rachel is buried, a thought occurred to him which came from the heart rather than the head, namely, that this woman eager to have another child might die, if you will pardon the expression, at his hands, and before she could even get to know him. Without so much as a word or a glance, one body separates itself from another, as indifferent as the fruit that drops from a tree. Then an even sadder thought came to him, namely, that children die because their fathers beget them and their mothers bring them into the world, and he took pity on his own son, who was condemned to die although innocent. As he stood, filled with confusion and anguish, before the tomb of Jacob's beloved wife, carpenter Joseph's shoulders drooped and his head sank, and his entire body broke out in a cold sweat, and now there was no one passing on the road to whom he could turn for help. For the first time in his life he doubted whether the world had any meaning, and said in a loud voice, like one who has lost all hope, This is where I will die. Perhaps these words, in other circumstances and if spoken with the courage and conviction of those who commit suicide, words devoid of sorrow and weeping, would suffice to open the door by which we depart the land of the living. But most men are inconstant and can be distracted by a cloud on high, by a spider weaving its web, a dog chasing a butterfly, a hen scratching the soil and clucking to its chicks, or something as commonplace as a sudden itch on one's face, which one scratches, wondering, Now what was I thinking about. For this reason Rachel's tomb instantly reverted to a small, windowless whitewashed building, a building like a discarded die forgotten because not needed for the game under way. On the stone at the entrance there are marks left by the sweaty and grimy hands of pilgrims, who have been coming here since ancient times, and the tomb is surrounded by olive trees, which were perhaps already old when Jacob chose this spot for the poor mother's last resting place and felled as many trees as were necessary to clear the ground. When all is said and done, we can confidently say that destiny exists and each man's destiny is in the hands of others. Then Joseph moved on, but not before saying a prayer suited to the time and place. He said, Praise be to You, O Lord our God and God of our forefathers, God of Abraham, God of Isaac, God of Jacob, great, almighty, and wondrous God, praise be to You.

Returning to the cave, he went to look at his little son,

asleep in the manger, before telling his wife that he had found work. He thought to himself, He'll die, he must die, and his heart grieved, but then he reflected that by the natural order of things he himself would die first and that his departure from the land of the living would bestow on his son a limited eternity, a contradiction in terms, an eternity that allows one to go on for a little longer when those whom we know and love no longer exist.

Joseph had been careful not to mention to the head carpenter that he would be staying only a few weeks, five at the most, enough time to take his son to the Temple to complete Mary's purification, and to pack their belongings. He said nothing rather than be turned away, which shows that the carpenter from Nazareth was not familiar with working conditions in his own country, no doubt because he thought of himself, and rightly, as his own master and took little interest in the rest of the working community, which then consisted almost entirely of casual labor. He kept careful count of the remaining days, twenty-four, twenty-three, twenty-two, and to avoid making mistakes he improvised a calendar on one of the cave walls, nineteen, drawing lines that he then erased one at a time, sixteen, watched by an admiring Mary, fourteen, thirteen, who thanked the Lord for having given her, nine, eight, seven, six, such a clever husband, who could turn his hand to anything. Joseph told her, We'll leave after we go to the Temple, for it's time I got back to my work in Nazareth, where I have customers waiting, and she tactfully suggested, rather than appear to be criticizing him, But surely we cannot leave without first thanking the woman who owns the cave and the slave who helped deliver our child and who still calls every day to see how he's coming along. Joseph made no reply. He'd never admit to having overlooked such an act of common courtesy, although he had intended to load the donkey beforehand, tie it up during the ceremony, then set off for Nazareth without wasting any time on thanks and farewells. Mary was right, it would have been ill-mannered to go away without so much as a word of gratitude, but if truth, poor thing, were to be known, Joseph was somewhat lacking in manners. To be reminded of this omission caused him to sulk and become irritable with his wife, behavior which usually served to ease his conscience and silence remorse. So they would stay on for two or three days, make their farewells as was only fit and proper, and leave the inhabitants of Bethlehem with a favorable impression of this devout family from Galilee, courteous and dutiful, notably different when one considers the low opinion the inhabitants of Jerusalem and its environs generally have of people from Galilee.

The memorable day finally arrived when the child Jesus was carried to the Temple in the arms of his mother, who rode the patient donkey that had accompanied and assisted this family since the beginning. Joseph led the donkey by the halter, he was in a hurry to get there, anxious not to lose a whole day's work, even though their departure was imminent. The next day they were on the road as dawn dispersed the last vestiges of night. Rachel's tomb was already some distance behind. When they passed it, the façade had taken on the fiery hue of a pomegranate, so unlike its appearance at night, when it became opaque, or in the light of the moon, when it looked deathly pale. After a while the infant Jesus woke up, and had scarcely opened his eyes when his mother wrapped him for the journey, and he cried to be fed in that plaintive voice, the only voice he has so far. One day, like the rest of us, he will learn to speak with other voices, which will enable him to express other forms of hunger and experience other tears.

On the steep slopes not far from Jerusalem the family merged with the pilgrims and vendors who were flocking to the city, all intent on being the first to arrive but cautiously slowing down and curbing their excitement when they came face to face with the Roman soldiers who were moving through the crowd in pairs, or with a detachment of Herod's mercenary troops, who recruited every imaginable race, many Jews, as one might expect, but also Indumaeans, Galatians, Thracians, Germans, Gauls, and even Babylonians, who are unrivaled as archers. A carpenter who handles only peaceful weapons such as the plane, adze, mallet, or hammer, Joseph becomes filled with such fear and revulsion when he runs into these louts that he can no longer behave naturally or disguise his true feelings. He keeps his eyes lowered, and it is Mary, who has been shut away in the cave for weeks with no one to talk to apart from the female slave, it is Mary who takes a good look around, her dainty little chin held high with understandable pride, for she is holding her firstborn, a mere woman yet capable of giving children to God and her husband. She looks so radiant and happy that some Gauls, fierce, fair, with large whiskers, their weapons at the ready, smile as the family passes, their cruel hearts softened by the sight of the young mother with her first child. Smiling at this renewal of the world, they bare rotten teeth, but it's the thought that counts.

There is the Temple. Viewed at close quarters, the building gives one vertigo, a mountain of stones upon stones which no earthly power seems capable of dressing, lifting, laying, and fitting, yet there they are, joined together by their own weight, without mortar, as if the entire world were a set of building blocks. The uppermost cornices, seen from below, appear to graze the sky, like another but quite different Tower of Babel, which even God will be unable to save because it is doomed to the same destruction, confusion, and bloodshed. Voices will ask, Why, a thousand times, believing there must be an answer, but eventually they will die away, because it is better to be silent. Joseph goes off to tether the donkey in the caravansary set aside for the animals. During Passover and other religious feasts the place gets so crowded that there is not enough room for a camel to shake the flies from its tail, but it is easier now that the last day of the census has passed and travelers have returned to their homes. In the Court of the Gentiles, however, which is bordered by colonnades on all four sides, with the temple precinct in the center, there is a large crowd, money changers, bird catchers, merchants trading lambs and kids, pilgrims gathered here for one reason or another, and numerous foreigners curious to visit the famous Temple built by King Herod. But the court is so spacious that anyone on the far side looks no bigger than an insect, as though Herod's architects, seeing through God's eyes, wanted to show the insignificance of men in the presence of the Almighty, especially if they happen to be Gentiles. As for the Jews, unless they have come for a leisurely stroll, their goal is the middle of the court, the center of their world, the navel of navels, the Holy of Holies. That is where the carpenter and his wife are heading, that is where Jesus is carried after his father purchases two turtledoves from the steward of the Temple, if such a title is appropriate for one who benefits from the monopoly on these religious transactions. The poor birds are ignorant of the fate that awaits them, though the smell of flesh and singed feathers lingering in the air does not deceive anyone, to say nothing of the much stronger stench of blood and excrement as oxen, dragged away to be sacrificed, foul themselves in terror. Joseph cradles the doves in the palms of his callused hands, and the poor birds, in their innocence, peck with satisfaction at his fingers, which he curves to form a cage. It is as if they were trying to tell him, We are happy with our new master. But Joseph's skin is far too rough to feel or decipher the affectionate nibbling of the two doves.

They enter by the Wooden Gate, one of thirteen entrances to the Temple. It has an inscription in Greek and Latin carved into the stonework, which reads as follows,

It is forbidden for any Gentile to cross this threshold and the balustrade surrounding the Temple, trespassers will be put to death. Joseph and Mary enter, carrying Jesus between them, and in due course will make a safe exit, but the doves, as we know, must be killed according to the law before Mary's purification can be acknowledged and ratified. Any ironic or irreverent disciple of Voltaire will find it difficult to resist making the obvious remark that, things being what they are, purity can be maintained only so long as there are innocent creatures to sacrifice in this world, whether turtledoves, lambs, or others. Joseph and Mary climb the fourteen steps to the platform of the Temple. Here is the Court of the Women, on the left the storehouse for the oil and wine used in the liturgy, on the right the Chamber of the Nazirites, priests who do not belong to the tribe of Levi and who are forbidden to cut their hair, drink wine, or go near a corpse. On the opposite side, to the left and right, respectively, of the door facing this one, are the chamber where the lepers who believe themselves cured wait for the priests to come and examine them, and the storehouse where the wood is kept and inspected daily, because rotten and worm-eaten wood must not be thrown on the altar fire. Mary has not much farther to go, she still has to climb the fifteen semicircular steps leading to the Nicanor Gate, also known as the Gate Beautiful, but there she will stop, because women are not permitted to enter the Court of the Israelites, which lies beyond this gate. At the entrance, the Levites receive those who have come to offer sacrifice, but the atmosphere is less pious, unless piety at that time had another meaning. It is not just the smoke rising from the burning fat or the smell of fresh blood and incense but also the shouting of the men, the howling, bleating, and lowing of the animals waiting to be slaughtered, and the last raucous squawk of a bird once able to sing. Mary tells the Levite in attendance that she has come for purification, and Joseph hands over the doves. For one brief moment Mary places her hands over the birds, her only gesture before the Levite and her husband turn away and disappear through the gate. She will not stir until Joseph returns, she simply steps aside so as not to obstruct the passage, and waits, holding her son in her arms.

Within the Court of the Israelites there is a furnace and a slaughterhouse. On two sizable stone slabs, larger animals such as oxen and calves are killed, also sheep, ewes, and male and female goats. There are tall pillars alongside the tables, where the carcasses are suspended from hooks set into the stonework, and here one can watch the frenzied activity as the butchers wield their knives, cleavers, axes, and handsaws, the air filled with fumes rising from the wood and the singed hides, and with the smell of blood and sweat. Anyone witnessing this scene would have to be a saint to understand how God can approve of such appalling carnage if He is, as He claims, the father of all men and beasts. Joseph has to wait outside the balustrade that separates the Court of the Israelites from that of the priests, but from where he stands he has a good view of the high altar, four times higher than the tallest man, and of the Temple proper beyond, for the arrangement is like one of those Chinese boxes with each chamber leading into another. We see the building from afar and think to ourselves, Ah, the Temple, then we enter the Court of the Gentiles and once more think, Ah, the Temple, and now the carpenter Joseph, leaning on the balustrade, looks up and says, Ah, the Temple, and he is right, there is the wide front, with its four columns set into the wall, the capitals festooned with laurel leaves in the Greek style, and the great gaping entrance, which has no door, but to enter that Temple of Temples inhabited by God would be to defy all prohibitions, to pass through the holy place called Hereal, and finally come into Debir, which is the last chamber of all, the Holy of Holies, an awesome stone chamber as empty as the universe, windowless and dark as the tomb, where the light of day has never and will never penetrate, until the hour of its destruction, when all the stones are reduced to rubble. The more remote He is, the more holy he becomes, while Joseph is merely the father of a Jewish child among many. He is about to witness the sacrifice of two innocent doves, that is, the father not the son, for the son, who is just as innocent, is in his mother's arms, perhaps thinking, if such a thing is possible at his age, that this is how the world must always be.

By the altar, which is made of massive slabs of stone untouched by tools since hewn from the quarry and set up in this vast edifice, a barefooted priest wearing a linen tunic waits for the Levite to hand over the turtledoves. He takes the first one, carries it to a corner of the altar, and with a single blow knocks the head from its body. The blood spurts everywhere. The priest sprinkles blood over the lower part of the altar and then places the decapitated bird on a dish to drain the rest of the blood. At the end of the day he will retrieve the dead bird, for it now belongs to him. The other turtledove has the honor of being wholly sacrificed, which means it will be incinerated. The priest ascends the ramp leading to the top of the altar, where the sacred fire burns. On the righthand edge of the altar he beheads the bird, sprinkles its blood over the plinth adorned on each corner with sheeps' horns, then plucks out the entrails. No one pays any attention to what is happening, for this is a death of no consequence. Craning his neck, Joseph tries to identify, amid all the smoke and smells, the smoke and smell of his own sacrifice, when the priest, having poured salt over the bird's head and carcass, tosses the pieces into the fire. Joseph cannot be sure. Crackling in the billowing flames fueled by fat, the limp, disemboweled carcass of the little dove would not even fill a cavity of one of God's teeth. At the foot of the ramp three priests are waiting. A calf topples to the ground, felled by a cleaver, my God, my God, how fragile You have made us and how vulnerable to death. Joseph has nothing more to accomplish here, he must withdraw, collect his wife and child, and return home. Mary is pure once more, not in the strict sense of the word, because purity is something to which most human beings, and above all women, can scarcely hope to aspire. With time and a period of seclusion, her fluxes and humors have settled down, everything has returned to normal, the only difference being that there are now two doves fewer in the world and one more child, who caused their death. The family leaves the Temple by the same gate they entered, Joseph goes to fetch the donkey, and Mary, stepping on a large stone, climbs onto the animal's back while Joseph holds the child. This is not the first time, but perhaps the memory of that turtledove having its entrails plucked out causes him now to linger before handing Jesus back to his mother, as if convinced that no arms can protect his son better than his own. He accompanies his wife and child to the city gate before returning to the Temple site. He will also be here tomorrow to finish his week's work, and then, God willing, they'll be off to Nazareth with all haste.

That same night, the prophet Micah revealed what he had hitherto withheld. As King Herod, by now resigned to his tortured dreams, waited for the apparition to disappear after the usual ranting and raving, which no longer had much effect, the prophet's formidable shape suddenly grew bigger, and he uttered words he had never spoken before, It is from you, Bethlehem, so insignificant among the families of Judah, that the future ruler of Israel has come. And at that moment the king awoke. Like the deepest chord of a harp, the prophet's words continued to resound through the room. Herod lay with his eyes open, trying to fathom the meaning of this revelation, if there was indeed any meaning, and was so absorbed that he scarcely felt the ants gnawing under his skin or the worms tunneling in his entrails. The prophecy was familiar to every Jew and revealed nothing Herod did not already know. Besides, he was never one to waste his time worrying about the sayings of the prophets. What bothered him was a vague disquiet, a sense of agonizing strangeness, as if the prophet's utterance had another meaning and that somewhere in those syllables and sounds lay an imminent and fearsome threat. He tried to rid himself of this obsession and go back to sleep, but his body resisted, aching to the marrow. Thinking offered some measure of relief. Staring up at the beams on the ceiling, where the decoration appeared to vibrate in the light of aromatic torches shielded by fire screens, King Herod searched for an answer but could find none. He then summoned the chief eunuch from among those guarding his bedside and ordered him to fetch at once from the Temple a priest bearing the Book of Micah.

This coming and going from palace to Temple and from Temple to palace went on for almost an hour. Read, ordered Herod when the priest entered the king's bedchamber, and the priest began, The word of the Lord as spoken to Micah of Maresheth in the days of Jotham, Ahaz, and Hezekiah, kings of Judah. He continued reading until Herod told him, Read further on, and the priest, puzzled and uncertain as to why he had been summoned, jumped to another passage, Woe to those who plot evil and lay plans for wicked deeds as they lie abed, but here he stopped, horrified at this involuntary impudence, became tongue-tied, and, hoping Herod might forget what had just been said, he went on, In the end it will come to pass that the Lord's great mansion will rise above the hills. Further on, snarled Herod, impatient to get to the passage that interested him, and the priest finally came to it, But it is from you, Bethlehem, so insignificant among the families of Judah, that the future ruler of Israel will come. Herod raised his hand, Repeat that passage, he insisted, and the priest obeyed. Once more, he ordered him, and the priest read it a third time. That's enough, said the king after a pro-

76

longed silence, You may withdraw. All was now clear. The book announced a future birth, nothing else, while the ghost of Micah had come to warn him that this birth had already taken place. Your words, like those of all prophets, could not have been clearer, even when we interpret them badly. Herod thought and thought again, his expression more and more grim and menacing. He then summoned the commander of the guards and gave him an order to be carried out forthwith. When the commander returned to report, Mission fulfilled, Herod gave another command to be carried out at daybreak, now only hours away. So we shall soon know what has been ordered, unlike the priest, who was brutally assassinated by soldiers before he reached the Temple. There is reason to believe that this was the first of the two orders, so close are the likely cause and the logical effect. As for the Book of Micah, it disappeared, and imagine what a loss that would have been had there been only one copy.

A CARPENTER AMONG CARPENTERS, JOSEPH HAD FINISHED eating his lunch, and he and his companions still had some free time before the overseer gave the signal to get back to work. Joseph could sit for a while, stretch out and take a nap or indulge in pleasant thoughts, imagine himself on the open road, wandering the countryside amid the hills of Samaria or, better still, looking down from a great height on the village of Nazareth, which he sorely missed. His soul rejoiced as he told himself that this long separation would soon be over and he would be on his way with only the morning star in the sky, singing praises to the Lord who protects our homes and guides our footsteps. Startled, he opened his eyes, afraid that he had dozed off and missed the overseer's signal, but he had only been daydreaming, his companions were still there, some chatting, others taking a nap, and the jovial mood of the overseer suggested that he might give his workers the rest of the day off. The sun is overhead, sharp gusts of wind drive the smoke from the sacrificial fires in the opposite direction. In this ravine, which looks onto the site where a hippodrome is under construction, not even the gabbling of the vendors in the Temple can be heard. The machine of time appears to have come to a halt, as if it too were awaiting a signal from the mighty overseer of universal space and time. Joseph suddenly became uneasy, after feeling so happy only a moment ago. He looked around him and saw the same familiar building site, to which he had grown accustomed in recent weeks, slabs of stone and wooden planks, a thick layer of white dust everywhere, and sawdust that never seemed to dry. He tried to find some explanation for this unexpected gloom, it was probably the natural reaction of a man who had to leave his work unfinished, even if this particular job was not his responsibility and he had every reason for leaving. Rising to his feet, Joseph tried to calculate how much time was left. The overseer did not even turn to glance in his direction, so Joseph decided to take one last look at the section of the building on which he had worked, to bid farewell, as it were, to the timbers he had planed and the joists he had fitted, if they could possibly be identified, for where is the bee that can claim, This honey was made by me.

After taking a good look around, Joseph was heading back to the site when he paused for a moment to admire the city on the opposite slope, built up in stages, with stones baked to the color of bread. The overseer must have given the signal by now, but Joseph was in no hurry, he gazed at the city, waiting for who knows what. The minutes passed and nothing happened. Joseph muttered to himself, Well, I might as well get back to work, when he heard voices on the path below the spot where he was standing, and, leaning over the stone wall, he saw three soldiers. They must have been walking along the path and decided to stop for a break, two of them were resting on their lances and listening to the third man, who looked older and was probably their officer, although it was not easy to tell the difference unless you were familiar with the various uniforms and knew the significance of the many insignia, stripes, and braids denoting rank. The words, which Joseph could barely make out, sounded like a question, something like, And when will that be, and one of the younger men answered in a clear voice, At the beginning of the third hour, when everyone is indoors. Whereupon the other soldier asked, How many of us are being dispatched, only to be told, I don't know yet but enough men to surround the village. Has an order been given to kill all of them. No, not all of them, only those under the age of three. It's difficult to tell a two-year-old from a four-year-old. And how many will that make, the second soldier wanted to know. According to the census, the officer told them, there must be around twenty-five. Joseph's eyes widened as if they could grasp this conversation better than his ears could, and he trembled from head to foot, because it was clear that these soldiers were talking about killing people. People, what people, he asked himself, bewildered and distressed, No, no, not people, or rather, people, but children. Children under the age of three, the officer in charge said, or perhaps it was one of the junior soldiers, but where, where could this be. Joseph could not very well lean over the wall and ask, Is there a war going on. He felt his legs shaking. He could hear one of the men say gravely, though with relief, How fortunate for us and our children that we don't live in Bethlehem. Does anyone know why they've chosen to kill the children of Bethlehem, one of the soldiers asked. No, the commander didn't say and I'll wager he doesn't know himself, the order came from the king, and that's all we need to know. Tracing a line on the ground with his lance, as if dividing and parceling out destiny, the other soldier said, Wretched are we who not only practice the evil that is ours by nature but must also serve as an instrument of evil for those who abuse their power. But these words went unheard by Joseph, who had stolen away from his vantage point, cautiously at first and then in a mad rush, like a frightened goat, scattering pebbles in all directions as he ran. Unfortunately, without Joseph's testimony we have reason to doubt the authenticity of this soldier's philosophical remark, both in form and content, given the obvious contradiction between the aptness of the sentiment and the humble station of the person who expressed it.

Delirious, bumping into everything, overturning fruit stalls and bird cages, even a money changer's table, and oblivious to the cries of fury from the vendors in the Temple, Joseph is concerned only that his child's life is in danger. He cannot imagine why anyone would want to do such a thing, he is desperate, he chose to father a child and now someone wants to take it from him, one desire is as valid as another, to do and undo, to tie and untie, to create and destroy. Suddenly he stops, realizing the risk he is running if he continues in this reckless flight, the Temple guards might appear and arrest him, he is surprised they have not already been alerted by the uproar. Dissembling as best he can, like a louse taking refuge in the seams of a garment, he disappears into the crowd and instantly becomes anonymous, the only difference being that he walks a little faster than others, but this is hardly noticed amid the labyrinth of people. He knows he must not run until he reaches the city gate, but he is distressed at the thought that the soldiers may already be on their way, ominously armed with lance, dagger, and unprovoked hatred. If they are traveling on horseback, he will never catch up with them, and by the time he gets there, his son will be dead, poor child, sweet little Jesus. At this moment of deepest anguish a foolish thought occurs to him, he remembers his wages, the week's wages he stands to lose, and such is the power of these vile material things that, without exactly coming to a halt, he slows down just long enough to ponder whether he can rescue both his money and his child's life. Quick as it surfaced, this unworthy thought

81

disappears, leaving no sense of shame, that feeling which often, but not often enough, proves our most reliable guardian angel.

Joseph finally puts the city behind him. There are no soldiers on the road for as far as the eye can reach, no crowds gathered as one might expect them to for a military parade, but the most reassuring sight of all is that of children playing innocent games, with none of the wild enthusiasm they display when flags, drums, and horns go marching by. If any soldiers had passed this way, there would be no boys in sight, they would have followed the detachment at least to the first bend in the road, as is the time-honored custom, and perhaps one child, his heart set on becoming a soldier someday, accompanied them on their mission and so learned the fate that awaited him, namely, to kill or be killed. Now Joseph can run as fast as he likes, he takes advantage of the slope, is hampered only by his tunic, which he hitches up over his knees. As in a dream, he has the agonizing sensation that his legs cannot keep up with the rest of his body, with his heart, head, and eyes, and his hands, eager to offer protection, are so painfully slow in their movement. Some people stop on the road and shake their heads disapprovingly at this undignified performance, for these people are known for their composure and noble bearing. The explanation for Joseph's extraordinary behavior in their eyes is not that he is running to save his child's life but that he is Galilean, one of a lot with no real breeding, as has often been observed. He has already passed Rachel's tomb, and that good woman could never have suspected that she would have so much cause to weep for her children, to cover the nearby hills with her cries and lamentations, to claw at her face, tear out her hair, and then beat her bare skull.

Before he comes to the first houses on the outskirts of Bethlehem, Joseph leaves the main road and goes cross-country, I am taking a shortcut, he would reply if we were to question this sudden change of direction, a route that might be shorter but is certainly much less comfortable. Taking care not to encounter any laborers at work in the fields, and hiding behind boulders whenever he sees a shepherd, Joseph makes for the cave where his wife is not expecting him at this hour and his son, fast asleep, is not expecting him at all. Halfway up the slope of the last hill, from where he can already see the dark chasm of the grotto, Joseph is assailed by a terrible thought, suppose his wife has gone to the village, taking the child with her, nothing more natural, knowing what women are, than for her to take advantage of being on her own to make a farewell visit to Salome and several families with whom she has become acquainted in recent weeks, leaving Joseph to thank the owners of the cave with all due formality. He sees himself running through the streets and knocking on every door, Is my wife here. It would be foolish to inquire anxiously. Better, Is my son here, in case some woman, carrying a child in her arms, for example, should ask, on seeing him distressed, Is something wrong. No, nothing, he would reply, Nothing at all, it's just that we have to set off at first light and we still haven't packed. The village, seen from here, with its identical roof terraces, reminds Joseph of the building site, stones scattered everywhere until the workers assemble them, one on top of another, to erect a watchtower, an obelisk to commemorate some victory, or a wall for lamentations. A dog barks in the distance, others bark in response, but the warm evening silence continues to hover over the village like a blessing about to lose its effect, like a wisp of a cloud on the point of vanishing.

This pause was short-lived. In one last spurt the carpenter reached the entrance to the cave and called out, Mary, are you there. She called in reply, and Joseph realized that his legs were weak, probably from all the running, but also from the sheer relief of knowing his child was safe. Inside the cave Mary was chopping vegetables for the evening meal, the child asleep in the manger. Joseph collapsed on the ground but was soon back on his feet, We must leave, we must get out of this place. Mary looked at him in dismay, Are we leaving, she asked, Yes, this very minute, But you said, Be quiet and start packing while I harness the donkey. Aren't we going to eat first. No, we'll eat something on the way. But it will soon be dark and we might get lost, whereupon Joseph lost his temper, Be quiet, woman, I've already told you we're leaving, so do as I say. Tears sprang to Mary's eyes, this was the first time her husband had ever raised his voice to her. Without another word she began gathering their scant possessions. Be quick, be quick, he kept repeating as he saddled the donkey and tightened the straps and crammed whatever came to hand into the baskets, while Mary looked on dumbfounded at this husband she barely recognized. They were ready to leave, the only thing left to be done now was put out the fire with earth. Joseph signaled to his wife to wait until he took a look outside.

The ashen shadows of twilight merged heaven and earth. The sun had not yet set, but the heavy mist, while too high to obscure the surrounding fields, kept the sunlight from them. Joseph listened carefully, took a few steps, his hair on end. A scream came from the village, so shrill that it scarcely sounded human, its echo resounding from hill to hill, and it was followed by more screams and wailing, which could be heard everywhere. These were not weeping angels lamenting human misfortune, these were the voices of men and women maddened by grief beneath an empty sky. Slowly, afraid of being heard, Joseph stepped back to the cave, and collided with Mary, who had disregarded his warning. She was trembling. What are those screams, she asked, but he pushed her back inside without replying and hastily began throwing earth on the fire. What are those screams, Mary asked a second time, invisible in the darkness, and Joseph eventually answered, People are being put to death. He paused and then added in a whisper, Children, by order of Herod, his voice breaking into a dry sob, That's why I said we should leave. There was a muffled sound of clothing and hay being disturbed, Mary was lifting her child from the manger and pressing him to her bosom, Sweet little Jesus, who would want to harm you, her words drowned in tears. Be quiet, said Joseph, don't make a sound, perhaps the soldiers won't find this place, they've been ordered to kill all the children in Bethlehem under the age of three. How did you find out. I overheard it in the Temple and that's why I ran back. What do we do now. We're on the outskirts of the village, the soldiers aren't likely to look inside these caves, they've been ordered to carry out a house-to-house search, so let's hope no one reports us and we're spared. He took another cautious look outside, the screaming had stopped, nothing could be heard now except a wailing chorus, which gradually subsided. The massacre of the innocents had ended.

The sky was still overcast. The advancing darkness and the mist overhead had erased Bethlehem from the sight of those inhabiting heaven. Joseph warned Mary, Don't move from here, I'm going out to the road to see if the soldiers have gone. Be careful, said Mary, forgetting that her husband was in no danger, only children under the age of three, unless someone else had gone out to the road with the intention of betraying him, telling the soldiers, This is Joseph, the carpenter, whose child is not yet three, a boy called Jesus, who could be the child mentioned in the prophecy, for our children cannot be destined for glory now that they are dead.

Inside the cave one could touch the darkness. Mary, who had always feared the dark, was used to having a light in the house, from either the fire or an oil lamp, or both, and the feeling, all the stronger now that she was hiding here in the earth, that fingers of darkness would reach out and touch her lips, filled her with terror. She did not want

85

to disobey her husband or expose her child to danger by leaving the cave, but she was becoming more terrified by the minute. Soon the fear would overpower her fragile defenses of common sense, it was no good telling herself, If there was nothing in the cave before we put out the fire then why should there be anything now, although this thought gave her just enough courage to grope her way to the manger, where she settled her child, and then, carefully creeping around until she found the spot where the fire had been, she poked the ashes with a piece of firewood until a few embers appeared that had not yet completely died. Her fear vanished at once as, remembering the luminous earth, she watched this tremulous glow with crisscrossing flashes like a torch that darts over the ridge of a mountain. The image of the beggar came to her, only to be pushed aside by the urgent need to create more light in that terrifying cave. Fumbling, Mary went to the manger to fetch a handful of straw. Guided by the faint glow on the ground, she was back in an instant and soon had the oil lamp set up in a corner, where it could cast a pale but reassuring light on the nearby walls without attracting the attention of anyone outside. Mary went to her child, who continued to sleep, indifferent to fears, cares, and violent deaths. Taking him in her arms, she went and sat near the lamp and waited.

Time passed. Her child woke without fully opening his eyes, and when Mary saw he was about to cry, she opened her tunic and brought the child's avid mouth to her breast. Jesus was still feeding at his mother's breast when she heard footsteps. Her heart almost stopped beating. Could it be soldiers. But these were the footsteps of one person, and soldiers on a search normally went in pairs at least so that one could aid the other in the event of an attack. It must be Joseph, she thought, and feared he would scold her for having lit the lamp. The steps came closer, Joseph was entering the cave, but suddenly a shiver went up Mary's spine, those were not Joseph's firm, heavy steps, perhaps it was some itinerant laborer seeking shelter for the night, as had happened twice before, although Mary had not been afraid on those occasions, because it never occurred to her that anyone, however heartless and cruel, would harm a woman with a child in her arms. She thought of the infants slaughtered in Bethlehem, some perhaps in their mothers' arms, just as Jesus lies in hers, innocent babes still sucking the milk of life as swords pierced their tender flesh, but then those assassins were soldiers, not vagrants. No, it was not Joseph, and it was not a soldier looking for an exploit he would not have to share, and it was not a laborer without work or shelter. It was the man, again in the guise of a shepherd, who had appeared to her as a beggar, claiming to be an angel, not revealing, however, whether he came from heaven or hell. At first Mary thought it could not possibly be he, but she now realized it could be no one else.

The angel said, Peace be with you, wife of Joseph, and peace be with your child, how fortunate for both of you to have found shelter in this cave, otherwise one of you would now be broken and dead and the other broken though still alive. Mary told him, I heard cries for help. The angel said, One day those cries will be raised to heaven in your name, and even before then you will hear thousands of cries beside you. Mary told him, My husband went to the road to see if the soldiers have left, he must not find you here when he comes back. The angel said, Don't worry, I'll be gone before he returns, I only came to tell you that you will not see me again for some time, that all that was decreed in heaven has come to pass, that these deaths were as inevitable as Joseph's crime. Mary asked, What crime, my husband has committed no crime, he is an honest man. The angel told her, An honest man who committed a crime, you have no idea how many honest men have committed crimes, their crimes are countless, and contrary to popular belief these are the only crimes that cannot be forgiven. Mary asked, What crime did my husband commit. The angel replied, Should I tell you, surely you don't want to share his guilt. Mary said, I swear I am innocent. The angel told her, Swear if you will, but any oath taken before me is a puff of wind that knows not where it's going. Mary pleaded, What crime have we committed. The angel replied, Herod's cruelty unsheathed those swords, but your selfishness and cowardice were the cords that bound the victims' hands and feet. Mary asked, What could I have done. The angel told her, You could not have done anything, for you found out too late, but the carpenter could have done something, he could have warned the villagers that the soldiers were coming to kill their children when there was still time for parents to gather them up and escape, to hide in the wilderness, for example, or flee to Egypt and wait for Herod's death, which is fast approaching. Mary said, Joseph didn't think. The angel retorted, No, he didn't think, but that hardly excuses him. Mary tearfully implored, Angel that you are, forgive him. The angel replied, I am not an angel who grants pardons. Mary pleaded, Forgive him. The angel was unswayed, I've already told you, there's no forgiveness for this crime, Herod will be forgiven sooner than your husband, for it is easier to forgive a villain than a deserter. Mary asked, What are we to do. The angel told her, You will live and suffer like everyone else. Mary asked, And what about my son. The angel said, A father's guilt falls on the heads of his children, and the shadow of Joseph's guilt already darkens his son's brow. Mary sighed, Wretched are we. Indeed, said the angel, and there is nothing to be done. Mary lowered her head, pressed her child closer to her bosom, as if protecting him from the promised evil, and when she turned around, the angel had vanished. But this time there was no sound of footsteps. He must have flown away, Mary thought to herself. She got up and went to the entrance of the cave to see if there was any trace of the angel's flight through the sky or any sign of Joseph nearby.

The mist had cleared, the first stars glittered like metal, and wailing voices could still be heard from the village. Then a thought as presumptuous as spiritual pride itself blotted out the angel's dark warning and caused Mary's head to spin. Suppose her son's salvation was a sign from God, for surely the child's escape from a cruel death must mean something when so many others who perished could do nothing but wait for the opportunity to ask God himself, Why did you kill us, and be satisfied with whatever reply He might choose to give. Mary's delirium soon passed, and the thought occurred to her that she too could be holding a dead child like all those other mothers in Bethlehem, and she shed a flood of tears for the welfare and salvation of her soul. She was still weeping when Joseph returned. She heard him coming but did not stir, did not care if he rebuked her, she was crying now with the other women, all of them seated in a circle with their children on their laps awaiting resurrection. Joseph saw that she wept, understood, and said nothing.

Inside the cave, he did not appear to notice the burning oil lamp. A fine layer of ash now covered the embers, but in the center there was still a faint flicker of flame struggling to survive. As he began unloading the donkey, Joseph reassured Mary, We're no longer in danger, the soldiers have gone, we might as well spend the night here. We'll leave before dawn, avoid the main road, and take a shortcut, and where there are no roads we'll find a way somehow. Mary murmured, All those dead children, which provoked Joseph into asking brusquely, How do you know, have you counted them, and Mary continued, I even knew some of those children. You ought to be thanking God for having spared your own son. I will. And stop staring at me as if I'd committed some crime. I wasn't staring at

89

you. Don't answer in that accusing tone of voice. Very well, I won't say another word. Good. Joseph tethered the donkey to the manger, where there was still some hay. The donkey cannot complain, it has had lots of fodder and plenty of fresh air, but it is not hungry, it is preparing itself for the arduous journey back with a full load. Mary put her child down and said, I'll get the fire going. What for. To prepare some supper. I don't want a fire in here to attract the attention of some passerby, let's eat whatever there is that doesn't need to be cooked. And so they ate.

The light from the lamp made the cave's four inhabitants look like ghosts, the donkey motionless as a statue, not eating though its nose was buried in the straw, the child dozing, the man and woman satisfying their hunger with a few dry figs. Mary laid out the mats on the sandy ground, threw a cover over them, and, as usual, waited for her husband to go to bed. First Joseph went to take another look at the night sky, all was peaceful in heaven and on earth, and no more cries or lamentations could be heard in the village. Rachel only had strength enough left to sigh and whimper inside the houses where doors and souls were tightly closed. Stretched out on his mat, Joseph felt exhausted after all his worry and panic, and he could not even say that his wild chase had saved his son's life. The soldiers had strictly carried out their orders, Kill the children of Bethlehem, without taking any further initiative, such as searching all the caves in the vicinity to ferret out families in hiding or families making their homes there. Normally Joseph did not mind that Mary came to bed only after he had fallen asleep, but on this occasion he could not bear to think of her watching him, in her sorrow, as he lay sleeping. He told her, I do not want you waiting up, come to bed. Mary made no protest. After making sure, as usual, that the donkey was securely tethered, she lay down with a sigh on her mat, closed her eyes, and waited for sleep to come.

In the middle of the night, Joseph had a dream. He was riding down a road leading into a village, when the first houses came into view. He wore a military uniform and was armed with sword, lance, and dagger, a soldier among soldiers. The commanding officer asked him, Where do you think you're going, carpenter, to which Joseph replied, proud of being so well prepared for the mission entrusted to him, I'm off to Bethlehem to kill my son, and as he said those words, he woke with a fearsome growl, his body twitching and writhing with fear. Mary asked him in alarm, What's wrong, what happened, as Joseph kept repeating, No, no, no. Suddenly he broke into bitter sobs. Mary got up, fetched the lamp, and held it near his face, Are you ill, she asked. Covering his face with his hands, he shouted, Take that lamp away at once, woman, and still sobbing, he went to the manger to see if his child was safe. He is fine, Master Joseph, do not worry, in fact the child gives no trouble, good-natured, quiet, all he wants is to be fed and to sleep, and here he rests as peaceful as can be, oblivious to the dreadful death he has miraculously escaped, just think, to be put to death by the father who gave him life, for though death is the fate that awaits all of us, there are many ways of dying. Afraid that the dream might come back, Joseph did not lie down again. Wrapped in his mantle, he sat at the entrance to the cave, beneath an overhanging rock that formed a natural porch, and the moon above cast a black shadow over the opening, a shadow the faint glow of the oil lamp within could not dispel. Had Herod himself been carried past by his slaves, escorted by legions of barbarians thirsting for blood, he would have told them calmly, Don't bother searching this place, continue on, there is nothing here but stone and shadow, what we want is the tender flesh of newborn babes. The very thought of his dream made Joseph shiver. He wondered what it could possibly mean, for, as the heavens could testify, he had raced like a madman down that slope,

91

a Via Dolorosa if ever there was one, he had scaled rocks and walls in his haste to rescue his child, like a good father, yet in the dream he saw himself as a fiend intent on murder. How wise the proverb that reminds us that there is no constancy in dreams. This must be the work of Satan, he decided, making a gesture to drive out evil spirits.

The piercing trill of an unseen bird filled the air, or perhaps it was a shepherd whistling, but surely not at this hour, when the flocks are asleep and only the dogs are keeping watch. Yet the night, calm and remote from all living creatures, showed that supreme indifference which we associate with the universe, or that other absolute indifference, the indifference of emptiness, which will remain, if there is such a thing as emptiness, when all has been fulfilled. The night ignored the meaning and rational order that appear to govern the world in those moments when we can still believe the world was made to harbor us and our insanity. The terrifying dream grew unreal and absurd, was dispelled by the night, the shining moon, and the presence of his child asleep in the manger. Joseph was awake and as much in command of himself and his thoughts as any man could be, his thoughts were now charitable and peaceful, yet just as capable of monstrosity, for example his gratitude to God that his beloved child had been spared by the soldiers who had butchered so many innocents. The night that descends over carpenter Joseph descends also over the mothers of the children of Bethlehem, forgetting their fathers, and even Mary for a moment, since they do not figure here for some strange reason. The hours passed quietly, and at first light Joseph got up, went to load the donkey, and, taking advantage of the last moonlight before the sky turned clear, the whole family, Jesus, Mary, and Joseph, were soon on their way back to Galilee.

Stealing from her master's house, where two infants had been killed, the slave Salome rushed to the cave that morning, convinced that the same sad fate had befallen the child she helped bring into the world. She found the place deserted, nothing remained except footprints and the donkey's hoofprints. Dying embers beneath the ashes, but no bloodstains. Gone, she said, little Jesus has escaped this first death.

Eight months had passed since that happy day when Joseph arrived in Nazareth with his family safe and sound despite many dangers, the donkey less so, for it was limping slightly on its right hoof, when the news came that King Herod had died in Jericho, in one of his palaces where he took refuge to escape the rigors of the Jerusalem winter, which spares neither the weak nor the infirm. There were also rumors that the kingdom, now robbed of its mighty monarch, would be divided among three of his sons who had survived the feuding and destruction, namely, Herod Philip, who would govern the territories lying east of Galilee, Herod Antipas, who would inherit Galilee and Peraea, and Archelaus, who would rule Judaea, Samaria, and Idumaea. One day a passing muleteer with a flair for narrating tales both real and fictitious will give the people of Nazareth a graphic description of Herod's funeral, which he will swear he witnessed. The body, placed in a magnificent sarcophagus made of the purest gold and inlaid with precious stones, was transported on a gilded carriage draped with purple cloth and drawn by two white oxen. The body was also covered with a purple cloth, all that could be seen was a human shape with a crown resting where the head was. Behind followed musicians playing flutes and the professional mourners, who could not avoid the overpowering stink, and as I stood there at the roadside even I felt queasy, then came the king's guards on horseback, then foot soldiers armed with lances, swords, and daggers as if marching to war, an endless procession wending its awesome way like a serpent with no head or tail in sight. In horror I watched those soldiers marching behind a corpse but also to their own death, to that death which sooner or later knocks on every door. Time to leave, promptly comes the order to kings and vassals alike, making no distinction between the rotting body at the head of the procession and those in the rear choking on the dust of an entire army, they are still alive but heading for a place where they will remain forever. Clearly this muleteer would be more at home as an Aristotelian scholar strolling beneath the Corinthian capitals of some academy rather than prodding donkeys along the roads of Israel, sleeping in smelly caravansaries, and narrating tales to rustics such as these of Nazareth.

Among the crowd in the square in front of the synagogue was Joseph, who happened to be passing and had stopped to listen. He did not pay much attention to the descriptive details of the funeral procession, and lost interest when the poet began to strike an elegiac note, for grim experience had made the carpenter wise about that particular chord on the harp. One had only to look at him, his composure when he concealed his youth by becoming solemn and thoughtful, the bitterness that marked him with lines deeper than scars. But what is really disturbing about Joseph's face are the eyes, which are dull and expressionless except for a tiny flicker caused by insomnia. It is true that Joseph gets little sleep. Sleep is the enemy he confronts each night, as if fighting for his very life, and it is a battle he invariably loses, for even when he seems to be winning and falls asleep from sheer exhaustion, he no sooner closes his eyes than he secs a detachment of soldiers appearing on the road, with Joseph himself riding in their midst, sometimes brandishing a sword above his head, and it is just at that moment, when terror overwhelms him, that the leader of the expedition asks, Where do you think you're going, carpenter. And the poor man, who would rather not say, resists with all his might, but the malignant spirits in the dream are too strong for him, and they prise open his mouth with hands of steel, reducing him to tears and despair as he confesses, I'm on my way to Bethlehem to kill my son. We won't ask Joseph if he remembers how many oxen pulled the carriage bearing Herod's corpse or whether they were white or dappled. As he heads for home, all he can think of are the closing phrases of the muleteer's tale, when the man described the multitude accompanying the procession, slaves, soldiers, royal guards, professional mourners, musicians, governors, princes, future kings, and all the rest of us, whoever we might be, doing nothing else in life but searching for the place where we will stay forever. If only it were so, mused Joseph, with the bitterness of one who has given up all hope. If only it were so, he repeated to himself, thinking of all those who never left their place of birth yet death went there to find them, which only proves that fate is the only real certainty. It is so easy, dear God, we need only wait for everything in life to be fulfilled to say, It was fate. Herod was fated to die in Jericho and be borne on a carriage to the fortress of Herodium, but death exempted the infants of Bethlehem from having to travel anywhere. And Joseph's journey, which in the beginning seemed part of some divine plan to save those holy innocents, turned out to be futile. The carpenter listened and said nothing, he ran off to rescue his own child, leaving the others to their fate. So now we know why Joseph cannot sleep, and when he does, it is only to awaken to a reality that will not allow him to forget his dream, even when awake he dreams the same dream night after night, and when asleep, though trying desperately to avoid it, he knows he will encounter that dream again, for it hovers on the threshold between sleep and waking and he must pass it when he enters and when he leaves. This confusion is best defined as remorse. Yet human experience and the practice of communication have shown throughout the ages that definitions are an illusion, like having a speech defect and trying to say love but unable to get the word out, or, better, having a tongue in one's head but unable to feel love.

Mary is pregnant again. No angel disguised as a beggar came knocking at the door this time to announce the child's arrival, no sudden gust of wind swept the heights of Nazareth, no luminous earth was discovered in the ground. Mary told Joseph in the simplest words, I'm with child. She did not say to him, for example, Look into my eyes and see how our second child is shining there, nor did he reply this time, Don't think I hadn't noticed, I was waiting for you to tell me. He just listened, remained silent, and eventually said, Is that so, and carried on planing a piece of wood with apparent indifference, but, then, we know that his thoughts are elsewhere. Mary also knows, since that night of torment when her husband blurted out the secret he had kept to himself, and she was not altogether surprised, she had been expecting something like this after the angel told her in the cave, You will have a thousand cries all around you. A good wife would have said to her husband, Don't fret, what's done is done, and besides, your first duty was to rescue your own child. But Mary has changed and is no longer what one would normally refer to as a good wife, perhaps because she heard the angel utter those grave words that excluded no one, I am not an angel who grants pardons. Had she been allowed to discuss these deep matters with Joseph, who was so well versed in Holy Scripture, he might have pondered the nature of this angel who appeared from nowhere to announce that he did not grant pardons, a statement which seems superfluous, since everyone knows that the power to pardon belongs to God alone. For an angel to say that he does not grant pardons is either meaningless or much too meaningful. An angel of judgment, perhaps, might exclaim, You expect me to forgive you, what a silly idea, I did not come to forgive, I came only to punish. But angels, by definition, leaving aside those cherubim with flaming swords who were posted by the Lord to guard the path to the tree of life lest our first parents or we, their descendants, try to return to steal the fruits, angels, as we were saying, are not vigilantes entrusted with the corrupt albeit socially necessary enforcement of repression. Angels exist to make our lives easier, they protect us when we are about to fall down a well, help us cross the bridge over the precipice, pull us to safety just as we are about to be crushed by a runaway chariot or a car without brakes. An angel worthy of the name could have spared Joseph all this torment simply by appearing in a dream to the fathers of the children of Bethlehem to warn them, Gather your wife and child and flee to Egypt and stay there until I tell you to return, for Herod means to slaughter your child. In this way the children could have all been saved, Jesus hidden in the cave with his parents and the others on their way to Egypt, where they would remain until the same angel returned to tell the fathers, Arise, gather your wife and child and return to Israel, for he who tried to kill your children is dead. Thus the children would return to the places where they came from and where eventually they would meet their deaths at the appointed hour, because angels, however powerful, have their limitations, just like God. After much thought, Joseph might have reached the conclusion that the angel who appeared in the cave was an infernal creature, an agent of Satan disguised this time as a shepherd, and further proof of the weakness and gullibility of women, who can be led astray by a fallen angel. If Mary could speak, if she were less secretive and revealed the details of that strange annunciation, things would be different, Joseph would use other arguments to support his theory, most important, the fact that this so-called angel did not proclaim, I am an angel of the Lord, or, I come in the name of the Lord. He simply said, I am an angel, before adding cautiously, Keep this to yourself, as if afraid for anyone else to know. Some may argue that such details contribute nothing new to our understanding of what is an all-too-familiar story, but as far as this narrator is concerned, it is crucial to know, when interpreting past and future events, whether the angel came from heaven or from hell. Between angels of light and angels of darkness there are differences not just of form but also of essence, substance, and content, and while it is true that whoever created the former also created the latter, He subsequently attempted to correct His mistake.

Mary, like Joseph, but for different reasons, often looks distracted, her expression becomes blank, her hands drop in the middle of some task, her gestures are suddenly interrupted, she stares into the distance, not so surprising for a woman in her condition, were it not for the various thoughts that occupy her mind and that can be summed up in the following question, Why did the angel announce the birth of Jesus yet say nothing of this second child. Mary looks at her firstborn crawling on all fours as children do at that age, she studies him and tries to perceive a special trait, some mark or sign, a star on his forehead, a sixth finger on his hand, but she sees a child like any other, who slobbers, gets dirty, and cries, the only difference being that he is her son. His hair is black like that of his parents, his irises are already losing that whitish tinge inaccurately called milky and assuming their natural, inherited color, a dark brown which gradually turns a somber green if one can so describe a color, but these features are hardly unique, important only when the child belongs to us, or, as in this case, to Mary. Within weeks he will be making his first attempts to stand up and walk, he will fall on his hands countless times, stay there staring, lifting his head with some difficulty as he hears his mother say, Come here, come here, my child. And he will begin to feel the urge to speak, sounds will form in his throat, at first he will not know what to do with them, he will get them mixed up with sounds he already knows and makes, such as gurgling and crying, until he begins to realize that they must be articulated in a different and more deliberate way, and he will move his lips as his father and mother do, until he succeeds in pronouncing his first word, perhaps da or dada or daddy, or perhaps even mummy, in any case after that little Jesus will not have to poke the forefinger of his right hand into the palm of his left hand if his mother and her neighbors ask him for the hundredth time, Where does the hen lay her egg. This is just another of those indignities to which a human being is subjected, trained like a lapdog to respond to certain sounds, a tone of voice, a whistle, or the crack of a whip. Now Jesus is able to answer that the hen can lay her egg wherever she wishes so long as she does not lay it in the palm of his hand. Mary looks at her little son, sighs, downhearted that the angel is not likely to return. You will not see me again for a while, he told her, but if he were to appear now, she would not be as intimidated as before, she would ply the angel with questions until he gave her an answer. Already a mother and expecting her second child, Mary is no innocent lamb, she has learned, to her cost, what suffering, danger, and worry mean, with all that experience on her side she can easily tip the scales to her advantage. It would not be enough for the angel to reply, May the Lord never allow you to see your child as you see me now, with nowhere to lay my head. First, the angel would have to identify this Lord in

100

whose name he claimed to speak, secondly, convince her that he told the truth when he said he had no place to lay his head, which seemed unlikely for an angel unless he meant it only in his role as beggar, thirdly, what future did those dark, threatening words augur for her son, and finally, what was the mystery surrounding that luminous earth buried near the door, where a strange plant had grown after their return from Bethlehem, nothing but stalk and leaves, which they had given up pruning after trying to pull it up by the roots, only to have it reappear with even greater vigor. Two of the elders of the synagogue, Zacchaeus and Dothan, came to inspect the phenomenon, and although they knew little about botany, they were in agreement that the seed must have been in the mysterious soil and then sprouted at the right moment, for as Zacchaeus observed, Such is the law of the Lord of life. Once she became accustomed to this stubborn plant, Mary decided it added a festive touch at the entrance to the house, while Joseph, still suspicious, moved his carpenter's bench to another part of the yard rather than have to look at the thing. He cut it back with an ax and saw, poured boiling water over it, even scattered burning coals around the stalk, but superstition prevented him from taking a spade and digging up the bowl of luminous earth that had been the cause of so much trouble. This was how matters stood when their second child, whom they named James, was born.

Over the next few years there were not many changes in the family, apart from the arrival of more children, including two daughters, while the parents lost the last vestiges of youth. In the case of Mary that was not surprising, for we know how childbearing, and she had borne many children, gradually saps whatever freshness and beauty a woman possesses, causing her face and body to age and wither, suffice it to say that after James came Lisa, after Lisa came Joseph, after Joseph came Judas, after Judas came

Simon, then Lydia, then Justus, then Samuel, and if any more followed, they perished without trace. Children are the pride and joy of their parents, as the saying goes, and Mary did her utmost to appear contented, but after carrying for months on end all those fruits that greedily consumed her strength, she often felt impatient, resentful, but in those days it would never have occurred to her to blame Joseph, let alone Almighty God who governs the life and death of His creatures and assures us that the very hairs of our heads are counted. Joseph had little understanding of the begetting of children, apart from the practical rudiments, which reduce all enigmas to one simple fact, namely, that if a man and woman come together, he will likely impregnate her, and after nine months, or on rare occasions after seven, a child is born. Released into the female womb, the male seed, minute and invisible, transmits the new being chosen by God to continue populating the world He has created. Sometimes, however, this fails to happen, and the fact that the transmission of seed into womb is not always sufficient to create a child is further evidence of the impenetrability of God's design. Allowing the seed to spill onto the ground, as did the unfortunate Onan, whom the Lord punished with death for refusing in this way to give his brother's widow children, rules out any possibility of the woman's becoming pregnant. On the other hand, time and time again, as someone once said, the pitcher goes to the fountain until there is no more water and it comes back empty. For it was clearly God who put Isaac into the little seed that Abraham was still able to produce, and God who poured it into Sarah's womb, because she was past conceiving children. Looking at things from a theogenetic angle, as it were, we may conclude without offending logic, which must preside over everything in this and every other world, that it was God Himself who spurred Joseph to keep having intercourse with Mary, so that they might have lots of children, helping Him assuage the remorse that plagued Him ever since He permitted, or willed, without considering the consequences, the massacre of those innocent children of Bethlehem. But the strangest thing of all, and which goes to show that the ways of the Lord are not only inscrutable but also disconcerting, is that Joseph truly believed he was acting of his own accord and obeying God's will, as he made strenuous efforts to beget more and more children, to compensate for all those killed by Herod's soldiers, so that the numbers would tally in the next census. God's remorse and Joseph's were one and the same, and, if people in those days were already familiar with the expression God never sleeps, we now know that the reason He never sleeps is that He made a mistake which no man would be forgiven. With every child begotten by Joseph, God raised His head a little higher, but He will never raise it fully, because twenty-seven infants were massacred in Bethlehem, and Joseph did not live long enough to impregnate one woman with that many children, and Mary, worn out in body and soul, could never have withstood that many pregnancies. The carpenter's house and yard, though full of children, might as well have been empty.

On reaching the age of five, Joseph's son started going to school. Each morning his mother took him to the synagogue and left him in the charge of the steward who taught beginners, and it was there in the synagogue-and-classroom that Jesus and the other little boys of Nazareth under the age of ten observed the wise man's precept, The child must be instructed in the Torah just as the ox is bred in the corral. The lesson ended at the sixth hour, which we now refer to as midday. Mary would be waiting for her child, and the poor woman was not allowed to ask him what he was learning, even this simple right was denied her, for as the wise man's maxim categorically states, Better that the law go up in flames than it be entrusted to women. Besides, if by any chance little Jesus had already been taught the true status of women in this world, including mothers,

103

he might have given her the wrong answer, the kind of answer that reduces one to insignificance. Take Herod, for example, with all his wealth and power, yet if we were to see him now, we would not even be able to say, He is dead and rotting, because he is nothing but mold, dust, bones, and filthy rags. When Jesus arrived home, his father asked him, What did you learn today, and Jesus, having been blessed with an excellent memory, repeated word for word and without a moment's hesitation the lessons of the day. First the children were taught the letters of the alphabet, then the most important words, and finally whole sentences and passages from the Torah, which Joseph accompanied, beating out the rhythm with his right hand and slowly nodding his head. Standing aside, Mary looked on and learned things she was forbidden to ask, a clever stratagem on the part of women and practiced to perfection throughout the ages. Listening, they soon learn everything, even the difference between falsehood and truth, which is the height of wisdom. But what Mary did not understand, or understand completely, was the mysterious bond between her husband and Jesus, although even a stranger would have noticed the look of wistful tenderness on Joseph's face when he spoke to his firstborn, as if he was thinking to himself, This beloved son of mine is my sorrow. All Mary knew was that Joseph's nightmares, like a scourge on his soul, refused to go away, and were now so frequent that they became as much a habit as sleeping on the right side or waking up with thirst in the middle of the night. Mary, as a good and dutiful wife, still worried about her husband, but for her the most important thing of all was to see her son alive and well, a sign that Joseph's crime had not been too serious, otherwise the Lord would have punished him without mercy, as was His wont. Take Job, broken and leprous, yet he had always been an honest, upright, and God-fearing man. Job's misfortune was that he became involuntarily the cause of a dispute between Satan and God Himself, each clinging tenaciously to his own idea and prerogative. And yet they are surprised when a man despairs and cries out, Perish the day I was born and the night in which I was conceived, let that day turn to darkness and be erased from the calendar and that night become sterile and void of all happiness. It is true that God compensated Job by repaying him twice as much as He had taken, but what of all those other men, in whose name no book was ever written, men deprived of everything and given nothing in return, to whom everything was promised and nothing fulfilled.

But in this carpenter's house life was peaceful, and however frugal their existence, there was always bread on the table and enough food to keep body and soul together. As for possessions, the only thing Joseph had in common with Job was the number of sons. Job had seven sons and three daughters, while Joseph had seven sons and two daughters, giving the carpenter the merit of having put one woman less into the world. However, before God doubled his possessions, Job already owned seven thousand sheep, three thousand camels, five hundred yokes of oxen, and five hundred donkeys, not to mention slaves, of which he had many, whereas Joseph has only his donkey and nothing else. And there's no denying that it is one thing to feed two mouths, then a third, even if only indirectly during the first year, and quite another to find yourself saddled with a houseful of children who need more and more food when they start growing. Since Joseph's earnings were not enough to allow him to hire an apprentice, it was only natural that he make his children work. Besides, this was his fatherly duty, for as the Talmud says, Just as a man must feed his children, he must also teach them to work, otherwise he turns his sons into good-for-nothings. And recalling the precept of the rabbis that the artisan must never think himself inferior to the greatest scholar, we can imagine how proudly Joseph began instructing his older sons one after another as they came of age, first Jesus, then James, then Joseph, then Judas, in the secret skills of the carpenter's trade, ever mindful of the ancient proverb, A child's service is little, yet he is no little fool that despises it. When Joseph returned to work after the midday meal, his sons lent him a hand, a good example of domestic economy and a way to establish a whole dynasty of carpenters for future generations, if God in His wisdom had not decreed otherwise.

As if the humiliation inflicted on the Hebrew race for more than seventy years was not enough to satisfy the shameless arrogance of the empire, Rome decided, using the division of the former kingdom of Herod as a pretext, to update the previous census. This time, however, the men would not have to register in their places of origin, and thus they were spared the damaging effect on agriculture and commerce and all the other upheavals we witnessed Joseph and his family enduring earlier. The new decree ruled that the censors go from village to village, town to town, and city to city and summon all the men, whatever their status, to the main square or other suitable open-air site, where their names, occupations, and taxable wealth would be entered into the public record under the surveillance of guards. Now, it must be said that such procedures are not viewed with favor in this part of the world, which is nothing new, for Holy Scripture narrates the unfortunate decision of King David when he ordered Joab, the leader of his army, Go through all the tribes of Israel from Dan to Beersheba and carry out a census of the people, and since a royal command was never questioned, Joab silenced his doubts, gathered together his army, and set off to do the king's bidding. Nine months and twenty days later Joab returned to Jerusalem with the results of the census, which had been carefully tabulated and verified. There were eight hundred thousand armed soldiers in Israel and five hundred thousand in Judah. Now, we all know that God does not like anyone usurping His authority, especially when it comes to His chosen people, whom He will never allow to be ruled by any other lord or master, least of all by Rome, who bows to false gods and men, first because false gods do not really exist and secondly because of the sheer vanity of that pagan cult. But let us forget Rome for a moment and return to King David, whose heart sank the moment the leader of his army began reading the report, but it was too late, and he confessed, I have committed a grave sin, but I beg you, Lord, forgive your humble servant's folly. And next morning, a prophet named Gad, who was in a manner of speaking the king's soothsayer and his intermediary with Almighty God, came to David as he was rising and told him, The good Lord wishes to know whether you prefer three years of famine on earth, three months of persecution at the hands of your enemies, or three days of plague throughout the land. David did not inquire how many people would have to die in each case, he reckoned that in three days, even with plague, fewer would die than in three years of war or famine. So he prayed, God willing, let there be plague. And God sent a plague, and seventy thousand people died, not counting the women and children, who had not been registered. The Lord finally agreed to lift the plague in exchange for an altar, but the dead were dead, either God had forgotten them or it was not convenient to have them resurrected, since we can safely assume that innumerable inheritances and divisions of property were already being debated and contested, because there is no reason why God's

108

chosen people should disclaim worldly goods that rightfully belong to them, whether acquired by the sweat of their brow, in litigation, or as the spoils of war. The outcome is what matters.

But before passing judgment on human and divine actions, we must also bear in mind that God, who lost no time in making David pay dearly for his mistake, now appears to be unaware of the humiliation being inflicted by Rome on His chosen children, and, more perplexing still, He seems indifferent to this blatant lack of respect for His name and authority. When such a thing happens, that is to say, when it becomes clear that God is showing no sign of coming soon, man has no choice but to take His place, to leave home and restore order in this poor old world of ours, which belongs to God. The censors, as we said earlier, were strutting around with all the arrogance of those in power, backed by a military escort, in other words the soldiers were there to protect them from insults and assault when people started to rebel in Galilee and Judaea. Testing their strength, some protest, quietly at first, then gradually they become more aggressive and defiant, an artisan bangs on the censor's table and swears they will never get a name out of him, a merchant takes refuge in his tent with his entire family and threatens to smash everything and tear off all his clothes, a farmer sets fire to his harvest and brings a basket of ashes, saying, This is the money Israel will pay to those who offend her. Such troublemakers were arrested immediately, thrown into prison, flogged and humiliated, and since human resistance has its limits, frail creatures that we are, their courage soon failed them, the artisan shamelessly revealed his most intimate secrets, the merchant was prepared to sacrifice several daughters in addition to paying his taxes, the farmer covered himself in ashes and offered himself as a slave. The few who still resisted were put to death, while others, who had long ago learned that the only good invader is a dead one, took up arms and fled into the mountains. The arms in question were stones, slings, sticks, clubs and cudgels, a few bows and arrows, hardly enough to wage a war, and the odd sword or lance captured in brief skirmishes but unlikely to do the rebels much good, accustomed as they were, since David's reign, to the primitive weapons of placid shepherds rather than to those of trained warriors. But whether a man is Jewish or not, he takes more readily to war than to peace, especially if he finds a leader who shares his convictions. The insurrection against the Romans began when Joseph's firstborn was eleven years old, and it was led by a man called Judas, who hailed from Galilee and was therefore known as Judas the Galilean or Judas of Galilee. This simple method of naming people was common at the time, as we can see from names such as Joseph of Arimathaea, Simon of Cyrene or the Cyrenian, Mary Magdalene or Mary from Magdala. And if Joseph's son had lived and prospered, he would have been called Jesus of Nazareth or the Nazarene or perhaps something even simpler. But this is mere conjecture, we must never forget that fate is a casket like no other, open and closed at the same time. We can look inside and see all that has happened, the past transformed into fulfilled destiny, but we have no way of seeing into the future, apart from an occasional presentiment or intuition, as we find in this gospel, which could not have been written were it not for those signs and prodigies forecasting a destiny perhaps greater than life itself. But to return to what we were saying, Judas the Galilean had rebellion in his blood. His father, old Hezekiah, had participated in the popular revolts waged against Herod's presumed heirs after his death and before Rome could acknowledge the division of the kingdom and the authority of the new tetrarchs. This is beyond our understanding, for, while we are all made of the same all-too-human substance, the same flesh, bones, blood, skin and laughter, tears and sweat, some of us become cowards and others heroes, some are aggressive and others passive. The same substance used to make a Joseph also made a Judas, and while the latter passed on to his sons the thirst for battle he had inherited from his own father, giving up a peaceful existence in order to defend God's rights, the carpenter Joseph remained at home with his nine young children and their mother, confined to his workbench in order to eke out a living and provide food for his family. For no one can tell who will triumph tomorrow, some say God, others say nobody, one hypothesis is as good as the other, because to speak of yesterday, today, and tomorrow is simply to give different names to the same illusion.

But the men of the village of Nazareth, most of them youths, who went to join the guerrilla force of Judas the Galilean, all disappeared without warning, without a trace, their families sworn to secrecy, and this silence was so strictly observed that no one would have dreamt of asking, Where's Nathanael, I haven't seen him for days, if Nathanael failed to appear at the synagogue or among the reapers in the fields, there was simply one man missing and the others carried on as if Nathanael had never existed, well, not quite, for some saw him entering the village under cover of darkness and leaving again before dawn. Although the only proof of his arrival and departure was the smile on the face of his wife. A smile can be most revealing, a woman may be standing motionless, staring into space, at the horizon, or simply at the wall in front of her, then suddenly she smiles, a pensive smile, like an image coming to the surface and playing on restless water, one would have to be blind to think that Nathanael's wife spent the night without her husband. But human nature is so perverse that some women who were never without their husband at their side began sighing as they imagined those encounters, and they hovered around Nathanael's wife like bees around a flower heavy with pollen. Mary's situation was different, with nine children to care for and a husband who spent his nights tossing and turning in anguish, often waking up the little ones and scaring them out of their wits. After a time they grew used to it, more or less, but the eldest boy, whose own dreams were disturbed by some mysterious presence, was forever waking up. In the beginning he would ask his mother, What's wrong with Father, and she would brush the question aside, reassuring him, It's only a nightmare. She could not very well tell her son, Your father dreamt he was marching with Herod's soldiers along the road to Bethlehem. Which Herod. The father of the present king. Was that why he was groaning and shouting. Yes, that's right. I can't see how being the soldier of a king who's dead can give one nightmares. Your father was never one of Herod's soldiers, he's been a carpenter all his life. Then why does he have nightmares. People don't choose their dreams, dreams choose people, not that I've ever heard that said, but it must be so. And what about all that groaning, Mother. It's because your father dreams he's on his way to kill you. Obviously Mary could never have brought herself to say such things, revealing the cause of her husband's nightmare to Jesus, who like Abraham's son Isaac was cast in the role of the victim who escaped, yet is inexorably condemned.

One day, when he was helping his father make a door, Jesus summoned his courage and questioned him. After a long pause and without raising his eyes, Joseph told him, My son, you are aware of your duties and obligations, perform them and you will be worthy in the eyes of God, but examine your conscience and ask yourself if there are not other duties and obligations waiting to be performed. Is this what you dream, Father. No, the fear that I might have neglected some duty, or worse, that is the cause of my dreams. What do you mean by worse. I didn't think, and the dream itself, the dream is the thought that wasn't thought when it should have been, and now it haunts me night after night and I can't forget it. And what should you have thought. Not even you have the right to ask me that question, and I have no answer to give you. They were working in the shade in the yard, for it was summer and the sun was blazing. Jesus' brothers played nearby, except for the youngest, who was indoors being fed at his mother's breast. James had also been helping, but he soon got tired and bored, little wonder, for the year between them made all the difference, Jesus will soon be old enough for more advanced religious study, he has finished his elementary schooling. In addition to his study of the Torah, the written law, he is already being initiated in the oral law, which is much more difficult and complicated. This explains why at such an early age he was able to conduct a serious conversation with his father, using words properly and debating with reflection and logic. Jesus is almost twelve, on reaching manhood he will perhaps resume this interrupted conversation, if Joseph can find the courage to confide in his son and confess his guilt, that courage which failed Abraham when he was confronted by Isaac, but for the moment Joseph is content to acknowledge and praise the power of God. There can be no doubt that God's upright handwriting bears no resemblance to the crooked lines of men. Just think of Abraham, to whom the angel appeared and said at the last minute, Lay not your hand upon the child, and think of Joseph, who failed to seize the opportunity to save the children of Bethlehem when God sent an officer and three loquacious soldiers instead of an angel to warn him. If Jesus continues as well as he has started, one day he will get around to asking why God saved Isaac and did nothing to protect those poor children, who were as innocent as Abraham's son yet were shown no mercy before the throne of the Lord. And then Jesus will be able to say to Joseph, Father, you mustn't take all the blame, and deep down, who knows, he might dare to ask, When, O Lord, will You come before mankind to acknowledge Your own mistakes.

113

While the carpenter Joseph and his son Jesus debated these important matters in private, the war against the Romans went on. It had been going on for more than two years, and now and then news of casualties reached Nazareth. Ephraim was killed, then Abiezer, then Naphtali, then Eleazar, but no one knew for certain where their bodies lay, between two stones on a mountain, or at the bottom of a ravine, or swept downstream by the current, or beneath the futile shade of a tree. Unable to hold a funeral for those who had died, the villagers of Nazareth eased their conscience by insisting, We neither caused nor witnessed this bloodshed. News also arrived of great victories. The Romans had been driven out of the nearby city of Sepphoris, also from vast regions of Judaea and Galilee where the enemy dared not venture now, and even in Joseph's own village no Roman soldiers had been sighted for more than a year. Who knows, perhaps this is what prompted the carpenter's neighbor, the inquisitive and obliging Ananias, whom we have not mentioned for some time, to turn up in the yard one day and whisper in Joseph's ear, Follow me outside, and no wonder, because these houses are so tiny that it is impossible to have any privacy, everyone is crammed into one room day and night, whatever the circumstances or occasion, so that when the Day of Judgment finally comes, the Lord God should have no difficulty recognizing his own. So the request did not surprise Joseph, not even when Ananias added furtively, Let us go into the desert. Now, the desert is not simply that barren place, that vast expanse of sand or sea of burning dunes we generally picture when we read or hear the word. Desert, as understood here, can also be found in the green land of Galilee, for it means uncultivated fields, where there are no signs of human habitation or labor. Such places cease to be desert when humans arrive on the scene. But since there are only two men walking across this scrubland and Nazareth is still in sight as they head for three great

114

boulders crowning the summit of the hill, there is no suggestion of the place's being populated, and when the men have gone, the desert will be desert again.

Ananias sits on the ground with Joseph at his side. There is the same age difference between them as there has always been, but, while time passes for everyone, the results can vary. Ananias did not look his years when we first met him, but now seems much older, though the years have also left their mark on Joseph. Ananias hesitates, the decisive manner with which he entered the carpenter's house changed once they were on the road, and Joseph has to coax him to speak without appearing to pry. We've come a long way, he remarked, giving Ananias his cue. This isn't something I could have discussed in your house or mine, explained Ananias, but now, in this remote place, they can converse freely without fear of being overheard. You once asked me to look after your house in your absence, Ananias reminded him. Yes, replied Joseph, and I deeply appreciated your help. Then Ananias continued, Now the time has come for me to ask you to look after my house while I'm gone. Are you taking your wife. No, I'm going alone. But surely if Shua is staying behind, there's no need. She'll be staying with relatives who live in a fishing village. Do you mean to tell me you're divorcing your wife. No, if I didn't divorce her when I found that she couldn't give me a son, why should I divorce her now, it's just that I will be away for a while and I'd prefer Shua to be with relatives. Will you be gone long. I don't know, much depends on how long the war lasts. What does the war have to do with your absence, asked Joseph in surprise. I'm going off to look for Judas the Galilean. What do you want from him. To ask him if he'll allow me to join his army. I don't believe it, a peace-loving man like you, Ananias, getting involved in the war against the Romans, have you forgotten what happened to Ephraim and Abiezer. And also to Naphtali and Eleazar. Precisely, so

115

listen to the voice of reason. No, you listen to me, Joseph, and to the voice that comes from my lips, I've now reached the age at which my father died, and he achieved much more in life than this son of his who couldn't even beget children, I'm not as learned as you or likely to become an elder in the synagogue, all I have to look forward to is death, and I'm tied to a woman I don't even love. Then why not divorce her. Divorcing Shua is no problem, the problem is how to divorce myself, and that's impossible. But how much fighting can you do at your age. Don't worry, I'll go into battle as determined as if I were about to get a woman pregnant. I never heard that expression before. Nor I, it came into my head this very minute. Very well, Ananias, you can rely on me to look after your house until you return. Should I not return and news reaches you that I've been killed, promise me you'll send for Shua so that she can claim my possessions. You have my promise. Let's return now that my mind is at peace. At peace, when you've decided to go to war, I really don't understand you. Ah, Joseph, Joseph, for how many centuries will we have to go on studying the Talmud before we begin to understand the simplest things. Why did we have to come all this way. I wanted to speak to you in the presence of witnesses. The only witnesses we need are Almighty God and this sky that covers us wherever we may be. And what about these stones. These stones are deaf and dumb and cannot bear witness. That may be so, but if you and I were to give a false account of our conversation, these stones would accuse us and go on accusing us until they turned to dust and we to nothingness. Shall we go back. Yes, let's go.

As they went, Ananias turned around several times to look at the stones, until finally they disappeared behind a hillock, then Joseph asked him, Does Shua know. Yes, she knows. And what did she have to say. At first not a word, then she told me I should have abandoned her years ago and left her to her fate. Poor Shua. Once she's with rela-

116

tives, she'll forget me, and if I die in battle, she'll forget me forever, forgetting is all too easy, that is life. They entered the village, and when they arrived at the carpenter's house, which was the first of two houses on one side, Jesus, who was playing in the road with James and Judas, told them his mother was with the neighbor next door. As the two men turned away, the voice of Judas could be heard announcing solemnly, I am Judas the Galilean, whereupon Ananias looked around and said with a smile to Joseph, Take a look, there goes my leader, but before the carpenter had time to reply, the voice of Jesus could be heard saying, Then you don't belong here. Joseph felt a sword pierce his heart, as if those words were addressed to him, as if the game being played by his son was meant to convey another truth. Then he thought of the three boulders and tried, without knowing why, to imagine what life would be like if henceforth he were obliged to speak every word and perform every action in their presence, and suddenly, remembering God, he was stricken with fear. In Ananias's house they found Mary consoling a distressed Shua, who dried her tears the moment the men arrived, not because she had stopped weeping but because women know from bitter experience when to hide their tears. Hence the well-known saying, They're either laughing or weeping, but it simply is not true, because they weep quietly to themselves. But there was nothing quiet about Shua's grief, and when Ananias departed, she sobbed her heart out. One week later Shua's relatives came to fetch her. Mary accompanied her to the edge of the village, where they embraced and said good-bye. Shua was no longer weeping, but her eyes would never be dry again. Nothing can ease her sorrow or extinguish the flame that burns her tears before they surface and roll down her cheeks.

THE MONTHS PASSED, AND NEWS OF THE WAR CONTINUED
to arrive, sometimes good, sometimes bad, but while the
good news never went beyond vague allusions to victories
that always turned out to be modest, the bad news spoke
of much bloodshed and heavy losses for the rebel army of
Judas the Galilean. One day news came that Eldad had been
killed when the Romans made a surprise attack on a guerrilla ambush, there were many casualties, but Eldad was
the only one from Nazareth to lose his life. Another day
someone said he had heard from a friend, who had been
told by someone else, that Varus, the Roman governor of
Syria, was on his way with two legions to put an end once
and for all to this intolerable insurrection that had been
dragging on for three years. The statement, Varus is on
his way, and the lack of any precise details spread panic
among the people. They expected the dreaded insignia of
war, which bore the initials SPQR, the Senate and People
of Rome, to appear at any moment, heralding the arrival
of a punitive force. Under this symbol and that flag, men
go forth to kill one another, and the same can be said of

118

those other well-known initials, INRI, Jesus of Nazareth, King of the Jews, but we must not anticipate events, for the dire consequences of Jesus' death will emerge only in the fullness of time. Everywhere there is talk of imminent battle, those with more faith in God predict that before the year is out, the Romans will be expelled from the Holy Land of Israel, but others, less confident, sadly shake their heads and foresee nothing but doom and destruction. And so it turned out.

Following the news that Varus's legions were advancing, nothing happened for several weeks, which allowed the rebels to intensify their attacks on the dispersed troops they were fighting, but the tactics behind this Roman passivity soon became clear, when the scouts of Judas the Galilean reported that one of the legions was heading south in a circular movement, skirting the bank of the river Jordan, then turning right at Jericho to repeat the maneuver northward, like a net cast into the water and retrieved by an experienced hand, or a lasso thrown to capture everything around. And the other legion, carrying out a similar maneuver, was now heading south. A strategy that could be described as a pincer movement, but it was more like two walls closing in simultaneously, knocking down those unable to escape, and finally crushing them. Throughout Judaea and Galilee, the legions' advance was marked with crosses, to which Judas's men had been nailed by their wrists and feet, their bones broken with hammers to hasten their death. The soldiers looted the villages and searched every house. No evidence was needed for them to arrest suspects and execute them. These unfortunates, if you will pardon the irony, had the good fortune to be crucified near their homes, so relatives could remove their bodies once they were dead. And what a sad spectacle it was, as mothers, widows, young brides, and weeping orphans watched the bruised corpses being gently lowered from the crosses, for there is nothing more pitiful for the living than the sight

119

of an abandoned body. The crucified man was then carried to his grave to await the day of resurrection. But there were also men wounded in combat, in the mountains or in some other lonely spot, who, though still alive, were left by the soldiers in the most absolute of all deserts, that of solitary death, and there they remained, slowly burnt by the sun, exposed to birds of prey, and after a time stripped of flesh and bone, reduced to repugnant remains without shape or form. Those questioning if not skeptical souls, who resist the facile acceptance of gospels such as these, will ask how it was possible for the Romans to crucify such a large number of Jews in vast arid regions devoid of trees, apart from the rare stunted bush on which you could barely crucify a scarecrow. But they are forgetting that the Roman army has all the professional skills and organization of a modern army. A steady supply of wooden crosses has been maintained throughout the campaign, as witnessed by all these donkeys and mules following the troops and laden with posts and crossbars, which can be assembled on the spot, and then it is simply a question of nailing the condemned man's extended arms to the crossbar, hoisting the post upright, forcing him to draw in his legs sideways, and securing his two feet, one on top of the other, with a single long nail. Any executioner attached to the legion will tell you that this operation may sound complicated, but it is in fact much more difficult to describe than to carry out.

The pessimists who predicted disaster were right. From north to south and from south to north, men, women, and children flee before the advancing legions, some because they might be accused of having collaborated with the rebels, others simply in terror, for, as we know, they are in danger of being arrested and put to death without a trial. One of these fugitives interrupted his retreat for a few moments to knock on Joseph's door with a message from Joseph's neighbor, Ananias, who had been severely wounded back in Sepphoris. Ananias wanted Joseph to know, The war is lost and there is no hope of escape, send for my wife and tell her to claim my possessions. Is that all he said, asked Joseph. Nothing more, replied the messenger. Why couldn't you have brought him here with you, when you knew you had to pass this way. In his condition he would have been a hindrance, and I had to put my family's safety first. First, perhaps, but surely not to the exclusion of everyone else. What are you trying to say, you yourself are surrounded by children, and if you remain here, that can only be because you are in no danger. There's no time to lose, be on your way and may God go with you, for without Him there is always danger. You sound like a man without faith, for you should know the Lord is everywhere. Indeed, but He often ignores us, and don't speak to me about faith after abandoning my neighbor to his fate. Well, then, why not go and rescue him yourself. That's exactly what I intend to do. This conversation took place in the middle of the afternoon. It was a fine, sunny day, with a few white clouds drifting across the sky like unmanned barges. Joseph went to untie the donkey, called his wife, and told her without further explanation, I'm off to Sepphoris to look for our neighbor, Ananias, who's been badly wounded and cannot make the journey on his own. Mary simply nodded in reply, but Jesus clung to his father and pleaded, Take me with you. Joseph looked at his son, placed his right hand on the boy's head, and told him, You stay here, I'll be back soon, if I make good time, I should be back before dawn, and he could be right, for the distance between Nazareth and Sepphoris cannot be much more than five miles, about the same distance as from Jerusalem to Bethlehem, additional proof that the world is full of coincidences. Joseph did not mount the donkey, he wanted the animal to be fresh for the return journey, firm

121

and steady on its feet and prepared to carry a sick man gently, or, to be precise, a wounded soldier, which is not quite the same thing.

At the foot of the hill where, almost a year before, Ananias had told him of his decision to join the rebel army of Judas the Galilean, the carpenter looked up at the three enormous boulders on the summit, which reminded him of segments of a fruit. Perched on high, they appeared to be waiting for a reply from heaven and earth to the questions posed by all the creatures of this world, even though the creatures cannot voice them, What am I, Why am I here, What other world awaits me, this one being what it is. Were Ananias to ask such questions, we could tell him that at least the boulders remain unscathed by the wind, rain, and heat, and some twenty centuries hence they will probably still be here, and twenty centuries after that, while the world changes all around them. To the first two questions, however, there is no answer.

Throngs of fugitives were to be seen on the road, with the same look of terror on their faces as on that of the messenger sent by Ananias. They looked at Joseph in amazement, and one man, taking him by the arm, inquired, Where are you going, and the carpenter replied, To Sepphoris, to rescue a friend. If you know what's good for you, you'll do no such thing. Why not. The Romans are approaching, and there is no hope of defending the city. I must go, my neighbor is like a brother and there is no one else to fetch him. Heed my advice, and with that the wise counselor went on his way, leaving Joseph standing in the middle of the road, lost in thought, wondering whether his life was worth saving and whether he despised himself. After giving the matter thought, he decided he felt quite indifferent, like someone confronting a void that is neither near nor far, and where there is nowhere to rest one's eyes, for who can focus on emptiness. Then it occurred to him that as a father he had a duty to protect his children, that he ought to return home rather than chasing after a neighbor, and Ananias was no longer even that, for he had deserted his home and sent his wife away. But Joseph's children were safe, the Romans, engaged as they were in pursuing rebels, would do them no harm. Finally reaching a conclusion, Joseph heard himself say aloud, as if he were wrestling with his thoughts, And I am not a rebel either. Without further ado he gave his animal a slap on its haunch, exclaimed, Go, donkey, and continued on.

It was late evening when he arrived at Sepphoris. The long shadows of houses and trees that could be made out at first gradually disappeared into the horizon like dark, cascading water. There were few people on the streets of the city, no women or children, only weary men laying down their awkward weapons as they stretched out, panting for breath, and it was difficult to tell whether they were exhausted from combat or from flight. Joseph asked one of them, Are the Romans approaching. The man closed his eyes, slowly reopened them, and said, They'll arrive by tomorrow, and then, averting his gaze, he told Joseph, Get away from here, take your donkey and leave this place. But I'm searching for a friend who's been wounded, Joseph explained. If you counted all who have been wounded as your friends, you'd be the wealthiest man in the world. Where are the wounded. Here, there, everywhere. But is there some place in the city where they're being nursed. Yes, behind those houses you'll find a garrison where many wounded have been given shelter, perhaps you'll find your friend there, but hurry, for more corpses are being carried out than men brought in alive. Joseph knew the place well, he had been here often, both for work, which was plentiful in a city as rich and prosperous as Sepphoris, and for certain minor religious feasts that did not justify the long and arduous journey to Jerusalem. Finding the storehouse was easy enough, all one had to do was to follow the terrible stench of blood and pus that hung in the air, almost like a game of hide and seek, Hot, cold, hot, cold, it hurts, it doesn't, but now the pain was becoming unbearable. Joseph tethered the donkey to a long pole he found nearby and entered the storehouse, which had been converted into a dormitory. Between the mats on the floor were tiny lamps which provided hardly any light, twinkling stars against a black sky, which helped to guide one's faltering steps. Joseph walked slowly between the rows of wounded men in search of Ananias. There were other strong odors in the air, the smell of oil and wine used to heal wounds, the smell of sweat, excrement, and urine, for some of these unfortunate men were unable to move, and could not help evacuating then and there. He isn't here, Joseph thought to himself as he reached the end of the row. He retraced his steps, walking more slowly this time and looking carefully. Alas, they were all alike, with their long beards, hollow cheeks, sunken eyes, and unwashed bodies covered with sweat. Some of the wounded followed him with anxious expressions, hoping that this able-bodied man had come for them, but the momentary glimmer in their eyes soon disappeared and their long vigil, for who knows what or whom, continued. Joseph came to a halt before an elderly man with white beard and hair. It is he, he thought. Yet Ananias's appearance had changed since Joseph walked past the first time, his beard and hair, white as snow before, now looked dirty, and his eyebrows, still black, looked unnatural. The old man's eyes were closed, and he breathed heavily. In a low voice Joseph called, Ananias, then, moving closer, he repeated the name louder. Little by little, as if he were emerging from the depths of the earth, the old man's eyelids began to move, and when the eyes were fully open, there was no longer any doubt, this was Ananias, the neighbor who had abandoned his home and wife to go and fight the Romans, and here he lies with frightful abdominal wounds and stinking of rotting flesh. At first Ananias does not recognize Joseph, the poor light in this

124

makeshift infirmary does not help, and his eyesight is poorer anyway, but he recognizes him when the carpenter repeats his name in another tone of voice, which almost holds affection. The old man's eyes fill with tears, and he says over and over, It's you, it's you, what are you doing here, what have you come here for, and he tries to raise himself on one elbow and stretch out his arm, but cannot find the strength, his body sags, his whole face twisted with pain. I came for you, said the carpenter, my donkey is tethered outside, and we can be back in Nazareth in no time at all. You shouldn't have come here, the Romans are expected any minute, I can't leave this place, I'm done for, and with trembling hands he opened his tunic. Beneath the rags soaked with wine and oil were two gaping wounds which gave off such a nauseating smell that Joseph held his breath and looked away. The old man covered himself, his arms falling to his sides, as if the effort had been too much for him, Now you know why I can't leave this place, if you tried to move me, my guts would spill out. You'll be all right with a bandage tight around your belly and if we go slowly, insisted Joseph, unconvincingly, because it was obvious that even if he could get the old man onto the donkey's back, they would never make it to Nazareth. Ananias's eyes were shut again, and without opening them he told Joseph, You must go back, I'm warning you, the Romans will be here soon. Don't worry, they won't attack at night. Go home, go home, muttered Ananias, and in reply Joseph said, Try to get some sleep.

He watched over him all night long. Struggling to keep awake, he found himself wondering why he had come to this place, since there had never really been any deep friendship between Ananias and him. There was a considerable difference in their ages, and besides, he had always had certain reservations about Ananias and his wife, who could be nosy and meddlesome even while doing one a favor, and who always gave the impression of expecting to be paid back in kind. But he is my neighbor, Joseph thought, and could think of no better answer to silence his misgivings, he's my fellow creature, a man close to death, with his eyes already shut, as if to savor every minute of his dying, I can't abandon him now. He was sitting in the narrow space between the mat on which Ananias lay and that of a young boy who couldn't have been much older than his son Jesus, the poor lad was moaning quietly and muttering to himself, his lips cracked with fever. Joseph held his hand to comfort him, and Ananias's hand began fumbling as if reaching for a weapon to defend himself, and there the three of them remained, Joseph alive and well between two who were dying, one life between two deaths. Meanwhile the tranquil night sky sent stars and planets into orbit, and a shining white moon came floating through space from the other end of the world, shedding innocence over the whole of Galilee. It was only much later that Joseph emerged from the torpor into which he had reluctantly fallen. He awoke with a sense of relief, because this time he had not dreamed of the road to Bethlehem. Opening his eyes, he saw that Ananias, whose eyes were also open, was dead. At the last moment he had been unable to endure the vision of death, and his hand gripped Joseph's so tightly that Joseph felt his bones were being crushed. To ease the painful grip, he released his other hand, which was clasping the boy's, and noticed that the boy's fever had subsided. Joseph looked out through the open door, there was daylight, a sky in hues of sepia. Human forms stirred in the storehouse, those who could get up unaided went outside to watch the sunrise. They might well have asked one another or even the sky itself, What will this new dawn bring. One day we shall learn not to ask useless questions, but until that day comes, let us take this opportunity to ask ourselves, What will this new dawn bring. Joseph thought to himself, I may as well go, I can do nothing more here, but there was a questioning note in

126

these words that prompted him to think, I could take his body to Nazareth, and the idea seemed so obvious that he almost convinced himself this was why he had come, to find Ananias alive and carry him back dead. The boy asked for water. Joseph held an earthenware bowl to his lips, How do you feel, he asked him. Better. At least the fever seems to have passed. Let me see if I can stand up, said the boy. Be careful, said Joseph, trying to restrain him, then another idea occurred to him. All he could do for Ananias was bury him in Nazareth, but the boy's life could still be saved if Joseph delivered him from this death house, so that one human being could be substituted, in a manner of speaking, for another. He no longer felt compassion for Ananias, whose body now was an empty shell, his soul more remote each time Joseph looked at him. The boy appeared to sense that something good was about to happen to him, and his eyes shone, but before he could ask any questions, Joseph had already gone to bring the donkey. Blessed is the Lord who puts such splendid ideas into the heads of mankind. But the donkey was gone. All that remained was a bit of rope tied to the pole. The thief had wasted no time trying to untie the knot, using a sharp knife, he had simply cut through it.

This latest misfortune drained the strength from Joseph's body. Like one of those felled calves he had watched being sacrificed in the Temple, he dropped to his knees, covered his face with his hands, and shed all the tears that had been welling for the last thirteen years while he waited for the day he would be able to forgive himself or face the final condemnation. God does not forgive the sins He makes us commit. Joseph did not return to the storehouse, for he realized that his actions had become forever meaningless, that the world itself was meaningless. The sun was rising, but why, O Lord, were there thousands of tiny clouds scattered throughout the sky like stones in the desert. Anyone watching Joseph there, as he wiped his tears with the sleeve of his tunic, would have thought he was mourning the death of a relative found with the other wounded men in the storehouse, when the truth was that Joseph had just shed the last of his natural tears, the tears of life's sorrow.

After wandering through the city for more than an hour, hoping that he might still find the stolen animal, he was about to give up and return to Nazareth when he was arrested by Roman soldiers, who had taken Sepphoris. They asked him his name, I am Joseph, son of Eli, and then where he lived, In Nazareth, and where he was going, Back to Nazareth, and what brought him to Sepphoris, Someone told me a neighbor of mine was here, and who was this neighbor, Ananias, and had he found him, Yes, and where had he found him, In a storehouse with others, and what others might they be, Wounded men, and in which part of the city, Over in that direction. They took him to a square where a group of men were assembled, twelve or fifteen sitting on the ground, some of them wounded, and the soldiers ordered him, Join the others. Realizing that the men sitting there were rebels, he protested, I am a carpenter and a man of peace, and one of the rebels spoke up and said, We don't know this man, but the officer in charge of the prisoners refused to listen and, giving Joseph one mighty push, sent him flying to the ground, where he ended up among the others. The only place you're going is to your death, the officer told him. The double shock of this misfortune and the fate awaiting him left Joseph stunned. But once he regained his composure, he felt a great tranquillity, convinced that it was all a nightmare which would soon pass and that there was no point tormenting himself over these threats, for they would vanish the moment he opened his eyes. Then he remembered that when he dreamed of the road to Bethlehem, he was also convinced he would wake up, and he began to tremble as the cruel certainty of his fate finally dawned on him, I'm going to die, to die even though I'm innocent. He felt a hand on his

128

shoulder, the hand of the prisoner beside him, When the commanding officer comes, we'll explain you're not one of us, and he'll order your release. And what about the rest of you. The Romans have crucified every rebel they've captured so far, and they're not likely to treat us any better. God will save you. Surely you're forgetting that God saves souls rather than bodies. The soldiers arrived with more prisoners, in twos and threes, and then a large group of about twenty. The inhabitants of Sepphoris had gathered in the square, and there were even women and children in the crowd. A restless murmur could be heard, but no one dared move without the permission of the Roman soldiers, who were still looking for anyone who might have helped the rebels. After a while another man was dragged into the square, and the soldiers who had captured him announced, That's all for now, whereupon the officer in charge shouted, On your feet, you lot. The prisoners guessed that the commanding officer of the cohort was approaching, and the man sitting beside Joseph told him, Prepare yourself, what he meant was, Prepare yourself for release, as if one needed to prepare oneself for freedom, but if someone came, it was not the commanding officer, nor did anyone learn who it was, because the officer in charge suddenly gave an order in Latin to the soldiers. Needless to say, everything said so far by the Romans has been in Latin, because it would be unthinkable for the descendants of the she-wolf to speak in barbarian tongues, they have interpreters for that purpose, but since the conversation here was between the soldiers themselves, no translation was required. Obeying their superior's orders, the soldiers quickly rounded up the prisoners, Forward march, and the procession of condemned men made its way out of the city, with the crowd trailing behind. Forced to march with the other prisoners, Joseph had nowhere to turn for mercy. He raised his arms to heaven and called out, Save me, I'm not one of them, help me, I'm innocent,

129

at which point a soldier prodded him from behind with the butt of a lance, almost knocking him to the ground. In despair, Joseph felt hatred for Ananias, the one who had got him into this predicament, but the feeling soon passed, giving way to emptiness. He thought to himself, There is nowhere else to go, but he was wrong, and he would soon be there. Strange as it may seem, the certainty of death calmed him. He looked around at his companions in misfortune, who seemed quite composed, some, naturally, were downcast, but others defiantly held their heads high. Most were Pharisees. Then, for the first time, Joseph remembered his children, and for one fleeting moment even his wife, but all those faces and names were too much for his tired brain. In need of sleep and food, he felt weak, could not concentrate, the only image that remained was that of Jesus, his firstborn and his final punishment. He recalled their conversation about his dream and remembered telling Jesus, It just isn't possible for you to ask me all the questions, or for me to give you all the answers, but now the time for answering questions was over.

On a stretch of high ground overlooking the city forty thick posts strong enough to take a man's weight had been erected in rows of eight. At the foot of each post lay a crossbar long enough to allow a man to spread his arms. At the sight of these instruments of torture, some of the prisoners tried to escape, but the soldiers, baring their swords, drove them back. One rebel attempted to impale himself on a sword, but to no avail, he was dragged off at once to be crucified. Then the laborious task began of nailing the wrists of each condemned man to a crossbar before hoisting him up on the upright posts. The screams and moans could be heard throughout the countryside, and the people of Sepphoris wept before this sad spectacle, which they were obliged to watch as a warning. One by one, the crosses went up, a man hanging from each, his legs drawn in as we saw before, who knows for what reason, perhaps

130

an order from Rome intended to make the job easier and save on materials, because one does not need to know much about crucifixions to see that a cross made to the measurements of the average man would require more work and be heavier to carry and more awkward to handle, not to mention the serious disadvantage to the victim, since the closer his feet to the ground, the easier it is to lower his body afterward, without having to use a ladder, thus allowing him to pass directly, as it were, from the arms of the cross into the arms of his family, if he has any, or of the appointed gravedigger, who will not just leave him lying there. It so happened that Joseph was the last to be crucified, and this meant he had to look on as his thirty-nine unknown companions were tortured one by one and put to death. When his turn finally came, he was resigned to his fate and no longer protested his innocence, thus missed his last opportunity to save himself, when the soldier doing the hammering said to the officer in charge, This is the man who said he was innocent. The officer paused for a moment, giving Joseph just enough time to cry out, I'm innocent, but instead Joseph chose to remain silent. The officer looked up and probably decided that the symmetry would be destroyed if the last cross was not raised, and that forty made a nice round figure, so he gave the signal, the nails were driven in, Joseph let out a scream and went on screaming, then they hoisted him up, his weight held by the nails that pierced his wrists, and there were more cries of pain as a long nail was driven through his feet. Dear God, this is the man You created, blessed be Your holy name, since it is forbidden to curse You. Suddenly, as if someone had given another signal, panic gripped the inhabitants of Sepphoris, not because of the crucifixions they had just witnessed but at the sight of flames spreading rapidly through the city, fire destroying the houses and public buildings and even the trees in the inner courtyards. Indifferent to the blaze set by their comrades, four soldiers

131

from the cohort moved between the rows of dying men, methodically breaking their shinbones with iron rods. Sepphoris was burning wherever one looked, as the crucified men expired one after another. The carpenter named Joseph, son of Eli, was a young man in his prime, having just turned thirty-three.

WHEN THIS WAR ENDS, AND IT WILL NOT BE LONG NOW, for as we can see it is already almost over, there will be a final reckoning of those who lost their lives, so many here, so many there, some near, some farther away, and if it is true that with the passage of time the number of those killed in ambushes or open warfare loses all importance and is forgotten, those crucified, who number around two thousand, according to the most reliable statistics, will long be remembered by the people of Judaea and Galilee, even after more wars have broken out and more blood has been spilled. Two thousand crucified is a lot, but it seems even more if we imagine them set out a mile apart along a highway or encircling, for example, the country that one day will be known as Portugal, which has a perimeter more or less that length. Between the river Jordan and the sea, widows and orphans weep, an ancient custom, that is why they are widows and orphans, so that they may weep, and when the boys grow up and go to fight a new war, there will be more widows and orphans to take their place, and even if customs change, if black becomes the color of mourning instead of white, or if women wear black mantillas instead of tearing their hair out, tears of sincere grief will never change.

So far Mary is not weeping, but in her soul she has a presentiment, for her husband has not returned, and in Nazareth it is rumored that Sepphoris was burned and men were crucified. Accompanied by her eldest son, she retraces the route taken by Joseph yesterday. Very likely, at one point or other, her feet will touch the footprints left by her husband's sandals, for this is not the rainy season and there is nothing but the gentlest breeze to disturb the soil. Joseph's footprints are like the prints of a prehistoric animal that inhabited these parts in some bygone age, for we say, Only yesterday, and we might as well say, A thousand years ago, because time is not a rope one can measure from knot to knot, time is a pitched and undulating surface which only memory can make accessible. A group of villagers from Nazareth accompany Mary and Jesus, some moved by compassion, others simply curious, and there are distant relatives of Ananias, but they will return home as uncertain as they left, for since they have not found a body, he may still be alive. It never occurred to them to search the debris of the storehouse, where they might have recognized his body among the charred remains. These Nazarenes had gone half the way, when they met a detachment of soldiers that had been sent to search their village, so some turned back, worried about what might happen to their property, for one can never predict what soldiers will do when they knock on a door and find no one at home. The officer in charge asked why these villagers were on their way to Sepphoris, and they replied, We wanted to see the fire, an explanation which the officer accepted, because fires have had an irresistible attraction for mankind since the world began, there are even those who say that fire is a kind of inner call, an instinctive memory of the original fire, as if ashes somehow preserve

134

what was burned, thus explaining, by this theory, the look of fascination in our faces as we watch a camp fire or the flickering of a candle in a dark room. If we humans were as foolhardy or daring as butterflies, moths, and other winged insects, and threw ourselves, all together, into the flames, then who knows, perhaps the blaze would be so fierce and the light so strong that God would open His eyes and be roused from His torpor, too late, of course, to recognize us, but in time to see the impending void after we went up in smoke.

Although she had left behind a house full of children with no one to look after them, Mary refused to turn back, and she was easy in her mind, because it is not every day that soldiers invade a village and start slaughtering young children. Besides, these Romans were not only willing but even eager to see the children grow up, provided they remained servile and paid their taxes on time. Mother and son are walking along the road by themselves, because Ananias's relatives, some half dozen of them, are so busy chatting that they have fallen behind. Mary and Jesus have only words of anguish to exchange and so prefer to remain silent rather than distress each other. A strange silence hangs everywhere, no birds are singing, the wind has died down, there is nothing but the sound of footsteps, and even that withdraws, like a polite intruder who has entered an empty house by mistake. Sepphoris comes into sight suddenly as they turn a bend in the road. Several houses are still burning, thin columns of smoke rise here and there, walls are blackened, trees scorched from top to bottom, the foliage intact but the color of rust. And there on our right, the rows of crosses.

Mary started running, but they were still some distance away and she had to slow down and catch her breath. As a result of giving birth to all those children without letup, her heart is weaker. Jesus, a respectful son, would like to accompany his mother, remaining at her side, now and later, so that they can share the same joys and sorrows, but she walks so slowly, dragging her feet, At this rate, Mother, we'll never get there. She makes a gesture as if to say, You go ahead and I'll catch up. Leaving the road, Jesus sprints across the field to save time, Father, Father, he calls, hoping that his father will not be there, fearing that he will find him. He reaches the first row, some of the crucified men are still hanging from the crosses, others have already been taken down and lie waiting on the ground. Few have relatives to gather around them, for most of these rebels came from afar, part of a mixed contingent which made its last united assault and is now finally dispersed, each man left to confront alone the ineffable solitude of death. Jesus does not see his father, his heart would rejoice but his reason tells him, Wait, we haven't got to the end of the row. But in fact the end is right here. Stretched out on the ground is the father he has been seeking, there is little blood, only the open wounds on the wrists and feet, You could be sleeping, Father, but no, you are not asleep, how could you possibly sleep with your legs twisted in that position, how charitable of them to remove you from the cross, but there are so many bodies here that the good souls who removed you had no time to straighten your broken bones. The boy named Jesus kneels beside his dead father and weeps, he cannot bring himself to touch the corpse, but then grief overcomes his fear and he embraces the motionless body. Father, Father, he sobs aloud, and another cry accompanies his, What have they done to you, Joseph, it is the voice of Mary, who has arrived at last, exhausted and sobbing her heart out, for when she saw her son come to a halt in the distance, she knew what to expect. Mary's tears overflow when she sees the pitiful state of her husband's legs. We do not know what happens to life's sorrows after death, especially those last moments of suffering, it is possible that everything ends with death, but we cannot be certain that the memory of suffering does not linger at least for several hours in this body we describe as dead, nor can we rule out the possibility that matter uses putrefaction as a last resort to rid itself of the suffering. With a tenderness she would never have permitted herself to show while her husband was alive, Mary pulled down Joseph's tunic after trying to straighten the broken legs that gave him the grotesque appearance of a puppet coming apart. Jesus helped his mother pull the tunic down over the thin shinbones, perhaps the most vulnerable part of the human body and a painful reminder of our fragile state. The feet hung sideways, and flies, drawn by the smell of blood, kept swarming around the wounds inflicted by the nail. Joseph's sandals had fallen to the ground beside the thick trunk of which he was the last fruit. Worn and covered with dust, they would have lain there forgotten if Jesus had not recovered them without thinking. As if obeying an order, and unnoticed by Mary, he tucked the sandals under his belt, a gesture of perfect symbolism, Joseph's firstborn claiming his inheritance, for certain things begin as simply as this, and even today people say, In my father's shoes I become a man.

From a discreet distance Roman soldiers kept a lookout, ready to intervene in the event of disorderly behavior among those mourning and tending to the bodies. But these people showed no sign of making trouble, they were doing nothing but praying as they went from body to body, and this took more than two hours. Rending their garments, they recited the prayer for the dead over each corpse, relatives on the left, others on the right, their voices breaking the evening silence as they chanted, Lord, what is man that You are mindful of him, and the son of man that You should visit him, man is but a puff of wind, his days pass like a shadow, he lives and fails to see death and saves his soul by escaping to the tomb, man born of woman is given little time and much disquiet, he blossoms like a flower and like a flower perishes, what is man that You are mindful of him, and the son of man that You should visit him. And yet, after acknowledging man's utter insignificance in the eyes of God, in tones so deep that they seemed to come from within rather than from the voices themselves, the chorus soared in exaltation to proclaim before Almighty God our unsuspected worth, Do not forget, O Lord, that You made man a little lower than the angels and have crowned him with glory and honor. When the mourners reached Joseph, whom they did not know and who was the last of the forty, they passed on quickly, but the carpenter had taken with him to the other world everything he needed. Their haste was justified, because the law does not allow the crucified to remain unburied until the following day, and the sun was already going down. Jesus, given his youth, did not have to rend his garments, he was exempt from this ceremony of mourning, but his strong, clear voice could be heard above all the others when he intoned, Blessed be the Lord, our God, King of the Universe, who created you with justice, kept you alive with justice, nourished you with justice, who with justice allowed you to know this world, and with justice will resurrect you, blessed be the Lord, who resurrects the dead. Stretched out on the ground, Joseph, if he can still feel the pain of the nails, may perhaps also hear these words, and he must know what part God's justice played in his life, now that he can no longer expect anything more from either the one or the other. The mourners, finished praying, now had to bury their dead, but there were so many dead, and with night fast approaching it was impossible to find a fitting place for all of them, that is to say a real tomb covered with a stone, and as for wrapping the bodies in mortuary cloth or even a simple shroud, there was no hope of that. So they decided to dig a long trench to hold them, which was not the first time nor would it be the last that men were buried where they lay. Jesus too was given a spade, and he set about digging vigorously beside the grown-ups.

138

Destiny in its wisdom decreed that Joseph be buried in a grave dug by his own son, thus fulfilling the prophecy, The son of man will bury man, while he himself remains unburied. However enigmatic these words seem at first, they merely state the obvious, for the last man, by virtue of being last, will have no one to bury him. But this will not be true of the boy who has just buried his father, the world will not end with him, and we shall be here for thousands and thousands of years in a constant succession of births and deaths, and if man has always been the implacable foe and executioner of man, all the more reason for him to go on being the gravedigger of man.

The sun has now disappeared behind the mountain. Enormous dark clouds over the valley of Jordan move slowly westward, as if pulled by this fading light that tinges their upper edges crimson. It has suddenly become cooler, and rain seems likely tonight although unusual for this time of the year. The soldiers have withdrawn, taking advantage of the waning light to return to their encampment some distance away, where their comrades-in-arms have probably arrived after carrying out a similar search in Nazareth. This is how a modern war should be fought, with the utmost coordination, not in the haphazard fashion of Judas the Galilean's rebel force, and the outcome is there for all to see, thirty-nine of his men crucified, the fortieth an innocent man who came with the best of intentions and met a miserable death. The people of Sepphoris will look among the ruins of their burnt-out city for somewhere to spend the night, and at daybreak each family will salvage what possessions they can from their former homes, then go off to make a new life for themselves elsewhere, because not only has Sepphoris been razed to the ground but Rome will make sure the city is not rebuilt for some time. Mary and Jesus are two shadows in the midst of a dark forest consisting of nothing but trunks. The mother draws her son to her bosom, two frightened souls searching as

139

one for courage, and the dead beneath the ground, it seems, wish to detain the living. Jesus suggested to his mother, Let's spend the night in the city, but Mary told him, We cannot, your brothers and sisters are all alone and they must be famished. They could scarcely see where they were treading. After much stumbling, they finally reached the road, which in the dark stretched out like a parched riverbed. No sooner did they leave Sepphoris than it started raining, heavy drops to begin with, making a gentle sound as they hit the thick dust on the ground. The rain became more insistent, oppressive, the dust soon turned to mud, and Mary and her son had to remove their sandals to avoid losing them. They walk in silence, the mother covering her son's head with her mantle, they have nothing to say to each other, perhaps they are even thinking vaguely that Joseph is not dead after all, that when they get home, they will find him tending to the children as best he can, and he will ask his wife, What on earth possessed you to go out without asking my permission, but the tears have welled up again in Mary's eyes, not only because of her grief but also because of this infinite weariness, this continuous, persistent rain, the grim darkness, all much too sad and black for any hope that Joseph is still alive.

One day someone will tell the widow about the miracle witnessed at the gates of Sepphoris, when the tree trunks used to crucify the prisoners took root again and sprouted new leaves, and miracle is the right word, first because the Romans were in the habit of taking the crosses with them when they left, and secondly because trunks that have been chopped top and bottom have no sap left or shoots capable of transforming a thick, bloodstained post into a living tree. The credulous attributed this wonder to the blood of the martyrs, the skeptics said it was the rain, but no one had ever heard of blood or rain reviving trees once they were made into crosses and abandoned on a mountain slope or the plain of a desert. That it had been willed by God was something no one dared suggest, not only because His will, whatever that may be, is inscrutable, but also because no one could think of any good reason why the crucified of Sepphoris should be the beneficiaries of this peculiar manifestation of divine grace, which was really more in keeping with the style of pagan gods. These trees here will survive a long time, and the day will come when this episode will be forgotten, and since mankind seeks an explanation for everything, whether it be true or false, tales and legends will be invented, containing facts to begin with, then moving gradually away from the facts, until they become pure fantasy. Then eventually the trees will die of old age or be cut down to make way for a road, a school, a house, a shopping center, or a military base, the excavators will unearth the skeletons buried for two thousand years, and the anthropologists will appear on the scene, and an expert in anatomy will examine the remains and announce to a shocked world that there is conclusive evidence that men were crucified in those days with their legs bent at the knee. And people will be unable to refute these scientific findings though they find them aesthetically deplorable.

When Mary and Jesus arrived home drenched to the skin, covered with mud, and shivering with cold, they found the children in better spirits than one might have expected, thanks to the resourcefulness of James and Lisa, who were older than the others. They remembered to light the fire when the night turned cold, and sat huddled against one another around it and tried to forget the pangs of hunger. Hearing someone knocking outside, James went to open the door. The rain poured in as their mother and brother crossed the threshold, it seemed to flood the house. The children stared, and knew their father would not be coming back when Jesus closed the door, but they said nothing until James finally asked, Where is Father. The ground slowly absorbed the water that dripped from wet clothes, and all that broke the silence was the damp wood crackling in the hearth. The children stared at their mother. James repeated the question, Where is Father. Mary opened her mouth to speak, but the word, like a hangman's noose, choked her, forcing Jesus to intervene, Father is dead, he told them, and without knowing why, perhaps as proof that Joseph was dead, he took the wet sandals from his belt and showed them, I brought these back. The older children were already close to tears, but the sight of those forlorn sandals was too much for all of them, and the widow and her nine children were soon crying their hearts out. Not knowing which of them to comfort, she sank to her knees, exhausted, and her children gathered around her, like a cluster of grapes that did not need to be trampled to release the colorless wine of tears. Only Jesus remained standing, clasping the sandals to his bosom, musing that one day he would wear them, or this minute if he could summon the courage. One by one the children stole away from their mother, the older children tactfully leaving her to grieve, the younger ones following their example. Unable to share their mother's sorrow, they simply wept, in this respect young children are like the very old, who cry for nothing, cry even when they no longer feel or because they are incapable of feeling.

Mary knelt in the middle of the room, as if awaiting a decision or sentence. She became aware of her wet clothes, got to her feet, shivering, opened a chest, and took out an old, patched tunic that had belonged to her husband. Handing it to Jesus, she told him, Remove that wet tunic, put this on, and go sit by the fire. Then she called her two daughters, Lisa and Lydia, and made them hold up a mat to form a screen while she too changed, before starting to prepare supper with the few provisions left in the house. Jesus, in his father's tunic, sat by the fire. The tunic was too long for him at the hem and sleeves, in other circumstances his brothers would have laughed at him for looking like a scarecrow, but this was not the time for jesting, not only because they were in mourning but also because of the air of superiority that emanated from the boy, who suddenly appeared to have grown in stature, and this impression became even stronger when, slowly and deliberately, he took his father's wet sandals and held them in front of the fire. James went and sat beside Jesus and asked him in a low voice, What happened to Father. They crucified him with the other rebels, Jesus whispered. But why. Who knows, there were forty men there, and Father was one of them. Perhaps he too was a rebel. Who are you talking about. Father, of course. Impossible, he was always here at home, working at his bench. And what about the donkey, did you find it. Nowhere to be seen, alive or dead. Supper was ready, and they all sat around the common bowl and ate what little food there was. By the time they finished eating, the younger children were nodding off to sleep, their spirits still troubled but their bodies in need of rest. The boys' mats were laid out along the wall at the far end of the room. Mary told the two girls, You will sleep here with me, one on either side to avoid any jealousy. Cold air came through the gap in the door, but the house stayed warm, there was still heat coming from the fire. Huddling up against one another, the children gradually fell asleep despite their sighs. Holding back her tears, Mary waited for them to sleep, for she wished to grieve alone, her eyes were wide open as she contemplated a future without a husband and with nine mouths to feed. But unexpectedly the sorrow left her soul, and her body succumbed to fatigue, and then they were all asleep.

In the middle of the night Mary was awakened by the sound of moaning. She thought she dreamed it, but she had not been dreaming, she heard it a second time, louder. Taking care not to disturb her daughters, she sat up and looked around her, but the light from the oil lamp did not reach the far end of the room. Which of them could it be,

143

she wondered, but knew in her heart it was Jesus who moaned. She got up quietly, went to fetch the lamp from its nail on the door, and raising it above her head, she examined the children one by one. Jesus tossed and turned, muttering to himself as if having a nightmare, he must be dreaming about his father, a mere boy and yet he has already witnessed so much suffering, death, blood, and torture. Mary thought to rouse him, to stop this agony, but changed her mind, she did not want to know what her son was dreaming, and then she noticed he was wearing his father's sandals. She found this strange, it worried her, how foolish, quite uncalled for and so disrespectful, wearing his father's sandals on the very day of the poor man's death. Not knowing what to think, she returned to her mat. Perhaps because of those sandals, and the tunic, her son was reliving his father's fatal adventure from the day Joseph left home, and thus the boy had passed into the world of men, to which he already belonged by the law of God, he was now heir to Joseph's few possessions, a much-mended tunic and a pair of worn sandals, and his dreams, Jesus retracing his father's last steps on earth. It did not occur to Mary that her son might be dreaming about something else.

Day broke with a clear sky. It was warm and bright, and there was no sign of further rain. Mary set out early with all her sons of school age, accompanied by Jesus, who as we mentioned earlier has already finished his studies. At the synagogue she informed the elders of Joseph's death and the probable circumstances that led to his crucifixion, cautiously adding that as many of the burial rites as possible were observed, despite the haste and improvisation with which everything had to be done. Finding herself alone with Jesus as they headed home, she thought to ask him why he had decided to wear his father's sandals, but something dissuaded her at the last moment. He might be at a loss to explain, might feel embarrassed. And unlike the

144

child who gets up in the middle of the night to steal food and is caught in the act, he could not very well make the excuse that he was feeling hungry, unless he meant a kind of hunger unknown to us. Another idea occurred to Mary. Now that her son was the head of the household, it was only right that as his mother and dependent she should show him respect, consideration, take an interest in the dream that disturbed his sleep, Were you dreaming about your father, she asked, but Jesus pretended not to hear, he turned his face away, but his mother, undeterred, repeated the question, Were you dreaming. She was taken aback when her son replied, Yes, then almost immediately said, No, his expression clouding over as if he was seeing his dead father once more. They walked on in silence. When they got home, Mary set about carding wool, thinking to herself that she should make the most of her skills and take on extra work to support her family. Meanwhile Jesus, after looking up at the sky to see if the good weather would hold, fetched his father's workbench from the shed, checked the jobs that still had to be finished, and examined the various tools. Mary was pleased to see her son taking his new responsibilities so seriously. When the younger boys returned from the synagogue and they all sat down to eat, only the most careful observer would have guessed that this family had just lost a husband and father. Jesus's dark, twitching eyebrows betrayed anxiety, but the others, including Mary, seemed tranquil and composed, for it is written, Make bitter weeping and make passionate wailing, and let your mourning be according to his desert for one day or two, lest evil be spoken of you, and so be comforted of your sorrow, for it is also written, Give not your heart unto sorrow, put it away remembering the last end, forget it not, for there is no returning again, him you shall not profit, and will only hurt yourself. There will be a time to laugh and rejoice, as surely as one day follows another, one season another, and the best lesson of all comes

145

from the Book of Ecclesiastes, where it is written, There is nothing better for man in this world than that he should eat, drink, and be merry even as he labors. For to the man who is virtuous in His eyes God gives wisdom and knowledge and joy. That same afternoon, Jesus and James went onto the terrace to repair the roof, which had been leaking throughout the night, and in case anyone is wondering why this minor domestic problem was not mentioned earlier, let me remind him that the death of a human being takes precedence over all else.

Night returned, and another day would soon dawn. The family supped as best they could, then settled down on their mats to sleep. Mary woke with a start in the early hours, no, it was not she who was dreaming but Jesus. It was heartbreaking to hear his moans, which awakened the older children, but it would have taken much more to rouse the little ones, who were enjoying the deep sleep of the innocent. Mary found her son tossing and turning on his mat, his arms raised as if fending off a sword or lance, but he gradually quieted down, either because his attackers had withdrawn or because his life was ebbing away. Jesus opened his eyes and wept in his mother's arms like a little child, even grown men become children again when they are frightened or upset, they do not like to admit it, poor things, but there is nothing like a good cry to relieve one's sorrow. What's wrong, my son, what troubles you, Mary asked in distress, and Jesus could not or would not answer, there was nothing childlike about those pursed lips. Tell me what you were dreaming about, insisted Mary, and trying to encourage him to speak, she asked, Did you see your father. The boy shook his head, released his arms, and fell back on his mat. Try to get some sleep, he told her, and then turning to his brothers, It's nothing, go back to sleep, I'll be all right. Mary rejoined her daughters but lay awake until morning, expecting Jesus' dream to return at any moment. She wondered what this dream could be

that caused him so much anguish, but nothing more happened. It did not occur to her that her son might also be
lying awake, to keep from dreaming again. What a strange
coincidence, she thought, that Jesus, who had always slept
peacefully, should start having nightmares immediately after
his father's death, God forbid that it should be the same
dream, she prayed inwardly. If her common sense assured
her that dreams were neither bequeathed nor inherited, she
was much deceived, because fathers do not need to confide
their dreams to their sons for them to have the same dream
at the same hour.

Day finally dawned, and the morning light streamed
through the chink in the door. On opening her eyes, Mary
saw that Jesus was no longer lying on his mat, Where can
he have gone, she asked herself. She got up and went to
look outside. He was sitting on a bed of straw in the shed,
his head buried in his arms. Chilled by the cool morning
air and the sight of her son's solitude, she went up to him,
Are you ill, she asked. The boy raised his eyes, No, I'm
not ill. Then what's ailing you. It's these dreams I keep
having. Dreams, you say. No, the same dream for the last
two nights. Did you dream of your father on the cross.
No, I already told you, I dream about my father but don't
see him. You told me you weren't dreaming about him.
That's because I don't see him, but he is in my dreams.
And what is this dream that never stops tormenting you.
Jesus did not reply immediately, he looked at his mother
helplessly, and Mary felt as if a finger had touched her
heart, here was her son looking like a little boy, with the
wan expression of one who had not slept, but the first
signs of a beard, which invited affectionate teasing, this
was her firstborn, on whom she would rely for the rest of
her life. Tell me everything, she pleaded, and Jesus finally
spoke, I dream that I'm in a village that isn't Nazareth and
that you are with me, but it's not you, because the woman
who's my mother in the dream looks very different, and

there are other boys my age, difficult to say how many, with women who could be their mothers, someone has assembled us in a square and we're waiting for soldiers who are coming to kill us, we can hear them on the road, they're nearer, but we can't see them, and I'm still not frightened, I know it's only a dream, then suddenly I feel sure Father is coming with the soldiers, I turn to you for protection, though you may not really be my mother, but you're no longer there, all the mothers have gone, leaving only us children, no longer boys but tiny babies, I'm lying on the ground and start to cry, and all the others are crying too, but I'm the only one whose father is accompanying the soldiers, we look at the opening into the square where we know they will enter, but there's no sign of them, we wait but nothing happens, though their footsteps are getting closer, they're here, no, not yet, then I see myself as I am now, trapped inside the infant, I struggle to get out, it's as if my hands and feet are tied, I call to you, but you're not there, I call to my father, who's coming to kill me, and that's when I woke up, both last night and the night before. As he spoke, Mary shuddered with horror, lowered her eyes in anguish, her greatest fear had been confirmed, somehow, inexplicably, Jesus had dreamed his father's dream, although it was slightly different. She heard her son ask, What was the dream father used to have every night. It was just a nightmare like any other. But what was it about. I don't know, your father never told me. Come now, Mother, don't hide the truth from your own son. It's best forgotten, not good for you to know. How do you know what's good or bad for me. Show some respect for your mother. Of course I respect you, but why hide things that concern me. Don't make me say any more. One day I asked Father why he was haunted by that dream, and he told me that I had no right to ask and that he had nothing to tell me. Well, then, why not accept your father's words. I did accept them while he was alive, but

148

now I am a man, I've inherited his tunic, a pair of sandals, and a dream, and with these I can go out into the world, but I must know more about the dream. Perhaps it won't come back. Staring into his mother's eyes, Jesus told her, I will not insist on knowing so long as the dream does not come back, but if it does, swear to me you'll tell me everything. I swear it, replied Mary, yielding to her son's insistence and authority. From her full heart a silent plea went up to God, a prayer without words, which might have sounded as follows, O Lord, send this dream to haunt my nights until the day I die, but I beseech You, spare my son, spare my son. Jesus warned her, Don't forget your promise. I won't forget, Mary assured him, repeating to herself, Spare my son, O Lord, spare my son.

But he was not spared. Night came, a black cock crowed at dawn, the dream returned, the head of the first horse appeared around the corner. Mary heard her son moan but did not go to comfort him. Shaking with fear and covered with sweat, Jesus knew that his mother was lying there awake and listening. What will she tell me, he wondered, while Mary for her part thought, What will I say to him, and she tried desperately to think how not to tell him everything. In the morning she was readying her sons for the synagogue when Jesus said, I'll come with you, then we can talk in the desert. Mary was so nervous, she kept dropping things as she tried to prepare some food, but the wine of affliction has been poured and now must be drunk. Once the younger children were taken to school, Mary and Jesus left the village, and in the desert they sat beneath an olive tree where no one except God, should He chance to be around, could possibly overhear their conversation. For stones, as we know, cannot speak, even if we strike them one against the other, and as for the earth below, that is where all words turn to silence. Jesus said, Now you must keep your promise, and Mary told him outright, Your father dreamt he was a soldier marching with other soldiers on their way to kill you. To kill me. Yes, to kill you. But that's my dream. I know, she told him, with a sigh of relief, It is easier than I imagined, she thought before saying aloud, Now that you know, let's go home, dreams are like clouds, they come and go, you only inherited this dream because you were so fond of your father, he didn't want to kill you, nor could he ever have done such a thing, even if the Lord Himself ordered him to do so, an angel would have stayed his hand, as happened to Abraham when he was about to sacrifice his son Isaac. Don't speak of things you know nothing of, said Jesus bluntly, and Mary realized that the bitter wine would have to be drunk to the dregs. What I do know, my son, is that the Lord's will must be done, whatever that will may be, and if He ordains one thing now and something quite different later, there's nothing we can do. As she finished speaking, Mary folded her hands in her lap and sat waiting. Jesus asked her, Will you answer all my questions. Of course, she said. When did Father start having this dream. Many years ago. How many years. From the day you were born. Did he have the dream every night. Yes, I believe he did, after a while he didn't bother calling me, people get used to nightmares. Tell me, Mother, was I born in Bethlehem of Judaea. That's right. What happened when I was born that my father should dream he was going to kill me. It didn't happen when you were born. But you just said so. The dream started some weeks later. Later than what. Herod ordered that all infants under the age of three should be slaughtered, why, I wish I knew. Did Father know. If he did, he never told me. So how did Herod's soldiers miss me. We were living in a cave on the outskirts of the village. You mean the soldiers didn't kill me because they couldn't find me. Yes. Was Father a soldier. Never. What did he do, then. He worked on the site of the Temple. I don't understand. I'm trying to answer your questions. But if the soldiers didn't find me because we lived outside the

150

village, and if Father wasn't a soldier and therefore not guilty, and if he had no idea why Herod wanted the infants killed. That's right, your father couldn't understand why Herod ordered the deaths of those children. Then. There's nothing more to tell, and unless you have more questions to ask, I've told you all I know. You're hiding something from me. Perhaps it's that you are blind.

Jesus said nothing more, felt his authority evaporate like moisture in the soil, and sensed the presence of an unworthy thought in his mind, still wavering but monstrous from the moment of its birth. He saw a flock of sheep crossing the slopes of the opposite hill, and both the shepherd and the sheep were the color of earth, like earth moving over earth. Surprise crept into Mary's tense face, that tall shepherd, that manner of walking, so many years later and just at this moment, was it an omen, but then she stared hard and felt less certain, for now the shepherd looked like any other shepherd from Nazareth as he led his tiny flock to pasture, the animals as halting as their owner. The thought that came to Jesus, that struggled to be spoken, until finally he blurted it, was, Father knew those children were going to be slaughtered. It was not a question, so there was no need for Mary to answer. How did he know, and this time it was a question. Your father was working on the Temple site in Jerusalem when he overheard some soldiers discussing what they'd been ordered to do. And then. He ran to save you. And then. He decided there was no need for us to flee so long as we didn't leave the cave. And then. That was all, the soldiers carried out their orders and left. And then. Then we returned to Nazareth. And when did the dream start. The first time was in the cave. Beside himself with grief, Jesus covered his face and cried out, Father murdered the children of Bethlehem. What are you saying, my son, they were murdered by Herod's soldiers. No, Father was to blame, Joseph son of Eli was to blame, because he knew those children were to be killed

151

and did nothing to warn their parents. Once these words were spoken, all hope of consolation was lost forever. Jesus threw himself to the ground and wept. Those children were innocent, innocent, he said bitterly, incredible that a simple boy of thirteen should react so strongly when one thinks how selfish children can be at that age and how indifferent most people are to the misfortunes of others. But people are not all alike, there are exceptions for better and for worse, and this is clearly one of the best, a young boy weeping his heart out because his father did wrong so many years ago, but he could also be weeping on his own account if, as it would appear, he loved this father who was guilty. Mary put out her hand to comfort him, but Jesus drew away, Don't touch me, I am wounded. Jesus, my son. Don't call me your son, you are also guilty. Such are the hasty judgments of adolescence, because Mary was as innocent as the slaughtered infants, it is the men, as every woman knows, who make the decisions, my husband came and said, We're leaving, then changed his mind and without going into details told me, We're not leaving after all, and I even had to ask him, What is that screaming I hear outside. Mary made no attempt to defend herself. It would have been easy to prove her innocence, but she thought of her crucified husband, he too had been killed though innocent, and she realized to her shame and sorrow that she loved him even more now than when he was alive, so she said nothing, for one person's guilt can be assumed by another. She simply said, Let's go home, we have nothing more to discuss here, and her son replied, You go, leave me by myself. There were no tracks of shepherd or sheep to be seen, the desert was truly deserted, and even the few scattered houses on the slope below looked like slabs of stone at an abandoned building site, gradually sinking into the ground. When Mary disappeared from sight into the gray depths of the valley, Jesus fell to his knees and called out, his entire body burning as if he were sweating blood,

Father, Father, why have You forsaken me, because that was how the poor boy felt, forsaken, lost in the infinite solitude of another wilderness, without father, mother, brothers, or sisters, and already following a path of death. Concealed by his sheep, the shepherd sat watching him from afar.

Two days later, Jesus left home. During this time he said very little. Unable to sleep, he spent the nights awake. He could picture the awful massacre, the soldiers entering the houses and searching for cradles, their swords striking, stabbing the tender little bodies, mothers in despair, fathers roaring like chained bulls, and he also had a vision of himself inside a cave he had never seen before. At such moments, as if great waves were slowly engulfing him, he wished he were dead or at least no longer alive. One question that he had not asked his mother bothered him, How many children lost their lives. In his mind's eye they were piled high on top of one another, like beheaded lambs thrown into a heap and about to be cremated in a huge bonfire, and when reduced to ashes, they would go up to heaven in smoke. But since he had not asked this when his mother made her revelation, he felt he could not go to her now and say, By the way, Mother, I forgot to ask you the other day how many of those infants in Bethlehem passed on to a better life, to which she would reply, Ah, my son, try to put it out of your mind, there could not have been

154

more than thirty, and if they died, it was the will of the Lord, for He could have prevented the massacre had He so desired. But Jesus could not stop wondering, How many. He would look at his brothers and ask himself, How many. How many bodies, he wanted to know, did it take to tip the scales against his own salvation. On the morning of the second day, he said to his mother, I can find no rest or peace of mind in this house, you stay here with my brothers, for I am going away. Mary raised her hands to heaven, horrified and close to tears, What are you saying, my eldest son, ready to abandon your widowed mother, whoever heard of such a thing, what is the world coming to, how can you think of leaving your home and family, what will become of us without you. James is only one year younger than me, he'll take my place and provide for all of you, as I did after your husband died. My husband was your father. I don't want to talk about him, I have nothing more to say, give me your blessing for the journey, but with or without it I am off. And where are you going, my son. I'm not sure, perhaps Jerusalem, perhaps Bethlehem, to see the land where I was born. But no one knows you there. Probably just as well, but tell me, Mother, what do you think would happen if anyone recognized me. Hush, your brothers might hear you. One day they too will have to know the truth. But have you thought of the risk, traveling at a time like this, with Roman soldiers on all the roads searching for the rebels of Judas the Galilean. The Romans are no worse than the soldiers who served under the late Herod, and they're not likely to kill me with their swords or nail me to a cross, after all, I've done nothing wrong, I'm innocent. So was your father and look what happened to him. Your husband may have been wrongfully crucified, but his life was not innocent. Jesus, my son, the devil's taken possession of your tongue. How do you know it isn't God. Don't take the name of the Lord in vain. Who can tell when the name of God is taken in

155

vain, neither you nor I, God alone can tell, and I doubt whether we'll ever understand His reasons. My son, where on earth did you pick up such ideas at your age. Who knows, perhaps men are born carrying the truth inside them, but do not speak it because they're not completely sure it is the truth. You've decided, then, to leave us. Yes. Will you come back. I don't know. If that dream is troubling you, by all means go to Bethlehem, and go to the Temple in Jerusalem and consult the teachers, they will advise you and put your mind at rest, then you can come back to your mother and brothers, who need you. I can't promise to return. But how will you survive, your poor father didn't live long enough to teach you everything he knew. Don't worry, I'll work in the fields or tend sheep or persuade some fishermen to take me out to sea with them. Wouldn't you prefer to be a shepherd. Why. I don't know, a feeling, that's all. We'll see what turns up, and now, Mother, I must be on my way. But you can't go like this, let me get you some food for the journey, we haven't much money, but take some, and take your father's pack, which fortunately he left behind. I'll take the food but not the pack. Your father didn't have leprosy. I cannot. One day you'll weep for your father and be sorry you didn't take it. I've already wept for him. You'll weep even more, and you won't be asking then what sins he committed. Jesus made no attempt to reply to these words. The older children, unaware of the conversation between him and their mother, gathered around Jesus and asked, Are you really going away, and James said, I wish I were going with you, for the boy dreamed of adventure, travel, of doing something challenging and different. You must stay here, Jesus told him, someone has to look after our widowed mother, the word widowed slipped out involuntarily and he bit his lip to suppress it, but what he couldn't suppress were his tears, because the vivid memory of his father suddenly caught him like a ray of dazzling light.

156

After the family had eaten together, Jesus departed. He bade his brothers farewell one by one, embraced his tearful mother, and told her, without knowing why, One way or another I shall always come back, and adjusting his pack on his shoulder, he crossed the yard and opened the gate to the street. There he stopped, as if reflecting. How often we find ourselves on the point of crossing a threshold or making a decision, when further consideration causes us to change our mind and turn back. Mary's face lit up with jubilant surprise, but her joy was short-lived. Jesus lay down his pack, stood mulling over something, then turned back, passed between his brothers without looking at them, and went into the house. When he reappeared a few moments later, he had his father's sandals in his hand. Silently, his eyes lowered as if modesty or some hidden shame prevented him from looking anyone in the eye, he put the sandals into the pack, and without another word or gesture walked off. Mary ran to the gate and her children followed, the older ones indifferent, it seemed, no one waved good-bye, because Jesus didn't look back even once. A neighbor who was passing and saw Jesus leave asked, Where's your son off to, Mary, and Mary replied, He's found work in Jerusalem and he'll be staying there for a while, a barefaced lie as we know, but this matter of telling the truth or lying is complicated, better to make no hasty moral judgments, because if one waits long enough, the truth becomes a lie and a lie becomes the truth.

That night, as everyone in the house lay asleep except for Mary, who could not help wondering how and where her son was at that hour, whether he was safe in a caravansary, or huddled under a tree, or between the rocks of some dark ravine, or, God forbid, taken prisoner by the Romans. She heard the outside gate creak, and her heart leaped, It's Jesus coming back, she thought, momentarily overcome with joy and confusion. What should I do, she was reluctant to open the gate, to appear triumphant, to greet him with words such as, It didn't take you long to come back after giving your mother a sleepless night. That would be humiliating, better to say nothing, pretend to be asleep, let him creep in quietly, and if he lies down on his mat without even saying I'm back, tomorrow I'll pretend to be surprised that the prodigal son has returned. However brief his absence, her happiness is great, for absence too is a kind of death, the difference being that with absence there is still hope. But he's so slow in coming to the door, who knows, perhaps he changed his mind again, Mary cannot bear the suspense any longer, she will peer through the chink in the door without being seen and run back to her mat should her son decide to enter, and if he shows signs of leaving again, she'll be able to stop him. Tiptoeing on bare feet, she went to the door and looked out. The moon was bright, and the yard shone like water. A tall, dark figure, moving slowly, came toward the door, and the moment Mary saw him, she put her hands to her mouth to keep from screaming. It was not her son, it was the beggar, covered with rags as when she first saw him, but now, perhaps because of the moonlight, those rags were suddenly like sumptuous robes that stirred in the breeze. Terrified, she locked the door, What can he want from me, she muttered with trembling lips. The man who had claimed to be an angel moved to one side, was now right at the door, yet made no attempt to enter, Mary could hear him breathing, and then she heard the sound of something ripped open, as if the earth was being split to reveal an enormous abyss. The massive shadow of the angel appeared again, for a brief moment it blocked the entire countryside from her sight, and then, without so much as a glance at the house, he walked to the gate, taking with him, uprooted, the mysterious tree that had sprouted outside the door some thirteen years before, on the very spot where the bowl was buried. Between the opening and closing of the gate, the angel changed back into a beggar and disappeared behind the wall, this time in total silence, dragging the leafy branches with him as though the tree were a plumed serpent. Mary opened the door cautiously and looked out. The world was bright beneath a remote sky. Near the wall of the house was a hole where the plant had been pulled out, and from there to the gate a trail of soil sparkled like the Milky Way, if that term existed in those days. She thought about her son but without heartache now, surely no harm could come to him under such a beautiful sky, serene and unfathomable, and this moon like manna made from light, nourishing the earth's roots and springs. Her soul at peace, she crossed the yard and, fearlessly treading the stars on the ground, went to open the gate. She looked outside, saw that the trail ended a short distance away, as if the iridescence of the leaves had been extinguished or as if, another flight of fancy on the part of this woman who can no longer make the excuse that she is pregnant, the beggar had reverted to his angel form and finally made use of his wings to mark this special occasion. Mary pondered these strange events, and they seemed to her as simple and natural as her own hands in the moonlight. She returned to the house, took the oil lamp from its hook on the wall, and went to take a closer look at the deep hole where the plant had been. At the bottom of it lay the empty bowl. She reached in and lifted it out, the same plain bowl she remembered but with little earth left inside and no longer shining, an ordinary household utensil restored to its proper function. From now on it will be used to serve milk, water, or wine, according to one's taste and means, and how true the saying which reminds us that everyone has his hour and everything its time.

Jesus found shelter on the first night of his travels. It was dusk when he came to a tiny hamlet just outside the city of Jenin, and fate, which had predicted so much ill fortune since the day he was born, relented on this occasion. The owners of the house where, with little hope, he sought shelter turned out to be hospitable people who could never have forgiven themselves if they left a boy of his age out in the open all night, especially at a time like this, with so much fighting and violence everywhere, men being crucified and innocent children hacked to death for no reason. Although Jesus told his kind hosts that he hailed from Nazareth and was on his way to Jerusalem, he did not repeat the shameful lie he had heard his mother tell when she said he left to do a job. He told them he was on his way to consult the teachers of the Temple about a point of holy law that greatly concerned his family. The head of the household expressed his surprise that such an important mission should be entrusted to a mere boy, however advanced in his religious studies. Jesus explained that he was entrusted with this matter as the eldest son, but made no mention of his father. He ate with the family, then settled down under the lean-to in the yard, which was the best they could offer a passing traveler. In the middle of the night the dream returned to haunt him, although this time his father and the soldiers did not get quite so close and the horse's nose did not appear around the corner. Do not imagine, however, that the dream was any less terrifying, put yourself in Jesus' place, suppose you dreamed that the father who gave you life was pursuing you with drawn sword. Those asleep inside were completely unaware of the drama taking place in the yard, for Jesus had learned to hide his fear even while he slept. When the fear became unbearable, he would instinctively cover his mouth with a hand to muffle the cry of anguish throbbing in his head. In the morning, he joined the family for breakfast, then thanked them for their hospitality with such courtesy and eloquence that the whole family felt they were momentarily sharing in the ineffable peace of the Lord, humble Samaritans though they were. Jesus said good-bye and departed, his host's parting words ringing in his ears, Blessed be You, O Lord our God, King of the Universe, who guides our footsteps, words he repeated to himself, praising that same Lord, God, and King, provider of all our needs, as can clearly be seen from everyday experience, in accordance with that most just rule of direct proportion, which says that more should be given to those who have more.

The rest of the journey to Jerusalem was not so easy. In the first place, there are Samaritans and there are Samaritans, which means that even in those days one swallow was not enough to make a summer, it took two, two swallows, that is, not two summers, provided there was a fertile male and female and they had offspring. No more doors opened when Jesus knocked, so our traveler had to find somewhere to sleep outdoors, once under a fig tree of the large spreading variety that resemble a dirndl skirt, on another occasion by joining a caravan which, fortunately for Jesus, had to pitch tent in the open countryside because the nearby caravansary was full. We say fortunately because before this, while crossing some uninhabited mountain, the poor boy was attacked by two cowardly thieves, who took the little money he possessed, which meant that Jesus had no hope of finding lodgings at any of the inns, where everything had to be paid for. Anyone witnessing that episode would have looked with pity on the lad, abandoned to his fate by those heartless rogues, who went off laughing at his plight. He lay there in a lamentable state, with nothing but the sky overhead and the surrounding mountains, the infinite universe stripped of moral significance and peopled with stars, thieves, and executioners. One might argue that a boy of thirteen could not have had sufficient knowledge of science and philosophy, or even sufficient experience of life, for such thoughts, and that this boy in particular, notwithstanding his religious studies in the synagogue and his natural talent for debate, was not capable of the words and deeds attributed to him. There is no lack of carpenters' sons in these parts, or of sons whose fathers were crucified, but even if another man's son had been chosen, we are confident that whoever he was, he would have given us just as much food for thought as young Jesus. First because it is well known that every man is a world unto himself, by the path either of transcendence or immanence, and secondly because this land has always been different from any other, one need only consider how many people, both rich and poor, have traveled here to preach and prophesy, from Isaiah to Malachi, nobles, priests, shepherds, men from every conceivable walk of life, which teaches us to be cautious about jumping to conclusions, the humble origins of a carpenter's son do not give us the right to dismiss him. This boy who is on his way to Jerusalem at an age when most children do not venture outside the front door may not be a genius or luminary, but he deserves our respect. His soul, as he himself confessed, has been deeply wounded, and since the wound is unlikely to heal quickly, given his reflective nature, he has gone out into the world, perhaps to combine his scars into one definitive sorrow. It may seem inappropriate to put the complex theories of modern thinkers into the head of a Palestinian who lived so many years before Freud, Jung, Groddeck, and Lacan, but if you will pardon our presumption, it is not all that foolish, when one considers that the scriptures from which the Jews derive their spiritual nourishment consistently teach that a man, no matter the age in which he lives, is the equal in intellect of all other men. Adam and Eve are the only exceptions, not just because they were the first man and woman but because they had no childhood. And while biology and psychology may be invoked to prove that the human mind as we know it today can be traced back to Cro-Magnon man, that argument is of no interest here, inasmuch as Cro-Magnon man is not even mentioned in the Book of Genesis, which is all Jesus knew about the beginning of the world.

Distracted by these reflections, which are not entirely

irrelevant to the gospel we have been telling, we forgot, to our shame, to accompany Joseph's son on the last leg of his journey to Jerusalem, where he is just now arriving, penniless but safe. Although his feet are badly blistered after the long trip, he is as steadfast as when he left home three days ago. He has been here before, so his excitement is no greater than one might expect from a devout man whose God is about to manifest himself. From this mountain known as Gethsemane, or the Mount of Olives, one can get a view of Jerusalem's magnificent architecture, of the city's Temple, the towers, palaces, and houses, which give the impression of being within reach, but this impression depends on the degree of mystical fervor, which can lead the faithful to confuse the limitations of the body with the infinite power of the universal spirit. The evening is drawing to a close, and the sun is setting over the distant sea. Jesus begins his descent into the valley, wondering where he will spend the night, whether inside or outside the city walls. On other occasions, when he accompanied his parents at Passover, the family spent the night outside the walls, in a tent thoughtfully provided by the civic and military authorities to receive pilgrims, all of them segregated, needless to say, the men with the men, the women with the women, and the children divided according to sex. When Jesus reached the city walls, the night air had already turned chilly. He arrived just as the gates were being closed, but the watchmen allowed him to enter, and as those great wooden crossbars slammed into position, Jesus may have begun to feel remorse for some past sin, imagining himself caught in a trap, its iron teeth about to snap shut, a web imprisoning a fly. At the age of thirteen, however, he cannot have sins that numerous or serious, he is not at an age yet to be killing or stealing or bearing false witness, to be coveting his neighbor's wife or house or fields, his neighbor's male or female slave or ass or ox or any other thing that belongs to his neighbor, therefore this boy walks pure

163

and undefiled, though he may have lost his innocence, for no one can witness death without being affected.

The roads become deserted at this hour as families gather for supper, and on them there are only beggars and vagabonds, who will also retreat into their dens and hideaways, because any minute now Roman soldiers will be scouring the streets in search of malefactors that venture even into the capital of Herod Antipas's kingdom to commit every manner of crime and iniquity despite the severe sentences that await them if they are caught, as we saw in Sepphoris. At the end of the road a night patrol with torches blazing marches past amid the clang of swords and shields and to the rhythm of feet clad in military sandals. Hiding in a dark corner, the boy waited for the soldiers to disappear, then went to look for a place to sleep. He found one among the many building sites around the Temple, a gap between two great stone slabs, with another slab on top to form a roof. There he munched what remained of his hard, moldy bread, along with some dry figs he found at the bottom of his pack. He was thirsty but resigned himself to going without water. Stretching out on his mat, he covered himself with the little mantle he carried as part of his baggage and, curling up to protect himself from the cold, which penetrated from both sides of his precarious refuge, he managed to fall asleep. Being in Jerusalem did not prevent him from dreaming, but perhaps because he was close to God's holy presence, his dream was merely a repetition of familiar scenes that merged with the arrival of the patrol he encountered earlier. He awoke as the sun was rising. Wrapped in his mantle, he dragged himself out of that hole cold as a tomb and saw the houses of Jerusalem before him, low-lying houses made of stone, their walls painted pale crimson by the morning light. Then, with great solemnity, coming as it did from the lips of one who after all is still a boy, he offered up a prayer of thanksgiving, Thanks be to You, O Lord our God, King of the Universe, who through the power of Your mercy restored my soul. There are certain moments in life that should be arrested and protected from time, and not simply be transmitted in a gospel or a painting or, as in this modern age, a photograph, film, or video. How much more interesting it would be if the person who lived those moments could remain forever visible to his descendants, so that those of us alive today could go to Jerusalem and see with our own eyes young Jesus, son of Joseph, all wrapped up in his little threadbare mantle, beholding the houses of Jerusalem and giving thanks to the Lord who mercifully restored his soul. Since his life is just beginning at the age of thirteen, one can assume there are brighter and darker hours in store for him, moments of greater joy and despair, pleasure and grief, but this is the moment we ourselves would choose, while the city slumbers, the sun is at a standstill, the light intangible, and a young boy wrapped in a mantle looks wide-eyed at the houses, a pack at his feet and the entire world, near and far, waiting in suspense. Alas, he has moved, the instant is gone, time has carried us into the realm of memory, it was like this, no, it was not, and everything becomes what we choose to invent.

Now Jesus walks through the narrow, crowded streets, it is still too early to go to the Temple, the teachers, as in all ages and places, only start appearing later. Jesus is no longer cold, but his stomach is rumbling, those two remaining figs served only to whet his appetite, Joseph's son is famished. Now he could do with the money those rogues stole from him, for city life is quite unlike that leisurely existence in the country, where one goes around whistling and looking for what may have been left behind by God-fearing laborers who carry out His commandments to the letter, When you are harvesting your fields and leave a sheaf behind, do not turn back to retrieve it, When you pick olives, do not go back to collect those still hanging on the branches, When you gather grapes from

your vineyard, do not go rummaging for any you overlooked, leave them to be gathered by the stranger, orphan,
or widow, and always remember that you were once a
slave in the land of Egypt. Now, because it is a large city,
and despite God's decree that His earthly dwelling be built
here, these humanitarian precepts are not observed in Jerusalem, so that for anyone arriving without thirty or even
three pieces of silver in his pocket the only recourse is to
beg and almost certainly be refused, or to steal and run the
risk of being flogged, imprisoned, or worse. But this youth
is incapable of stealing and much too shy to beg. His mouth
waters as he stares at the stacks of loaves, the pyramids of
fruits, the cooked meats and vegetables set out on stalls up
and down the streets, and the sight of all that food after
three days of fasting, if we don't count the Samaritan's
hospitality, almost makes him faint. It is true that he is
heading for the Temple, but notwithstanding the claims of
those mystics who believe in fasting, his mind would be
in better condition to receive the word of the Lord if his
body were fed. Fortunately, a Pharisee who happened to
be passing noticed the boy's weak condition and took pity
on him. Posterity will unjustly give the Pharisees the worst
possible reputation, but at heart they were decent people,
as this encounter clearly shows, Where are you from, asked
the Pharisee, and Jesus replied, I'm from Nazareth of Galilee. Are you hungry, the man asked, and the boy lowered
his eyes, there was no need to say anything, hunger was
written on his face. Have you no family. Yes, but I'm
traveling on my own. Did you run away. No, and it is
true, he did not run away. We must not forget that his
mother and brothers bade him an affectionate farewell at
the gate, and the fact that he did not turn back even once
does not mean he fled. The words we use are like that, to
say yes or no is the most straightforward answer possible
and in principle the most convincing, yet the world demands that we start indecisively, Well no, not really, I didn't

exactly run away, at which point we have to hear the story all over again, but do not worry, this is unnecessary, first because the Pharisee, who reappears in our gospel, does not need to hear it and, secondly because we know the story better than anyone else. Just think how little the main characters of this gospel know about one another, Jesus does not know everything about his mother and father, Mary does not know everything about her husband and son, and Joseph, who is dead, knows nothing about anything. Whereas we know everything that has been done, spoken, and thought, whether by them or by others, although we have to act as if we too are in the dark, in that sense we are like the Pharisee who asked, Are you hungry, when Jesus' pinched, wan face spoke for itself, No need to ask, just give me something to eat. And that is exactly what the compassionate man did, he bought two loaves still hot from the oven and a bowl of milk, and without a word handed them to Jesus. As the bowl passed between them, it so happened that a little milk spilled on their hands, whereupon they both made the same gesture, which surely comes from the depths of time, each lifted his wet hand to his lips to suck the milk, like kissing bread when it has fallen to the floor. What a pity these two will never meet again after they have sealed such an admirable and symbolic pact. The Pharisee went about his affairs, but not before taking two coins from his pocket and saying, Take this money and return home, the world is much too big for someone like you. The carpenter's son stood there clutching the bowl and the bread, no longer hungry, or perhaps still hungry but not feeling anything. He watched the Pharisee walk away, and only then did he say, Thank you, but in such a low voice that the Pharisee could not possibly have heard him, and if the man expected to be thanked, then he must have thought to himself, What an ungrateful boy. In the middle of the road, Jesus suddenly regained his appetite. He lost no time in eating his bread

167

and drinking his milk, then gave the empty bowl to the vendor, who told him, The bowl is paid for, keep it. Is it the custom in Jerusalem to buy the bowl with the milk. No, but that's what the Pharisee wanted, though you can never tell what's on a Pharisee's mind. So I can keep it. I already told you, it's paid for. Jesus wrapped the bowl in his mantle and tucked it into his pack while thinking that he would have to handle it carefully. These earthenware bowls are fragile and easily broken, they are only made of a little clay on which fortune has precariously bestowed a shape, and the same could be said of mankind. His body nourished and his spirits revived, Jesus set off in the direction of the Temple.

A LARGE CROWD HAD ALREADY GATHERED ON THE CON-
course facing the steep stairway that led up to the entrance.
Ranged along the walls on either side were the tents of the
peddlers and traders selling animals for sacrifice, and here
and there were money changers at their stalls, groups of
people engaged in conversation, gesticulating merchants,
Roman soldiers on foot and on horseback, keeping a watchful eye, slave-borne litters, camels and donkeys laden with
baggage, and frenzied shouting everywhere, interrupted
by the feeble bleats of lambs and goats, some carried in
people's arms or on their backs like tired children, others
dragged by a rope around their neck, but all destined
to perish by sword or fire. Jesus passed the bathhouse
used for purification, climbed the steps, and without stopping crossed the Court of the Gentiles. He entered the Court
of the Women through the door between the Chamber of
the Holy Oils and the Chamber of the Nazirites, and there
he found what he was looking for, the assembly of elders
and scribes who traditionally gathered to discuss holy law,
answer questions, and dispense advice. They stood in

169

groups, and the boy joined the smallest of these just as a man was raising his hand to ask a question. The scribe invited him to speak, and the man asked, Can you tell me if we should accept, word for word, the commandments given by the Lord to Moses on Mount Sinai, when He promised peace on earth and told us no one would disturb our sleep, when He promised that He would banish dangerous animals from our midst, that the sword would not pass through our land, and that if our enemies pursued us, they would fall under our sword, for as the Lord Himself said, Five of you will pursue a hundred men, a hundred of you ten thousand, and your enemies will fall under your sword. The scribe eyed the man suspiciously and, thinking he might be a rebel in disguise sent by Judas the Galilean to stir up trouble with wicked insinuations about the Temple's passive resistance to Roman rule, he replied brusquely, Those words were spoken by the Lord when our forefathers were in the desert, having fled the Egyptians. The man raised his hand a second time and asked another question, Are we to understand, then, that the Lord's words on Mount Sinai were meaningful only so long as our forefathers did not enter the promised land. If that is how you interpret them, you are not a good Israelite, the words of the Lord must prevail in every age, past, present, and future, for they were in His mind before He uttered them and remained there after He spoke. But it was you yourself who said what you forbid me to think. And what do you think. That the Lord allows that our swords should not be raised against this military force which oppresses us, that a hundred of our men lack the courage to face five of theirs, that ten thousand Jews cower before a hundred Romans. Let me remind you that you are in the Temple of the Lord and not on some battlefield. The Lord is the God of legions. True, but do not forget that God imposed His condition. What condition. The Lord said, So long as you observe my laws and keep my commandments. But

170

what are these laws and commandments we have ignored, that we should accept Roman rule as just and necessary punishment for our sins. The Lord must know. Yes, the Lord must know, and how often man sins without knowing, but would you care to explain why the Lord should make use of the Roman army to punish us instead of confronting His chosen people and punishing us Himself. The Lord knows His intentions and chooses His means. So you're trying to tell me that the Lord wants the Romans to govern Israel. Yes. Well, if that is so, then the rebels fighting the Romans are opposing the Lord and His holy will. You jump to the wrong conclusion. And you, scribe, contradict yourself. God's will may be not-to-will, and that not-to-will may be His will. So the will of man is genuine yet of no importance in the eyes of God. That's right. So man is free. Yes, free so that he might be punished. A murmur went up among the bystanders, some stared at the person who had asked the questions, based on the texts yet politically inopportune, and they looked at him accusingly, as if he were the one who should answer for the sins of all Israel, while the skeptical were reassured by the victory of the scribe, who acknowledged their praise and applause with a complacent smile. The scribe looked around him confidently and asked if there were other questions, like a gladiator who, having dispatched a weak opponent, seeks a more worthy opponent in order to gain greater glory. Another hand went up, and a different question was raised, The Lord spoke to Moses and told him, The stranger in your midst shall be treated as one of your own and you will love him as you love yourselves, for you were strangers in the land of Egypt. But before the man could finish speaking, the scribe, still flushed from his victory, interrupted in a sarcastic voice, I hope you are not about to ask me why we do not treat the Romans as our compatriots since they, too, are foreigners. No, what I want to ask is whether the Romans would treat us as their compatriots if

171

both sides spent less time arguing about the differences between their laws and gods. So you too have come here to anger the Lord with blasphemous interpretations of His holy word, said the scribe. On the contrary, all I ask is whether you truly believe that we are obeying the holy word of the Lord when strangers are strangers not so much to the land in which we live as to the religion we profess. To which strangers do you refer. To some in our own day and age, to many in the past, and probably many more in the years to come. I've no time to waste on enigmas and parables, make yourself clear. When we arrived from Egypt, there were other nations living in the land we now call Israel, whom we had to fight, and in those days we were the strangers, and the Lord commanded us to exterminate the people who opposed His will. The land was promised to us but had to be conquered, we did not buy it, nor was it offered to us. And now we find ourselves living under foreign rule, we have lost the land we made our own. Israel lives forever in the spirit of the Lord, so that wherever His people may be, whether united or dispersed, there the land of Israel will be. In other words, wherever we Jews find ourselves, others will always be the stranger. Certainly, in the eyes of the Lord. But the stranger who lives among us, according to the word of the Lord, must be our compatriot and we must love him as we love ourselves, for we were once strangers in Egypt. That is what the Lord said. In that case, the stranger we are expected to love must also be those who, living among us, are not so powerful that they can rule us, as at present with the Romans. Yes, I agree. Then tell me, do you believe that if one day we become powerful, the Lord will permit us to oppress the stranger He commanded us to love. All Israel can do is obey the will of the Lord, and since the children of Israel are His chosen people, the Lord wills only what is good for them. Even if it means not loving those we should. Yes, if so willed. Willed by whom, the Lord or

Israel. By both, for they are one and the same. Thou shalt not violate the stranger's rights, says the Lord. When that stranger has rights and we acknowledge them, replied the scribe. Once again, those present murmured their approval, and the scribe's eyes gleamed like those of a champion wrestler, discus thrower, gladiator, or charioteer.

Jesus raised his hand. No one present found it strange that a boy his age should come forward to question a scribe or doctor of the Temple, the young have been plagued by doubts ever since the time of Cain and Abel, they tend to ask questions to which adults respond with a condescending smile and a pat on the shoulder, When you grow up, young man, you'll stop worrying about such matters, while the more understanding will say, When I was your age, I thought the same. Some moved away, and others were preparing to do so, which vexed the scribe, who did not want to see his attentive audience leave, but Jesus' question caused many to turn back and listen, What I want to discuss is guilt. You mean your own guilt. No, guilt in general, but also the guilt a man may feel without having sinned himself. Explain yourself more clearly. The Lord said that parents will not die for their children or children for their parents and that each man will be judged for his own crime. This was a precept for those ancient times when an entire family, however innocent, paid for the crime of any one of its members. But if the word of the Lord is forever, there is no end to guilt, and as you yourself just said, saying man is free so that he might be punished, then one is right to believe that the father's guilt, even after his punishment, does not cease but is passed on to his children, just as all of us who are alive today have inherited the guilt of Adam and Eve, our first parents. I am amazed that a boy of your age and humble circumstances should know so much about the scriptures and be able to debate these matters with such ease. I only know what I was taught. Where are you from. From Nazareth of Galilee. I thought

173

as much from your manner of speaking. Please answer my question. We may assume that the gravest sin of Adam and Eve, when they disobeyed the Lord, was not eating the fruit of the tree of the knowledge of good and evil but, rather, its consequence, because their sin prevented the Lord from carrying out the plan He had in mind when He created first man and then woman. Whereupon the second man who asked a question challenged the scribe with another gem of sophistry, which the carpenter's son would never have had the courage to voice in public, Do you mean to say that every human act, such as that of the disobedience in Eden, can interfere with God's will, which is like an island in the ocean assailed on all sides by the turbulent waves of human will. Not exactly, the scribe replied cautiously, the will of the Lord is not content only to prevail over all things, His will makes everything what it is. But you yourself said that it is because of Adam's disobedience that we do not know the plan God conceived for him. That is what our reason tells us, but the will of God, the creator and ruler of the universe, embraces all possible wills, His own as well as that of every man born into this world. If this is so, intervened Jesus with sudden insight, then each man is a part of God. Probably, but even if all men were united as one, that combined part would be but a grain of sand in the infinite desert that is God. Sitting on the ground surrounded by men who watch him with mixed feelings of awe and fear, as if they are in the presence of a magician who has unwittingly conjured up powers greater than his own, the scribe looks less complacent. With drooping shoulders and doleful expression, his hands resting on his knees, his entire body seems to ask that he be left alone with his anguish. People in the group started rising to their feet, some made their way to the Court of the Israelites, some to join other groups still engaged in discussion. Jesus said, You didn't answer my question. The scribe stared at him like someone coming out of a trance, then after a long, tense silence replied, Guilt is a wolf that eats her cub after devouring its father. The wolf of which you speak has already devoured my father. Then it will soon be your turn. And what about you, were you ever devoured. Not only devoured but also spewed up.

Jesus rose to his feet and left. Heading for the gate through which he had entered, he paused and looked back. The column of smoke coming from the sacrificial fires climbed into the heavens, where it dispersed and vanished, as if sucked in by God's mighty lungs. It was mid-morning, more and more people were arriving, while inside the Temple sat a man broken by a sense of emptiness, waiting to regain his composure so that he could reply calmly to one who came wanting to know if the pillar of salt that Lot's wife turned into was rock salt or sea salt, or if Noah got drunk on white wine or red wine. Outside the Temple, Jesus asked the way to Bethlehem, his second destination. He lost his way twice amid the confusion of streets and people before he found the gate through which he had passed while inside his mother's womb thirteen years earlier, almost ready to enter the world. But this was not in Jesus' mind, because the obvious, as we all know, clips the wings of the restless bird of imagination, if any reader of this gospel were to look at a photograph of his pregnant mother when she was carrying him, for example, could he possibly imagine himself inside that womb. Jesus descends in the direction of Bethlehem, now he can reflect on the scribe's answers not just to his own question but also to the questions raised by others. What worries him is the feeling that all those questions were really one question, and that the reply given to each answered all, especially the last reply, which summed up the rest, the insatiable hunger of the wolf of guilt that is forever gnawing, devouring, and spewing up. Thanks to the fickleness of memory we often do not know, or know but try to forget, what caused our guilt, or, speaking metaphorically like the scribe, the lair of the wolf that pursues us. But Jesus knows, and that is where he is going. He has no idea what he'll do when he gets there, but this is better than announcing, I am here, and waiting for someone to ask, What do you want, punishment, pardon, or oblivion.

Like his father and mother before him, he stopped at Rachel's tomb to pray. Then, feeling his heart beat faster and faster, he resumed his journey. The first houses of Bethlehem were within sight, this is the main road into the village, taken by his homicidal father and the soldiers in his dream night after night. In daylight it doesn't seem a place of horror, even the tranquil white clouds drifting across the sky are benevolent gestures from God, and the very earth slumbers beneath the sun, as if bidding us, Let's leave things as they are, there's nothing to be gained by digging up the past, and before a woman with a child in her arms appears at a window asking, Who are you looking for, turn back, erase your footprints, and pray that the endless motion of the hourglass of time will quickly obliterate with its dust all memory of those events. Too late. There is a moment when a fly about to brush past the web still has time to escape, but once it touches the web and finds its wing caught, then the slightest movement suffices to trap and paralyze it completely, forever, however indifferent the spider to its new victim. For Jesus, that moment has passed. In the middle of a square with a spreading fig tree stands a tiny square building, and one does not have to look twice to see it is a tomb. Jesus approached, walked around it slowly, paused to read the faded inscription on one side, and this was enough, he had found what he was looking for. A woman crossed the square, leading a five-year-old child by the hand. She stopped, looked inquisitively at the stranger, and asked him, Where do you come from, and to justify her question added, You're not from these parts. No, I'm from Nazareth in Galilee. Have you relatives here. No, I was visiting Jerusalem, and it seemed a good opportunity to take a look at Bethlehem. Are you passing through. Yes, I'll return to Jerusalem later this afternoon, when it gets cooler. Lifting the child onto her left arm, the woman told him, May the Lord go with you, then turned to leave, but Jesus detained her, asking, Whose tomb is this. The woman pressed the child to her bosom, as if to protect it from some threat, and replied, Twenty-five little boys, who died years ago, are buried here. How many. Twenty-five. I mean how many years ago. Oh, about fourteen. So many. I think that's right, they would be your age if they were alive today. Yes, but what about the little boys. One of them was my brother. You have a brother buried here. Yes. And this child in your arms, is he your son. He's my firstborn. Why did they kill only the little boys. No one knows, I was only seven at the time. But you must have heard your parents and the other grown-ups talking about it. There was no need, I myself saw some of the children being killed. Your brother as well. Yes, my brother. And who killed them. The king's soldiers came searching for little boys up to the age of three, and they killed all of them. Yet you don't know why. No one knows to this day. And after Herod died, did anyone go to the Temple to ask the priests to investigate. I really don't know. If the soldiers had been Romans, one might understand it, but to have our own king ordering his people slaughtered, mere babes, seems very strange, unless there was some reason. The will of kings is beyond our understanding, may the Lord go with you and protect you. It's a long time since I was three. At the hour of death men go back to being children, replied the woman before departing.

Once alone, Jesus knelt beside the boulder covering the entrance to the tomb, took the last piece of stale bread from his pack, rubbed it into crumbs between his palms, and sprinkled the crumbs all along the entrance, as if making an offering to the invisible mouths of the innocents buried there. As he finished, another woman appeared from around the corner, but this woman was very old and bent and walked with the aid of a stick. No longer able to see clearly, she had caught only a fuzzy glimpse of what the boy did. She stopped, watched him carefully, saw him get to his feet and bow his head as if praying for the repose of the souls of those unfortunate infants, and although it is customary, we will refrain from adding the word eternal to souls, for our imagination failed us on the one and only occasion we tried to picture eternal rest. Jesus ended his prayer and looked around him, blank walls, closed doors, nothing except the old woman standing there, dressed in a slave's tunic and leaning on her stick, the living image of that third part of the sphinx's famous enigma about the animal that walks on four feet in the morning, two at mid-day, and three in the evening, It is man, replied astute Oedipus, who forgot that some do not even get as far as midday, and that in Bethlehem alone twenty-five infants were cut down. The old woman drew closer, hobbling at a snail's pace, and now she stands before Jesus, twists her neck to get a better view of him, and asks, Are you look-ing for someone. The boy did not answer immediately, in fact he was not looking for anyone, those he sought are all dead, buried here, and are not even what you could call someone, mere infants still in diapers and with pacifiers in their mouths, whimpering, their noses running, yet death struck and turned them into an enormous presence that cannot be contained in any ossuary or reliquary, these are bodies that come out of their graves each night, if there is any justice, to show their wounds, the holes that, opened at sword point, allowed life to escape, No, replied Jesus, I am not. The old woman did not go, she seemed to be waiting for him to continue, so Jesus confided, I was born in this village, in a cave, and was curious to see the place. She stepped back unsteadily and strained her eyes to get a better look, her voice trembling as she asked him, What is your name, where do you come from, who are your parents. No one needs to answer a slave, but the elderly, however low their station, deserve our respect, we must never forget that they have little time left for asking questions, it would be cruel in the extreme to ignore them, after all we might possess the very answer they have been waiting for. My name is Jesus and I come from Nazareth of Galilee, the boy told her, and he seems to have been saying nothing else since he left home. The old woman stepped forward again, And your parents, what are their names. My father's name was Joseph, my mother is Mary. How old are you. I'm almost fourteen. The woman looked around her, as if seeking a place to sit, but a square in Bethlehem of Judaea is not the same as a garden in São Paulo de Alcântara, with its park benches and pleasant view of the castle, here we have to sit on the dusty ground, at best on a doorstep or, if there's a tomb, on the stone by the entrance put there for the respite of the living who come to mourn their loved ones, and perhaps also for those ghosts who leave their rest to shed any remaining tears, as does Rachel, in the tomb nearby, where it is written, Here lies Rachel who weeps for her children and seeks no consolation, for one does not need to be as shrewd as Oedipus to see that this place befits the circumstances, and Rachel's weeping the cause of her grief. The old woman lowered herself onto the stone with effort, and the boy went to help her, but too late, for halfhearted gestures are never made in time. I know you, the old woman told him. You must be mistaken, said Jesus, I've never been here before and I never saw you in Nazareth. The first hands to touch you were not your mother's but mine. How is that, old woman. My name is Salome, and I was the midwife who delivered you. Acting on impulse, which only goes to prove the sincerity of gestures made spontaneously, Jesus fell to his knees at the old woman's feet, wanting both to know everything and to show his gratitude for bringing him out

179

of a limbo without memory into a world that would mean nothing without memory. My mother never mentioned you, said Jesus. There was no need, your parents appeared on my master's doorstep, and I was asked to help, since I had some experience as a midwife. Was that when the innocents were massacred. That's right, you were fortunate they didn't find you. Because we lived in a cave. It was either that or because you'd already left, I never found out, for when I went to see what had happened to you, the cave was empty. Do you remember my father. Yes, I remember him well, at that time he was in his prime, a fine figure of a man, and honest. He's dead. Poor man, he didn't live long, but if you're his heir, what are you doing here, for I assume your mother is still alive. I came to see the place where I was born, also to learn more about the children who were slaughtered here. God alone knows why they had to die, the angel of death, disguised as Herod's soldiers, descended into Bethlehem and slew them. So you believe it was God's will. I'm only an old slave, but all my life I've heard people say that everything that happens in this world can happen only by the will of God. So it is written. God may decide to take me any day now, that I can understand, but these were innocent little children. Your death will be decided by God in His own good time, but it was a man who ordered that the children be killed. The hand of God, then, can do precious little if it cannot come between the sword and little children. You mustn't offend the Lord, good woman. An ignorant old woman like me isn't likely to cause any offense. Today in the Temple I heard it said that every human action, however insignificant, interferes with the will of God, and that man is free only in order to be punished. My punishment doesn't come from being free, it comes from being a slave, the old woman told him. Jesus fell silent. He hardly heard Salome's words, because it suddenly dawned on him that man is a mere toy in the hands of God and forever subject to His will, whether he imagines himself to be obeying or disobeying Him.

The sun was going down, and the fig tree's evil shadow lengthened and came closer. Jesus spoke to the old woman. Salome raised her head with effort, What do you want, she asked. Take me to the cave where I was born, or at least tell me how to get there, if it's too far for you to walk. I'm not very steady on my feet, but you won't find it unless I show you. Is it far from here. No, but there are many caves and they all look alike. Let's go, then. As you wish, she said. Anyone who happened to be watching that day, when Salome and the unknown boy passed by, must have asked himself where those two could have met. But no one ever knew, because the old slave revealed nothing to the day she died, and Jesus never again returned to the land of his birth. Next morning Salome went to the cave where she had left the boy. No sign of him. She was relieved, because even if he had still been there, they would have had nothing more to say to each other.

Much has been said about life's coincidences but little or nothing about the everyday encounters that guide the course of life, although one could argue that an encounter, strictly speaking, is a coincidence, which obviously does not mean that all coincidences have to be encounters. Throughout this gospel there have been many coincidences, and if we look carefully at the life of Jesus, especially after he left home, we can see that there has been no lack of encounters either. Leaving aside his unfortunate adventure with the thieves, since it is too early to tell what the consequence of that might be in the future, Jesus' first journey on his own has resulted in many meetings, such as the providential appearance of the Pharisee, thanks to whom the boy not only satisfied his hunger but, by eating in haste, reached the Temple in time to listen to the questions and answers that prepared the ground, as it were, for his question about guilt, the question that brought him all the way from Nazareth. When critics discuss the rules of effective narration, they insist that important encounters, in fiction as in life, be interspersed with others of no importance, so that the hero of the story does not find himself transformed into an exceptional being to whom nothing ordinary ever happens. They argue that this narrative approach best serves the ever desirable effect of verisimilitude, for if the episode imagined and described is not, and is not likely to become or supplant, factual reality, there must at least be some similitude, not as in the present narrative, where the reader's credence has clearly been put to the test, Jesus having taken himself to Bethlehem only to come face-to-face as soon as he arrives, with Salome, who assisted at his birth, as if that other encounter, with the woman carrying a child in her arms, whom we deliberately planted there to fill in the story, had not been license enough. The most incredible part of our story, however, is yet to come, after the slave Salome accompanies Jesus to the cave and leaves him there at his request, Leave me alone between these dark walls, that I may hear my first cry in the deep silence, if echoes can last that long. These were the words the woman thought she heard, and so they are recorded here, at the risk of once more offending verisimilitude, but, then, we can always blame the unreliable testimony of a senile old woman. Unsteady on her feet, Salome hobbled off, moving cautiously, one step at a time and leaning heavily on her staff, which she gripped with both hands. It would have been a nice gesture on the boy's part to help this poor, suffering creature return home, but such is youth, selfish and thoughtless, and there is nothing to suggest that Jesus was different from other boys his age.

He sat on a stone, and on a stone beside him was an oil lamp casting its dim light on the cave's rough walls, the dark heap of coals where once there was a fire, and his limp hands and pensive face. This is where I was born, he thought, I once slept in that manger, my father and mother once sat on this very stone I am sitting on now, this is where we took refuge as Herod's soldiers searched the village and slaughtered infants. But hard as I try, I will never hear the cry of life I gave at birth, or the cries of those dying children and the parents who watched them die, there is nothing but silence in this cave where a beginning and an end came together. As I learned in the Temple, parents pay for the sins they have committed, and their children for the sins they may one day commit, but if life is a sentence and death a punishment, there was never a more innocent town than Bethlehem, infants who died in perfect innocence, parents who had done no wrong, nor was there ever a more guilty man than my father, who remained silent when he should have spoken, and now I, whose life was saved so that I could learn of the crime that saved my life, and even if I commit no other offense, this will suffice to kill me. Amid the shadows of the cave Jesus got to his feet, as if to flee, but after a few faltering steps his legs gave way, and he put his hands to his eyes to catch his tears, poor boy, writhing in the dust, tormented by a crime he never committed, condemned to remorse for the rest of his life. This flood of bitter tears will leave its mark in Jesus' eyes forever, a dull glimmer of sadness and despair, always as if he has just stopped crying. Time passed, the sun outside began to set, the earth's shadows grew, the prelude to the great shadow that descends at dusk. The darkness penetrated the cave, where shadows were already threatening to extinguish the lamp's tiny flame, the oil is clearly running out, this is what it will be like when the sun finally disappears, when men say to one another, We are losing our sight, unaware that their eyes are no longer of any use to them.

Jesus is now asleep, yielding to the merciful exhaustion of recent days, his father's horrible death, the inherited nightmare, his resigned mother, and then the journey to Jerusalem, the daunting vision of the Temple, the discouraging words uttered by the scribe, the descent to Bethlehem, the fateful encounter with Salome, who appeared from the depths of time to reveal the circumstances of his birth, therefore it is not surprising that his weary body should have overcome his spirit, he appears to be resting now, but his spirit stirs, in his dream it rouses his body so that they may go together to Bethlehem and there, in the middle of the square, confess their heinous crime. Through the physical instrument of voice his spirit declares, I am he who brought death to your children, judge me, condemn this body I bring before you, abuse and torture it, for only by mortifying the flesh can we hope to gain absolution and the rewards of the spirit. In his dream Jesus sees the mothers of Bethlehem bearing tiny bodies, only one of the infants is alive, and its mother is the woman who spoke to Jesus with a child in her arms, it is she who replies, Unless you can restore their lives, be silent, for who needs words in the presence of death. In self-abasement his soul shrinks into itself like a tunic folded three times, surrendering his defenseless body to the mercy of the mothers of Bethlehem, but his body is spared, because just as the woman with the child is about to tell him, You're not to blame, you may go, a flash of lightning fills the cave and wakes him with a start. Where am I, was his first thought. Struggling to his feet from the dusty ground, tears in his eyes, he saw a giant of a man towering over him with head aflame, then he realized his mistake, the man held a torch in his right hand, the fire almost touched the ceiling of the cave. But the head was so huge, it could have been the head of Goliath, there was nothing hostile about the face, however, with its gratified expression of one who has been searching and found what he wanted. Jesus got to his feet and backed against a wall of the cave, to get a better look at the giant, who was not that big after all, perhaps a span taller than the tallest man of Nazareth. Such optical illusions, without which there can be no prodigies or miracles, were discovered ages ago, and the only reason Goliath did not become a basketball player is that he was born before his time. And who are you, the man asked. Resting his torch on a jutting rock, he stood the two sticks he was carrying against the wall, one with great knots smoothed by constant use, the other still covered with bark and recently cut from a tree. Then, seating himself on the largest stone, he began pulling the vast mantle he wore down over his shoulders. I am Jesus of Nazareth, the boy replied. What are you doing here if you're from Nazareth. Although I'm from Nazareth, I was born in this cave, and I came to see the place where I was born. Where you were born, my lad, was in your mother's belly, and you'll never be able to crawl back in there. Unaccustomed to such language, Jesus blushed at the man's words and could think of nothing to say. Did you run away from home, the man asked. As if searching in his heart to see if his departure could be described as running away, the boy hesitated before answering, Yes. Did you quarrel with your parents. My father's dead. Oh, was all the man said, but Jesus had the strange feeling that the man already knew this, and everything, and all that had been said and all that remained to be said. You didn't answer my question, the man insisted, What question, Did you quarrel with your parents, It's not your business. Don't be rude to me, boy, unless you want a good thrashing, not even God will hear your cries for help in this place. God is eye, ear, and tongue, He sees and hears everything, and it's only because He chooses not to that He doesn't speak everything. What does a boy your age know about God. What I learned in the synagogue. You never heard anyone in the synagogue say that God is eye, ear, and tongue. I myself decided that if this were not so, then God would not be God. And why do you think God has an eye and an ear and not two eyes and two ears like the rest of us. So that one eye cannot deceive the other, or one ear the other, and as for the tongue, there is no problem, because we only have one tongue. The tongue of man is also two-sided, serving both truth and falsehood. God cannot lie. Who's to prevent Him. God Himself, otherwise He'd deny Himself. Have you ever seen Him, Seen who, Seen God, Some have seen Him and announced His coming. The man stared at the boy in silence, as if looking for some familiar trait, then said, True, some believed they've seen Him. He paused, then continued with a mischievous smile, You still haven't answered my question. What question. Did you quarrel with your parents. I left home because I wanted to see the world. You've mastered the art of lying, my boy, but I know who you are, you were born to a simple carpenter named Joseph and a wool carder named Mary. How do you know. I found out one day and have remembered ever since. I don't understand. I'm a shepherd and have spent nearly all my life breeding and caring for my sheep and goats, and I happened to be in these parts when the soldiers came to slaughter the children of Bethlehem, so as you can see, I've known you since the day you were born. Jesus looked at the man nervously and asked, What is your name. My sheep don't know me by a name. But I am not one of your sheep. Who knows. Tell me what you're called. If you insist on giving me a name, call me Pastor, that will be enough to summon me if you ever need me. Will you take me with you to help with the flock. I was waiting for you to ask. Well then. Yes, you may join the flock. The man stood, lifted his torch, and went outside. Jesus followed.

It was darkest night, and the moon had still not risen. Gathered near the entrance to the cave, sheep and goats waited in silence, except for the faint jingling of bells from time to time. Patiently they awaited the outcome of the conversation between the shepherd and his latest helpmate. The man raised the torch, revealing the black heads of the goats and the white snouts of the sheep, some sheep scrawny with sparse hair, others plump with woolly coats, and he told him, This is my flock, take care not to lose even one of these animals. Jesus and the shepherd sat at the entrance to the cave beneath the flickering light of the torch and ate

187

cheese and stale bread from their packs. Then the shepherd went inside and returned with the new stick, the one still covered with bark. He lit a fire and, deftly turning the wood in the flames, slowly scorched the bark until it peeled off in long strips, and then he smoothed down the knots. Allowing the stick to cool, he plunged it back into the fire, but turned it briskly this time so the wood would not burn, darkening and strengthening the surface until it took on the appearance of seasoned wood. Handing the stick to Jesus when it was ready, he said, Here's your shepherd's crook, strong and straight and as good as a third arm. Jesus, although his hands were hardly delicate, dropped the stick with a howl. How could the shepherd hold anything so hot, he asked himself. When the moon finally appeared, they went into the cave to get some sleep. A few sheep and goats followed and lay down beside them. At first light, the shepherd shook Jesus, Time to get up, the flock has to be fed, from now on you'll take them out to pasture, as important a job as you're ever likely to be entrusted with. Walking as fast as their tiny steps allowed, the flock moved on, the shepherd in front, his helpmate at the rear. The cool, transparent dawn seemed to be in no hurry for the sun, envious of that splendor heralding a world reborn. Hours later, an old woman, going slowly with the aid of a stick, emerged from the houses of Bethlehem and entered the cave. She was not surprised that Jesus was no longer there, besides they would have had nothing more to say to each other. Amid the eternal shadows inside the cave a tiny flame continued to shine, because the shepherd had filled the lamp with oil.

Four years from now, Jesus will meet God. This unexpected revelation, which is probably premature according to the rules of effective narration referred to above, is intended simply to prepare the reader for some everyday scenes from pastoral life which will add little of substance to the main thread of our story, thus excusing anyone who might be tempted to jump ahead. Nevertheless, four years is four years, especially at an age when there are so many physical and mental changes in a youth, when his body grows so fast, the first signs of a beard, a swarthy complexion becoming even darker, the voice turning as deep and harsh as a stone rolling down a mountain slope, and that faraway look, as if he is daydreaming, always reprehensible but especially when one has a duty to be vigilant, like sentinels in barracks, castles, and encampments or, lest we stray from our story, like this shepherd boy who has been warned to keep a watchful eye on his master's goats and sheep. Although we do not really know who that master is. Tending sheep at this time and in these parts is work for a servant or slave, who under pain of punishment must give a regular account of milk, cheese, and wool, not to mention the number of animals, which should always be on the increase so that neighbors can see that the eyes of the Lord are looking down with favor on the pious owner of such abundant possessions, and if the owner wishes to conform to the rules of this world, he must have greater trust in the Lord than in the genetic strength of the mating rams of his flock. Yet how strange that Pastor, as he asked to be called, does not seem to have any master over him, for during the next four years no one will come to the desert to collect the wool, milk, or cheese, nor will Pastor ever leave the flock to give account of his duties. All would be well if Pastor were the owner of these goats and sheep. Though it is hard to believe that any owner would allow such an incredible amount of wool to be lost, shearing his sheep only to prevent them from suffocating from the heat, or would use the milk, if at all, only to make the day's supply of cheese, then barter the rest for figs, dates, and bread, or, mystery of mysteries, would never sell lambs and kids from his flock, not even during Passover, when they are much in demand and fetch such high prices. Little wonder, therefore, that the flock continues to grow bigger, as if obeying, with the persistence and enthusiasm of those who feel their life span is guaranteed, that famous mandate given by the Lord, who may have lacked confidence in the efficacy of sweet natural instinct, Go forth and multiply. In this unusual and wayward flock the animals tend to die of old age, but Pastor himself serenely lends a hand by killing those who can no longer keep up with the others because of disease or age. Jesus, the first time this occurred after he started working for Pastor, protested at such cruelty, but the shepherd said, Either I kill them as I've always done, or I leave them to die alone in this wilderness, or I hold up the flock, wait for the old and sick to die, and risk letting the healthy animals starve to death for lack of pasture. So tell me what you would do if you were in my shoes and had power of life and death over your flock. Jesus did not know what to say and changed the subject by asking, Since you don't sell the wool, have more milk and cheese than we need in order to live, and never take the lambs and kids to market, why do you allow this flock to become bigger and bigger, one of these days your goats and sheep will cover every hill in sight and there will be no land left for pasture. Pastor told him, The flock was here and somebody had to look after the animals and protect them from thieves, and that person happened to be me. What do you mean by here. Here, there, everywhere. Are you asking me to believe that this flock has always been here. More or less. Did you buy the first sheep and goat, No, Who then. I simply found them, I don't know if anyone bought them, there was already a flock when I came here. Were they given to you. No one gave them to me, I found them, and they found me. So you are the owner. No, I'm not the owner, nothing in this world belongs to me. For everything belongs to the Lord, as you know, True, How long have you been a shepherd. I was a shepherd before you were born, How many years, Difficult to say, perhaps if

190

we multiplied your age by fifty. Only the patriarchs before the great flood lived that long, and no one nowadays can hope to reach their age. No need to tell me. Yet if you insist you've lived that long, don't expect me to believe you're human. I don't. Now, if Jesus, who was as skilled in the art of interrogation as any disciple of Socrates, had asked, What are you, then, if you are not a man, Pastor would most probably have answered, An angel, but don't tell anyone. This often happens, we refrain from asking a question because we are unprepared or simply too afraid to hear the answer. And when finally we summon the courage to ask, no answer is forthcoming, just as Jesus one day will refuse to answer when asked, What is truth. A question that remains unanswered to this day.

Jesus knows without having to ask that his mysterious companion, whatever he may be, is not an angel of the Lord, because the angels of the Lord forever sing His glory, while men praise Him only out of obligation and on prescribed occasions, although it is worth pointing out that angels have greater reason for singing Glory since they live in intimacy, as it were, with the Lord in His heavenly kingdom. What surprised Jesus from the beginning was that when they left the cave at first light, Pastor, unlike him, did not praise the Lord with all the usual blessings, such as having restored man's soul and having endowed the cock with intelligence, and when obliged to step behind a rock to relieve himself, Pastor did not thank the Lord for the providential orifices and vessels that help the human body function and without which we would be in a sorry state. Pastor looked at heaven and earth as one does on getting out of bed, he muttered something about the fine day ahead, and putting two fingers to his lips, gave a shrill whistle which brought the entire flock to its feet as one. And that was all. Jesus thought he might have forgotten, always possible when one's mind is on other things, such as how to teach this boy, accustomed to the easy life of a carpenter, the rudiments of tending sheep and goats. Now, as we know, in a normal situation among ordinary people, Jesus would not have had to wait long to discover the extent of his master's piety, since Jews in those days gave thanks to the Lord some thirty times a day and on the slightest pretext, as indeed we have often seen in this gospel. But the day passed, and Pastor showed no sign of offering prayers of thanksgiving, dusk fell, and they settled down to sleep out in the open, and not even the majesty of God's sky above touched the shepherd's heart or brought so much as a word of praise or gratitude to his lips, after all, it could have been raining and it was not, a clear sign that the Lord was watching over His creatures. Next morning, after they had eaten and his master was preparing to inspect the flock to make sure that they were all there and that some restless goat had not decided to wander off, Jesus announced in a firm voice, I am leaving. Pastor stopped, looked at him without any change of expression, and said, Have a good journey, but you don't need to tell me, you're not my slave and there is no legal contract between us, you can leave whenever you like. But don't you want to know why I'm leaving. I'm not all that curious. Well, I'll tell you just the same, I'm leaving because I do not want to work with a man who doesn't perform his obligations to the Lord. What obligations. The simplest obligations, such as offering up prayers of thanksgiving. Pastor said nothing, his eyes half smiling, then finally he spoke, I'm not a Jew and therefore have no such obligations to perform. Deeply shocked, Jesus backed away. That the land of Israel was swarming with foreigners and worshipers of false gods he knew all too well, but this was the first time he had actually slept beside such a person and shared his bread and milk. As if holding a sword and shield before him, he exclaimed, The Lord alone is God. Pastor's smile faded and his mouth became twisted and grim, Certainly if God exists, He must be only one, but it would be

192

better if He were two, then there would be a god for the wolf and one for the sheep, a god for the victim and one for the assassin, a god for the condemned man and one for the executioner. God is one, whole, and indivisible, exclaimed Jesus, almost weeping with pious indignation, whereupon Pastor retorted, I don't know how God can live, but he got no further, because Jesus, with all the authority of a teacher in the synagogue, interrupted him, God does not live, God exists. These fine distinctions escape me, but I'll tell you this, I wouldn't like to be a god who guides the dagger in the hand of the assassin while he offers the throat that is about to be cut. You offend God with these irreverent thoughts. You overestimate my importance. Remember, God never sleeps, and one day He will punish you. Just as well He doesn't sleep, so He can avoid the nightmares of remorse. Why speak to me of the nightmares of remorse. Because we're discussing your god. And which god do you serve. Like my sheep, I have no god. But sheep, at least, produce lambs for the altars of the Lord. And I can assure you that their mothers would howl like wolves if they knew. Jesus turned pale and could think of no reply.

All was silent as the flock gathered around them attentively. The sun had already risen, its light casting a crimson glow on the fleecy coats of the sheep and the horns of the rams. Jesus said, I'm off, but didn't move. Pastor waited, leaning on his crook, as composed as if he had all the time in the world. At last Jesus took a few steps, opening a path through the sheep, then suddenly stopped and asked, What do you know about remorse and nightmares. That you are your father's heir. These words were too much for Jesus, his legs buckled, and the pack slipped from his shoulder, and either by chance or necessity his father's sandals fell out, and he could hear the Pharisee's bowl shatter into pieces. Jesus began weeping like a lost child, but Pastor made no attempt to comfort him, he merely said from

193

where he was standing, Do not forget that I've known about you since the day you were born, and now you had better decide whether you're going or staying. First tell me who you are. The time has not yet come for you to know. And when will I know. If you stay, you'll regret not having left, and if you leave, you'll regret not having stayed. But if I leave, I will never know who you are. You're wrong, your hour will come, and when it does, I will be there to tell you, and that's enough conversation for now, the flock can't stand here all day waiting for you to make up your mind. Jesus gathered up the broken pieces of the bowl, looking at them as if he couldn't bear to part with them, but for no good reason, yesterday at this hour he had not yet met the Pharisee, besides, what had happened was only to be expected, earthenware breaks so easily. He scattered the pieces on the ground like sowing seeds, and Pastor said, You will have another bowl, but the next won't break while you are alive. Jesus didn't hear him, he held Joseph's sandals in his hand and was trying to decide if he should wear them. Not so long ago they would have been much too big for him, but time, as we know, can be deceptive, Jesus felt as if he had been carrying his father's sandals in his pack for ages, he would have been very surprised to find they were still too big for him. He slipped them on and, without knowing why, packed his own. Pastor said, Once feet have grown, they don't shrink again, and you will have no sons to inherit your tunic, mantle, and sandals, but Jesus did not discard them, their weight helped keep the almost empty pack on his shoulders. There was no need to give Pastor the answer he wanted, Jesus took his place behind the flock, his heart divided between a vague sense of terror, as if his soul were in peril, and another, even vaguer sense of somber fascination. I must find out who you are, murmured Jesus, choking on the dust raised by the flock as he chased after a sheep that lagged behind, and this, he believed, was the reason he had decided to stay with the mysterious shepherd.

That was the first day. No more was said about matters of faith and blasphemy, about life, death, and inheritance, but Jesus, who had started to watch Pastor, his every attitude and gesture, noticed that each time the shepherd offered up prayers of thanksgiving to the Lord, he got down and placed the palms of his hands on the ground, lowering his head and shutting his eyes, without uttering a word. One day, when he was still a little boy, Jesus had heard some elderly travelers who were passing through Nazareth relate that deep in the earth were vast caverns where one could find cities, fields, rivers, forests, and deserts just like those on the surface of the world, and that this underworld, a perfect image and likeness of the one we live in, was created by the devil after God threw him down from the heavens as punishment for his rebellion. Since God had initially befriended the devil and looked on him with favor, causing the angels to comment that there had never been so close a friendship in the universe, the devil witnessed the birth of Adam and Eve. Having learned how it was done, he repeated the process in his underworld and created a man and woman for himself, with the one difference that, unlike God, he forbade them nothing, which explains why there has never been such a thing as original sin in the devil's world. One of the old men even dared suggest, And because there was no original sin, there was no other kind of sin either. After the men were sent on their way with the help of some persuasive stones thrown by outraged Nazirites, who soon realized what these irreverent old fools were getting at with their remarks, there was a sudden tremor, nothing serious, a mere sign of confirmation coming from the bowels of the earth, which made young Jesus think, capable as he was, even as a boy, of linking cause and effect. And now, watching Pastor kneel

before him with his head lowered and palms resting lightly
on the ground to feel every grain of sand, every pebble
and rootlet and blade sprouting on the surface, Jesus was
reminded of that story. Perhaps this man inhabited the
hidden world created by the devil in the image and likeness of the visible world. What is he doing here, Jesus asked
himself, but he didn't dare probe any further. When Pastor
eventually got to his feet, Jesus asked him, What are you
doing. I want to be sure the earth is still beneath me. Surely
you can tell with your feet. My feet perceive nothing, only
my hands can tell me, when you adore your God, you
don't raise your feet to Him, you raise your hands, even
though you could raise other parts of your body, for example what is between your legs, unless you happen to be
a eunuch. Overcome with shame and horror, Jesus turned
beet red. Do not offend the God you do not know, he told
Pastor severely when he had recovered, but Pastor asked,
Who created your body. It was God, of course. Just as it
is now, Yes, And did the devil play any part in creating
your body. None whatsoever, man's body is God's creation. So all the parts of your body are equally worthy in
the eyes of God, Obviously, So God isn't likely to disown
what you have between your legs, for example. No, I suppose not, but then the Lord created Adam, yet expelled
him from Paradise even though he was His creation. Just
give me a straight answer, boy, and stop talking like a
teacher in the synagogue. You're trying to make me give
the answers you want, but I can tell you, if you wish, all
the cases in which man is forbidden by the Lord, under
pain of death, to expose his own or another's nakedness,
which proves that certain parts of the body are in themselves sinful. No more sinful than the mouth when it utters falsehood and slander, that same mouth with which
you praise your Lord before uttering falsehood and after
spreading slander. That's enough, I don't want to hear another word. You must hear me out, if only to answer my

question. What question. Can God disown what you have between your legs as something not of His making, just answer yes or no. No, He can't, Why not, Because the Lord cannot undo what He has willed. Slowly nodding his head, Pastor said, In other words, your God is the only warden of a prison where the only prisoner is your God. The final echo of these momentous words was still ringing in Jesus' ears when Pastor went on to say in an almost natural voice, You must choose a sheep. What, asked Jesus in bewilderment. I said choose a sheep, unless you prefer a goat. Whatever for. Because you'll need it, unless you really are a eunuch. When Pastor's meaning sank in, the boy was stunned, but worst of all was the surge of vile sensuality once he had suppressed his embarrassment and revulsion. Covering his face with both hands, he said in a hoarse voice, This is the word of the Lord, The man who copulates with an animal will be punished with death and the animal slaughtered, and the Lord also said, Cursed is the man who sins with an animal of any species. Did your Lord say all that. Yes, and now leave me alone, abominable creature, for you are not of God but belong to the devil. Pastor listened impassively, waiting for Jesus' curse to have its full effect, whatever that might be, an apparition, leprosy, the sudden destruction of body and soul. But nothing happened. Wind came playing between the stones, raising a cloud of dust that swept across the wilderness, then nothing, silence, the universe quietly watching men and animals, perhaps waiting to see what meaning they can find, recognize, or construe in those words, it consumes itself in this vigil, the primordial fire is already reduced to ashes, but the response is slow in coming. Then Pastor raised his arms and called out to his flock in a commanding voice, Listen, my sheep, hear what this learned boy has come to teach us, God has forbidden anyone to copulate with you, so fear not, but as for shearing you, neglecting you, slaughtering you, and eating you, all these

197

things are permitted, because for this you were created by God's law and are sustained by His providence. He gave three long whistles and, waving his crook over his head, he cried, Be off, be off with you, whereupon the flock began moving toward the spot where the column of smoke disappeared. Jesus stood watching until the tall figure of Pastor all but vanished from sight and the resigned rumps of the animals merged with the color of the earth. I'm not going with him, Jesus said, but he went. He adjusted the pack on his back, tightened the straps of the sandals that had belonged to his father, and followed the flock at a distance. He caught up with them at nightfall and, emerging from the shadows into the light of the campfire, announced, I'm here.

TOMORROW IS ANOTHER DAY IS A WELL-KNOWN SAYING AND to the point, yet not as simple as it may seem to one who is satisfied with the approximate meaning of words, whether taken separately or together, because everything depends on how a thing is said, which varies according to the mood of the person speaking. When the words are expressed by one whose life is going badly and who hopes for better times, they are not the same as when one utters them as a threat, promising vengeance at some future date. The most extreme case would be one who sighs, Tomorrow is another day, because he is a pessimist by nature and given to expecting the worst. It would not be entirely plausible for Jesus to go around saying this at his age, whatever his meaning or tone of voice, but for us, yes, because like God we know everything about what has been and what is to come, so we can say, mutter, or whisper these words as we watch Jesus go about his tasks as a shepherd boy, crossing the hills of Judah, or, later, descending into the valley of Jordan. And not just because we are writing about Jesus but because every human being is constantly

199

confronted with good and bad, one thing coming after another, day following day. Since this gospel was never meant to dismiss what others have written about Jesus or to contradict their accounts, and since Jesus is clearly the hero of our story, it would be easy for us to go up to him and predict his future, tell him what a wonderful life lies ahead, the miracles he will perform to provide food and restore health, even one to conquer death, but that would hardly be wise, because young Jesus, notwithstanding his aptitude for religious studies and his knowledge of patriarchs and prophets, enjoys the healthy skepticism one associates with youth, so he would send us away with scorn. Yes, he will change his mind when he meets God, but it is much too soon for that great encounter, and before then Jesus will have to go up and down many a mountain slope, milk many a goat and sheep, help make cheese, and barter wares in the villages. He will also kill animals that are diseased or have outlived their usefulness, and he will mourn their loss. But fret not, all you sensitive souls, he will never engage in the horrid vice suggested by Pastor, of coupling with a goat or sheep or both to relieve and satisfy the corrupt flesh that houses his pure soul. This is neither the time nor the place, however, to ponder how often the soul, in order to be able to boast of a clean body, has burdened itself with sadness, envy, and impurity.

Although their initial exchanges on ethical and theological matters remained unresolved, Pastor and Jesus got along well enough with each other, the shepherd patiently teaching him how to tend the flock, the boy listening intently, as if it were a matter of life and death. Jesus learned how to send his crook whirling through the air to land on the rump of an animal that in a moment of distraction or daring had strayed from the flock, but his apprenticeship was painful, because one day, while he was still struggling to master the technique, he threw the crook too low and accidentally hit the tender neck of a newborn kid, with such force that he killed the poor thing outright. Such accidents can happen to anyone, even an experienced and skillful shepherd, but Jesus, who was already burdened with so many sorrows, stiffened with horror as he lifted the little kid, still warm, into his arms. There was nothing to be done. Even the mother goat, after sniffing her child for a moment, moved away and resumed grazing, pawing at tufts of grass, which she pulled at with quick movements of her head, recalling the familiar refrain, A bleating goat doesn't chew much grass, which is another way of saying, You can't cry and eat at the same time. Pastor came to see what happened, Bad luck, no need for you to feel guilty. But I killed the poor little animal, Jesus said mournfully. So you did, but if he'd been an ugly, smelly old billy goat you wouldn't have felt much pity, put him on the ground and let me deal with this while you go attend to that ewe over there that looks as if she's about to give birth. What will you do with the kid. Skin it, of course, unless you expect me to work a miracle and bring it back to life. I swear I'll never touch that meat. Eating the animal we kill is our only way of showing respect, what is wrong is to eat what others have been forced to kill. I refuse to eat it. Please yourself, there will be all the more for me. Pastor drew a knife from his belt, looked at Jesus, and said, This is something else you'll have to learn sooner or later, to study the entrails of the animals created to serve and feed us. Jesus looked away and turned to go, but Pastor, knife in hand, went on to say, Slaves exist to serve us, perhaps we should open them up to see if they carry slaves inside, or open up a monarch to see if he has another monarch in his belly, I'll bet if we met the devil and he allowed us to open him up, we might be surprised to find God jumping out. Pastor still liked to provoke Jesus with these outrageous remarks. Jesus had gradually learned that the best way to deal with this was ignore it and say nothing. For Pastor might have gone even further, suggesting that on

201

opening up God one might find the devil inside. Jesus went off in search of the ewe about to give birth, here at least there were no surprises awaiting him, a lamb like any other would appear, in the image and likeness of its mother, who in turn was identical to her sisters, for the one thing we can expect from these creatures is a smooth continuity of the species. The sheep had already given birth. The newborn lamb, lying on the ground, seemed to be all legs as its mother tried to help it to its feet, gently nudging with her nose, but the poor, dazed creature could only cock its head, as if trying to find the best angle to take in this strange new world. Jesus helped hold it steady on its feet, his hands sticky with the afterbirth, but he did not mind, one gets used to such things when one is in constant contact with animals, and this lamb arrived at the right moment, so pretty with its curly coat and its pink little mouth already searching avidly for milk from those teats, which it is seeing for the first time and could never have imagined from inside its mother's womb. No one has any grounds for complaining about God, when we discover so many useful things from the moment we are born.

Within sight, Pastor stretches the kid's pelt on a wooden frame in the form of a star, the skinned carcass already in his pack, wrapped in cloth. He will salt it later, when the flock settles down for the night, except for the piece Pastor intends to have for his supper, since Jesus is adamant he will not touch the meat of an animal he killed. These scruples on the part of Jesus place him in conflict with the religion he observes and the traditions he respects, including the slaughter of all those other innocent animals sacrificed daily on the altars of the Lord, especially in Jerusalem, where the victims are counted in hecatombs. Given the time and place, Jesus' attitude does seems odd, but perhaps it is really a question of vulnerability, for we must not forget Joseph's tragic death and Jesus' recent discovery of the appalling massacre that took place in Bethlehem almost fifteen

202

years ago, enough to disturb any young mind, not to mention those terrifying nightmares, which we have not mentioned lately, although they still trouble him and refuse to go away. When he can no longer bear the thought that Joseph is coming to kill him, his cries wake the flock in the middle of the night, and Pastor gives him a gentle shake, What's this, what's going on. Delivered from his nightmare, Jesus falls into the shepherd's arms, as if Pastor were his unfortunate father. Soon after joining Pastor, Jesus had confided in him that he had nightmares, though not giving the reason, but Pastor said, Save your breath, I know everything, even what you're hiding from me. This was about the time Jesus rebuked Pastor for his lack of faith and his wickedness, particularly, if you'll forgive my laboring the point, in sexual matters. But Jesus realized that he had no one else in the world, besides the family he had abandoned and forgotten, but not the mother who gave him life, although he often wished she hadn't, and, after his mother, only his sister Lisa, which he couldn't explain, but then memory is like that, it has its own reasons. So gradually Jesus began to enjoy Pastor's company, and it is easy to imagine his relief at not having to live alone with his remorse, at having someone at his side who understood, who would not pretend to forgive what could not be forgiven, someone who would treat him with both kindness and severity in accordance with his innocence and his guilt. We felt this needed explaining, so that the reader would find it easier to understand and accept why Jesus, so different in character and outlook from his ill-bred master, decided to stay with him until the prophesied encounter with God, which promises to be momentous, because God is not likely to appear to a simple mortal without good reason.

But before that, the circumstances and coincidences which we have discussed at length dictate that Jesus meet his mother and some of his brothers in Jerusalem during

203

Passover, which he thought he would be celebrating for the first time without his family. That Jesus wanted to celebrate Passover in Jerusalem might have angered Pastor, for they were in the hills and the flock needed all their attention. Besides, Pastor was not a Jew and had no other god to honor, so he could well have refused Jesus permission, telling him, Oh no, you don't, you'll stay right here, I'm the one who gives the orders, and there's work to be done. Yet none of this happened, Pastor simply asked, Will you be coming back, but from the tone of his voice he seemed certain that Jesus would return, and indeed, the boy replied without a moment's hesitation, although he was surprised that the words came out so quickly, Yes, I'll be back. Then pick yourself a clean lamb, Jesus, and take it to be sacrificed, since you Jews attach so much importance to such practices. Pastor was putting him to the test, to see if the boy could lead to its death a lamb from the flock they had worked so hard to maintain and protect. No one warned Jesus, no tiny, invisible angel whispered in his ear, Be careful, it's a trap, don't trust him, this man is capable of anything. His gentle nature provided him with a good answer, or perhaps it was the memory of the dead kid and the newborn lamb. I want no lamb from this flock, he said. Why not. I cannot lead to its death an animal that I myself raised. Please yourself, but I hope you realize that you'll have to get a lamb from some other flock. I suppose so, since lambs don't fall from heaven. When are you thinking of leaving, Early tomorrow morning, And you'll be coming back, Yes, I'll be back. They said no more on the subject, although it was difficult to see how Jesus would find enough money to buy a paschal lamb when he could barely scrape together a living. One may presume that, not given to vices that cost money, he still had the few coins given him by the Pharisee almost a year ago, but they didn't amount to much, and, as we said, at this time of the year the prices of livestock in general and of lambs especially rise out of all proportion, so that one really has to put one's trust in God. Despite all the misfortunes that have befallen him, one is tempted to say that a lucky star guides this boy, but it would be feebleminded of this or any other evangelist to believe that celestial bodies so remote from our planet could have any appreciable influence on a human life, however much the devout Magi may have invoked, studied, and compared the stars. For, if what we are told is true, they must have traveled here some years ago, only to see what they saw and to go away again. What we are simply trying to say in this long-winded passage is that our Jesus must somehow find a way to present himself worthily in the Temple with a little lamb, thus fulfilling what is expected of him. For he has proved himself a good Jew even in difficult situations, such as those tense exchanges with Pastor.

About this time the flock was enjoying the rich pastures of the valley of Aijalon, situated between the cities of Gezer and Emmaus. In Emmaus, Jesus tried to earn enough money to buy the much-needed lamb, but he soon saw that after a year of tending sheep and goats he no longer had the aptitude for any other kind of work, not even for carpentry, in which, from lack of practice, he had made no progress. So he took the road that leads up from Emmaus to Jerusalem, wondering what he should do, he had no money to buy the lamb, stealing was out of the question, and it would be more miracle than luck if he found a stray lamb on the road. There are plenty of lambs in sight, some with ropes around their necks following their owners, others fortunate enough to be carried in loving arms. Imagining themselves on an outing, these innocent creatures are excited and nervous, they are curious about everything, and because they cannot ask questions, they use their eyes in the hope of making sense of a world made of words. Jesus sat on a stone by the roadside to think of a solution to this material problem that prevented him from carrying out his spiritual duty, if only another Pharisee, or even the same one, who probably gives alms daily, were suddenly to appear and ask him, Are you in need of a lamb, just as the man had previously asked him, Are you hungry. On that first occasion Jesus did not have to beg in order to receive, but now, with little hope of being given anything, he will have to beg. He already has his hand out, a gesture so eloquent that it dispenses with all explanations, and so expressive that we nearly always avert our eyes rather than be confronted with an unsightly wound or distressing obscenity. A few coins were dropped into Jesus' palm by less distracted travelers, but so few that at this rate the road from Emmaus will never bring him to the gates of Jerusalem. When he adds up what money he already has and what he just collected, there isn't enough to buy even half a lamb, and the Lord, as everyone knows, does not accept an animal on His altars unless it is perfect and whole, He refuses those that are blind, crippled, mutilated, diseased, or contaminated. You can imagine the scandal in the Temple if we were to present ourselves at the sacrificial altar with the hindquarters only, or, if by any misfortune the testicles have been crushed, broken, or cut, that too would exclude it. No one asks this boy why he needs money, but wait, an elderly man with a long white beard now approaches Jesus while his family pauses in the middle of the road, respectfully waiting for the patriarch to rejoin them. Jesus thought he would receive another coin, but he was mistaken. The old man asked, Who are you, and the boy stood up to answer, I am Jesus of Nazareth. Have you no family. Yes, I have. Then why are you not with them. I came to work as a shepherd in Judaea, a deceitful way of telling the truth, or putting the truth at the service of a lie. The old man looked at him quizzically and asked, Why are you begging for alms if you have a trade. I earn my keep but cannot save enough money to buy a lamb for Passover. So that is why you beg. Yes, whereupon the patriarch ordered one of the men in his group, Give this boy a lamb, we can buy another when we get to the Temple. There were six lambs tied to the same rope, the man untied the last of them and handed it to the old man, who told Jesus, Here's your lamb so that you too may offer sacrifice to the Lord this Passover, and without waiting to be thanked, he returned to his family, who received him with smiles and admiration. Before Jesus could thank the old man, he was gone, then suddenly the road was mysteriously empty, between one bend and the next there was only Jesus and the lamb, who had finally found each other on the road from Emmaus thanks to the generosity of an elderly Jew. Jesus clutched the end of the cord, the animal looked up at his new master and started to bleat me-e-e-e in that nervous, tremulous way of young lambs before they are sacrificed to placate the gods. This bleating, which Jesus had heard thousands of times since becoming a shepherd's helpmate, touched his heart, and he felt as if his limbs were dissolving with pity. Here he was, with power as never before over the life of another creature, this immaculate white lamb that had no will and no desire, its trusting little face looking up at him anxiously, its pink tongue showing each time it bleated, and pink flesh beneath its soft hairs, and pink inside its ears, and pink nails on its feet, just as humans have, but nails that would never harden and be called hooves. Jesus stroked the lamb's head, it responded by stretching its neck and rubbing its moist nose against the palm of his hand, sending a shiver up his spine. The spell broke as suddenly as it had begun. At the end of the road, from the direction of Emmaus, other pilgrims appeared in a swarm of fluttering tunics, of packs and staffs, with more lambs and prayers of thanksgiving to the Lord. Jesus lifted his lamb into his arms and started walking.

He had not been back to Jerusalem since that distant day he came out of necessity to discover the burden of sorrow and remorse in life, whether shared like an inheritance or kept entirely to oneself like death. The crowd filling the streets resembled a muddy brown river about to flood the concourse before the steps of the Temple. Holding the lamb in his arms, Jesus watched the people file past, some coming, some going, some carrying animals to be sacrificed, some returning without them, looking joyful and exclaiming, Alleluia, Hosanna, Amen, or saying none of these things, feeling it was inappropriate to walk around shouting Hallelujah or Hip hip hurrah, because there is really not much difference between the two expressions, we use them enthusiastically until with the passage of time and by dint of repetition we finally ask ourselves, What does it mean, only to find there is no answer. The endless column of smoke spiraling above the Temple indicated for miles around that all who had come to offer sacrifices were direct and legitimate descendants of Abel, that son of Adam and Eve who in his day offered to the Lord the firstborn of his flock and their fat, which were favorably received, while his brother Cain, who had nothing to offer but the simple fruits of nature, saw that the Lord for some reason did not so much as look at him. If this was Cain's motive for killing Abel, then we can put our minds at rest, the worshipers here are not likely to kill one another, they all offer the same sacrifice, and how the fat spits and the carcasses sizzle as God in the sublime heavens inhales the odors of all this carnage with satisfaction. Jesus pressed his lamb to his breast, unable to fathom why God could not be appeased with a cup of milk poured over His altar, that sap of life which passes from one being to another, or with a handful of wheat, the basic substance of immortal bread. Soon he will have to part with the old man's generous gift, his for such a short time, the poor little lamb will not live to see the sun set this day, it is time to mount the stairs of the Temple, to deliver it to the knife and sacrificial fire, as if it were no longer worthy of existence or being punished by the eternal guardian of myths and fables for having drunk from the waters of life. Then Jesus decided, in defiance of the law of the synagogue and the word of God, that this lamb would not die, that what he had received to deliver to the altar would continue to live and that he would leave Jerusalem a greater sinner than when he arrived. As if his previous offenses were not enough, he was now committing this one too, but the day will come when he has to pay for all his sins, because God never forgets. The fear of punishment made him hesitate for a moment, but suddenly, in his mind's eye, he saw a horrifying vision, a vast sea of blood, the blood of the countless lambs and other animals sacrificed since the creation of mankind, for that is why men have been put on this earth, to adore and to offer sacrifice. And he saw the steps of the Temple awash with red, as blood came streaming down them, and he saw himself standing in a pool of blood and raising the lifeless body of his beheaded lamb to heaven. Deep in thought, Jesus stood inside a sphere of silence, but then the sphere shattered, and once more he was plunged into the clamor of invocations and blessings, pleas, cries, chants, and the pitiful bleating of lambs, until all was silenced in an instant by three low blasts from the shofar, the long, spiral horn of a ram made into a trumpet. Covering the lamb with his pack, Jesus ran from the concourse and disappeared into a labyrinth of narrow alleyways without worrying where he might end up. When he finally stopped for breath, he was on the outskirts, having left the city by the northern gate, known as that of Ramah, the same gate by which he had entered when he arrived from Nazareth. He sat beneath an olive tree by the side of the road and took the lamb out of his pack, no one would have found it strange to see him sitting there, they would simply have thought, He has traveled a long way and is recovering his strength before taking his lamb to the Temple, how endearing, we do not know whether the person thinking this means the lamb or

Jesus. We find both of them endearing, but if we had to make a choice, the prize would almost certainly go to the lamb, on the condition that it does not grow any bigger. Jesus lies on his back, holding the end of the cord to prevent the lamb from escaping, an unnecessary precaution, the poor animal has no strength, not only because of its tender age but also because of all the excitement, the constant motion back and forth, not to mention the meager food it was given this morning, for it is considered neither fitting nor decent for anyone, lamb or martyr, to die with a full belly.

Stretched out on the ground, Jesus gradually recovers and starts breathing normally again. Between the branches of the olive tree, as it sways gently in the wind, he can see the sky, the sun's rays filtering through gaps in the foliage and playing on his face, it must be about the sixth hour, the sun directly overhead shortens the shadows, and who would ever think that night will come to extinguish this dazzling light. Some people pass on the road, more follow behind, and when Jesus looks again at that group, he receives such a shock that his first impulse is to flee, but how can he, for coming toward him is his own mother accompanied by some of his brothers, the older sons, James, Joseph, and Judas, and Lisa too, but she is a girl and should be mentioned separately rather than listed according to age, which would place her between James and Joseph. They still have not seen him. Jesus goes into the road to meet them, once more carrying his lamb in his arms, but one suspects this is only to make sure his arms are full. First to notice him is James, who waves before turning to their mother in great excitement, and now Mary is looking, they start walking faster, and Jesus too feels obliged to hasten toward them, though he cannot run with the lamb in his arms. We are taking so long over this that the reader might get the impression we do not want them to meet, but this is not so, maternal, fraternal, and filial love should give

them wings, yet there are reservations and certain con-
straints, we know how they separated, we do not know
the effect of all those months apart without news of each
other. If one keeps walking, one eventually arrives, and
there they are, face-to-face, Jesus says, Your blessing,
Mother, and his mother says, May the Lord bless you, my
son. They embraced, then it was his brothers' turn, then
Lisa's, followed by an awkward silence, all of them at a
loss for words, Mary was not going to say to her son,
Such a surprise, what on earth are you doing here, nor
Jesus to his mother, I never expected to find you here,
what brings you to the city, the lamb in his arms and the
one they have brought speak for themselves, this is the
Passover of the Lord, the difference being that one lamb is
going to die and the other has been saved. We waited and
waited to hear from you, Mary said at length, bursting
into tears. Her eldest son stands before her, so tall, so
grown-up, with the beginnings of a beard and the weather-
beaten complexion of one who has spent his days in the
open, exposed to the sun, wind, and dust of the desert.
Don't cry, Mother, I have work. I'm a shepherd now. A
shepherd. Yes, a shepherd. But I was hoping you'd follow
your father and take up the trade he taught you. Well, as
things turned out, I became a shepherd, and that's what I
am. When are you coming home. I don't know, one day,
I suppose. At least accompany your mother and brothers
to the Temple. Mother, I'm not going to the Temple. Why
not, you have your lamb there. This lamb isn't going to
the Temple either. Is there something wrong with it. No,
nothing, but he will die a natural death when his time
comes. My son, I don't understand. You don't have to
understand, if I save this lamb, it's so that someone may
save me. Then why not come with your family. I was
leaving. Where to, Back to the flock where I belong, Where
did you leave it, At present it's in the valley of Aijalon,
Where is this valley of Aijalon, On the other side, What

211

other side, On the other side of Bethlehem. Mary stepped back and turned quite pale, how she has aged although barely thirty, Why do you mention Bethlehem, she asked. That's where I met the shepherd who is my master. Who is this man, and before Jesus had time to reply, she said to the others, You go on ahead and wait for me at the entrance. Then taking Jesus by the hand, she led him to the side of the road, Who is this man, she asked a second time. I don't know, Jesus answered. Doesn't he have a name. If he has, he's never told me, I call him Pastor and that's all. What does he look like, He's big, And where did you meet him, In the cave where I was born, Who took you there, A slave named Salome, who told me she helped deliver me, And this man, What about him, What did he say to you, Nothing you don't already know. Mary slumped to the ground, as if a heavy hand were pushing her, That man is a demon. How do you know, did he tell you so. No, the first time I saw him, he told me he was an angel and asked me not to say a word to anyone. When did you see him. The day your father learned I was pregnant, he appeared at our door disguised as a beggar and told me he was an angel. Did you ever see him again. On the road when your father and I traveled to Bethlehem for the census, then in the cave where you were born, and the night after you left home, he walked into the yard, I thought it was you, and peering through the gap in the door, I saw him uproot the plant in the yard, you remember that bush which grew at the very spot where the bowl of bright earth was buried. What bowl, what earth. You were never told, but the beggar gave it to me before he went away, when he returned the bowl after he had finished eating, there was luminous earth inside. For earth to shine, he must have been an angel. At first I believed so, but the devil too has magical powers. Jesus sat beside his mother and left the lamb to roam at will. Yes, I've learned that when they are both in agreement, it's almost impossible to tell the difference between an angel of the Lord and an angel of Satan, he told her. Stay with us, don't go back to that man, do this for your mother's sake. No, I promised to return, and I will keep my word. People make promises to the devil only in order to deceive him. This man, who I'm certain is no man but an angel or demon, has been haunting me since the day I was born, and I want to know why. Jesus, my son, come to the Temple with your mother and brothers, by taking this lamb to the altar you'll fulfill your obligation and the lamb its destiny, and there you can ask the Lord to deliver you from the powers of Satan and all evil thoughts. This lamb will die only when his time comes. But this is its day for dying. Mother, the lambs you gave birth to must die, but you should not make them die before their time. Lambs are not people, and even less so when those people are sons. When the Lord ordered Abraham to kill his son Isaac, no distinction was made then. My son, I'm a simple woman, I have no answer to give you, but I beseech you, give up these evil thoughts. Mother, thoughts are but passing shadows, neither good nor bad in themselves, actions alone count. Praised be the Lord who blessed this poor, ignorant woman with such a wise son, yet I cannot believe this is the wisdom of God. One can learn also from the devil. And I fear you are in his power. If his power saved this lamb, then something has been gained in the world today. Mary made no attempt to reply. They saw James approaching from the city gate. Mary got to her feet, I find my son only to lose him again, she said, to which Jesus replied, If you haven't already lost him, you will not lose him now. He put his hand into his pack and took out the money he had been given as alms, This is all I have. You've worked all those months for so little. I work to earn my keep. You must be very fond of that master of yours to be satisfied with so little. The Lord is my shepherd. Don't offend God, living with a demon. Who knows, Mother, who knows, he could be an angel serving another God who reigns in another heaven. The Lord said, I am the Lord and you will worship no other god. Amen, responded Jesus. He gathered the lamb into his arms and said, I see James approaching, farewell, Mother, and Mary said, One would think you had more affection for that lamb than for your own family. Right now I do, said Jesus. Choking with grief and anger, Mary turned away and ran to meet her other son. She did not look back.

Outside the city walls, Jesus took a different route across the fields before beginning the long descent into the valley of Aijalon. He stopped at a village and bought food with the money his mother had refused, some bread and figs, milk for himself and the lamb, sheep's milk, and if there was any difference, it wasn't noticeable, it's possible, at least in this case, that one mother is as good as another. Anyone surprised that Jesus spends money on a lamb that by rights should now be dead will be told that the boy once owned two lambs, one was sacrificed and lives on in the glory of the Lord, while this other lamb was rejected because it had a torn ear, Take a look, But there's nothing wrong with its ear, they might say, to which Jesus would reply, Well, then, I'll tear it myself, and lifting the lamb to his back, he went on his way. He caught sight of the flock as the evening light began to wane and the sky became overcast with dark, low clouds. The tension in the air spoke of thunderstorms, and indeed lightning rent the sky just as Jesus saw the flock. But there was no rain, it was one of those dry thunderstorms, all the more frightening because they make you feel so vulnerable, without the shield of rain and wind, as it were, to protect you in the naked battle between a thundering heaven that tears itself apart and an earth that trembles and cowers beneath the blows. A hundred paces from Jesus, another blinding flash split an olive tree, which immediately caught fire and blazed like a torch. A loud burst of thunder shuddered across

214

the sky as if ripping it open from end to end, and the impact knocked Jesus to the ground and left him senseless. Two more bolts struck, here, there, like two decisive words, then little by little the peals of thunder grew remote and finally became a gentle murmur, an intimate dialogue between heaven and earth. The lamb, having survived the storm unharmed and no longer afraid, came up to Jesus and put its mouth to his lips, there was no sniffing, one touch was all that was needed. Jesus opened his eyes, saw the lamb, then the livid sky like a black hand blocking whatever light remained. The olive tree still burned. His bones ached when he tried to move, but at least he was in one piece, if that can be said of a body so fragile that it takes only a clap of thunder to knock it to the ground. He sat up with some effort and reassured himself, more by touch than by sight, that he was neither burned nor paralyzed, none of his bones were broken, and apart from a loud buzzing in his head as insistent as the drone of a trumpet, he was all right. He drew the lamb to him and said, Don't be afraid, He only wanted to show you that you would have been dead by now if that was His will, and to show me that it was not I who saved your life but He. One last rumble of thunder slowly tore the air like a sigh, while below, the white patch of the flock seemed a beckoning oasis.

Struggling to overcome his weakness, Jesus descended the slope. The lamb, kept on its cord simply as a precaution, trotted at his side like a little dog. Behind them, the olive tree continued to burn, and the light it cast in the twilight allowed Jesus to see the tall figure of Pastor rise before him like a ghost, wrapped in a mantle that seemed endless and holding a crook that looked as though it might touch the clouds were he to raise it. Pastor said, I was expecting that thunderstorm. I'm the one who should have expected it, replied Jesus. Where did you get the lamb. I didn't have enough money to buy one for Passover, so I stood by the roadside and begged, then an old man came and gave me this lamb. Why didn't you offer it in sacrifice. I couldn't, I just couldn't bring myself to do it. Pastor smiled, Now I begin to understand, He waited for you, let you come to the flock safely, in order to show His might before my eyes. Jesus did not reply, he had more or less said the same thing to the lamb, but having just arrived, he had no desire to get into a discussion about God's motives and acts. So what will you do with your lamb. Nothing, I brought it here so that it could join the flock. The white lambs all look alike, tomorrow you won't even recognize it among the others. My lamb knows me. The day will come when it forgets you, besides the lamb will soon grow tired of always having to come and look for you, better to brand it or cut off a piece of its ear. Poor little beast. What's the difference, after all they branded you when they cut your foreskin so that people would know to whom you belong. It's not the same thing. It shouldn't be, but it is. As they were speaking, Pastor gathered up wood and was now busily trying to light a fire with a flint. Jesus told him, It would be easier to go and fetch a branch from the burning olive tree, whereupon Pastor replied, One should always leave heavenly fire to burn out by itself. The trunk of the olive tree was now one great ember glowing in the darkness, the wind made sparks fly from it and sent incandescent strips of bark and burning twigs into the air, where they soon went out. The sky remained heavy and strangely oppressive. Pastor and Jesus ate together as usual, which led Pastor to remark ironically, This year you're not partaking of the paschal lamb. Jesus listened and said nothing, but deep inside he felt uneasy, from now on he would face the awkward contradiction between eating lambs and refusing to kill them. So what's to be done, asked Pastor, is the lamb to be branded or not. I couldn't do it, said Jesus. Give it to me, then, and I'll do it. With a firm, quick flick of the knife Pastor removed the tip of one of its ears, then holding it up, he asked, What shall I do with this, bury it or throw it away. Without thinking, Jesus replied, Let me have it, and dropped it into the fire. That's exactly how they disposed of your foreskin, said Pastor. Blood dripped from the lamb's ear in a slow trickle that would soon stop. The smoke from the flames gave off the intoxicating smell of charred young flesh. And so at the end of a long day, in which much time had been wasted on childish and presumptuous gestures of defiance, the Lord finally received His due, perhaps because of those intimidating blasts of thunder and lightning, which surely made enough of an impression to persuade these stubborn shepherds to show obedience. The earth quickly swallowed the last drop of the lamb's blood, for it would have been a great shame to lose the most precious drop of all from this much-disputed sacrifice.

Transformed by time into an ordinary sheep, distinguishable from the others only by the missing tip of one ear, this same animal came to lose itself three years later in the wild country bordering the desert south of Jericho. In so large a flock, one sheep more or less may not seem to make much difference, but we must not forget that this flock is like no other, even its shepherds have little in common with shepherds we have heard about or seen, so we should not be surprised if Pastor, looking from a hilltop, noticed that an animal was missing without having to count them. He called Jesus and told him, Your sheep is missing from the flock, go and look for it, and since Jesus himself did not ask Pastor, How do you know the sheep is mine, we will also refrain from asking Jesus. What matters now is to see where Jesus, who is unfamiliar with this region where few have ventured, will go on the broad horizon. Since they came from the fertile land of Jericho, where they had decided not to stay, preferring to wander at their leisure rather than be trapped among people, a person or sheep intent on getting lost was much more likely to choose a place where the effort of searching for food would not interfere with his precious solitude. By this logic, it was clear that Jesus' sheep had deliberately lagged behind the others and even now was probably grazing on the fertile banks of the Jordan, within sight of Jericho for greater safety. Logic, however, is not everything in this life. Often what you expect, as the most feasible outcome of a sequence of events or else foreseeable for some other reason, comes about in the most unlikely way. If this is so, then our Jesus should seek his lost sheep not in those rich pastures back there but in the scorched and arid desert before him. No one need argue that a sheep would not stray off to die of hunger and thirst, first because no one knows what goes on inside a sheep's head, and secondly because you must keep in mind what we just said about the uncertain nature of the foreseeable. And so we find Jesus already making his way into the desert. Pastor showed no surprise at his decision, he said nothing, only gave a slow and solemn nod of the head, which, oddly, looked also like a gesture of farewell.

The desert in this region is not one of those vast tracks of sand with which we are all familiar, here it is more a great sea of parched, rugged dunes straddling one another and creating an inextricable labyrinth of valleys. A few plants barely survive at the foot of these slopes, plants consisting of only thorns and thistles, which a goat might be able to chew but will tear the sensitive mouth of a sheep at the slightest contact. This desert is far more intimidating than one formed by smooth sands and constantly shifting dunes, here every hill announces the threat lurking on the next hill, and when we arrive there in fear and trembling, at once we feel the same threat at our back. In this desert our cries will raise no echo, all we will hear in reply are the hills themselves calling out, or the voice of the mysterious force hidden there. Jesus, carrying nothing but his crook and pack, entered the desert. He had not gone far, had barely crossed the threshold of this world, when he became aware that his father's old sandals were coming apart under his feet. They had been often patched, but Jesus' mending skills could no longer save what had walked so many roads and pressed so much sweat into the dust. As if obeying a commandment, the last of the fibers disintegrated, the patches came undone, the laces broke in several places, and soon Jesus was practically barefoot. The boy Jesus, as we have grown used to calling him, although being Jewish and eighteen years of age, he is more adult than adolescent, suddenly remembered the sandals he had been carrying all this time in his pack, and he foolishly thought they might still fit. Pastor was right when he warned him, when feet grow, they will not shrink again, and Jesus could scarcely believe that once he could slip his feet into these tiny sandals. He confronted the desert in his bare feet, like Adam expelled from Eden, and like Adam he hesitated before taking his first painful step across the tortured earth that beckoned him. But then, without asking himself why he did it, perhaps in memory of Adam, he dropped his pack and crook, and lifting his tunic by the hem pulled it over his head to stand as naked as Adam himself. Pastor cannot see him here, no inquisitive lamb has followed him, only birds venturing beyond this frontier can catch a glimpse of him from the sky, as can the insects from the ground, the ants, the occasional centipede, a scorpion that in panic lifts its tail with its poisonous sting. These tiny creatures cannot remember ever having seen a naked man before and have no idea what he is trying to prove. If they were to ask Jesus, Why did you take off your clothes, perhaps he would tell them, One must walk into the desert naked, a reply beyond the understanding of insects of the genus Hemiptera, Myriapoda, or Arachnida. We ask ourselves, Naked, with all those thorns to graze bare skin and catch in pubic hair, naked, with all those sharp thistles and that rough sand, naked under that

scorching sun which can make a man dizzy and blind, naked, to find that lost sheep we branded with our own mark.
The desert opens to receive Jesus, then closes behind him,
as if cutting off any path of retreat. Silence echoes in his
ears like the noise from one of those dead, empty shells
which, washed ashore, absorb the vast sound of the waves
until some passerby brings it slowly to his ear, listens, and
says, The sea. Jesus's feet are bleeding, the sun pushes aside
the clouds and stabs him, thorns prick his legs like clawing
nails, thistles scratch him. Sheep, where are you, he calls,
and the hills pass on his words, Where are you, where are
you. This would be a perfect echo, but the prolonged, faraway sound of the shell imposes itself, murmuring God,
Go-o-od, Go-o-od. Then, as if the hills were suddenly swept
away, Jesus emerged from the maze of valleys into a flat
and sandy arena, his sheep right in the center. He ran to it
as fast as he could on his blistered feet, but a voice restrained him, Wait.

Slowly billowing upward like a column of smoke, a
cloud twice as tall as any man appeared before him. The
voice came from this cloud. Who speaks, Jesus asked in
terror, already knowing the reply. The voice said, I am
the Lord, and Jesus understood why he had felt the need
to remove his clothes at the edge of the desert. You brought
me here, what do You want with me. For the moment
nothing, but the day will come when I will want everything. What is everything. Your life. You are the Lord,
You always take from us the life You gave us. There is no
other way, I cannot allow the world to become overcrowded. Why do You want my life. You will know when
the time comes, therefore prepare your body and your soul,
because the destiny that awaits you is one of great good
fortune. My Lord, I do not understand what You mean or
what You want with me. I will give you power and glory.
What power, what glory. You will learn when I summon
you again. And when will that be. Do not be impatient,

220

live your life as best you can. My Lord, I stand here before You, You have brought me here naked, I beg You, give me today what You would give me tomorrow. It is not a gift. You said you would give. An exchange, nothing more than an exchange. My life in exchange for what. For power. And for glory, You said, but until I know more about this power, until You tell me what it is, over whom and in whose eyes, Your promise comes too soon. You will find Me again when you are ready, but My signs will accompany you henceforth. Lord, tell me. Be quiet, ask no more questions, the hour will come, not a second sooner or later, and then you will know what I want of you. To hear You, Lord, is to obey, but I have one more question. Stop asking Me questions. Please, Lord, I must. Very well then, speak. Can I save my sheep. So that's what's bothering you. Yes, that's all, may I. No. Why not. Because you must offer it in sacrifice to Me to seal our covenant. You mean this sheep. Yes. Let me choose another from the flock, I'll be right back. You heard Me, I want this one. But Lord, can't you see, its ear has been clipped. You are mistaken, take a good look, the ear is perfect. It isn't possible. I am the Lord, and with the Lord all things are possible. But this is my sheep. Again you are mistaken, the lamb was Mine and you took it from Me, now you will recompense Me with the sheep. Your will be done, for You rule the universe, and I am Your servant. Then offer this sheep in sacrifice, or there will be no covenant. Take pity on me, Lord, I stand here naked and have neither cleaver nor knife, said Jesus, hoping he might still be able to save the sheep's life, but God said, I would not be God if I were unable to solve this problem, here. No sooner had He finished speaking than a brand-new cleaver lay at Jesus' feet. Now quickly, said God, for I have work to do and cannot stay here chatting all day long. Grasping the cleaver by the handle, Jesus went to the sheep. It raised its head and hardly recognized him, never having seen him naked before, and as everyone knows, these animals do not have a strong sense of smell. Do you weep, God asked. The cleaver went up, took aim, and came down as swiftly as an execution-er's ax or the guillotine, which has not yet been invented. The sheep did not even whimper. All one could hear was, Ah, as God gave a deep sigh of satisfaction. Jesus asked Him, May I go now. You may, and don't forget, from now on you are tied to Me in flesh and blood. How should I take my leave of You. It doesn't matter, for Me there is no front or back, but it's customary to back away from Me, bowing as you go. Tell me, Lord. What a tiresome fellow you are, what's bothering you now. The shepherd who owns the flock, What shepherd, My master, What about him, Is he an angel or a demon, He's someone I know. But tell me, is he an angel or a demon. I've already told you, for God there is no front or back, good-bye for now. The column of smoke was gone, and the sheep too, all that remained were drops of blood, and they were trying to hide in the soil.

When Jesus returned, Pastor stared at him and asked, Where's the sheep, and he explained, I met God. I didn't ask you if you met God, I asked you if you found the sheep. I offered it in sacrifice. Whatever for. Because God was there and I had no choice. With the tip of his crook Pastor drew a line on the ground, a furrow deep as a pit, insurmountable as a wall of fire, then told him, You've learned nothing, begone with you.

How can I go anywhere with my feet in this condition, thought Jesus as he watched Pastor move to the other side of the flock. God, who had so efficiently disposed of the sheep, had not favored poor Jesus with any divine spittle from that cloud to anoint and heal the cuts on his feet, whose oozing blood glistened on the stones. And Pastor is not going to help him, he has withdrawn, expecting his command to be obeyed, he has no intention of watching Jesus prepare to leave, let alone of bidding him farewell. On hands and knees Jesus crawled to the shelter where they stored the tools for handling the sheep, the receptacles for the milk, the cheese presses, and the sheepskins and goatskins they cured before trading them for what they needed, a tunic, a mantle, provisions of every kind. Jesus thought no one would object if he used the skins to make himself a pair of shoes. The thongs he fashioned from strips of goatskin, which were less hairy and therefore more pliable, but on adjusting the shoes, he was uncertain whether the hair should be on the inside or the outside, he ended up using it as padding because of the wretched state of his feet. It would be uncomfortable if the hairs stuck to the sores, but he would be traveling along the banks of the Jordan and needed only put his shod feet into the water for the congealed blood to dissolve. The weight of those clumsy boots, for that is what they look like, when they are soaked in water, will keep the hair from adhering to the scabs without disturbing those protective crusts that are gradually forming. The color of the blood that seeped from the sores showed, a pleasant surprise, that they were not yet infected. On the slow journey northward Jesus stopped twice and sat on the riverbank to plunge his feet into the cool water, which was as good as medicine. It grieved him to be sent away in this manner, after having met God, an event unprecedented in the fullest sense of the word, for to the best of his knowledge there was not a single man in all Israel who could boast of having seen God and lived. It is true that Jesus did not exactly see Him, but if a cloud appears in the desert in the form of a pillar of smoke and says, I am the Lord, and then holds a conversation that is not only logical and sensible but so compelling that it can only be divine, then to have even the slightest doubt is unpardonable. The answer He gave when questioned about Pastor proved that He was indeed the Lord, His tone of contempt as well as of a certain intimacy, and His refusal to say whether Pastor was an angel or a demon. But the most interesting thing was that Pastor's words, unfeeling and seemingly irrelevant, actually confirmed the supernatural character of the encounter, I didn't ask you if you met God, as if to say, That much I knew already, as if the news was no surprise. But Pastor clearly blamed him for the sheep's death, those final words, You've learned nothing, begone with you, could have no other meaning, and the way he moved to the other side of the flock, his back to Jesus, until he disappeared from sight. On one of the occasions when Jesus allowed his mind to ponder what the Lord might want from him when they met again, Pastor's words suddenly came back to him as loudly and sharply as if the shepherd were standing right beside him, You've learned nothing, and at that moment the feeling of loss and solitude was so great as he sat by himself on the bank of the Jordan, watching his feet in the transparent river, a fine thread of blood suspended in the water, from a heel, that suddenly the blood and the heel no longer belonged to him, it was his father who had come there, limping on pierced feet, to find relief in the cool water of the river, and he repeated what Pastor had said, You must start all over again, for you've learned nothing. As if lifting a long, heavy iron chain from the ground, Jesus recalled his life so far, link by link, the mysterious annunciation of his conception, the earth that shone, his birth in the cave, the massacred innocents of Bethlehem, his father's crucifixion, the nightmare he had inherited, the flight from home, the debate in the Temple, the revelation of Salome, the appearance of the shepherd, his experiences with the flock, the rescued lamb, the desert, the dead sheep, God. And as if this last word was too much for his mind to encompass, he concentrated on one question, Why should a lamb rescued from death eventually die as a sheep, an absurd question if ever there was one, it might make more sense if rephrased as follows, No salvation lasts, and damnation is final. And the last link in the chain is sitting now on the bank of the Jordan, listening to the mournful song of a woman who cannot be seen from here, she is hidden among the rushes, perhaps washing clothes, perhaps bathing, while Jesus tries to understand how all these things are connected, the living lamb that became a dead sheep, his feet bleeding his father's blood, and the woman singing, naked, lying on her back in the water, firm breasts above the surface, dark pubic hair ruffled by the breeze, for though it is true that Jesus never saw a naked woman before, if a man can predict, just by encountering a simple column of smoke, what it will be like to be with God when the time comes, then why should he not be able to visualize a naked woman in every detail, assuming she is naked, merely by listening to the song she sings, even though the words are not addressed to him. Joseph is no longer here, he has returned to the common grave in Sepphoris, while Pastor, not so much as the tip of his shepherd's crook is to be seen, and God, if He is everywhere, as people say, perhaps He is now in that current, in the very water where the woman is bathing. Jesus's body received a signal, the place between his legs began to swell, as with all humans and animals, the blood rushing there, causing his sores to dry up at once. Lord, this body has such strength, yet Jesus made no attempt to go in search of the woman, and his hands resisted the violent temptation of the flesh, You are no one until you love yourself, you will not reach God until you love your body. No one knows who spoke these words, God could not have spoken them, for they are not beads from His rosary, Pastor could well have uttered them, except he is far away, so perhaps they were the words of the song the woman sang. Jesus thought, How I wish I could go there and ask her to explain, but the singing had stopped, perhaps swept away by the current, or possibly the woman simply stepped from the water to dry herself and dress, thus silencing her body. Jesus put on his wet shoes and rose to his feet, dripping water everywhere like a sponge. The woman will have a good laugh if she passes this way and sees him wearing this grotesque footwear, but she will stop laughing when her eyes take in the shape beneath his tunic and stare at length into those eyes saddened by sorrows past and present, but looking troubled now for quite a different reason. With few or no words she will remove her clothes again and offer to do what one might expect in such cases, she will take off his shoes with the utmost care and tend those sores, kissing each of his feet and then covering them with her own damp hair, as if protecting an egg or cocoon. No sign of anyone coming down the road,

Jesus looks around him, sighs, looks for a spot to conceal himself, heads there, but comes to a sudden halt, remembering in time that the Lord punished Onan with death for spilling his seed on the ground. Now, Jesus could have provided a more sophisticated interpretation of this old episode, as was his wont, and not been deterred by the Lord's inflexibility, for two reasons, the first being that he had no sister-in-law by whom he was legally bound to provide an heir for a deceased brother, the second and perhaps more compelling reason being that the Lord, according to what He told him in the desert, had definite plans for his future which were yet to be revealed, therefore it would be neither practical nor logical to forget the promise made and risk losing everything, just because an uncontrolled hand strayed where it should not have, for the Lord knows our corporal needs, which are not confined to food and drink, there are other forms of abstention just as hard to endure. These and similar reflections should have encouraged Jesus to follow his natural inclinations and find a quiet spot to satisfy his urge, but instead they distracted him and confused him so much that he soon lost the desire to yield to wicked temptation. Resigned to his own virtue, Jesus lifted the pack to his shoulder, took up his staff, and went on his way.

On the first day of his journey along the banks of the Jordan, Jesus, accustomed to a lonely existence after four years of solitude, kept clear of inhabited places. But as he approached the Lake of Gennesaret, it became increasingly difficult to avoid passing through villages, especially since they were surrounded by cultivated fields that barred his way, moreover his rough appearance aroused the suspicions of the laborers. So Jesus decided to enter the world of men, and was pleasantly surprised by what he found there, all that really bothered him was the noise, which he had forgotten. In the first village he came to, a group of rowdy urchins roared with laughter at the sight of his

227

sandal boots, no great problem, Jesus had enough money to buy new ones, remember that he has not touched any of the money he has been carrying with him since he was given two coins by the Pharisee, to live four years with few needs and no expenses has proved the greatest fortune one could have wished from the Lord. Now after buying the sandals he is left with two coins of little value, but poverty does not worry him, soon he will arrive at his destination, Nazareth, the home where he is certain to return, for on the day he left, and he feels as if he has been away forever, he said, One way or another I shall always come back. Following the thousand bends in the road along the Jordan, he travels at an easy pace, his feet are really in no condition for such a journey, but something else is slowing him down, something deep within, a vague premonition which might be expressed, The sooner I get there, the sooner I must leave. As he proceeds northward along the shore of the lake, he is already on the latitude of Nazareth, should he decide to make straight for home, all he need do is turn toward the setting sun, but he lingers by the waters of the lake, blue, wide, tranquil. He loves sitting on the shore watching the fishermen cast their nets, as a little boy he often came here with his parents, but he never stopped to watch the labors of these men who smell of fish as if they themselves lived in the sea.

As he went, Jesus earned enough to eat by doing what jobs he knew, which were none, or could do, which were few, pulling a boat ashore or pushing it into the water, helping to drag in a full net, and the fishermen, seeing how hungry he looked, would offer him a couple of fish in payment. At first Jesus felt shy and would go off to cook and eat them on his own, but after several days the fishermen invited him to join them. On the third and last day Jesus went out on the lake with two brothers, Simon and Andrew, both older than he, already in their thirties. When they were out on the open water, Jesus, who knew nothing about fishing, laughing at his own awkwardness, tried at the insistence of his new friends to cast the net with that broad gesture which seen from a distance resembles a blessing or a challenge, but he had no success, and once almost fell into the water. Simon and Andrew roared with laughter, well aware that Jesus only knew how to handle goats and sheep, and Simon said, Life would be much easier for us if this flock could be gathered and led, to which Jesus replied, At least they don't go astray or get lost, they are all here in the lake, escaping the net or falling into it day after day. The catch was disappointing, the bottom of the boat almost empty, and Andrew said, Brother, let's turn back, we're not likely to catch more fish today. Simon agreed, You're right, brother, let's go. He slipped the oars into the oarlocks and was about to start rowing to the shore when Jesus suggested, not out of any inspiration or special insight but simply from inexplicable good spirits, that they try three more times, Who knows, perhaps this watery flock, led by its shepherd, has moved to our side. Simon laughed, That's another good thing about sheep, they're visible, and turning to Andrew, told him, Cast the net over there, nothing ventured, nothing gained, whereupon Andrew cast the net and it came back full. The fishermen gasped in amazement, and their amazement turned to awe when the net was cast a second and third time and came back full both times. From water that earlier seemed devoid of fish suddenly there came pouring forth, like a fountain, fish such as never were seen before, gleaming torrents of gills, scales, and fins that left one dazed. Simon and Andrew asked Jesus how he knew that the fish would gather there, and Jesus told them he didn't know, it was impulse when he said to try again. The two brothers had no reason to doubt him, pure chance can work such miracles, but Jesus trembled inside and in the silence of his soul asked, Who did this. Simon said, Give us a hand to sort them, and we should explain now that it was

229

not from the Sea of Galilee that the ecumenical proverb originated which says, Everything that falls into the net is fish. Here different criteria prevail, the net may have caught fish, but the law, as elsewhere, is quite unambiguous, Behold what you may eat of the various aquatic species, you may eat anything in the waters, seas, and rivers that has fins and scales, but that which has neither fins nor scales, whether they be creatures that breed or that live in the water, you will shun and abhor them for all time, you will refrain from eating the flesh of everything in the water that has neither fins nor scales, and treat them as abomination. And so the despised fish with smooth skins, those that cannot be served at the table of the people of the Lord, were returned to the sea, many of them so accustomed to this by now that they no longer worried when caught in the nets, for they knew they would soon be back in the water and out of danger. With their fish mentality, they believed themselves the recipients of some special favor from the Creator, perhaps even of a special love, so that in time they came to consider themselves superior to other fish, for those in the boats must have committed grievous sins beneath the dark water for God to let them perish so mercilessly.

When the three finally reached the shore, taking every precaution not to sink, for the waters of the lake came up to the edge of the boat as if about to swallow it, the people there were dumbfounded. They could not understand how this happened, the other fishermen had returned with empty boats, but by tacit and mutual agreement the three lucky men said nothing of what had brought about their prodigious catch. Simon and Andrew did not want to see their reputations as fishermen diminished in public, while Jesus had no desire to find himself in demand as a lookout for other crews, which, it must be said, would have been only just and fair, if we could abolish once and for all the favoritism that has caused so much harm in this world. Which thought led Jesus to announce that same night that, after four years of constant trial and tribulation which could have been sent only by Satan, he would depart tomorrow for Nazareth, where his family were expecting him. This decision saddened Simon and Andrew, who regretted losing the best lookout ever celebrated in the annals of Gennesaret. And two other fishermen felt regret, these were James and John, the sons of Zebedee, two simple lads whom people used to ask in jest, Who is the father of the sons of Zebedee, throwing both of them into mortified confusion, though they knew the answer, they were obviously his sons. They regretted Jesus' departure not only because it meant no more prodigious catches but because, being younger, and John was even younger than Jesus, they had hoped to form a crew that could compete with the older men. Their simplicity had nothing to do with being stupid or retarded, they simply went through life with their thoughts elsewhere, so that they were always caught by surprise when someone asked them who was the father of the sons of Zebedee, and were always puzzled by the merriment that broke out when they replied, Zebedee, of course. John tried to dissuade Jesus, he went up to him and said, Stay with us, our boat is bigger than Simon's and we can catch more fish, to which Jesus, wise and compassionate, replied, The measure of the Lord is not that of men but the measure of His justice. John went off, crestfallen, and the evening passed without any further approaches from interested parties. Next day, Jesus bade farewell to the first friends he ever made, and with his pack replenished he turned his back on the Lake of Gennesaret where, unless he was mistaken, God had given him a sign, and set out for the mountains that led to Nazareth.

Fate decreed, however, that as he passed through the town of Magdala, a troublesome sore on his foot should open, and it looked as if it would never stop bleeding. Fate

231

also decreed that this misfortune should occur at the very edge of Magdala, directly in front of a house that stood apart, away from the other houses, as if ostracized. When the blood showed no sign of stopping, Jesus called, Anyone home, and a woman appeared in the doorway as if expecting to be called, from the lack of surprise on her face we might assume she is accustomed to people walking into the house without knocking, but on careful reflection we know this is not the case, for the woman is a prostitute, and the respect she owes her profession requires that she close her front door when she receives a client. Jesus, who was sitting on the ground and pressing the open sore, looked up as the woman approached, Help me, he said, and taking hold of her outstretched hand, he struggled to his feet and made a few faltering steps. You're in no state to be walking, she told him, come inside and let me bathe your foot. Jesus did not say yes or no, the woman's perfume was so powerful that the pain vanished as if by magic, and with one arm around her shoulders and another arm, which obviously could not be his, around his waist, he felt turmoil surge through his body, or more precisely through his senses, because it was in his senses, or at least in one of them, which is neither sight nor smell nor taste nor touch, though all of these play some part, that he felt it most, God help him. The woman helped him into the yard, closed the gate, and made him sit. Wait here, she said. She went inside and returned with an earthenware basin and a white cloth. Filling the basin with water, she wet the cloth, knelt at Jesus' feet, rested the injured foot in the palm of her left hand, and washed it gently, removing the dirt and softening the broken scab, which oozed blood and disgusting yellow pus. The woman told him, It will take more than water to heal this, but Jesus said, All I ask is that you bandage my foot so I can reach Nazareth. He was on the point of saying, My mother will treat it, but stopped himself in time, he did not wish to give the impression of being a mama's boy who has only to stub his toe on a stone and he is crying to be comforted and nursed, It's nothing, child, look, it's better already. It's a long way from here to Nazareth, the woman told him, but if that's what you want, let me rub in a little ointment. She went back into the house and seemed to take longer this time. Jesus looks around him in surprise, for he has never seen such a clean and tidy yard. He suspects the woman is a prostitute, not because he is particularly good at guessing people's professions at first glance, besides, not that long ago he himself would have been identified as a shepherd by the smell of goat, yet now everyone would say, He's a fisherman, for he lost one smell only to replace it with another. The woman reeks of perfume, but Jesus, who may be innocent, has learned certain facts of life by watching the mating of goats and rams, he also has enough common sense to know that just because a woman uses perfume, it does not necessarily mean she is a whore. A whore should smell of the men she lies with, just as the goatherd smells of goat and the fisherman of fish, but who knows, perhaps these women perfume themselves heavily because they want to conceal, disguise, or even forget the odor of a man's body. The woman reappeared with a small jar, and she was smiling, as if someone in the house had told her something amusing. Jesus saw her approach, but unless his eyes deceived him, she walked very slowly, the way it is often in dreams, her tunic flowing and revealing the curves of her body as she walked, her hips swaying, her black hair loose over her shoulders and tossing like corn silk in the wind. Her tunic was unmistakably a whore's, her body a dancer's, her laughter a whore's. Deeply troubled, Jesus searched his memory for some apt maxims by his famous namesake, Jesus the son of Sirach, and his memory obliged, whispering discreetly in his ear, Stay away from loose women lest you fall into their snares, Have nothing to do with female dancers lest you succumb to their charms, and

233

finally, Do not fall into the hands of prostitutes lest you lose your soul and all your possessions, and Jesus' soul may well be in danger now that he has reached manhood, but as for his possessions, they are in no danger, for, as we know, he possesses nothing. So he will be quite safe when the moment comes to fix a price and the woman inquires, How much money do you have.

Jesus was prepared and showed no surprise when the woman asked him his name as she rubbed ointment into the sores on his foot, which rested on her lap. I am Jesus, he replied, without adding, of Nazareth, for he had said so earlier, just as the woman who lived here was clearly from Magdala, and when he asked her name, she replied only, Mary. Having carefully examined and dressed his injured foot, Mary Magdalene tied the bandage with a firm knot, That should do, she said. How can I thank you, asked Jesus, and for the first time his eyes met hers, eyes black and bright as coals, also like water running over water, veiled with a sensuality that Jesus found irresistible. The woman did not answer at once, she looked at him as if weighing him, the boy obviously had no money, at length she said, Remember me, that is all I ask, and Jesus assured her, I will never forget your kindness, and then, summoning his courage, Nor will I forget you. Why do you say that, she asked, smiling. Because you are beautiful. You should have seen me in my youth. You are beautiful as you are. Her smile faded, Do you know what I am, what I do, how I earn my living. I do. You only had to look at me, and you knew everything. I know nothing. Not even that I'm a prostitute. That I know. I sleep with men for money. Yes. Then, as I said, you know everything about me. That is all I know. The woman sat down beside him, gently stroked his hand, touched his mouth with the tips of her fingers, If you really want to thank me, spend the day here with me. I cannot, Why, I have no money to pay you, That's no surprise. Please do not mock me. You may

234

not believe me, but I'd sooner mock a man with a full purse. It's not only a question of money. What is it, then. Jesus fell silent and turned his face away. She made no attempt to help him, she could have asked, Are you a virgin, but said nothing and waited. The silence was so great, only their hearts could be heard beating, his louder and faster, hers restless and agitated. Jesus said, Your hair reminds me of a flock of goats descending the mountain slopes of Gilead. The woman smiled but said nothing. Then Jesus said, Your eyes are like the pools of Heshbon by the Gate of Bath-Rabim. The woman smiled again but still said nothing. Then Jesus slowly turned to look at her and said, I have never been with a woman. Mary held his hands, This is how everyone has to begin, men who have never known a woman, women who have never known a man, until the day comes for the one who knows to teach the one who does not. Do you wish to teach me. So that you may thank me a second time. In this way, I will never stop thanking you. And I will never stop teaching you. Mary got to her feet, went to lock the gate, but only after hanging a sign outside, to tell any clients who might come looking for her that she had closed her window because it was now the hour to sing, Awake, north wind, and come, you south, blow upon my garden, that the spices thereof may flow out, let my beloved come into his garden and eat his pleasant fruits. Then together, Jesus' hand once more on the shoulder of Mary, this whore from Magdala who dressed his sores and is about to receive him in her bed, they went inside, into the welcome shade of a clean, fresh room. Her bed was no primitive mat on the floor with a coarse sheet on top, the sort Jesus remembered from his parents' house, this was a real bed, as once described elsewhere, I have adorned my bed with covers and embroidered sheets of Egyptian linen, I have perfumed my couch with myrrh, aloes, and cinnamon. Leading Jesus to the hearth, with its floor of brick, Mary Magdalene insisted on removing his tunic and washing him herself, stroking his body with her fingertips and kissing him softly on the chest and thighs, first one side, then the other. The delicate touch of hands and lips made Jesus shiver, the nails grazing his skin gave him gooseflesh, Don't be frightened, she whispered. She dried him and led him to the bed, Lie down, I'll be with you in a moment. She drew a curtain, there was the sound of splashing water, a pause, perfume filled the air, and Mary reappeared, completely naked. Jesus too was naked, lying as she had left him, he thought, This must be right, for to cover the body she had uncovered would give offense. Mary lingered at the side of the bed, gazed on him with an expression both passionate and tender, and told him, You are so handsome, but to be perfect you must close your eyes. Jesus hesitantly closed them, opened them again, and in that moment he understood the true meaning of King Solomon's words, Your thighs are like jewels, your navel is like a round goblet filled with scented wine, your belly is like a heap of wheat set about with lilies, your breasts are like two fawns that are the twins of a gazelle, and he understood them even better when Mary lay down beside him and took his hands in hers, and drew them to her, and guided them slowly over her body, her hair, face, neck, shoulders, her breasts, which he gently squeezed, her belly, navel, her lower hair, where he lingered, twining and untwining it with his fingers, then the curve of her smooth thighs, and as she moved his hands, she repeated in a whisper, Come, discover my body, come discover my body. Jesus breathed so fast, for one moment he thought he would faint when her hands, the left hand on his forehead, the right hand on his ankles, began caressing him, slowly coming together, meeting in the middle, then starting all over again. You've learned nothing, begone with you, Pastor had told him, and who knows, perhaps he meant to say that Jesus had not learned to cherish life. Now Mary Magdalene instructed him, Discover my body, and she said it again, but in a different way, changing one word, Discover your body, and there it was, tense, taut, roused, and she, naked and magnificent, was above him and saying, There is nothing to fear, do not move, leave this to me. Then he felt part of him, this organ, disappearing inside her, a ring of fire around it, coming and going, a shudder passed through him, like a wriggling fish slipping free with a shout, surely impossible, fish do not shout, no, it was he, Jesus, crying out as Mary slumped over his body with a moan and absorbed his cry with her lips, with a hungry kiss that sent a second, unending shudder through him.

For the rest of that day no one came to knock on Mary Magdalene's door. For the rest of that day she instructed the youth from Nazareth who came to ask her if she could relieve his pain and heal the sores which, unbeknownst to her, began with that other encounter, when Jesus met God in the desert. God had told him, Henceforth you are tied to me in flesh and blood, and the devil, if that is who he was, had spurned him, You've learned nothing, begone with you, and Mary Magdalene, the perspiration running down her breasts, her loose hair seeming to give off smoke, her lips swollen, her eyes dark pools, said, You won't stay with me because of what I taught you, but sleep here tonight. And Jesus, on top of her, replied, What you taught me is no prison but freedom. They slept together, and not only that night. When they woke, it was morning, and after their bodies sought and found each other once more, Mary examined Jesus' foot, It looks much better, but you should wait before journeying home, walking will only make it worse, not to mention all that dust. I cannot stay any longer, you yourself said my foot is much better. Of course you can stay, it's a question of wanting to, and as for the gate in the yard, that will remain locked for as long as we please. What about your life here. My life now is you. But why. Let me answer in the words of King

237

Solomon, My beloved put in his hand by the hole of the door and my heart trembled. But how can I be your beloved if you don't know me, I am simply someone who came to ask your help, on whom you took pity for his misfortune and ignorance. That is why I love you, because I helped and instructed you, but you will never love me, having neither helped nor instructed me. But you are not in pain. You will find my wound if you look carefully. What wound might that be. This open door through which others have entered, but not my beloved. You said I am your beloved. That is why the door closed behind you as you entered. There is nothing I can teach you, only what I learned from you. Teach me, so that I may know what it is like to learn from you. We cannot live together. You mean you cannot live with a whore. Yes. While you live with me, I will not be a whore, I stopped being one the moment you came into this house, and it is up to you whether or not I continue living as one. You ask too much. Nothing that you cannot give me for one or two days, or for as long as it takes your foot to heal, so that my wound may open once more. It took me eighteen years to get here. A few days more won't make much difference, you're still young. So are you. Older than you, younger than your mother. Do you know my mother, No, Then why did you mention her, Because I'm too young to have a son your age, How stupid of me. No, you're not stupid, only innocent, But I'm no longer innocent, Just because you've been with a woman, No, I lost my innocence before you. Tell me about yourself, but not just yet, for the moment all I want is to feel your left hand under my head and your right hand embracing me.

Jesus stayed in Mary Magdalene's house a week, sufficient time for new skin to form beneath the scabs. The gate remained locked. Several men, driven by lust or wounded pride, knocked impatiently at it, ignoring the sign that told them to keep away. They were curious to see this

238

fellow who took so long, one joker called over the wall, Either he isn't up to it or he has no idea what to do, open the gate, Mary, and I'll show him how it's done. Mary Magdalene went out into the yard to curse him, Whoever you are, boaster, your days of male prowess are over, so be off with you. Damned whore. That's just where you're wrong, for you won't find a woman anywhere more blessed than me. Whether it was because of this incident or because fate so decreed, no one else came knocking at the gate, most likely any man living in Magdala or passing through who heard of Mary's curse wanted to avoid the risk of being made impotent, for it is generally believed that an experienced prostitute can not only inflame a man but also kill his pride and desire forever. And so Mary and Jesus were left in peace for eight days, during which time the lessons given and received became one discourse of gestures, discoveries, surprises, murmurings, inventions, like the pieces of a mosaic that are nothing if taken one by one yet become everything when assembled and put into their proper places. Several times she asked her beloved to talk about himself, but he would change the subject and break into verses such as, I am come into my garden, my sister, my spouse, I have gathered my myrrh with my spice, I have eaten my honeycomb with my honey, I have drunk my wine with my milk, which he recited with passion before partaking of the poetic act itself, verily, verily, I say unto you, dear Jesus, this is no way to hold a conversation. But one day he told her about his father who was a carpenter and his mother who carded wool, about his brothers and sisters, and how he had started to learn his father's trade before going off to be a shepherd for four years, but now he was returning home. He also mentioned the few days he spent on the lake with some fishermen without mastering their skills. Then one evening, when they were eating out in the yard, Jesus took Mary Magdalene into his confidence, and from time to time they looked up at the rapid flight of swallows passing overhead with strident cries. The two, to judge from their silence, have nothing more to say to each other, the man has confessed all to the woman, but she asks, as if disappointed, Is that all, and nodding, he says, Yes, that's all.

The silence deepened, the circling swallows went elsewhere, and Jesus said, My father was crucified four years ago in Sepphoris, his name was Joseph. And you are his eldest son. Yes, I'm the eldest. Then I don't understand, surely you should be looking after your family. We quarreled, but don't ask me any more. No more about your family, then, but what about your time as a shepherd, tell me about that. There's nothing to tell, every day the same thing, goats, sheep, kids, lambs, and milk, lots of milk, milk everywhere. Did you enjoy being a shepherd. Yes, I did. Then why did you leave. I became restless, began to miss my family, felt homesick. Homesick, what is that. Sadness at being so far away. You're lying, Why do you think I'm lying, Because I see not sadness but fear and guilt in your eyes. Jesus did not reply, he got up, walked around the yard, then stopped in front of Mary, One day, if we should meet again, I'll tell you the rest if you promise not to tell anyone. Why not tell me now. I'll tell you when we meet again. You hope that by then I will have given up prostitution, you still don't trust me, you think I might sell your secrets for money or pass them on to the first man who turns up, for amusement or in exchange for a night of love more glorious than those you and I have shared. No, that's not the reason for my silence. Well, I promise you that Mary Magdalene, prostitute or not, will be at your side whenever you need her. Who am I to deserve this. Don't you know who you are.

That night the nightmare returned. It had been more bearable of late, a vague anguish that only occasionally disturbed his sleep, but this night, perhaps because it was the last night Jesus was to sleep in Mary's bed, perhaps be-

240

cause he had mentioned Sepphoris and the men crucified there, the nightmare began to uncoil in twists and turns like a huge snake awakening from hibernation, and to raise its hideous head. Jesus woke with a start, crying out in terror, his body covered with cold sweat. What's wrong, Mary asked in alarm. I was dreaming, only dreaming, he said evasively. Tell me, and those simple words were said with so much love and tenderness that Jesus could not hold back his tears, and after much weeping he revealed what he had hoped to withhold, I dream over and over that my father is coming to kill me. But your father is dead and you are still alive. In my dream I'm still a child back in Bethlehem of Judaea, and my father is coming to kill me. Why in Bethlehem. That's where I was born. Perhaps you think your father didn't want you to be born, and that is why you have this dream. You don't know what happened. No, I don't. Children in Bethlehem died because of my father. Did he kill them. He killed them because he made no attempt to save them, although his was not the hand that drew the sword. And in your dream, are you one of those children. I have died a thousand deaths. Poor man, poor Jesus. That is why I left home. I begin to understand, You think you understand, What more is there to know, What I cannot reveal yet, You mean what you will tell me when we meet again, That's right. Resting his hand on Mary's shoulder, his cheek on her breast, Jesus fell asleep. She stayed awake throughout the night, her heart aching, for it would soon be morning and time to separate. But her soul was at peace, she knew that this man in her arms was the one for whom she had been waiting all her life, the one who belonged to her and to whom she belonged, his body pure, hers defiled, but their world is just beginning. They have been together eight days, but only tonight was their union confirmed, and eight days is nothing compared to a whole future, for this Jesus who has come into my life is so young, and here am I, Mary

Magdalene, in bed with a man, as so often in the past, but this time deep in love and ageless.

They spent the morning preparing for the journey. One would have thought young Jesus was traveling to the end of the world, while in fact he had no more than twenty miles to cover, a distance any healthy man could walk between noon and dusk, notwithstanding the rough road from Magdala to Nazareth, with its steep slopes and rocky terrain. Take care, Mary warned him, you may run into rebel forces still fighting the Romans. After all this time, asked Jesus. You haven't lived here, this is Galilee. But I'm a native of Galilee, they're not likely to do me any harm. You can't be Galilean if you were born in Bethlehem of Judaea. My parents conceived me in Nazareth, and to be honest, I wasn't even born in Bethlehem, I was born in a cave in the earth, and now I feel reborn here in Magdala. Mothered by a whore. You're no whore in my eyes, said Jesus strongly. Alas, that is the life I've led. These words were followed by a long silence, Mary waiting for Jesus to speak, Jesus trying to still his uneasiness. Finally he asked her, Do you intend to remove the sign you hung on the gate to keep men from entering. Mary looked at him with a serious expression, then smiled mischievously, I could not possibly have two men in the house at the same time. What are you saying. Simply that you are leaving but will still be here. She paused, then added, The sign on the gate remains there. People will think you're with a man. And they'll be right, I'll be with you. Are you telling me no man will ever pass through that gate again. Yes, because this woman they call Mary Magdalene stopped being a prostitute the moment you walked into her house. But how will you live. Only the lilies in the fields thrive without working or spinning. Jesus took her hands and said, Nazareth isn't far from Magdala, one day I will return. If you come looking for me, you'll find me here. My desire is to find you all my life. You will find me even after death.

242

You mean I will die before you. I'm older than you, so most likely I will die first, but if you die before me, I will go on living so that you may find me. And if you die first. Then blessed be the woman who brought you into the world during my lifetime. After this conversation, Mary served Jesus food, and he did not have to tell her, Sit with me, for since their first day together behind locked doors this man and this woman have divided and multiplied between them feelings, gestures, spaces, and sensations without paying much attention to the rules and laws. They certainly would not know what to say if we were to ask them how they would behave outside the privacy of these four walls, where they have been free for some days to forge a world in the simple image and likeness of a man and a woman. A world that is more hers than his, let it be said, but since they are both so confident about meeting again, we need only have the patience to wait for the time when, side by side, they will confront the outside world, where people are already asking themselves anxiously, What's going on in there, and they don't mean the usual antics in the bedroom. After they had eaten, Mary helped Jesus into his sandals and told him, You must leave if you're to reach Nazareth before nightfall. Farewell, said Jesus, and taking up his pack and staff, he went out into the yard. The sky was covered with clouds as if lined with unwashed wool, the Lord must not be finding it easy today to keep an eye on His sheep from on high. Jesus and Mary Magdalene embraced a long time before exchanging a farewell kiss, which did not take long at all, and little wonder, for kissing was not the custom then.

243

THE SUN HAD JUST SET WHEN JESUS ARRIVED IN NAZARETH, four long years, give or take a week, from the day he left, a mere child driven by desperation to go out into the world in search of someone who might help him understand the unbearable truth about his birth. Four years, however long, may not be enough to heal one's sorrow, but they should bring some relief. He had asked questions in the Temple, traveled mountain paths with the devil's flock, met God, and slept with Mary Magdalene. Reaching Nazareth, he no longer gives the appearance of suffering, except for those tears in his eyes, but that could also be a delayed reaction to the smoke from the sacrifices, or sudden joy in his soul upon looking down at the town from a high pasture, or the fear of a man alone in the desert who has heard a voice say, I am the Lord, or, most likely, for most recent, yearning for the woman he left only a few hours ago, I have comforted myself with raisins, I have strengthened myself with apples, for I am swooning with love.

Jesus might recite these sweet words to his mother and brothers, but he pauses on the threshold to ask himself,

244

My mother and brothers, not that he does not know who they are, the question is, do they know who he is now, he who asked questions in the Temple, who watched the horizon, who met God, who has experienced carnal love and discovered his manhood. Before this same door once stood a beggar who claimed to be an angel, who if he really was an angel could have burst into the house with a great commotion of ruffled wings, yet he preferred to knock and to beg for alms like any pauper. The door is only latched. Jesus does not need to call out as he did in Magdala, he can walk calmly into his own home, the sores on his feet are completely healed, but then sores that bleed and fester are the quickest healed. There was no need to knock, but he did. He had heard voices over the wall, recognized the voice of his mother coming from farther away, yet could not summon the courage simply to push the door open and announce, I'm here, like one who knows his arrival is welcome and wishes to give a pleasant surprise. The door was opened by a little girl about eight or nine years old, who did not recognize the visitor, the voice of blood and kinship did not come to his assistance by telling her, This is your brother Jesus, don't you remember him. Instead he said, despite the four years that had passed since they last saw each other and despite the fading light, You must be Lydia, and she answered, Yes, amazed that a complete stranger should know her name, but the spell was broken when he said, I'm your brother Jesus, may I come in. In the yard under the lean-to adjoining the house he could see shadowy figures, probably his brothers, now they were looking in the direction of the door, and two of them, the oldest, James and Joseph, approached. They had not heard Jesus' words, but didn't need to go to the trouble of identifying the visitor, for Lydia was already calling out excitedly, It's Jesus, it's our brother, whereupon the shadows stirred and Mary appeared in the doorway, accompanied by Lisa, the other daughter, almost as tall now as her

245

mother, and both of them called out with one voice, My
son, My brother, and the next moment they were all embracing in joyful reunion in the middle of the yard, always
a happy event, but especially when it is the eldest son returning. Jesus greeted his mother, then each of his brothers, and was greeted warmly by all of them, Brother Jesus,
how good to see you again, Brother Jesus, we thought
you had forgotten us, but no one said, Brother Jesus, you
don't look any richer. They went inside and sat down to
the meal his mother had been preparing when he knocked
at the door. One could almost say to Jesus, coming as he
does from where he does, having indulged his sinful flesh
and kept bad company, one could almost say with the brutal frankness of simple people who suddenly see their share
of food diminish, When it's time to eat, the devil always
brings an extra mouth to feed. No one present dared put
this thought into words, and it would have been wrong if
he had, an extra mouth makes little difference when there
are already nine to feed. Besides, the new arrival has more
right to be here than any of them. During supper, the
younger children wanted to know about his adventures,
while the three older children and Mary observed that there
had been no change in his occupation since their meeting
in Jerusalem, for the smell of fish has long since disappeared, and the wind swept away the sensuous perfume of
Mary Magdalene, and don't forget all the sweat and dust
acquired on the road, unless one were to take a close sniff
at Jesus' tunic, but if his own family did not take such a
liberty, why should we. Jesus told them how he had tended
one of the largest flocks ever seen, how he had recently
been on a lake helping fishermen bring in the most extraordinary catch of fish, and that he had also experienced
the most wonderful adventure any man could imagine or
hope for, but he would tell them about it some other time
and then only some of them. The younger children pleaded,
Tell us, please tell us, and Judas, the middle brother, asked

him in all innocence, Did you make a lot of money while you were away, to which Jesus replied, Not so much as three coins, or two, or even one, nothing, and seeing disbelief on their faces, he emptied his pack without further ado. And truly, he had little to show for his labors, his only belongings a metal knife that was worn and bent, a bit of string, a chunk of bread as hard as a rock, two pairs of sandals reduced to tatters, the remnants of an old tunic. This belonged to your father, said Mary, stroking the tunic, then the larger pair of sandals, she told him, These too were his. The others lowered their heads in memory of their dead father.

Jesus was putting everything back into his pack when he felt a large, heavy knot in the hem of the tunic. The blood rushed to his face, it could only be money, money that he had denied possessing and that must have been put there by Mary Magdalene, and therefore earned not in the sweat of one's brow as dignity demands but with sinful groans and sweat of another kind. His mother and brothers looked at the knot, then all looked at him. Uncertain whether to try to conceal the proof of his deception or bluff his way out without really explaining, Jesus chose the more difficult way. He untied the knot and revealed the treasure, twenty coins the likes of which had never been seen in this house, and said, I had no idea this money was here. Their silent rebuke passed through the air like a hot desert wind, how shameful, the eldest son and caught telling such a lie. Jesus searched his heart but could not be angry with Mary Magdalene, he felt nothing but gratitude for her generosity, this touching act of giving him money she knew he would have been ashamed to accept openly, for it is one thing to say, Your left hand is under my head and your right hand embraces me, and another not to remember that other hands have embraced her. Now it is Jesus who looks at his family, defying them to doubt his word, I had no idea this money was here, which is true

247

but not quite the whole truth, daring them to ask him the question to which there is no answer, If you didn't know you had this money, how do you account for its being here now. He cannot tell them, A prostitute with whom I spent the last eight days put the coins here, money she received from the men she slept with before I came. Scattered on the soiled, threadbare tunic of the man who was crucified four years ago and whose remains were shamefully thrown into a common grave, the twenty coins shine like the luminous earth that one night struck terror in this same household, but no elders will come from the synagogue this time to say, The coins must be buried, just as no one here will ask, Where do they come from, lest the reply oblige us to give them up against our will. Jesus gathers the money into the palms of his hands and says once more, I didn't know I had these coins, as if giving his family one last chance, and then, glancing at his mother, says, It is not the devil's money. His brothers shuddered in horror, but Mary replied without showing any anger, Nor did it come from God. Jesus playfully tossed the coins into the air, once, twice, and said as naturally as if he were announcing he would return to his carpenter's bench the next day, Mother, we'll discuss God in the morning. Then turning to his brothers James and Joseph, he added, I also have something to say to you, and this was no condescending gesture, for both brothers are now of age according to their religion and therefore entitled to be taken into his confidence. But James felt that given the importance of the occasion, something ought to be said beforehand about the justification for the promised conversation, since no brother, however senior, can expect to appear unannounced and say, We must have a talk about God. So with a bland smile he said to Jesus, If, as you say, you traveled hill and dale four years as a shepherd, there couldn't have been much time to attend the synagogue and acquire so much knowledge that no sooner do you return home than

248

you want to talk to us about the Lord. Jesus sensed the barb beneath these words and replied, Ah, James, how little you understand God if you think we have to go in search of Him when He has decided to come to us. Am I right in thinking you refer to yourself. Save your questions until tomorrow, when I will tell you all I have to say. James muttered to himself, no doubt making some sour comment about people who think they know everything. Mary, turning to Jesus with a weary expression on her face, said, You can tell us tomorrow, or the day after tomorrow, or whenever you like, but for now tell us what you intend to do with this money, for we are in great difficulty. Don't you want to know where it came from. You said you didn't know. That's the truth, but I've been thinking and can guess how it got there. If the money doesn't taint your hands, then it won't taint ours. Is that all you have to say about this money. Yes. Then let us spend it, as is only right, on the family. There was a general murmur of approval, even James seemed satisfied with this decision, and Mary said, If you don't mind, we'll put some of the money aside for your sister's dowry. You didn't say anything about Lisa getting married. Yes, in the spring. Tell me how much you need. That depends on what those coins are worth. Jesus smiled and said, I'm afraid I don't know what they are worth, only their value. He laughed, amused by his own words, and the family looked at him in bewilderment. Only Lisa lowered her eyes, she is fifteen, still innocent, but has all the mysterious intuition of adolescence. Among those present, she is the most troubled about the money. Jesus gave a coin to his mother, You can change it tomorrow, then we'll know what it's worth. Someone is sure to ask me where it came from, thinking that whoever posesses such a coin must have others hidden away. Simply tell them that your son Jesus has returned, and that there is no greater fortune than the return of a prodigal son.

That night Jesus dreamed of his father. He had settled down to sleep in the lean-to rather than with all the others inside. He could not bear the idea of sleeping in the same room with ten people, each trying unsuccessfully to get a little privacy, they are no longer like a flock of little lambs but growing fast, all legs and arms and far from comfortable in such cramped quarters. Before falling asleep, he thought about Mary Magdalene and everything they had done together, which stirred him to such a pitch that he had to get up twice and walk in the yard to cool his blood, but when sleep finally came, he slept as peacefully as a small child, it was as if his body were floating slowly downstream while he watched branches and clouds pass overhead, and a silent bird flying back and forth. No sooner did the dream begin than he felt a slight jolt, as if he had brushed against another. He thought it was Mary Magdalene and smiled, and smiling turned his head in her direction, but the body drifting past, carried by the same current beneath the sky and branches and the fluttering silent bird, was that of his father. The usual cry of terror formed in his throat but stopped there, this was not his usual dream, he was not an infant in a public square in Bethlehem awaiting death with other children, there was no sound of footsteps, no neighing of horses or clanking and scraping of weapons, there was only the gentle murmur of water and the two bodies forming a raft as father and son were carried along by the river. All the fear went out of Jesus. Overcome with a feeling of exultation, he called out, Father, in his dream, Father, he repeated, awakening, but now with tears in his eyes, realizing he was alone. He tried to revive his dream, to repeat it, to feel again the brushing jolt and find his father beside him, so that they might float together on these waters to the end of time. He did not succeed that night, but the first dream never returned, from now on he will experience elation instead of fear, companionship instead of solitude, promised life instead of immi-

250

nent death. Now let the wise men of Holy Scripture explain, if they can, the meaning of Jesus' dream, the significance of this river, the overhanging branches, the drifting clouds, and the silent bird, which made it possible for father and son to be united even though the guilt of the one cannot be pardoned or the sorrow of the other relieved.

The following day Jesus offered to help James with some carpentry, but it soon became clear that good intentions were no substitute for the skills he lacked and had never fully acquired even by the time Joseph died. To meet their father's customers' needs, James had become a reliable carpenter, and even young Joseph, who was not yet fourteen, already knew enough to have been able to teach his eldest brother had such disrespect for seniority been allowed within the strict family hierarchy. James laughed at Jesus' clumsiness and told him, Whoever turned you into a shepherd led you astray, words of lighthearted irony that no one would have suspected of concealing any deeper meaning, but Jesus rose abruptly from the workbench, and Mary rebuked her second son, Speak not of perdition, lest you summon Satan and bring evil into our home. Taken aback, James protested, But I summoned no one, Mother, all I said was, We know what you said, interrupted Jesus, Mother and I heard what you said, it was Mother who linked the word shepherd with perdition, not you, and you don't know why, but she does. I warned you, Mary said. You warned me when the evil had already been done, if it was evil, for when I look at myself, I cannot see it, said Jesus, whereupon Mary told him, There are none so blind as those who will not see. These words annoyed Jesus, and he said reproachfully, Be quiet, Mother, if your son's eyes saw evil, they saw it after you, but these same eyes you call blind have also seen things you've never seen or are likely to see. Her son's authority and stern tone, and the strange thing he said, made Mary yield, but her reply conveyed a final warning, Forgive me, I didn't mean to offend you, may the Lord always protect the light in your eyes and soul. James looked at his mother, then at his brother, saw there was a disagreement but could not imagine what had caused it, clearly something from the past, because his brother had not been back long enough to start an argument. Jesus made for the house, but at the door he turned and said to his mother, Send the children out to play, I must talk to you in private along with James and Joseph. The others left, and the house, which had been so crowded a moment ago, suddenly seemed empty. Four now sat on the floor, Mary between James and Joseph, with Jesus facing them. A long silence followed, as if by common consent they were giving the children time to go far enough away. Finally Jesus spoke, pronouncing his words carefully, I have seen God. The first reaction on the faces of his mother and brothers was awe, followed by disbelief, and between the one and the other there was a hint of cynical mistrust in James's expression, of wonder in that of Joseph, of resigned bitterness in that of Mary. All three remained silent, and Jesus said a second time, I have seen God. If a moment of silence, as the saying goes, marks the passage of an angel, here angels are still passing. Jesus has said all there is to say, his family is at a loss for words, and soon they will rise to their feet and go about their affairs, wondering if this was all a dream. Yet silence, given enough time, has the power to make people speak. Unable to control himself any longer, James asked a question, the most innocent question of all, pure of rhetoric, Are you sure. Jesus did not reply, simply looked at James, perhaps as God had looked at him from within the cloud, and for the third time said, I have seen God. Mary, who had no questions to ask, said, You must have imagined it. Jesus replied, Mother, God spoke to me. James, having recovered his composure, decided this must be some kind of madness, a brother of his speaking to God, how ridiculous, Well, who knows, perhaps it was God who put the money in your pack, he said, smiling ironically. Jesus reddened but spoke coldly, Everything comes to us from the Lord, He is forever finding paths to reach us, and although this money may not have come from Him, it certainly came through Him. And what did the Lord say to you, where did you see Him, and were you asleep or keeping watch. I was in the desert looking for a stray sheep when He called out to me. Are you allowed to tell us what He said. That one day He will ask for my life. All lives belong to the Lord. That's what I told Him. And what did He say. That in exchange for the life I must give Him, I will have power and glory. You will have power and glory after you die, asked Mary, unable to believe her ears. Yes, Mother. What power and glory can be given to someone after death. I don't know. Were you dreaming. I was awake and looking for my sheep in the desert. And when is the Lord going to ask you for your life. I don't know, but He told me we would meet again when I was ready. James looked at his brother in dismay, The sun in the desert affected your brain, you've been suffering from sunstroke, but Mary suddenly asked, And what about the sheep, what happened to the sheep. The Lord ordered me to sacrifice it to seal our covenant. These words provoked James, You're offending the Lord, the Lord made a covenant with His people and He's not likely to make one with an ordinary man like you, the son of a carpenter, a shepherd, and who knows what else. Mary appeared to be following some thread of thought carefully, as if it might break, but by persevering she found the question she had to ask, What sheep was that. The lamb I had with me when we met in Jerusalem at the Gate of Ramah, in the end what I tried to keep from the Lord the Lord took from me. And God, what did God look like when you saw Him. A cloud. Open or closed, asked James. A column of smoke. You're mad, brother. If I am mad, God made me mad. You're in Satan's power, said Mary, shouting more than speaking. It wasn't Satan I met in the

253

desert, it was the Lord, and if it's true that I'm in Satan's power, then the Lord has so ordained. You've been in the clutches of Satan since the day you were born. You ought to know. Yes, I know all right, you chose to live with the devil for four long years rather than with God. And after spending four years with the devil, I met God. You're telling the most awful lies. I'm the son you brought into the world, either believe me or renounce me. I believe you, but not what you say. Jesus got to his feet, raised his eyes to heaven, and said, When the Lord's promise is fulfilled, you will have to believe what people say of me. He went to get his pack and staff and put on his sandals. Dividing the money in two parts, arranging the coins side by side on the ground, he said, This is Lisa's dowry when she marries, and added, The rest will be returned where it came from, and perhaps also be used as a dowry. He turned to the door, was about to leave without saying good-bye, when Mary remarked, I noticed you no longer carry a bowl in your pack. I had one, but it broke. There are four bowls over there, choose one and take it with you. Jesus hesitated, preferring to leave empty-handed, but he went to the hearth where the four bowls were stacked one on top of the other. Choose one, Mary said again. Jesus looked and chose, I'll take this one, which has seen better days. You picked the right one for you, said Mary. Why do you say that. It's the color of the black earth, it neither disintegrates nor breaks. Jesus put the bowl into his pack, tapped his staff on the ground, Tell me once more that you don't believe me. We don't believe you, said his mother, and now less than ever, because you chose the devil's symbol. What symbol are you talking about. That bowl. At that very moment Pastor's words came to Jesus from the depths of memory, You will have another bowl, but the next won't break while you are alive. A rope seemed to have been extended its full length, ending in a circle and tied with a knot. Jesus was leaving home for the second time, but this time he did not say, One way or another I shall always come back. As he turned his back on Nazareth and began descending the first mountain slope, an even sadder thought crossed his mind, What if Mary Magdalene did not believe him either.

This man who carries God's promise with him has nowhere to go except the house of a prostitute. He cannot return to his flock, Begone with you, were Pastor's last words to him, nor can he return home, We don't believe you, his family told him, and his steps begin to falter, he is afraid to proceed, to arrive. It is as if he were back in the desert, Who am I, but the mountains and valleys do not answer, nor the heavens, which ought to know everything. If he goes back now and repeats the question, his mother will say, You're my son, but I don't believe you, so the time has come for Jesus to sit on this stone that has been reserved for him since the world began, to sit and shed tears of misery and loneliness. Who knows, perhaps the Lord will appear to him once more, even if only in the form of smoke, all He has to say is, Come, there's no need for all this weeping and wailing, what's the matter with you, we all have our bad moments, and there's one important thing I should have mentioned earlier, everything is relative in life, and every misfortune becomes bearable when compared with something worse, so dry your tears and behave like a man, you've already made your peace with your father, what more do you want, and as for this friction with your mother, I'll deal with that when the time comes, what didn't please Me much was that business with Mary Magdalene, a common whore, but then you're still young and might as well enjoy life while you can, the one thing doesn't rule out the other, there's a time for eating and a time for fasting, a time for sinning and a time for repenting, a time for living and a time for dying. Jesus wiped his tears on the back of his hand, blew his nose, who knows where, and yes, there is no point spending the whole day here, the desert is what it is, it surrounds us, in some ways protects us, but when it comes to giving, it gives us nothing, it simply looks on, and when the sun suddenly clouds over, so that we find ourselves thinking, The sky mirrors our sorrow, we are being foolish, because the sky is quite impartial and neither rejoices in our happiness nor is cast down by our grief.

People are heading in this direction on their way to Nazareth, and Jesus, a grown man with a beard, does not wish to be seen crying like a child. From time to time a few travelers pass one another on the road, some going up, others coming down, they greet one another effusively, but only after they are certain of their mutual goodwill, for the bandits in these parts are of two types. There are those who assault travelers, like the heartless rogues who robbed Jesus some five years ago when the poor boy was on his way to Jerusalem to find solace. Then there are the rebels, who certainly do not make a habit of traveling the main roads, but they sometimes appear in disguise to spy on the movements of Roman troops before setting up the next ambush, or without any disguise they'll stop wealthy travelers collaborating with the Romans and strip them of their silver, gold, and other valuables, and even well-armed bodyguards are powerless to spare the travelers this outrage. It was natural for the eighteen-year-old Jesus to sigh for adventure as he gazed on those lofty mountains with the ravines and caves where the followers of Judas the Galilean continued to take refuge. He wondered what he would do if a band of rebels appeared from nowhere and invited him to join them, exchanging the amenities of peace for the glory of battle, for it is written that one day the Lord will bring forth a Messiah, who will deliver His people once and for all from oppression and give them strength against future enemies. A gust of mad hope and pride blows like a sign from the Spirit on Jesus' forehead, and for one spellbinding moment this carpenter's son sees himself as captain, leader, and supreme commander, with raised sword, his very presence striking awe and terror in the Roman legions, who throw themselves over precipices like pigs possessed by demons, so much for Senatus Populusque Romanus. Then Jesus remembered that he was promised power and glory, but only after his death, so he might as well enjoy life, and if he must go to war, let it be on one condition, that occasionally he will be allowed to leave the lines and spend a few days with Mary Magdalene, unless they allow one female companion for each soldier, anything more would lead to promiscuity and Mary has already said she has given that up. Let us hope so, for Jesus feels his strength redouble at the thought of the woman who cured his painful wound, which she replaced with the intolerable wound of desire. But here is the problem, how is he to face the locked gate with the sign unless he is absolutely certain he will find on the other side the woman he believes he left behind, who waits for him and him alone, in body and soul, because Mary Magdalene will not accept one without the other.

The day is drawing to a close, the houses of Magdala can be seen in the distance huddled together like a flock. Mary's house, the sheep that wandered off, cannot be seen from here, amid the great boulders that line the road bend after bend. Jesus remembers the sheep he had to kill in order to seal in blood the covenant demanded by the Lord, and his soul, now free of battles and victories, warms at the thought of searching once more for his sheep, not to kill it or lead it back to the flock but so that together they can climb to fresh pastures, which are still to be found if we look carefully enough in this vast and much traveled world, if we look even closer into those impenetrable gorges, sheep that we are. Jesus stopped in front of the door and discreetly confirmed that it was locked. The sign still hangs there, Mary Magdalene is not receiving anyone. Jesus need only call out, It's me, to hear her joyfully sing,

This is the voice of my beloved, behold him who has come leaping over mountains and jumping over hills, there he waits on the other side of this wall, behind this door, and it is true, but Jesus would rather knock on the door, once, twice, without uttering a word, waiting for someone to open. Who's there, what do you want, someone asked from within. Jesus disguised his voice, pretending to be an eager client with money to spend, using words such as, Open up, flower, you won't regret it, I'll pay and service you well, and if the voice was false, his words were true enough when he said, I'm Jesus of Nazareth. Mary Magdalene did not open, the voice did not quite match the words, besides she thought it unlikely that Jesus could be back so soon, when he had said, One day I'll come, Nazareth isn't far from Magdala, after all. People often say such things to please the listener, and one day might mean three months but never tomorrow. Mary Magdalene opens the door, throws herself into Jesus' arms, cannot believe her good fortune. In her excitement she foolishly imagines that he has come back because the sore on his foot reopened, so she leads him inside, sits him down, and fetches the lamp, Your foot, show me your foot, but Jesus tells her, My foot has healed, can't you see. She could have replied, No, I can't, which was true, for her eyes were filled with tears. She had to put her lips to the sole of his foot, which was covered with dust, untie carefully the thongs attaching the sandal to his ankle, and stroke with her fingertips the new skin which had formed, in order to verify that the ointment had done its work, though perhaps love too had played some part in the cure.

During supper she asked no questions, only wanted to know if he had had a good journey or encountered any unpleasantness on the road, small talk and nothing more. When they finished eating, there was a long silence, for it was not her turn to speak. Jesus regarded her, as if from a high rock he were weighing his strength against the sea, not because he feared man-eating fish or dangerous reefs beneath the smooth surface, he was simply putting his courage to the test. He has known this woman for a week, sufficient time to tell whether she will receive him with open arms, yet he is afraid to reveal, now that the moment has come, what has just been rejected by those of his own flesh and blood, who should have been with him also in spirit. Jesus hesitates, tries to find words, but all that comes out is a phrase to gain time, Weren't you surprised to see me back so soon. I began waiting for you the moment you left and did not count the hours between your leaving and returning, nor should I have counted them had you stayed away for ten years. Jesus smiled, he should have known there was no point being evasive with this woman. They sat on the ground, facing each other, a lamp in the middle and the leftovers from their supper. He took a piece of bread, broke it in two, and giving a piece to her, said, Let this be the bread of truth, let us eat it so that we may believe and never doubt, whatever is said and learned here. So be it, said Mary Magdalene. He ate his bread, waited for her to finish hers, and said, for the fourth time, I have seen God. Her expression did not change, she only fidgeted, her hands crossed on her lap, and asked, Was this what you said you would tell me when we met again. Yes, as well as all the other things that have happened to me since I left home four years ago, I feel they are all linked, although I cannot explain how or why. I am your lips and ears, replied Mary Magdalene, whatever you say, you will be saying it to yourself, for I am inside you. Now Jesus can begin to speak, for they have both partaken of the bread of truth, and there are few such moments in life. Night turned to dawn, the flame in the lamp died twice, and Jesus' entire history as we know it was related there, even including certain details we didn't consider worthwhile mentioning and countless thoughts that escaped us, not because he tried to conceal them but simply because this evangelist cannot be everywhere at once. As Jesus began telling in a weary voice what happened after he returned home, grief caused him to waver, just as dark foreboding had made him pause before knocking at the door. Breaking her silence for the first time, Mary Magdalene asked him in a voice of one who already knows the answer, Your mother didn't believe you. That's right, said Jesus. And so you came back to your other home. Yes. If only I could lie to you and tell you that I don't believe you. Why. So that you would do again what you've just done, leave as you left your home, and I, not believing you, would not have to follow you. That doesn't answer my question. True, it is not an answer, well then, if I did not believe you, I would not have to share the dreadful fate that awaits you. How do you know a dreadful fate awaits me. I know nothing about God, except that His pleasure is as terrifying as His displeasure. Whatever put that strange idea into your head. You have to be a woman to know what it means to live with God's contempt, and now you'll have to be more than a man to live and die as one of His chosen. Are you trying to frighten me. Let me tell you my dream, one night a little boy appeared to me and told me God was horrible, and with those words he disappeared, I have no idea who that child was, where he came from, or who he belonged to. It's only a dream. You of all people speaking of a dream that way. And then what happened. Then I turned to prostitution. But you've given that up. Not in the dream, not even after I met you. Tell me again what the child said. God is horrible. Jesus saw the desert, the dead sheep, the blood on the sand, heard the column of smoke sighing with satisfaction, and said, Yes, that could be, but it's one thing to hear it in a dream and another to experience it in real life. God forbid that you should ever experience it. Each of us has to fulfill his destiny. And you've been given the first solemn warning about yours. Studded with stars, the heavenly dome turns slowly over

Magdala and the wide world. Somewhere in the infinite that He occupies, God advances and withdraws the pawns of the other games He plays, but it is too soon to worry about this one, all He need do for the present is allow things to take their natural course, apart from the occasional adjustment with the tip of His little finger to make sure some stray thought or action does not interfere with the harmony of destinies. Hence His lack of interest in the rest of the conversation between Jesus and Mary Magdalene. And now what will you do, she asks him. You said you would follow me wherever I go. I will be with you wherever you are. What is the difference. None at all, but you can stay here as long as you like, if you don't mind living in what was once a house of sin. Jesus paused, reflected at length, and finally said, I will find work in Magdala, and we can live together as husband and wife. You promise too much, I'm quite content just to sit here at your feet.

Jesus found no work, and met with what he might have expected, jeers, ridicule, insults, which was not surprising, for here was a mere youth living with the notorious Mary Magdalene, It won't be long before we see him sitting at the front door waiting his turn like all her other clients. He tolerated their jibes for several weeks, but finally he said to Mary, I must get away from this place. But where can we go. Somewhere by the sea. They left before dawn, and the people of Magdala came too late to salvage anything from the flames.

MONTHS LATER, ON A COLD AND RAINY WINTER NIGHT, AN angel entered the house of Mary of Nazareth without disturbing anyone. Mary herself only noticed the visitor because the angel spoke to her as follows, Know, Mary, that the Lord mixed His seed with that of Joseph on the morning you conceived for the first time, and it was the Lord's seed rather than that of your husband, however legitimate, that sired your son Jesus. Much surprised, Mary asked the angel, So Jesus is my son and also the son of the Lord. Woman, what are you saying, show some respect for precedence, the way you should put it is the son of the Lord and also of me. Of the Lord and also of you. No, of the Lord and of you. You confuse me, just answer my question, is Jesus our son. You mean to say the Lord's son, because you only served to bear the child. So the Lord didn't choose me. Don't be absurd, the Lord was merely passing, as anyone watching would have seen from the color of the sky, when His eye caught you and Joseph, a fine, healthy couple, and then, if you can still remember how God's will was made manifest, He ordained that Jesus be born nine months later. Is there any proof that it was the Lord's seed that sired my firstborn. Well, it's a delicate matter, what you're demanding is nothing less than a paternity test, which in these mixed unions, no matter how many analyses, tests, and genetic comparisons one carries out, can never give conclusive results. There I was thinking the Lord had chosen me for His bride that morning, and now you tell me it was pure chance and He could just as easily have chosen someone else, well, let me tell you, I wish you hadn't descended to Nazareth to leave me in this state of uncertainty, besides, surely any son of the Lord, even with me as the mother, would have stood out at birth and, growing up, would have had the same bearing, appearance, and manner of speaking as the Lord himself, and though people say a mother's love is blind, my son Jesus looks ordinary enough to me. Your first mistake, Mary, is to think I came here only to discuss some sexual episode in the Lord's past, and your second mistake is to think that the beauty and speech of mankind resemble those of the Lord, when I can vouch, as someone close to Him, that the Lord's way of doing things is invariably the opposite of what humans imagine, and strictly between us, I'm convinced the Lord couldn't operate in any other fashion, and the word most frequently on His lips is not yes but no. But surely it's the devil who's the spirit of denial. No, my child, the devil only denies himself, and until you learn to tell the difference, you'll never know to whom you belong. I belong to the Lord. So you belong to the Lord, do you, well your third and biggest mistake is not to have believed your son. You mean Jesus. Yes, Jesus, for no other man saw God or is ever likely to see Him. Tell me, angel of the Lord, is it really true that my son Jesus saw God. Yes, like a child finding his first nest he came running to show you, and you, suspicious, mistrusting, told him that it couldn't be true, that if there was any nest, it was empty, if there were any eggs, they were hollow, and if there were

263

no eggs, a snake devoured them. Forgive me for having doubted. Now I cannot be sure whether you are talking to me or to your son. To him, to you, to both, what can I do to make amends for the harm done. Listen to your maternal heart. Then I should go and find him, tell him that I believe him, ask him to forgive me and come home, where the Lord will summon him when the time comes. I honestly don't know whether you will reach him in time, there is no one more sensitive than an adolescent, you risk being insulted and having the door slammed in your face. If that happens, the demon who bewitched and led him astray is to blame, and I cannot understand how the Lord, as a father, could have permitted such liberties and given the rascal so much freedom. To which demon are you referring. To the shepherd my son accompanied for four years and whose flock he tended for no good reason. Oh, that shepherd. Do you know him. We went to school together. And does the Lord let such a demon thrive and prosper. The harmony of the universe requires it, but the Lord will always have the last word, only we don't know when He will say it, but you'll see, one of these days we'll wake up and find there is no evil in the world, now if you'll excuse me I must be off, if you have any more questions to ask, this is your opportunity. Only one. Fine, go ahead. Why does the Lord want my son. Your son, in a manner of speaking. In the eyes of the world Jesus is my son. Why does the Lord want him, you ask, well there's an interesting question, but unfortunately I cannot answer it, at the moment that's between the two of them, and I don't believe Jesus knows any more than he has already told you. He told me he will have power and glory after death. Yes, I'm aware of that. But what must he do in life to merit this reward the Lord has promised. Come now, you're being stupid, surely you don't believe that such a word exists in the eyes of the Lord or that what you presumptuously refer to as merit has any value or meaning, it's incredible what you people get into your heads when you're nothing but complete slaves of God's absolute will. I'll say no more, for I am truly the servant of the Lord and would have Him do with me as He will, but tell me one thing, after all these months where am I to find my son. It is your duty to go in search of him just as he went in search of his lost sheep. In order to kill it. Don't worry, he won't kill you, but you will certainly kill him by not being present at the hour of his death. How do you know I won't die first. I am sufficiently close to the seat of power to know, and now I must bid you farewell, you've asked all the questions you wanted, except the one question you should have asked, but that's something which no longer concerns me. Explain. Explain it to yourself. And with these words the angel disappeared, and Mary opened her eyes.

The children were all fast asleep, the boys together in two groups of three, James, Joseph, and Judas, the three older boys, in one corner, in the other their younger brothers, Simon, Justus, and Samuel, and lying beside Mary were Lisa on one side, Lydia on the other. Troubled by the angel's words, Mary noticed with alarm and dismay that Lisa was practically naked, her tunic in disarray and pulled up over her breasts as she lay asleep with a smile on her face, the perspiration glistening on her forehead and upper lip, which appeared to be red from kissing. Had Mary not been certain that only one angel had entered, Lisa's appearance would have been enough to convince her that one of those incubuses who violate women in their sleep had secretly been having his way with the poor girl while her mother was engaged in conversation. This probably happens all the time without our knowing, these angels go around in pairs at their leisure, and while one diverts attention by telling fairy tales, the other carries out the wickedness, which strictly speaking is not all that wicked, and probably they will reverse their roles next time, so that the

265

salutary meaning of the duality of flesh and spirit will not be lost on either the dreamer or the person being dreamed about. Mary covered her daughter, pulled the tunic down before waking her and asking in a whisper, What were you dreaming. Taken by surprise, the girl had no time to invent a lie, she confessed that she dreamed of an angel who said nothing but looked at her with as gentle and sweet an expression as one could hope to find in paradise. Did he touch you, asked Mary, and Lisa replied, Mother, no one touches with their eyes. Not altogether convinced, Mary said in an even lower whisper, I too dreamed of an angel. And did your angel speak or was he also silent, Lisa asked in all innocence. He told me your brother Jesus was telling the truth when he said he saw God. Oh, Mother, how wrong we were not to believe Jesus, who is so good and patient, no one could have blamed him had he taken back the money for my dowry. Now we must try to put things right. But we don't know where to find him, he has sent no news, oh, if only we had asked the angel, after all, angels know everything. Of course, but the angel didn't offer to help, he just said it was our duty to look for your brother. Mother, if brother Jesus was truly with the Lord, then our life is going to be different from now on. Different, perhaps, but for the worse. Why. If we don't believe Jesus or his word, how can you expect others to believe, we can't very well go through the streets and squares of Nazareth proclaiming Jesus has seen the Lord, Jesus has seen the Lord, unless we want people chasing us with stones. But if the Lord himself chose Jesus, then surely He will protect us, his family. Don't be too certain, we weren't around when Jesus was chosen, and as far as the Lord is concerned, there are neither fathers nor sons, remember Abraham, remember Isaac. Oh, Mother, how terrible. It would be wise, my child, to keep this matter to ourselves and say as little as possible. Then what will we do. Tomorrow I'll send James and Joseph to look for Jesus. But

266

where, Galilee is so big, and so is Samaria, if he went there, and Judaea and Idumaea are at the end of the world. Your brother has probably gone to sea, remember what he told us when he came, that he had been helping some fishermen. Isn't it more likely that he returned to the flock. Those days are over. How do you know. Try to get some sleep, it's getting late. Who knows, we might dream of our angels again. Perhaps. Whether Lisa's angel, having given its companion the slip, visited her dream once more, no one ever discovered, but the angel who brought Mary tidings was unable to return, because her eyes remained open as she lay in the darkness, yet what she knew was more than enough, and what she suspected filled her with fear.

At daybreak the mats were rolled up, and Mary summoned all her children before her. She explained that she had been thinking seriously about their recent treatment of Jesus, Starting with myself, as his mother, I think we should have been kinder and more understanding, and I've come to the conclusion that it's only right that we go look for him and ask him to come home, for we believe in him and, God willing, will one day believe what he told us. This was what Mary told them, unaware that she was repeating the words used by Joseph, who had also been present during that dramatic moment of family rejection. Who knows, perhaps Jesus would still be here today if that quiet murmur, although we did not point it out at the time, for it was but a murmur, had been on everyone's lips. Mary said nothing about the angel and the angel's words, she just reminded her children of the respect they owed their oldest brother. James dared not question his mother's change of heart, but he continued to doubt his brother's sanity, unless Jesus had fallen under the spell of some dangerous charlatan. He asked, knowing her reply, And who is to go look for our brother Jesus. You must go, as the second oldest, and Joseph will accompany you, together you will travel more safely. Where should we begin. By the Sea of

Galilee, I'm sure you'll find him there. When do we leave. Jesus left months ago, so there's no time to lose. But the rains have started, Mother, and this is no time to be traveling. My son, the circumstances create the need, and the need, when it is great enough, creates the circumstances. Mary's children looked at her in surprise, unaccustomed to such deep maxims from their mother's lips and still too young to know that keeping company with angels can produce these and even more impressive results. Take Lisa, for example, who at this very moment is slowly nodding her head in a daze, the others suspecting nothing.

When the family meeting was over, James and Joseph took a good look at the sky to see if there was any chance of a dry day for their departure despite the recent bad weather. The sky must have noticed, for right over the Sea of Galilee it turned a watery blue which promised an afternoon without rain. Having discreetly made their farewells indoors, since Mary felt the neighbors should know as little as possible, the two brothers finally set out on their journey, not along the road to Magdala, for there was no reason to think Jesus had gone in that direction, but by another route, which would soon bring them to the new city of Tiberias. They went barefoot, with all the mud on the roads they could hardly wear sandals, so they kept them safely in their packs until the weather improved. James had two reasons for choosing the road to Tiberias. First because he was curious, coming from the provinces, to see the palaces and temples he had heard so much about, and secondly because he had been told that the city was situated about halfway up this side of the river. Since they would have to earn a living while searching, James hoped to find work on a building site there, despite what the devout Jews of Nazareth said about the place's being unhealthy because of the polluted air and sulphurous waters nearby. The brothers did not reach Tiberias that day, because the promising signs in the sky came to nothing, within an hour of their departure it started raining again. They were fortunate to come upon a cave big enough to shelter them before the floodwater could sweep them away. They slept in safety, but no longer trusted in the weather.

In Tiberias the only work they found at a building site was unskilled, carting stones, but after a few days they had earned enough to satisfy their modest needs, not that King Herod Antipas was generous to his workers. They inquired if anyone had seen a certain Jesus of Nazareth, perhaps only passing through, He's our brother, looks more or less like us, but we're not sure whether or not he's traveling alone. No one had seen him working there, so James and Joseph went around to all the boat houses. Clearly, if their brother had decided to rejoin the fishermen, he would not have wasted time slaving at a building site under some harsh foreman when the lake was right there. But no one had seen him. Now that the brothers had a little money, the next thing to consider was whether the search along the riverbank, village by village, crew by crew, boat by boat, should be carried out to the north or to the south. James finally decided they should travel south, that road was flatter, the northern road was much more uneven. The weather became stable, the cold bearable, the rain had passed, anyone with more experience of nature's cycle than these two youths had would have recognized, just by sniffing the air and feeling the soil, the first signs of spring. This mission to find their brother was turning into an agreeable country outing, a pleasant holiday by the lake, and James and Joseph were almost in danger of forgetting why they had come, when unexpectedly they met some fishermen who gave them news of Jesus, expressed in the strangest manner. One of the fishermen told them, Yes, we know him, and when you find him, tell him we wait for his return as eagerly as if we were waiting for our daily bread. The brothers were astounded, they could scarcely believe these men were talking about Jesus, perhaps the

269

fishermen had mistaken him for some other Jesus, Judging from your description, he's the same Jesus, but whether he came from Nazareth we cannot say, for he never mentioned it. And why do you wait for his return as eagerly as if waiting for your daily bread, James asked. Because whenever he was in the boat, the fish swam straight into our nets. But our brother knows nothing about fishing, so he can't be the same Jesus. We never said he knows anything about fishing, but he only has to say, Cast your nets on this side, and no sooner are the nets lowered than they come up full. Then why is he no longer with you. Because he moved on after a few days, saying he must help other fishermen, which is true, because he joined us on three occasions, always promising to return. And where is he now. We don't know, last time he left, he was heading south, but he may have gone north without our noticing, he comes and goes at will. James said to Joseph, Let's go south, at least we know our brother is somewhere on this side of the water. This seemed sensible, though they would miss Jesus if he happened to be out on the lake, on one of those miraculous fishing trips. We tend to overlook such details, but fate is not what we imagine, a thing determined according to some principle or other, note how certain encounters, such as the one we have just described, can occur only if the persons concerned happen to be in the same place at the same time, which is not always easy. If we pause for a moment to look up at a cloud in the sky, to listen to the song of a bird, to count the entrances and exits of an anthill, or are so preoccupied that we neither look nor listen nor count but continue on our way, we may miss the perfect opportunity. Believe me, brother Joseph, fate is the most difficult thing of all in this world, as you'll learn when you're my age. Forewarned, the two brothers kept a watchful eye, stopped often to see if any boat was late in returning, several times they even retraced their steps in the hope of taking Jesus by surprise in some unlikely place, till finally they reached the end of the lake. Crossing to the other side of the river Jordan, they asked the first fishermen they met if they knew anything about Jesus. Yes, of course the men had heard about his wondrous deeds, but no one had seen him. James and Joseph went back and headed north again, more observant this time, like fishermen dragging their nets in the hope of catching the king of fish. Whenever they spent the night by the road, they kept watch in turn, lest Jesus take advantage of the moonlight to steal from one place to another. Making inquiries as they went, they reached Tiberias, where they did not have to look for work, they still had some money left thanks to the generosity of the fishermen, who supplied them with fish, prompting Joseph to ask on one occasion, James, has it occurred to you that this fish we are eating might have been caught by our brother, and James replied, That won't improve the taste, unkind words coming from a brother but understandable when one considers James's frustration, God help him, as he wearily went on searching for a needle in a haystack.

They found Jesus an hour, that is to say, by our time, after leaving Tiberias. The first to spot him was Joseph, who has keen eyes and can see things from quite a distance, That's him, over there, he cried. In fact there are two persons coming in this direction, and one is a woman. No, says James, it can't be him. A young boy rarely contradicts an older brother, but Joseph is so overjoyed that he dispenses with the usual rules and conventions, I'm telling you, it's him, But I see a woman there, Yes, a woman with a man, and the man is Jesus. Along the riverbank and across a stretch of flat land between two hills that sloped practically to the water's edge, Jesus and Mary Magdalene could be seen approaching. James stopped and waited, and ordered Joseph to stay with him. The boy reluctantly obeyed, eager as he was to run to his long-lost brother, to embrace him and throw his arms around his neck. James,

271

however, was disturbed by the presence of the woman at Jesus' side. Who is she, he asked himself, refusing to believe that his brother already had carnal knowledge of a woman, the very idea created an enormous gulf between James and his older brother, as if Jesus, who boasted of having seen God, was now in a completely different realm, simply by having carnal knowledge of a woman. One reflection leads to another, though we often do not notice the connection between them, it is like crossing a river by a covered bridge, we walk without looking where we are going, passing over a river we did not know existed, and James too began to think it was not right to remain standing there, as if he were the eldest in the family and Jesus should come to him. No sooner did James stir than Joseph ran to Jesus with open arms and cries of joy, startling into flight a flock of birds that, concealed among the tall reeds, had been foraging in the marsh by the river. James walked faster, to prevent Joseph from delivering any messages that were his responsibility, and coming face-to-face with Jesus, he said to him, Thanks be to the Lord that we found you, brother, and Jesus replied, I am delighted to see both of you in such good health. Mary Magdalene, meanwhile, had lingered behind. Jesus asked, What brings you to these parts, and James suggested, Let's go over there, where no one can hear us. We can talk here, said Jesus, and if you're referring to the woman accompanying me, then let me assure you that whatever you have to say and that I may wish to hear can be said in her presence. The deep silence which followed was that of the sea and the mountains put together, not the silence of four human beings confronting one another and summoning their courage. Jesus seemed older, and his skin was tanned, but his feverish look had gone, and the expression behind his heavy, dark beard was composed, serene, despite the tension of this unexpected encounter. Who is that woman, asked James. Her name is Mary, and she is with me, said Jesus. Is she your wife.

Well, yes and no. I don't understand. That doesn't surprise me. I must talk to you. Go ahead. I've brought a message from Mother. I'm listening. I'd prefer to tell you in private. You heard what I said. Mary Magdalene stepped forward, I can stay out of the way until you've finished your conversation. No, said Jesus, you share all my thoughts, therefore you should know what my mother thinks of me, so I don't have to repeat it to you later. James flushed and made as if to turn away, giving Mary Magdalene a black look that betrayed mixed feelings of hatred and desire. Joseph stretched out his hands to keep them apart, all that he could do. James eventually calmed down, then remembered what he had to say, Mother sent us to find you and accompany you back home, for we believe you, and with God's help perhaps one day we'll believe what you told us. Is that all. Those were Mother's words. So, not willing to believe what I told you, you wait for the Lord to help you change your mind. Whether we believe or not depends on the Lord. You are mistaken, the Lord gave us legs that we might walk, and we walked, I've never heard of any man who waited for the Lord to say, Start walking, and it's the same with our mind, God gave us a mind to use according to our will and desire. I won't argue with you. Just as well, for you wouldn't win. What should I tell Mother. Tell her the message comes too late, that Joseph spoke those same words in time, but she paid no attention, and even should an angel of the Lord appear and convince her that everything I said was true, I have no intention of returning home. You're committing the sin of pride. A tree weeps when cut down, a dog howls when beaten, but a man matures when offended. She's your mother, and we are your brothers. Who are my mother and brothers, my mother and brothers are they who believe me when I speak, they are the fishermen who know that when I join them, they will catch more fish than ever, my mother and brothers are they who do not have to wait for the hour of my

273

death to take pity on my life. Have you no other message for Mother. That is all, but you will hear others speak of me, said Jesus, then turning to Mary Magdalene, Let us go, Mary, the boats are ready to leave, the fish are gathering, time to reap this harvest. As they walked away, James called out, Jesus, should I mention this woman to Mother. Tell her she is with me and her name is Mary, and the name echoed between the hills and over the lake. Crouching on the ground, young Joseph wept bitter tears.

WHEN JESUS GOES TO FISH WITH THE FISHERMEN, MARY
Magdalene waits for him, usually seated on a rock at the
water's edge, or on a nearby hill if there is one, from where
she can easily follow the route they sail. Fishing is no longer
a slow operation, for there have never been so many fish
in this lake, it's like putting one's hand in a bucket filled
with fish, but not for everyone, because if Jesus happens
to go elsewhere, then the bucket reverts to being almost
empty, and hands and arms soon tire of casting net after
net to find only an occasional fish or two trapped in the
mesh. In despair, the entire fishing community on the
western side of the Sea of Galilee goes to ask Jesus, to
implore Jesus, to demand that Jesus help them, and in some
places they even receive him with festivities and floral trib-
utes, as if it were Palm Sunday. But the bread of humanity
being what it is, a mixture of envy and malice with a little
charity here and there, the yeast of fear fermenting evil
while suppressing good, one group of fishermen began
quarreling with another, one village with another, they all
wanted Jesus, and let the others provide for themselves as

best they can. Whenever they started fighting, Jesus withdrew to the desert, returning only when the troublemakers repented and asked forgiveness for their rough behavior while protesting their love and devotion. But what we will never know is why the fishermen on the eastern side never sent delegates to discuss the drafting of a fair treaty that would benefit all parties, not including the large number of Gentiles of different races and persuasions who are to be found in this region. The fishermen on the other bank could also have sent a fleet with nets and pikes, under cover of darkness, to kidnap Jesus, reducing those on the western side to a meager existence just when they had grown accustomed to plenty.

But let us go back to the day James and Joseph came to ask Jesus to give up this existence and return home despite his newfound prosperity since he took up fishing. By now the two brothers, James in a rage, Joseph in tears, are quickly making their way back to Nazareth, where their mother continues to wonder whether the two sons who left will bring a third, but she is doubtful. Their homeward route from the spot on the shore where they met Jesus obliged them to pass through Magdala. James scarcely knew the town and Joseph not at all, the place didn't appear to have anything of interest to detain them there, so after a brief rest the brothers resumed their journey. As they passed the last of the houses before the wilderness began, they saw on their left the bare walls of a house that had been gutted by fire. The gate to the yard had been forced open but only partially destroyed, and it looked as if the fire had started inside. The passerby hopes that some treasure may be left among the ashes, and if there is no danger of a beam falling on his head, he cannot resist exploring further. Treading carefully, he pokes at the debris with one foot, looking for something shiny, a gold coin, an indestructible diamond, an emerald necklace. James and Joseph entered only out of curiosity, they are not so naive as to imagine that rapacious neighbors have not been here already to loot the place, although the house is so small that any prized possessions almost certainly have been removed by the owners. The roof of the oven had caved in, the brick floor was broken, and there were loose tiles underfoot. There's nothing here, said James, let's go, but Joseph asked, What's that. It was a bedstead, but the legs had been burned and the whole frame badly damaged, a phantom throne with bits of charred drapery hanging in tatters. It's a bed, said James, people like great lords and wealthy merchants actually sleep on such things. This doesn't strike me as a rich person's house, argued Joseph. Appearances can be deceptive, James wisely reminded him. As they left, Joseph noticed a cane hanging outside the gate, the sort used for gathering figs, no doubt it had originally been much longer. What is this doing here, he asked, and without waiting for a reply, either from himself or from his brother, he removed the useless cane and took it with him, a souvenir of a fire, of a house destroyed, of people unknown. No one had seen them enter, no one saw them leave, they are only two brothers going home in soiled tunics and with bad news, one brother frustrated by the memory of Mary Magdalene, the other thinking of the fun he will have playing with the broken cane.

Mary Magdalene, sitting on a rock and waiting for Jesus to return from fishing, thinks about Mary of Nazareth. Until today she simply thought of her as Jesus' mother, now she knows, after questioning him, that his mother is also named Mary, a coincidence of no great consequence when one considers the vast number of Marys on this earth and the many more to come if the fashion persists, but we are inclined to believe that there is nevertheless a sense of solidarity between those who share the same name, Joseph for example may think of himself no longer as the son of Joseph but more as his brother, and this could be God's problem, no one else bears His name. These reflections may

277

seem farfetched for someone like Mary Magdalene, but we are confident that she is perfectly capable of such ideas once her thoughts about the man she loves lead her to think of his mother. Mary Magdalene has never had a son of her own to love, but at long last she has learned what it means to love a man, having practiced the thousand and one deceptions of false love. She loves Jesus as a woman loves a man, but also wants to love him as a mother loves a son, perhaps because she is not much younger than his real mother, who sent a message asking her son to come home, only to be refused. Mary Magdalene wonders how Mary of Nazareth will feel when she receives his answer, but that is not the same as imagining how she herself would suffer were she to lose him, for she would be losing her man rather than her son. O Lord, punish me with both sorrows if necessary, murmured Mary Magdalene as she sat waiting for Jesus to return. And as the boat drew nearer and was pulled ashore, as the baskets laden with glistening fish were hauled in, as Jesus, his feet in the water, helped the fishermen and laughed like a child at play, Mary Magdalene saw herself in the role of Mary of Nazareth and, getting up, she went down to the water's edge and waded in to greet Jesus. Kissing him on the shoulder, she whispered, My son. No one heard Jesus say, Mother, for as we know, words that come from the heart are never spoken, they get caught in the throat and can only be read in one's eyes. Mary and Jesus were rewarded with a basket of fish, and as usual they retired to the house where they would spend the night, for they had no home of their own, going from boat to boat and from mat to mat. In the beginning Jesus often said to Mary, This is no life for you, let's find a house of our own where I can join you whenever possible, but Mary insisted, I don't want to wait behind, I prefer to be with you. One day he asked her if she had any relatives who might offer her shelter, and she told him that her brother Lazarus and sister Martha lived in the village of Bethany in Judaea, although she herself left home when she turned to prostitution, and to spare them embarrassment she moved farther and farther away, until she ended up in Magdala. So your name should really be Mary of Bethany if that's where you were born, said Jesus. Yes, I was born in Bethany, but you found me in Magdala, so I think of myself as being from Magdala. People don't refer to me as Jesus of Bethlehem although I was born there, and I don't think of myself as being from Nazareth, because people there don't want me and I certainly don't want them, perhaps I should say like you, I'm from Magdala, and for the same reason. Don't forget we destroyed our house. But not the memory, replied Jesus. No more was said about Mary's returning to Bethany, this stretch of shore is their whole world, and wherever Jesus may go, she will go with him.

How true, the saying which reminds us that there is so much sorrow in this world, misfortunes grow like weeds beneath our feet. Such a saying could only have been invented by mortals, accustomed as they are to life's ups and downs, obstacles, setbacks, and constant struggle. The only people likely to question it are those who sail the seas, for they know that even greater woe lies beneath their feet, indeed, unfathomable chasms. The misfortunes of seafarers, the winds and gales sent from heaven, cause waves to swell, storms to break, sails to rip, and fragile vessels to founder. And these fishermen and sailors truly perish between heaven and earth, a heaven hands cannot reach, an earth feet never touch. The Sea of Galilee is nearly always tranquil and smooth, like any lake, until the watery furies are unleashed, and then it is every man for himself, although sadly some drown. But let us return to Jesus of Nazareth and his recent worries, which only goes to show that the human heart is never content, and that doing one's duty does not bring peace of mind, though those who are easily satisfied would have us believe otherwise. One could say that thanks to the endless comings and goings of Jesus up and down the river Jordan, there is no longer any hardship, not even an occasional shortage, on the western shore, and not only fishermen have benefited, because the abundance of fish has brought down prices and provided people with more to eat. It is true that some attempts were made to keep prices high by the well-known corporate method of throwing part of the catch back into the sea, but Jesus threatened to go elsewhere if those responsible for this abuse did not apologize and change their ways. So everyone is happy, except Jesus. He is tired of the constant back and forth, the embarking and disembarking, the same routine day in and day out, and since the power of making fish appear clearly comes from the Lord, why should he be condemned to this monotony until the Lord is ready to summon him as promised. Jesus does not doubt that the Lord is with him, for the fish never fail to come when he calls them, which has led him to speculate whether the Lord might not be willing to concede him other powers, on the clear understanding that he put them to good use. For as we have seen, Jesus, who has achieved so much already with nothing but intuition to guide him, should have no difficulty meeting that condition. There was one way to find out, as easy as saying, Oh, and that was to try. If it worked, God approved, and if it didn't, God was showing His displeasure. The first problem was that of choice. Unable to consult the Lord directly, Jesus would have to risk choosing a power, one that would provoke the least objection, it could not be too obvious, yet not so subtle as to go unnoticed by those who would benefit, or by the world, for that would diminish the glory of God, which must be considered above all things. But Jesus could not make up his mind, he was afraid God might ridicule him, humiliate him as He had done in the desert, even now he shuddered at the thought of the embarrassment he would have suffered if the nets had come back empty when he first suggested, Cast your nets on this side. These matters worried him so much that one night he dreamed someone was whispering in his ear, Don't be afraid, remember God needs you, but when he woke up, he could not help wondering who had spoken, an angel, one of the many who go around delivering messages from the Lord, or was it a demon, one of the many who do Satan's bidding. Mary Magdalene was fast asleep beside him, so it could not have been her.

This was how things stood when Jesus set out one day, which seemed no different from any other, to perform the usual miracle. The clouds were low in the sky and there were signs of rain, but it takes more than rain to keep fishermen at home, they are used to every kind of weather. On this particular day the boat belonged to Simon and his brother Andrew, who had witnessed the first miracle, and it was accompanied by the boat of James and John, the sons of Zebedee, because one can never tell if a miracle will always have the same effect, a boat nearby may get some of the fish gathering there. The strong wind carries them swiftly out, and after lowering the sails the fishermen in both boats prepare their nets and wait for Jesus to tell them where they should cast them. At this point the situation starts getting difficult, a storm suddenly comes without warning from the overcast sky, it grows so fierce that the waves swell and rise, driven by the frenzied gale, and those two fragile nutshells are buffeted wildly as the elements unleash their wrath. The plight of the defenseless fishermen brought shouts and lamentations from the people watching on the shore. Wives, mothers, sisters, children, and the occasional good-hearted mother-in-law were gathered there, making such a din with their weeping and wailing that it must have been heard in heaven, Oh, my poor husband, Oh, my beloved son, Oh, my dear brother, Oh, my poor son-in-law, A curse on you, miserable sea, Holy Mother of the Afflicted, help us, Protectress of the

Voyager, come to our aid, but all the children could do was to weep. Mary Magdalene was there too, murmuring, Jesus, Jesus, but she did not pray for him, she knew the Lord was saving him for another occasion, not likely to let him perish in a mere storm at sea, where the only consequence was a few drowned men. She kept on repeating, Jesus, Jesus, as if the very sound of his name could rescue the fishermen, who certainly appeared close to meeting their fate. In the midst of the storm, Jesus watched the despair and destruction all around him, the waves sweeping over the boats and flooding them, the masts breaking, the sails flying through the air, the rain becoming a flood capable of sinking one of the emperor's own ships. Jesus watched and thought, It is not right that these men should die while I live, the Lord will rebuke me, saying, You could have saved those who were with you, yet you made no attempt to save them, as if your father's crime were not enough. To be reminded of that was so painful, Jesus jumped to his feet, and standing as firmly as if on solid ground, he commanded the wind, Be quiet, and told the sea, Be calm, and no sooner had he spoken than the sea and the wind abated, the clouds in the sky dispersed, and the sun appeared in all its glory, ever a wondrous sight in the eyes of us poor mortals. Impossible to describe the rejoicing in the boats, the kissing and embracing, the tears of joy ashore, those on the far bank were puzzled that the storm died down so quickly, those here, as if restored to life, could think of nothing but their lucky escape, and if some spontaneously exclaimed, Miracle, miracle, they seemed unaware that someone had to be responsible for it. A sudden silence fell over the water, the other boats surrounded that of Simon and Andrew, and all the fishermen looked at Jesus, too astonished to speak, for above the roar of the storm they had heard him call out, Be quiet, Be calm, and there he was, Jesus, the man who could summon fish from the sea, and now he had forbidden the sea to deliver men to the fish. Eyes lowered, Jesus sat on the oarsman's bench, his face showing both triumph and disaster, as if on reaching a mountain peak he was now beginning the sad and inevitable descent. Forming a circle, the men waited for him to speak. It was not enough to have tamed the wind and pacified the water, he had to explain how a simple Galilean, an obscure carpenter's son, could have achieved such a miracle, when God himself had abandoned them to death's cold embrace. Jesus rose to his feet and told them, What you have just witnessed was not my doing, the voice that quelled the storm was not mine but that of the Lord speaking through me, as through the prophets, I am only the mouth of the Lord. Simon, who was in the boat with him, said, Just as the Lord sent the storm, He could also have sent it away, but it was your word that saved our lives. Believe me, it was God's doing, not mine. Whereupon John, the younger son of Zebedee, spoke, proving that he was not at all simpleminded, It may have been God's doing, for in Him resides all power, but He acted through you, so clearly it is God's will that we should know you. But you already know me. Only that you came from who knows where and mysteriously filled our boats with fish. I am Jesus of Nazareth, the son of a carpenter who was crucified by the Romans, for a time I was a shepherd for a flock of sheep and goats, and now here I am with you, and perhaps I will go on being a fisherman until the hour of my death. Andrew, the brother of Simon, said, We will stay with you, because any man with your power is condemned to loneliness heavier than any millstone around one's neck. Jesus said, Stay with me if that is what your heart asks, and if the Lord, as John says, wishes that you should know me, but tell no one what has passed here, for the time has not yet come for Him to reveal my fate. Then James, the older son of Zebedee, who like his brother was no simpleton, said, Don't imagine people won't talk, just look at the crowd there on the shore, see how they're waiting to praise you, some so impatient that they're already pushing out their boats to come and join us, and even if we succeed in reining their enthusiasm and persuading them to keep our secret, how can you be sure that God will not continue to manifest Himself through you, however much you dislike the idea. The living image of sorrow, Jesus hung his head and said, We are all in the hands of the Lord. You more than the rest of us, replied Simon, for He has chosen you, but we shall follow you. To the end, said John. Until you have no further need of us, said Andrew. For as long as possible, said James. The boats were fast approaching, with much waving of arms and chanting of prayers and praise and thanks to the Lord. Resigned, Jesus told the others, Let's go, the wine is poured and we must drink it. He did not seek out Mary Magdalene, he knew she was waiting for him as always, it would take more than a miracle to stop her vigil, and the thought of her waiting for him filled his heart with gratitude and peace. Disembarking, he fell into her arms, and showed no surprise when she whispered in his ear, her cheek pressed against his wet beard, You will lose the war but win every battle. Arm in arm and accompanied by friends, they greeted the cheering spectators, who hailed Jesus as if he were a victorious general. Arm in arm, Jesus and Mary climbed the steep path to Capernaum, the village that overlooked the lake, where Simon and Andrew lived and where they had been offered hospitality.

James was right when he warned Jesus that the episode of the storm would be on everyone's lips. Within a few days people for miles around were discussing nothing else. Although, strange to relate, no one seems to have been aware of the storm in Tiberias, even though the lake there is not that wide, as we already mentioned, and from a height one can see from shore to shore on a clear day. When someone arrived with the news that a stranger accompanying the fishermen of Capernaum had quelled the storm just by speaking to it, he was asked to his amazement, What storm. But there was no lack of witnesses to testify that there had indeed been a storm, and there were those who had been involved directly or indirectly, among them some muleteers from Safed and Cana who chanced to be there in the course of their work. It was they who spread the news elsewhere, each man embroidering the story according to his fancy, but the news did not reach everyone, and we know what happens to such tales, they lose credibility after a while, by the time the news reached Nazareth, the tellers were no longer sure if there had been a genuine miracle or simply the lucky coincidence of a word's being tossed to the wind and a gale's growing tired of blowing. A mother's heart, however, is never deceived, and Mary had only to hear the dying echo of this prodigy that people were already questioning to know that her absent son was responsible. She grieved that the loss of her maternal authority had led her to conceal from Jesus the angel's revelation, confident that a message couched in a few words would bring home the son who had left with his own heart grieving. And now that Lisa was married and living in Cana, Mary no longer had anyone in whom to confide her bitterness. She could not turn to James, who had come back in a rage after the meeting with his brother. He spared Mary no details, and gave a withering account of the woman with Jesus, She's old enough to be his mother, and from the look of her there's nothing she doesn't know about life, to put it mildly. Not that James himself knows that much about life, here in this remote village. So Mary unburdened herself to Joseph, the son who in name and appearance reminded her most of her husband, but he gave her little comfort, Mother, we are paying for our mistake, after seeing Jesus, I fear he'll never come home, people say he calmed a storm, and the fishermen themselves told us that he fills their boats with fish as if by magic. Then the angel was right. What angel, asked Joseph, and Mary told

285

him everything that had happened, from the beggar who put glowing earth into the bowl to the appearance of the angel in her dream. They did not hold this conversation inside, for with such a large family it is almost impossible to have any privacy. When these people wish to disclose secrets, they go into the desert, where one might even meet God. Joseph and Mary were still deep in conversation when Joseph, looking over his mother's shoulder, saw a flock of sheep and goats with their shepherd pass over the distant hills. The flock did not appear to be very big or the shepherd very tall, so he watched without saying a word. And when his mother sighed, I will never see Jesus again, he replied pensively, Who knows.

Joseph was right. About a year later, Lisa sent a message to their mother, inviting her on behalf of her in-laws to come to Cana for the wedding of her husband's younger sister, and Mary was asked to bring as many of the children as she wished, they would all be most welcome. Despite this generous invitation Mary was reluctant to be a burden, for there is nothing more tiresome than a widow with a horde of children, so she decided to take her current favorite, Joseph, and Lydia, who like all other girls her age adored parties and celebrations. Cana is not far from Nazareth, little more than an hour away if calculated by our time, and with gentle autumn already here, this promised to be an agreeable outing, even without a wedding to look forward to. They left at sunrise, in order to arrive in Cana in time for Mary to assist in the final preparations for the festivities, for such labor is in direct proportion to the pleasure of the guests. Lisa ran out to meet her mother, brother, and sister, embracing them affectionately. She asked about their health, they asked if she was well and happy, but there was much work to be done, so they moved on quickly. Lisa and Mary went to the bridegroom's house, where the feast was traditionally held, to share the cooking with the other women of the family, and Joseph and Lydia remained in the yard with the children, the boys playing with the boys, the girls dancing with the girls, until it was time for the ceremony to begin. Then off they ran, boys and girls together, behind the men accompanying the bridegroom, friends carrying the customary torches although it was a bright, sunny morning, which shows that a little extra light, even from a torch, is not to be despised. Smiling neighbors came out to greet them, but saved their blessings for when the procession would return bringing the bride. Joseph and Lydia missed the rest of this, but then they have already seen a wedding in their own family, the bridegroom knocking at the door and asking to see the bride, the bride appearing surrounded by her friends, who carry little oil lamps, which are more suited to women than great flaming torches, and then the bridegroom lifts the bride's veil and shouts with joy on finding such a treasure there, as if he has not seen her thousands of times already during the last twelve months of courtship, and not gone to bed with her as often as he pleased. Joseph and Lydia missed all this, because Joseph, who happened to look down the street, saw two men and a woman in the distance. Recognizing Jesus and the woman with him, he felt a strange sensation for the second time, and called to his sister, Look, it's Jesus, and they ran to meet him, but then Joseph stopped, remembering his mother and the coldness with which his brother had received them by the lake, not so much James and him, it is true, as the message they had delivered. So Joseph, thinking to himself that he would eventually have to explain his behavior to Jesus, turned back. Before disappearing around the corner, he took another look and felt envy when he saw his brother gather Lydia into his arms like a feather in flight and smother her with kisses, while the woman and the other man looked on approvingly. Eyes filled with tears of frustration, Joseph ran, came to the house, crossed the yard, jumping to avoid the linen cloths and food set out on the ground and low tables, and called, Mother, Mother. Our own distinctive voices are our saving grace, otherwise mothers everywhere would be looking up only to see someone else's son. One look, and Mary understood when Joseph said to her, Jesus is coming this way. The color drained from her face, then she blushed, smiled, turned serious and pale once more, and these conflicting emotions brought her hand to her breast, as if her heart were no longer beating and she had backed into a wall. Who is with him, she asked, for she was certain someone was with him. A man and a woman, and Lydia, who's still with them, replied Joseph. Is that the woman you saw before. Yes, Mother, but I don't know the man. Lisa joined them, curious, unaware that there was something amiss, What's the matter, Mother. Your brother has arrived for the wedding. You mean Jesus is here in Cana. Yes, Joseph has just seen him. Lisa could not keep from smiling as she murmured to herself, My brother, and that quiet smile of hers betrayed the deepest satisfaction. Let's go and meet him, she said. You go, I'll stay here, her mother answered defensively, and turning to Joseph, she told him, Go with your sister. But Joseph felt resentful that Lydia had been the first to be embraced by Jesus, and Lisa did not have the courage to go on her own, so there they stood, like three criminals awaiting sentence and unsure of the judge's mercy, if the words judge and mercy mean anything here.

Jesus appeared in the doorway, carrying Lydia in his arms, and Mary Magdalene followed behind, but the first to enter was Andrew, the other man in the group and related to the bridegroom, as soon became apparent when he said to those who came smiling to welcome him, No, Simon couldn't come. And while many present were happily absorbed in this family reunion, others eyed one another over a chasm, asking themselves who would be first to set foot on that fragile, narrow bridge, which despite everything still joined the one side to the other. We shall not say, as a poet once said, that children are the greatest joy in this world, but it is thanks to them that adults sometimes succeed in taking difficult steps without losing face, even if they discover afterward that they have not gone very far. Lydia slipped from Jesus' arms and ran to her mother, and as in a puppet show one move led to another move, and another, Jesus went up to his mother and brother, greeted them in the sober, matter-of-fact tone of one who has seen them every day, then moved on, leaving them dumbfounded. Mary Magdalene followed him, and as she passed Mary of Nazareth, the two women, one upright, the other fallen, glanced at each other, not with hostility or contempt but with mutual recognition, which only those familiar with the labyrinthine ways of the feminine heart can understand. The procession was drawing near, shouts and applause could be heard, the tremulous vibration of tambourines, the scattered notes of gentle harps, the rhythm of dancing, the shrill sound of voices as everyone tried to speak at once. Then the guests poured into the yard, the bride and groom were almost swept in amid cheering and clapping as they went before parents and parents-in-law to receive their blessings. Mary was also there, waiting to give her blessing, just as she had blessed her daughter Lisa, then as now without her husband or eldest son at her side to take his rightful place as head of the family. As they sat down to eat, Jesus was offered a special seat, Andrew having quietly informed his relatives that this was the man who filled empty nets with fish and calmed storms, but Jesus refused the honor, choosing to sit with the guests farthest away from the bridal party. Mary Magdalene served Jesus, and no one questioned her presence there. Lisa too went to him several times, to make sure he was all right, and Jesus treated both women in exactly the same way. Watching this from afar, his mother's eyes met those of Mary Magdalene. Mary beckoned her to a quiet corner of the yard and without further ado told her, Take care of my son, for an angel warned me that great tribulations await him, and I can do nothing for him. You may count on me to protect and defend him with my life if necessary. What is your name. I'm known as Mary Magdalene, and I lived as a prostitute until I met your son. Mary said nothing but began to see things more clearly, certain details came back to her, the coins, the guarded statements made by Jesus when she asked where the money came from, James's indignant account of his meeting with Jesus, his remarks about the woman who was with his brother. Now she knew everything, and turning to Mary Magdalene, said, You will always have my blessing and gratitude for all the good you have done my son Jesus. Mary Magdalene leaned over and kissed Mary's shoulder as a mark of respect, but Mary threw her arms around her and held her tight, and there they remained for some moments, embracing each other in silence before returning to the kitchen, where there was work waiting to be done.

The festivities continued, one dish after another was brought in from the kitchen, wine flowed from the pitchers, guests began singing and dancing, when suddenly the steward came and whispered in the ear of the parents of the bride and groom, The wine is running out. They could not have been more dismayed had they been told the roof was falling in, What will we do now, how can we face our guests and tell them there's no more wine, by tomorrow everyone in Cana will know of our shame. My poor daughter, groaned the bride's mother, people will mock her, saying that even the wine ran dry on her wedding day, what have we done to deserve this, and what a bad start to married life. At the tables the guests were draining their goblets, many looking around for someone to serve them more wine, when Mary, who has now entrusted her maternal duties to another woman, decided to put Jesus' miraculous powers to the test before withdrawing into the silence of her own home, ready to depart this world, her mission on earth completed. She looked around for Mary Magdalene, saw her slowly nod her assent, so wasting no time, she went up to Jesus and said, There is no wine. Jesus turned to face his mother, looked at her as if she had spoken from a distance, and asked, Woman, what have I to do with you, shattering words that shocked and amazed those who overheard them, for no son treats in this manner the mother who brought him into the world. In time these words will be rephrased and interpreted in different ways to make them sound less brutal, some have even tried to change their meaning completely, insisting that what Jesus really said was, Why bother me with this, or, What has this to do with me, or, Who asked you to interfere, or, Why should we get involved, woman, or, Why can't you leave this to me, or, Tell me what you want and I'll see what can be done, or even, You can rely on me to do my best to please you. Mary did not flinch, she withstood Jesus' look of disdain and ended her challenge by saying to the servants, which put her son in an awkward position, Whatever he says, do it. As his mother went off, Jesus watched without saying a word or trying to stop her, aware that the Lord had used her, just as He had used the storm and the plight of the fishermen. Jesus raised his goblet, which still held some wine, and pointing to six stone jars of water used for purification, told the servants, Fill these with water, whereupon they filled them to the brim, and each jar held two to three measures. Bring them here, he told them, and they obeyed. Then into each jar Jesus poured a few drops of the wine in his goblet, and ordered the servants, Take them to the steward. Without knowing where the jars came from, the steward sampled the water, which the small quantity of wine had barely colored, and summoned the groom and told him, Every man serves good wine at the beginning, but when the guests have drunk their fill, serves that which is poorer, yet you have kept the best wine until now. The bridegroom, who had never before seen wine served in such jars and who knew, moreover, that the wine had run out, tasted it for himself and confirmed that it was wine by commenting, with an expression of false modesty, on the excellent quality of this vintage. Had it not been for the servants, who spread the news next day, this would have been a buried miracle, for the steward, ignorant of the transmutation, would have remained ignorant, while the groom would have been only too happy to take the credit, and no one expected Jesus to go around saying, I worked such and such a miracle, and Mary Magdalene, who was involved in the plan from the first, was unlikely to start boasting, He worked a miracle, and his mother even less so, because this was something between Mary and her son, the rest of it was a bonus in every sense of the word, as any guest who had his goblet refilled will testify.

Mary of Nazareth and her son conversed no more. Without saying good-bye to anyone, Jesus and Mary Magdalene left that same afternoon and set off for Tiberias. Joseph and Lydia, keeping out of sight, followed them to the outskirts of the village, where they stood watching until the couple disappeared around the bend in the road.

THEN THE LONG WAIT BEGAN. THE SIGNS BY WHICH THE Lord had manifested Himself in the person of Jesus were so far little more than magic tricks, clever, fascinating, with a few quick words of abracadabra, not unlike those performed with rather more style by Oriental fakirs, such as tossing a rope into midair and climbing it without any visible sign of support, no hooks, no hand of a mysterious genie. To work these wonders, Jesus had only to will them, and if anyone had asked him why, he would have had no answer other than that he could hardly ignore the misery of fishermen with empty nets, the danger of that raging storm, or the mortifying lack of wine at that marriage feast, for truly the hour has not yet arrived for the Lord to speak through his lips. Villagers dwelling on this side of Galilee said that a man from Nazareth was going around exercising powers that could only come from God, and that he did not deny it, but in the absence of any reason or explanation for his appearance among them, they might as well take advantage of this sudden abundance and ask no questions. Simon and Andrew were not of this opinion, nor

293

were the sons of Zebedee, but they were his friends and feared for his life. Each morning when he woke up, Jesus asked in silence, Perhaps today, and sometimes he even asked the question aloud, so that Mary Magdalene would hear him, but she said nothing, just lay there sighing, then put her arms around him and kissed him on the forehead and eyes while he breathed in the sweet, warm odor of her breasts. There were days when he went back to sleep, and days when he forgot the question and took refuge in Mary Magdalene's body, as if entering a cocoon from which he could be reborn in some other form. Later he would go down to the lake and to the waiting fishermen, many of whom would never understand him, they kept asking him why he didn't get himself a boat and fish independently, keeping the entire catch for himself. Sometimes, when they were out at sea and resting between catches, still necessary even though the fishing had become as easy as yawning, Jesus would have a sudden premonition, and his heart trembled, but instead of turning to heaven, where, as we know, God resides, his eyes settled with yearning on the lake's calm surface, on that smooth water that shone like the clearest skin, as if he waited with desire and fear to see rising from the depths not fish but the voice that was slow in coming. The day's fishing over, the boat returned laden, and Jesus, with lowered head, once more walked along the shore, Mary Magdalene behind him. And so the weeks and months passed, and the years, the only visible change taking place in Tiberias, where more buildings went up as the city prospered, otherwise things went on as usual in this land that seems to die with every winter and be reborn with every spring, a false observation and a deception on the part of the senses, for spring would be nothing without the sleep of winter.

Jesus was now twenty-five years old, and suddenly the entire universe awakened, there were signs, one after another, as if someone were anxiously trying to make up for lost time. True, the first sign was not exactly a miracle, after all there was nothing that remarkable about Simon's mother's falling ill with a fever and Jesus' going to her bedside and placing his hand on her forehead, something we have all instinctively done at one time or other, without expecting to cure the patient by this simple, natural gesture. But the fever subsided beneath his hand, as poisoned water is absorbed by the soil, and the old woman rose immediately and said, somewhat irrelevantly, Whoever befriends me befriends my son-in-law, then went about her household chores as if nothing had happened. This first sign was a private matter and took place indoors, but the second brought Jesus into open conflict with the written and observed law, though it was perhaps understandable, given human nature and the fact that Jesus was living in sin with Mary Magdalene. Seeing an adulteress about to be stoned to death in accordance with the law of Moses, Jesus intervened and said, Stop, he that is without sin among you, let him cast the first stone at her, as if to say, Were I not living with a prostitute and tainted by her in deed and thought, I might join you in carrying out this punishment. He was taking a big risk, because some of the more callous among the men could have turned a deaf ear to his rebuke and thrown stones, being themselves exempt from the law they were applying, which was meant only for women. What appears to have escaped Jesus, perhaps from lack of experience, is that if we wait for the arrival of sanctimonious judges who believe they alone have the right to condemn and punish, crime is likely to increase dramatically and wickedness to thrive, adulteresses will be on the loose, one minute with this man, the next with another, and adultery brings after it the thousand vices that persuaded the Lord to send down fire and brimstone on the cities of Sodom and Gomorrah, reducing them to ashes. But the evil that was born with the world, and from which the world has learned everything it knows, dear brethren, is like that famous phoenix that no one has ever seen and that even while appearing to perish in the flames is reborn from an egg hatched in its own ashes. Good is delicate, fragile, while Evil need only blow the hot breath of sin into the face of purity for it to be forevermore disfigured, for the stalk of the lily to break and the orange blossom to wither. Jesus told the adulteress, Go and sin no more, but in his heart he had serious doubts.

Another notable event took place on the opposite side of the lake, where Jesus decided he ought to go now and then, lest it be said that all his attention was given to the western shore. So he summoned James and John and suggested, Let's explore the other side, where the Gadarenes live, to see what fortune brings, and on the way back we can fish, so that we have something to show for our journey. The sons of Zebedee warmed to this idea, and after setting their boat on course, began to row, hoping that farther ahead there would be a breeze to help them on their way. And their prayer was answered, their satisfaction, however, soon turned to alarm when a storm came up that promised to be even more violent than the one they had experienced years ago, but Jesus chided the water and the sky, Now then, what's going on here, as if scolding a child, and the water calmed immediately, and the wind went back to blowing at the right speed and in the right direction. All three disembarked, Jesus walking first, James and John following him. They had never been to this region before and were surprised by everything they saw there, but the strangest sight of all on the road was the sudden appearance of a man, if one can use that word to describe the filthy creature with matted beard and wild hair. The stench he gave off was like that of a tomb, and little wonder, for as they soon learned, that was where the man took refuge whenever he managed to break the chains with which he was restrained. It is well known that a madman's strength is twice as great when he flies into a rage, yet he cannot be held with double the number of chains, this had been tried many times but to no avail, because the man was not simply a madman, the unclean spirit that possessed and ruled him made a mockery of all attempts to chain him. Day and night the possessed man went bounding over the mountains, fleeing from himself and his own shadow, and he hid among the tombs and often in them, from where he had to be dragged, to the horror of anyone who happened to be passing. This was how Jesus first saw him, the guards in pursuit, waving their arms at Jesus to get out of harm's way, but Jesus had come in search of adventure and was not going to miss this for anything. John and James, though terrified by the madman, did not abandon their friend, and so they were the first to hear words no one would ever expect to hear, words that undermined the Lord and His laws, as we are about to discover. The fierce man advances with outstretched claws and bared fangs from which hang the remains of rotten flesh, Jesus' hair stands on end with fright, but suddenly the possessed creature throws himself on the ground two paces away and cries out, What do you want of me, Jesus, son of the Almighty, I beseech you in the name of God to stop tormenting me. Now, this was the first time in public, not in private dreams which prudence and skepticism compel us to doubt, that a voice was raised, and a diabolical voice if ever there was one, proclaiming that Jesus of Nazareth was the son of God, something he himself was unaware of until this moment, for during his conversation with God in the desert the question of paternity never came up. I will need you later, was all the Lord said, and even that was suspect, considering that his heavenly father had appeared before him in the guise of a cloud and column of smoke. The possessed man writhed at his feet, and a voice within Jesus finally revealed what had hitherto been concealed, and at that moment, like one who sees himself reflected in another, he felt that he too was possessed and at the mercy

297

of powers which would lead him who knows where, but no doubt ultimately to the grave of graves. He asked the spirit, What is your name, and the spirit answered, Legion, for we are many. In commanding tones, Jesus said, Leave this man, unclean spirit. And no sooner had he spoken than a chorus of infernal voices went up, some reedy and shrill, others deep and hoarse, some as gentle as a woman's, others as harsh as the sound of a saw cutting through stone, some mocking and taunting, others pleading with the humility of paupers, some arrogant, others whining, some prattling like children learning their first words, others crying out like ghosts in distress, but all begging Jesus to allow them to remain, one word from him could drive them from this man's body, For pity's sake, the evil spirits begged, do not expel us. And Jesus asked them, Tell me, then, where do you want to go. Now as it happened, a large herd of pigs was grazing on the slopes of the mountain nearby, and the spirits implored Jesus, Allow us to enter the pigs. Jesus thought for a moment and decided it was the perfect solution, the pigs had to belong to Gentiles, since pork is unclean and forbidden to Jews, it never occurred to him that by eating the pigs the Gentiles would also eat the demons inside them and become possessed, and he failed to foresee the unfortunate events that would follow from this, but the fact is that not even the son of God, who is still not used to such elevated kinship, can see as on a chessboard all the consequences of one move or one decision. In great excitement the evil spirits made bets, awaiting Jesus' reply, and when he said, Yes, giving them permission to pass into the pigs, they cheered in triumph and inhabited the animals instantly. The pigs, either because of the shock of it or because they hated being possessed by demons, went wild and threw themselves over the cliff, all two thousand of them, and into the lake, where they drowned. The wrath of the swineherds tending these innocent animals was indescribable. One minute the poor things had been grazing at their leisure, grubbing in what soft soil they could find for roots and worms, and pawing at the sparse tufts of grass on the parched surface, the next minute they were down below in the water, a pitiful sight, some already lifeless and floating, others almost unconscious but making one last valiant effort to keep their ears above water, for as everyone knows pigs cannot close their eardrums, and once too much water gets in, the creatures drown. Enraged, the swineherds began throwing stones at Jesus and his companions, and were now coming after them, to demand compensation, so much per head multiplied by two thousand, a sum easy enough to calculate, not so easy to pay. Fishermen earn little money, they lead a meager existence, and Jesus could not even claim to be a fisherman. But the Nazarene decided to face the irate swineherds, to explain to them that there is no greater evil in this world than the devil, and that compared with Satan two thousand pigs is nothing, besides, we all suffer losses in this life, material or otherwise, So be patient, brethren, Jesus was prepared to urge them. But the last thing James and John wanted was a heated exchange with the swineherds, any show of friendship or goodwill was unlikely to appease the wrath of those rough characters intent on revenge. Reluctantly Jesus yielded to James and John's arguments, which grew more persuasive as the stones fell closer. They ran down the slope to the water's edge, jumped into their boat, and rowing at top speed, were soon out of danger. Swineherds, as a rule, do little fishing, and if the ones in pursuit had boats, they were nowhere in sight. Some pigs were lost, a soul was saved, the winner is God, said James. Jesus looked at him, his thoughts elsewhere, on something the two brothers watching him wished to hear about and discuss, the strange revelation by the demons that Jesus was the son of God, but Jesus turned to the bank from which they had escaped, gazed at the water, the pigs floating and rolling with the waves, two thousand innocent animals, and he felt an uneasiness rising within him, searching for an outlet, until he could no longer contain himself and exclaimed, The demons, where are the demons, and then he sent up a roar of laughter to heaven, Listen, Lord, either You chose poorly this son who must carry out Your plans, according to what those demons said, or there is something missing in Your powers, for otherwise You would be able to defeat the devil. What are you saying, asked John, appalled by this unthinkable challenge. I'm saying that the demons who possessed the man are now free, for demons as we know don't die, my friends, not even God can kill them, and for all the good I did there I might as well have struck the lake with a sword. On the shore a great crowd was descending, some jumped into the water to retrieve the pigs floating within reach, while others jumped into their boats and set off to gather any they could find.

That night, in the home of Simon and Andrew, which was near the synagogue, the five friends gathered in secret to discuss the extraordinary revelation by the demons that Jesus was the son of God. Greatly puzzled by what had happened, they agreed not to talk until after dusk, and the moment had now come to speak their minds. Jesus began by saying, One cannot trust the father of falsehood, clearly referring to the devil. Andrew said, Truth and falsehood pass through the same lips and leave no mark, the devil does not cease to be the devil just because he may have spoken the truth. Simon said, We knew you were no ordinary man, first there were the fish you helped us catch, then the storm that almost killed us, then the water you turned to wine, then the adulteress you saved from being stoned to death, and now these demons you exorcised. Jesus said, I am not the only one who has driven demons from people. That's true, said James, but you're the first they have addressed as the son of the Almighty. It didn't do much good, either, for in the end it was not they but I who was humiliated. That's not the point, interrupted John, I was there and heard everything, why didn't you tell us you were the son of God. But I'm not sure I am the son of God. How can the devil know if you don't. A good question, but they alone can answer it. Who do you mean by they. I mean God, whose son the devil claims I am, and the devil, who could only have been told by God. A silence fell, as if everyone was giving the powers invoked time to declare themselves, until finally Simon asked, What is there between you and God. Jesus sighed, That's the question I was afraid you would ask. Who would ever believe the son of God would choose to be a fisherman. I've already explained, I'm not even sure I am the son of God. Well, who are you then. Jesus covered his face with his hands, wondered how to begin the confession they wanted from him, his life suddenly seemed to be the life of someone else, perhaps that was it, if the demons spoke the truth, then everything which had happened to him took on a different meaning, and some of those events were only now becoming clear in the light of this. He lowered his hands, looked at his friends one by one with a pleading expression, as if asking them for trust to a greater degree than any man had a right to ask another, then after a long pause he told them, I have seen God. No one said a word, they waited. Lowering his eyes, he continued, I met Him in the desert, and He told me that when the hour came, He would give me power and glory in exchange for my life, but He never said I was His son. More silence. And how did God appear to you, asked James. Like a cloud, a column of smoke. You're sure it wasn't fire. No, not fire but smoke, and He said nothing else, only that He would return at the right moment. What moment is that. I really don't know, perhaps He meant the moment when I must sacrifice my life. And what about this power and glory, when will these be granted. Who knows. Again silence. The heat inside was stifling, yet they were all shivering. Then Simon asked

301

slowly, Are you the Messiah whom we should call the son of God because you have come to deliver God's people from bondage. I, the Messiah. No more incredible than your being the son of the Lord, said Andrew nervously. James said, Messiah or son of God, what I cannot understand is how the devil came to know it, when even the Lord did not confide in you. John said pensively, I wonder what the secret relationship is between the devil and God. Terrified of learning that truth, they eyed each other uneasily, and Simon asked Jesus, What are you going to do, and Jesus replied, The only thing I can do, wait for my hour to come.

And it is fast approaching, but until then Jesus will have two more opportunities to demonstrate his miraculous powers, although it might be better for us to draw a veil over the second, because it was a blunder on his part and resulted in the death of a fig tree as innocent of evil as those pigs the demons sent hurtling into the lake. The first of these two miracles, however, fully deserved to be brought to the attention of the priests of Jerusalem, that it might later be engraved in gold letters over the Temple door, for such a thing had never been witnessed before and indeed was never witnessed thereafter. Historians disagree as to why so many different races should have gathered in that place, whose exact location, let it be said in passing, has also been the subject of debate. Some historians claim the gathering was nothing more than a traditional pilgrimage, the origins of which are obscure, others say the crowd assembled there because of a rumor, later disproved, that an envoy had arrived from Rome to announce a reduction in taxes, there are also some historians who, not offering any hypotheses themselves, argue that only the simpleminded could believe in a tax reduction that would benefit taxpayers, and as for the pilgrimage of obscure origins, it could easily be verified if those who liked to spin such fantasies took the trouble to do a little research. What is beyond

dispute is that some four to five thousand people came together there, not counting women and children, and that
it turned out that they had nothing to eat. How such careful people, used to traveling and never without a well-
stocked pack even on the shortest journey, could have suddenly found themselves without so much as a crust of bread
or scrap of meat is something no one has ever been able to
explain. But facts are facts, and the facts say that there
were twelve to fifteen thousand, this time including women
and children, who had gone without food for hours and
would soon return to their homes and risk dropping from
sheer weakness on route, unless fortunate enough to be
rescued by a charitable passerby. The children, who are
always the first to complain in any crisis, grew impatient,
some of them whimpering, Mother, I'm hungry, and the
situation was quickly becoming intolerable. Jesus walked
among the multitude with Mary Magdalene, accompanied
by Simon, Andrew, James, and John, who since the episode of the pigs and its aftermath went everywhere with
Jesus, but unlike the rest of the crowd they had brought
some bread and fish and so had come provided. To have
set about eating in the presence of all these people, however, would not only have shown complete selfishness but
also have put them at some risk, for necessity knows no
law, and the most effective form of justice, as Cain taught
us, is that which we ourselves grab with both hands. Jesus
did not imagine for a moment that he could be of any help
to this vast assembly in need of food, but James and John
said to him, If you were able to drive demons from a man's
body, surely you can give these people the food they need.
And how am I to do this if we have no food other than
the few provisions we brought for ourselves. As the son
of God you must be able to do something. Jesus looked at
Mary Magdalene, who told him, There is no turning back
now, and her face was filled with compassion, although
Jesus did not know if it was meant for him or for the

famished multitude. He took the six loaves they had brought with them, broke each loaf in half, and gave them to his companions, then he did the same with the six fish, keeping a loaf and a fish for himself. Then he said, follow me and do as I do. And we know what he did, but will never know how he managed it. Going from person to person, he divided and distributed bread and fish, and each person received a whole loaf and a whole fish. Mary Magdalene and the four friends of Jesus did the same, and they passed through the crowd as a beneficent wind blows over the field of a farm and raises the drooping cornstalks one by one, to the sound of rustling leaves, which were mouths chewing and thanking. It is the Messiah, said some. He's a magician, insisted others, but it never dawned on anyone in the crowd to ask, Could this be the son of God. And to all of them Jesus said, Let those who have ears listen, for unless you divide, you will never multiply.

It was only right for Jesus to teach this rule when he had the opportunity. But he was wrong to apply it to the letter when it was inopportune, as in the case of the fig tree mentioned earlier. He was walking along a country lane when he began to feel hungry, and spotting a green fig tree in the distance, he went to see if it had any fruit on it. But coming closer, he found nothing but leaves, because it was too early for figs. Whereupon Jesus said to the tree, No more fruit will grow on your branches, and at that very moment the fig tree dried up. Mary Magdalene, who was with him, said, You must give to those in need but ask nothing of those with nothing to give. Filled with remorse, Jesus tried to revive the fig tree, but it was quite dead.

A MISTY MORNING. THE FISHERMAN RISES FROM HIS MAT, looks at the whiteness through a chink in the door, and says to his wife, I'm not taking the boat out today, in this kind of mist even the fish lose their way. All the other fishermen, from one shore to another, echo his sentiment, using more or less the same words, they are puzzled by the rare phenomenon of mist at this time of year. Only one man, who is not a fisherman by profession although he lives and works with fishermen, goes to his front door and sees that this is the day he has been waiting for. Looking up at the dull sky, he says, I'm going fishing. At his shoulder, Mary Magdalene asks, Must you, and Jesus replied, I've waited a long time for this day to come. Won't you eat something. Eyes are fasting when they open in the morning, but he embraced her and said, At last I will learn who I am and what is expected of me, then with surprising confidence, for he could not even see his own feet in the mist, he descended the slope to the water's edge, climbed into one of the boats moored there, and began rowing out toward the invisible space in the middle of the lake. The noise of the oars scraping against the sides of the boat and the bubbling and rippling of water around the wood blades carried over the surface, it kept awake those fishermen whose wives had told them, If you can't go out fishing, at least try to get some sleep. Restless and uneasy, the villagers stared at the impenetrable mist in the direction of the lake and waited for the noise of the oars to stop, so they could return to their homes and secure their doors with keys, crossbars, and padlocks, while knowing that if he in the mist is who they think he is and he decides to blow this way, a puff of air from him would knock them down. The mist allows Jesus to pass, but his eyes can see no farther than the tip of the oars and the stern, with its simple plank that serves as a bench. The rest is a blank wall, at first dim and gray, then, as the boat approaches its destination, a diffused light turns the mist white and lustrous, it quivers as if searching for a sound in the silence. The boat, moving into a circle of light, comes to a halt, it has reached the center of the lake. God is sitting at the stern, on the bench.

Unlike the first time, He does not appear as a cloud or column of smoke, which in this weather would be lost in the mist. This time He is a big man, elderly, a great flowing beard over His chest, head uncovered, hair hanging loose, a broad and powerful face, fleshy lips which barely move when He begins to speak. He is dressed like a wealthy Jew, in a long magenta tunic under a blue cape with sleeves and gold braiding, the thick sandals on His feet are those of one who walks a great deal, whose habits are anything but sedentary. When He is gone, we will ask ourselves, What was His hair like, unable to remember whether it was white, black, or brown, judging by His age it must have been white, but there are some whose hair takes a long time to turn white, and He might be one of them. Jesus raised the oars and rested them inside the boat, as if preparing for a lengthy conversation, and simply said, Here

306

I am. Slowly and methodically, God arranged the folds of the cape over His knees and added, Well, here we are. The voice suggested a smile, though His lips hardly moved, only the long hairs of His mustache and beard quivered like the vibration of a bell. Jesus said, I've come to find out who I am and what I must do henceforth to fulfill my part of the covenant. God said, These are two questions, let us take them one at a time, where would you like to start. With the first, said Jesus, and asked again, Who am I. Don't you know. Well, I thought I knew, I thought I was my father's son. Which father do you mean. My father, the carpenter Joseph, son of Eli, or was it Jacob, for I'm no longer certain. You mean the carpenter Joseph whom they crucified. I didn't know there was any other. A tragic mistake on the part of the Romans, that poor father died innocent, having committed no crime. You said that father, so there is another. I'm proud of you, I can see you're an intelligent lad and perceptive. There was no need for intelligence, I was told by the devil. Are you in league with the devil. No, I'm not in league with the devil, it was the devil who sought me out. And what did you hear from his lips. That I am Your son. Nodding His head slowly in agreement, God told him, Yes, you are my son. But how can a man be the son of God. If you're the son of God, you are not a man. But I am a man, I breathe, I eat, I sleep, and I love like a man, therefore I am a man and will die as a man. In your case I wouldn't be too sure. What do you mean. That's the second question, but we have time, how did you answer the devil when he said you were my son. I didn't answer, I simply waited for the day when I would meet You, then I drove Satan out of the possessed man he was tormenting, the man called himself Legion and said he was many. Where are they now. I have no idea. You said you exorcised those demons. Surely You know better than I that when demons are driven out of a body, nobody knows where they go. And what makes you

307

think I'm familiar with the devil's affairs. Being God, You must know everything. Up to a point, only up to a point. What point is that. The point where it becomes interesting to pretend I do not know. At least You must know how I came to be Your son and for what reason. I can see you are somewhat more confident, not to say impatient, than when I first met you. I was a mere boy then and rather shy, but I'm grown now. And you're not afraid. No. You will be, fear always comes, even to a son of God. You mean you have others. What others. Sons, of course. No, I only needed one. And how did I come to be Your son. Didn't your mother tell you. Does my mother know. I sent an angel to explain things to her, I thought she told you. And when was this angel with my mother. Let Me see, unless I'm mistaken it was after you left home for the second time and before you miraculously changed the water into wine at Cana. So, Mother knew and never said a word, when I told her I saw You in the desert, she didn't believe me, but she must have realized I was telling the truth after the angel's appearance, yet she did not confide in me. You know what women are like, after all you live with one, they have their little sensitivities and scruples. What sensitivities and scruples. Well, let Me explain, I mixed My seed with that of your father before you were conceived, it was the easiest way and the least conspicuous. If the seeds were mixed, how can You be sure I am Your son. I agree that it's usually unwise to be certain about anything, but I'm certain, there is some advantage in being God. And why did You want a son. I didn't have a son in heaven, so I had to arrange for one on earth, which is not all that original, even in religions with gods and goddesses, who can easily give one another children, we have seen some of them descend to earth, probably for a change of scenery, and at the same time they benefit mankind with the creation of heroes and other wonders. And this son who I am, why did You want him. Not, needless to say, for a change of scenery. Why, then. Because I needed someone to help Me here on earth. But surely, being God, You don't need help. That is the second question.

In the silence that followed, one could hear off in the mist, although from which direction one could not tell, the noise of a man swimming this way. To judge from the puffing and panting, he was no great swimmer and close to exhaustion. Jesus thought he saw God smiling and felt sure He was deliberately giving the swimmer time to reach the circle of clear air around the boat. The swimmer surfaced unexpectedly on the starboard side, Jesus was looking on the port side, it was a dark, ill-defined shape which at first he mistook for a pig, its ears sticking out of the water, but after it took a few more strokes he saw it was a man or a creature with human form. God turned His head to the swimmer, not out of idle curiosity but with real interest, as if encouraging him to make one last effort, and this turn of the head, perhaps because it came from God, had an immediate effect, the final strokes were rapid and regular, as if the swimmer had not covered all that distance from the shore. His hands clutched the edge of the boat, although his head was still half in the water, they were huge, powerful hands with strong nails, hands belonging to a body that had to be tall, sturdy, and advanced in years, like God's. The boat swayed, the swimmer's head emerged from the water, then his torso, splashing water everywhere, then his legs, a leviathan rising from the depths, and it turned out to be Pastor, reappearing after all these years. I've come to join you, he said, settling himself on the side of the boat, equidistant between Jesus and God, and yet oddly enough this time the boat did not tip to his side, as if Pastor had no weight or he was levitating and not really sitting, I've come to join you, he repeated, and hope I'm in time to take part in the conversation. We've been talking but still haven't got to the heart of the matter, replied God, and turning to Jesus, He told him, This is the devil whom we have just been discussing. Jesus looked from one to the other and saw that without God's beard they could have passed for twins, although the devil was younger and less wrinkled. Jesus said, I know very well who he is, I lived with him for four years when he was known as Pastor, and God replied, You had to live with someone, it couldn't be with Me, and you didn't wish to be with your family, so that left only the devil. Did he come looking for me or did You send him. Neither one nor the other, let's say we agreed that this was the best solution. So that's why, when he spoke through the possessed man from Gadara, he called me Your son. Precisely. Which means that both of you kept me in the dark. As happens to all humans. But You said I was not human. And that is true, but you have been what might technically be called incarnated. And now what do you two want of me. I'm the one who wants something, not he. But both of you are here, I noticed that Pastor's appearance came as no surprise, You must have been expecting him. Not exactly, although in principle one should always expect the devil. But if the matter You and I have to resolve affects only us, what is he doing here and why don't You send him away. One can dismiss the rabble in the devil's service if they become troublesome in word or deed, but not Satan himself. Then he's here because this conversation concerns him too. My son, never forget what I'm about to tell you, everything that concerns God also concerns the devil. Pastor, whom we shall sometimes refer to as such rather than constantly invoke the Enemy by name, overheard all this without appearing to listen or care, as if in contradiction of God's momentous statement. It soon became clear, however, that his inattentiveness was a sham, because when Jesus said, Let's now turn to the second question, Pastor immediately pricked up his ears.

God took a deep breath, looked at the mist around Him, and murmured in the hushed tone of one who has just made a curious discovery, This is not unlike being in the desert. He turned His eyes toward Jesus, paused awhile, then began speaking, as if resigning himself to the inevitable, Dissatisfaction, My son, was put into the hearts of men by the God who created them, I'm referring to Myself, of course, but this dissatisfaction, one of the qualities which make man in My image and likeness, I nursed in My own heart, and rather than diminish with time it has grown stronger, more pressing and insistent. God stopped for a moment to consider this preamble before going on to say, For the last four thousand and four years I have been the God of the Jews, a quarrelsome and difficult race by nature, but on the whole I have got along fairly well with them, they now take Me seriously and are likely to go on doing so for the foreseeable future. So, You are satisfied, said Jesus. I am and I am not, or rather, I would be were it not for this restless heart of Mine, which is forever telling Me, Well now, a fine destiny you've arranged after four thousand years of trial and tribulation that no amount of sacrifice on altars will ever be able to repay, for You continue to be the god of a tiny population that occupies a minute part of this world You created with everything that's on it, so tell Me, My son, if I should be satisfied with this depressing situation. Never having created a world, I'm in no position to judge, replied Jesus. True, you cannot judge, but you could help. Help in what way. To spread My word, to help Me become the god of more people. I don't understand. If you play your part, that is to say, the part I have reserved for you in My plan, I have every confidence that within the next six centuries or so, despite all the struggles and obstacles ahead of us, I will pass from being God of the Jews to being God of those whom we will call Catholics, from the Greek. And what is this part You have reserved for me in Your plan. That of martyr, My son, that of victim, which is the best role of all for propagating any faith and stirring up fervor. God made the words

311

martyr and victim seem like milk and honey on His tongue, but Jesus felt a sudden chill in his limbs, as if the mist had closed over him, while the devil regarded him with an enigmatic expression which combined scientific curiosity with grudging compassion.

You promised me power and glory, stammered Jesus, shivering with cold. And I intend to keep that promise, but remember our agreement, you will have them after your death. What good will it do me to have power and glory when I'm dead. Well, you won't be dead in the absolute sense of the word, for as My son you'll be with Me, or in Me, I still haven't decided. You haven't decided how I will not be dead. That's right, for example you'll be venerated in churches and on altars to such an extent that people will even forget that I came first as God, but no matter, abundance can be shared, what is in short supply should not be. Jesus looked at Pastor, saw him smile, and understood, Now I see why the devil is here, if Your authority extends to more people in more places, his power also spreads, for his territory will be the same as Yours. You're quite right, my son, and I'm delighted to see how quick you are, for most people overlook the fact that the demons of one religion are powerless to act in another, just as any god, confronting another, can neither vanquish him nor be vanquished by him. And my death, what will that be like. A martyr's death should be painful and, if possible, ignominious, that the believers may be moved to greater devotion. Come to the point and tell me what kind of death I can expect. A painful and ignominious death on a cross. Like my father. You're forgetting that I'm your father. Were I free to make a choice, I'd choose him despite his moment of shame. But you have been chosen and therefore have no say. I want to end our covenant, to have nothing more to do with You, I want to live like any other man. Empty words, My son, don't you see that you're in My power and that all these documents we call covenants, agree-

312

ments, pacts, or contracts, in which I figure, could be reduced to a single clause, wasting less paper and ink, a clause that bluntly says, Everything in the law of God is necessary, even the exceptions, and since you, My son, are an exception, you are as necessary as the law and I who made it. But with the power You have, wouldn't it be simpler and more honest for You to go out and conquer those other countries and races Yourself. Alas, I cannot, it is forbidden by the binding agreement between the gods ever to interfere directly, can you imagine Me in a public square, surrounded by Gentiles and pagans, trying to persuade them that their god is false while I am their real God, this is not something one god does to another, besides, no god likes another god to come and do in his house what the latter forbids in his own. So You make use of men instead. Yes, My son, man is a piece of wood that can be used for anything, from the moment he is born to the moment he dies, he's always ready to obey, send him and he goes, tell him to stop and he stops, tell him to withdraw and he withdraws, whether in peace or in war, man generally speaking is the best thing that ever happened to the gods. And the wood from which I'm made, since I'm a man, what use will it be put to, since I'm Your son. You will be the spoon I dip into humanity and bring out filled with people who believe in the new god I intend to become. Filled with people You will eat. There's no need for Me to eat those who eat themselves.

Jesus lowered his oars back into the water and said, Farewell, I'm going home, and you can both go back the way you came, you by swimming and You by disappearing as mysteriously as You appeared. Neither God nor the devil stirred, so Jesus added ironically, Then you prefer to go by boat, better still, I'll row you ashore myself so that everyone can see how alike God and the devil are and how well they get on together. Jesus turned the boat to face the direction from which he had come, and rowing vigorously, he entered the mist, which was so thick that he could no longer see God or the devil's face. Jesus felt alive, happy, and unusually strong. The prow of the boat rose with each stroke of the oars like the head of a horse in a race, and he rowed harder, they must be almost there, he wonders how people will react when he tells them, The one with the beard is God, the other is the devil. Glancing over his shoulder at the shore ahead, Jesus could make out a light, and he announced, We're here, and continued rowing, expecting any second to feel the bottom of the boat glide softly over thick mud, and the playful grazing of tiny loose pebbles, but the prow of the boat was pointing instead to the middle of the lake, and as for the light, it was now the same magic circle of light, the bright snare which Jesus thought he had escaped. His head fell, he crossed his arms over his knees in exhaustion, one wrist resting on the other, as if waiting to be bound, he even forgot to pull in the oars, convinced that any further action was futile. But he would not be the first to speak, he would not acknowledge defeat in a loud voice and ask to be forgiven for having defied God's will and also indirectly the devil's interests, the devil being the beneficiary of the consequences of His plan. The silence was short-lived. Sitting there on the bench, God arranged the folds of His tunic and the hood of His cape, then with mock solemnity, like a judge about to pass sentence, said, Let us start again, going back to where I revealed that you are in My power, for until you submit humbly to this truth you waste your time and Mine. Let us start again, agreed Jesus, but be warned, I refuse to work any more miracles, and without miracles Your plan will come to nothing, a mere sprinkle from heaven which cannot satisfy any real thirst. You would be right if it lay within your power not to work miracles. Don't I have that power. What an idea, I work miracles both great and small, naturally in your presence, so that you may reap the benefits on my behalf, but you are superstitious, believing the

314

miracle worker must stand at the patient's bedside for the thing to take place, yet if I so wished, a man dying alone, with no one at his side, without a doctor, nurse, or beloved relative within sight or hearing, if I so wished, I tell you, that man would be saved and go on living as if nothing had happened to him. Then why not do it. Because he would imagine he'd been cured by his own merit and start boasting, I am too good to die, and with all the presumption there already is in this world I've created, I have no intention of encouraging such nonsense. So all my miracles are Yours. All you have worked and will work, and even if you persist in opposing My will, and go out into the world and deny you are the son of God, I will cause so many miracles to occur wherever you pass that you will be obliged to accept the gratitude of those thanking you and thereby thanking Me. Then there is no way out. None whatever, and don't play the lamb taken to be sacrificed, who struggles and bleats pitifully, for your fate is sealed, the sword awaits. Am I that lamb. You are the lamb of God, My son, which God himself will carry to the altar we are preparing here.

Jesus looked to Pastor, not so much for help as for a signal, Pastor's understanding of the world must be different, he is not a man or ever has been, or a god, a glance or raised eyebrow might suggest a reply that would allow Jesus to extricate himself, at least momentarily, from this difficult situation. But all he reads in Pastor's eyes are the words the shepherd spoke to him when he banished him from the herd, You've learned nothing, begone with you. Now Jesus realizes that to disobey God once is not enough, that having refused to offer Him his sacrificial lamb, he must also refuse Him His own lamb, one cannot say yes to God and then say no, as if yes and no were one's left and right hands and the only good work the kind done with both. Because notwithstanding His manifestations of power, the universe and stars, lightning and thunder, voices and flames on mountaintops, God did not force you to slaughter the sheep, it was out of ambition that you killed the animal, and its blood could not be absorbed by all the sand in the desert, see how it has even reached us, that thread of crimson which will follow us wherever we go, you and God and me. Jesus said to God, I will tell men I am Your son, the only son God has, but I do not think that even in this land of Yours it will be enough to enlarge Your kingdom as much as You wish. At last you speak like a true son, you've given up those tiresome acts of rebellion which were beginning to anger Me, you've come around to My way of thinking, therefore know that whatever their race, color, creed, or philosophy, one thing is common to all men, only one, such that none of them, wise or ignorant, young or old, rich or poor, would dare to say, This has nothing to do with me. And what might that be, asked Jesus with interest. All men, replied God, as if imparting wisdom, whoever and wherever they may be and whatever they may do, are sinners, for sin is as inseparable from man as man from sin, man is like a coin, turn it over and what you see is sin. You haven't answered my question. Here is My answer, the only word no man can say does not apply to him is repentance, because all have succumbed to temptation, entertained an evil thought, broken a rule, committed some crime, serious or minor, spurned a soul in need, neglected a duty, offended religion and its ministers, or turned away from God, to all such men you need only say, Repent, repent, repent. But why sacrifice Your own son's life for so little, surely all You have to do is send a prophet. The time when people listened to prophets has passed, nowadays one must administer stronger medicine, shock treatment, to touch men's hearts and stir their feelings. Such as a son of God hanging from a cross. Yes, why not. And what else am I supposed to say to these people, besides urging them to repent, if they grow tired of hearing Your message and turn a deaf

316

ear. Yes, I agree, it may not be enough to ask them to repent, you may have to use your imagination, and don't make any excuses, look at the cunning way you avoided sacrificing your lamb. That was easy enough, the animal had nothing to repent. A subtle reply but meaningless, although meaninglessness too has its charm, people should be left perplexed, afraid that they don't understand and that it is their fault. So I'm to make up stories. Yes, stories, parables, moral tales, even if it means distorting holy law a little, don't let that bother you, the timid always admire it when liberties are taken, I myself was impressed by the way you saved that adulteress from death, and remember, it was I who put that punishment into the commandments I gave. It's a bad sign when You start allowing men to tamper with Your commandments. Only when it suits Me and is useful, you must not forget what I told you about the law and its exceptions, for whatever I will becomes instantly necessary. You said I must die on the cross. That is my will. Jesus looked askance at Pastor, who seemed to be preoccupied, as if contemplating a moment in the future, unable to believe his eyes. Jesus dropped his arms and said, Then do with me as You will.

God was about to rejoice, to rise to His feet and embrace His beloved son, when Jesus stopped Him with a gesture and said, On one condition. You know perfectly well you cannot set conditions, God replied angrily. Then let's call it a plea rather than a condition, the simple plea of a man sentenced to death. Tell me. You are God and therefore can speak only the truth when asked a question, and being God, You know the past, the present, what lies between them, and what the future will bring. That is so, I am time, truth, and life. Then tell me, in the name of all You claim to be, what will the future bring after my death, what will it contain that it would not had I refused to sacrifice myself to Your dissatisfaction and desire to reign far and wide. As if trapped by His own words, God made a

317

halfhearted attempt to shrug this off, Now then, son, the future is infinite and would take a long time to summarize. How long have we been out here in the middle of the lake, surrounded by mist, asked Jesus, a day, a month, a year, well then, let's stay another year, month, or day, allow the devil to leave if he wants to, for in any case his share is guaranteed, and if the benefits are proportional, as seems just, the more God prospers, the more the devil prospers. I'm staying, said Pastor, and these were the first words he spoke since revealing his identity. I'm staying, he said a second time, and added, I myself can see things in the future, but I'm not always certain if what I see there is true or false, in other words I can see my lies for what they are, that is, my truths, but I don't know to what extent the truths of others are their lies. This tortuous statement might have been clearer had Pastor said something more about the future he saw, but he abruptly fell silent, as if he had already said too much. Jesus, who kept his eyes on God, said with wistful irony, Why pretend not to know what You know, You realized I would ask this question, and You know very well You will tell me what I want to hear, so postpone no longer my time of dying. You began dying the moment you were born. True, but now I die all the sooner. God looked at Jesus with an expression which in a person we would describe as respectful, His whole manner became human, and although the one thing did not appear to have anything to do with the other, the mist came nearer the boat, surrounded it like a wall to keep from the world God's words about the consequences of the sacrifice of Jesus, who He claims is His son, with Mary, but whose real father is Joseph, if we go by the unwritten law that tells us to believe only in what we see, although as everyone knows, we mortals do not always see things in the same way, and this has undoubtedly helped preserve the relative sanity of the species.

God said, There will be a church, a religious society

founded by you or in your name, which comes to the same thing, and this church will spread throughout the world and be called Catholic, because universal, although sadly this will not prevent discord and misunderstanding among those who see you, rather than Me, as their spiritual leader, which will last no more than several thousand years, for I was here before you and will continue to be here after you cease to be what you are and what you will be. Speak more clearly, said Jesus. It's impossible, said God, human words are like shadows, and shadows cannot explain light, and between shadow and light stands the opaque body from which words are born. I asked You about the future. It's the future I speak about. What I want to know is how the men who come after me will live. Are you referring to your followers. Yes, will they be happier. Not in the true sense of the word, but they will have the hope of achieving happiness up in heaven, where I reign for all eternity and where they hope to live eternally with Me. Is that all. Surely it is no small thing to live with God. Small, great, or everything, we will only know at the day of final judgment, when You judge men according to the good or evil they have done, until then You reside alone in heaven. My angels and archangels keep Me company. But You have no human beings there. True, and you must be crucified in order that they come to Me. I want to know more, said Jesus, trying hard to shut out the mental image of himself hanging from a cross, covered with blood, dead, How will people come to believe in me and follow me, surely what I say to them or what those who come after me say to them in my name will not be enough, take the Gentiles and Romans, for example, who worship other gods, You don't expect me to believe they will give them up just like that to worship me. Not to worship you but to worship Me. But did You not say that You and me amounts to the same thing, let us not play with words, however, just answer my question. Whoever has faith will come to us. Just like that, as easily as You've just said. The other gods will resist. And You will fight them, of course. Don't be absurd, war occurs only on earth, heaven is eternal and peaceful, and men will fulfill their destiny wherever they may be. You mean men will die for You and for me. Men have always died for gods, even for false and lying gods. Can gods lie. They can. And You are the one and only true god among them. Yes, the one and only true god. Yet You are unable to prevent men from dying for You when they should have been born to live for You on earth rather than in heaven, where You have none of life's joys to offer them. Those joys too are false, for they come from original sin, ask your friend Pastor, he'll explain what happened. If there are any secrets You and the devil do not share, I hope one of them is what I learned from him, even though he says I learned nothing. There was silence, God and the devil faced each other for the first time, both giving the impression of being about to speak, but they didn't. Jesus said, I'm waiting. For what, asked God, as if distracted. For You to tell me how much death and suffering Your victory over other gods will cause, how much death and suffering will be needed in the battles men fight in Your name and mine. You insist on knowing. I do.

Very well then, the church I mentioned will be established, but its foundation, in order to be truly solid, will be dug in flesh, its walls made from the cement of renunciation, tears, agony, anguish, every conceivable form of death. At long last You speak so I can understand, go on. Let's start with someone you know and love, the fisherman Simon, whom you will call Peter, like you, he will be crucified, but upside down, Andrew too will be crucified, on a cross in the shape of an X, the son of Zebedee known as James will be beheaded. What about John, and Mary Magdalene. They will die of natural causes when their time comes, but you will make other friends, disciples, and apostles who will not escape torture, such as Philip,

320

who will be tied to a cross and stoned to death, Bartholomew, who will be skinned alive, Thomas, who will be speared to death, Matthew, the details of whose death I no longer remember, another Simon, who will be sawed in half, Judas, who will be beaten to death, James stoned, Matthias beheaded with an ax, also Judas Iscariot hanged from a fig tree by his own hand. Are all these men to die because of You, asked Jesus. If you phrase the question that way, the answer is yes, they will die for My sake. And then what. Then, My son, as I've already told you, there follows an endless tale of iron and blood, of fire and ashes, an infinite sea of sorrow and tears. Tell me, I want to know everything. God sighed, and in the monotonous tone of one who chooses to suppress compassion He began a litany, in alphabetical order so as not to hurt any feelings about precedence and importance, Adalbert of Prague put to death with a seven-pronged pikestaff, Adrian hammered to death over an anvil, Afra of Augsburg burned at the stake, Agapitus of Praeneste burned at the stake hanging by his feet, Agnes of Rome disemboweled, Agricola of Bologna crucified and impaled on nails, Agueda of Sicily stabbed six times, Alphege of Canterbury beaten to death with the shinbone of an ox, Anastasia of Sirmium burned at the stake and her breasts cut off, Anastasius of Salona strung up on the gallows and decapitated, Ansanus of Siena his entrails ripped out, Antonius of Pamiers drawn and quartered, Antony of Rivoli stoned and burned alive, Apollinaris of Ravenna clubbed to death, Apollonia of Alexandria burned at the stake after her teeth had been knocked out, Augusta of Treviso decapitated and burned at the stake, Aurea of Ostia drowned with a millstone around her neck, Aurea of Syria bled to death by being forced onto a chair covered with nails, Auta shot with arrows, Babylas of Antioch decapitated, Barbara of Nicomedia likewise, Barnabas of Cyprus stoned and burned at the stake, Beatrice of Rome strangled, Benignus of Dijon speared to death, Blaise of Sebaste thrown onto iron spikes, Blandina of Lyons gored by a savage bull, Callistus put to death with a millstone around his neck, Cassian of Imola stabbed with a dagger by his disciples, Castulus buried alive, Catherine of Alexandria decapitated, Cecilia of Rome beheaded, Christina of Bolsena tortured repeatedly with millstones tongs, arrows, and snakes, Clarus of Nastes decapitated, Clarus of Vienne likewise, Clement drowned with an anchor around his neck, Crispin and Crispinian of Soissons both decapitated, Cucuphas of Barcelona disemboweled, Cyprian of Carthage beheaded, young Cyricus of Tarsus killed by a judge who knocked his head against the stairs of the tribunal, and on reaching the end of the letter C, God said, And so on, it's all much the same, with a few variations and an occasional refinement which would take forever to explain, so let's leave it at that. No, continue, said Jesus, so reluctantly God continued, abbreviating wherever possible, Donatus of Arezzo decapitated, Eliphius of Rampillon scalped, Emerita burned alive, Emilian of Trevi decapitated, Emmeramus of Regensburg tied to a ladder and put to death, Engratia of Saragossa decapitated, Erasmus of Gaeta also called Elmo stretched on a windlass, Escubiculus beheaded, Eskil of Sweden stoned to death, Eulalia of Merida decapitated, Euphemia of Chalcedon put to the sword, Eutropius of Saintes beheaded with an ax, Fabian stabbed and spiked, Faith of Agen beheaded, Felicitas and seven sons beheaded with a sword, Felix and his brother Adauctus likewise, Ferreolus of Besançon decapitated, Fidelis of Sigmaringen beaten to death with a spiked club, Firminus of Pamplona beheaded, Flavia Domitilla likewise, Fortunas of Evora probably met the same fate, Fructoasus of Tarragon burned at the stake, Gaudentius of France decapitated, Gelasius likewise with iron spikes, Gengolf of Burgundy assassinated by his wife's lover, Gerard Sagreda of Budapest speared to death, Gerean of Cologne decapitated, the twins Gervase and Protase likewise,

Godleva and Ghistelles strangled, Gratus of Aosta decapitated, Hermenegild clubbed to death, Hero stabbed with a sword, Hippolytus dragged to his death by a horse, Ignatius of Azevedo murdered by the Calvinists, who are not Catholics, Januarius of Naples decapitated after being thrown to wild beasts and then into a furnace, Joan of Arc burned at the stake, John de Britto beheaded, John Fisher decapitated, John of Nepomuk drowned in the river Vltava, John of Prado stabbed in the head, Julia of Corsica whose breasts were cut off before she was crucified, Juliana of Nicomedia decapitated, Justa and Ruffina of Seville the former killed on the wheel and the latter strangled, Justina of Antioch thrown into a caldron of boiling tar and then beheaded, Justus and Pastor, not our Pastor but the one from Alcalá de Henares, decapitated, Kilian of Würzburg decapitated, Lawrence burned on a gridiron, Léger of Autun decapitated after his eyes and tongue were torn out, Leocadia of Toledo thrown to her death from a high cliff, Livinus of Ghent decapitated after his tongue was torn out, Longinus decapitated, Lucy of Syracuse beheaded after having her eyes plucked out, Ludmila of Prague strangled, Maginus of Tarragon decapitated with a serrated scythe, Mamas of Cappodocia disemboweled, Manuel, Sabel, and Ismael, Manuel put to death with an iron nail embedded in each nipple and an iron rod driven through his head from ear to ear and all three beheaded, Margaret of Antioch killed with a firebrand and an iron comb, Maria Goretti strangled, Marius of Persia put to the sword and his hands amputated, Martina of Rome decapitated, the martyrs of Morocco, Berard of Carbio, Peter of Gimignano, Otto, Adjuto, and Accursio, beheaded, those of Japan, all twenty-six crucified, speared, and burned alive, Maurice of Agaune put to the sword, Meinrad of Einsiedeln clubbed to death, Menas of Alexandria also put to the sword, Mercurius of Cappadocia decapitated, Nicasius of Rheims likewise, Odilia of Huy shot with arrows, Paneras beheaded,

323

Pantaleon of Nicomedia likewise, Paphnutius crucified, Patroclus of Troyes and Soest likewise, Paul of Tarsus, to whom you will owe your first church, likewise, Pelagius drawn and quartered, Perpetua and her slave Felicity of Carthage both gored by a raging bull, Peter of Rates killed with a sword, Peter of Verona his head slashed with a cutlass and a dagger driven into his chest, Philomena shot with arrows and anchored, Piaton of Tournai scalped, Polycarp stabbed and burned alive, Prisca of Rome devoured by lions, Processus and Martinian probably met the same fate, Quintinus nails driven into his head and other parts of his body, Quirinus of Rouen scalped, Quiteria of Coimbra decapitated by her own father, Reine of Alise put to the sword, Renaud of Dortmund bludgeoned to death with a mason's mallet, Restituta of Naples burned at the stake, Roland put to the sword, Romanus of Antioch strangled to death after his tongue was torn out, have you had enough, God asked Jesus, who retorted, That's something You should ask Yourself, go on. So God continued, Sabinian of Sens beheaded, Sabinus of Assis stoned to death, Saturninus of Toulouse dragged to his death by a bull, Sebastian pierced by arrows, Secundus of Asti decapitated, Servatius of Tongres and Maastricht killed by a blow to the head with a wooden clog, Severus of Barcelona killed by having nails embedded in his head, Sidwell of Exeter decapitated, Sigismund king of Burgundy thrown into a well, Sixtus decapitated, Stephen stoned to death, Symphorian of Autun decapitated, Taresius stoned to death, Thecla of Iconium mutilated and burned alive, Theodore burned at the stake, Thomas Becket of Canterbury a sword driven into his skull, Thomas More beheaded, Thyrsus sawed in half, Tiburtius beheaded, Timothy of Ephesus stoned to death, Torquatus and the twenty-seven killed by General Muça at the gates of Guimarães, Tropez of Pisa decapitated, Urbanus, Valeria of Limoges, and Valerian and Venantius of Camerino met the same fate, Victor decapitated, Victor of Marseilles beheaded, Victoria of Rome put to death after having her tongue pulled out, Vincent of Saragossa tortured to death with millstone, grid, and spikes, Virgilius of Trent beaten to death with a wooden clog, Vitalis of Ravenna put to the sword, Wilgefortis or Livrade or Eutropia the bearded virgin crucified, and so on and so forth, all of them meeting similar fates.

That's not good enough, said Jesus, to what others do You refer. Do you really have to know. I do. I refer to those who will escape martyrdom and die from natural causes after having suffered the torments of the world, the flesh, and the devil, and who in order to overcome them will have to mortify their bodies with fasting and prayer, there is even the amusing case of a certain John Schorn, who will spend so much time on his knees praying that he ends up with corns on his knees of all places, and some will say, this will interest you, he has trapped the devil inside a boot, ha ha ha. Me in a boot, said Pastor scornfully, these are old-wives' tales, any boot capable of holding me would have to be as vast as the world, besides, I'd like to see who would be capable of putting the boot on and taking it off afterward. Perhaps only with fasting and prayer, suggested Jesus, whereupon God replied, They will also mortify their flesh with pain and blood and grime and innumerable penances, hair shirts and flagellation, there will be some who never wash and others who throw themselves onto brambles and roll in the snow to suppress carnal desires that are the work of Satan, who sends these temptations to lure souls from the straight and narrow path that leads to heaven, sends visions of naked women, terrifying monsters, abominable creatures, because lust and fear are weapons the demon uses to torment wretched mankind. Is this true, Jesus asked Pastor, who replied, More or less, I simply took what God didn't want, the flesh with all its joys and sorrows, youth and senility, bloom and decay, but it isn't true that fear is one of my weapons, I don't recall having invented sin and punishment or the terror they inspire. Be quiet, God snapped, sin and the devil are one and the same thing. What thing is that, asked Jesus. My absence. How do your explain Your absence, is it because You withdraw or because mankind abandons You. I never withdraw, never. Yet You allow men to abandon You. Those who abandon Me come looking for Me. And when they do not find You, I suppose You blame the devil. No, he's not to blame, I'm to blame, because I cannot reach out to those who seek Me, words uttered by God with an unexpected, poignant melancholy, as if He had suddenly found a limitation to His power. Jesus said, Go on.

There are others, God continued slowly, who go into the wilderness, where they lead solitary lives in caves and grottoes, with nothing but animals for company, and others who choose a monastic existence, and others who climb to the top of high pillars and sit there year in year out, and others, His voice fell and died away, God was now contemplating an endless procession of people, thousands upon thousands of men and women throughout the world entering convents and monasteries, some buildings rustic, many palatial, There they will remain to serve you and Me from morning until night, with vigils and prayers, all with the same mission and the same destiny, to worship us and die with our names on their lips, they will call themselves Benedictines, Cistercians, Carthusians, Augustinians, Gilbertines, Trinitarians, Franciscans, Dominicans, Capuchins, Carmelites, Jesuits, and there will be so many of them that I should dearly like to be able to exclaim, My God, why so many. At this point the devil said to Jesus, Note from what He has told us that there are two ways of parting with one's life, through martyrdom and by renunciation, it isn't enough for all these people to wait until their time comes, they must run to meet their deaths, be crucified, disemboweled, beheaded, burned at the stake, stoned, drowned, drawn and quartered, skinned alive,

speared, gored, buried alive, sawed in two, shot with arrows, mutilated, tortured, or to die in their cells, chapter
houses, and cloisters, doing penance and mortifying the
flesh God gave them, without which flesh they would have
nowhere to put their souls, these punishments were not
invented by the devil who is talking to you. Is that all,
Jesus asked God. No, there are the wars and massacres.
No need to tell me of massacres, I almost perished in one,
and thinking it over, what a pity I didn't, for then I would
have been spared the crucifixion awaiting me. It was I who
led your other father to the place where he overheard the
soldiers' conversation and therefore I who saved your life.
You saved my life only in order to ordain my death at
Your pleasure and convenience, as if killing me twice. The
end justifies the means, My son. From what You have told
me so far I can believe it, renunciation, cloisters, suffering,
death, and now wars and massacres, what wars are they.
One war after another and unending, especially those waged
against you and Me in the name of a god who has yet to
appear. How can there possibly be a god who has yet to
appear, any true god can only have existed forever and
ever. I know it's difficult to understand or explain, but
what I'm telling you will come to pass, a god will rise up
against us and our followers, entire nations, no, there are
no words to describe the massacres then, the bloodshed
and slaughter, imagine my altar in Jerusalem multiplied a
thousandfold, replace the sacrificial animals with men, even
then you will have no idea what those crusades were like.
Crusades, what are they, and why do You refer to them
in the past if they have yet to take place. Remember, I am
time, for Me all that will happen has happened already, all
that has happened goes on happening every day. Tell me
more about the crusades. Well, My son, this region where
we now find ourselves, including Jerusalem, and other territories to the north and west, will be conquered by the
followers of the god I mentioned, who has been slow in

coming, the followers on our side will do everything possible to expel them from the places you have traveled and I constantly frequent. You haven't done much to rid this land of the Romans. Don't distract me, I'm talking about the future. Go on, then. Furthermore, you were born, you lived, and you died here. I'm not dead yet. That's irrelevant, because as I've just explained to you, for Me what will happen and what has happened are the same thing, and please stop interrupting, otherwise I'll say no more. All right, I'll be quiet. Now then, future generations will refer to this area as the holy places, because you were born, lived, and died here, so it didn't seem fitting that the cradle of the religion you represent should fall into the hands of infidels, this justified the coming of great armies from the west, who for almost two hundred years fought to conquer and preserve for Christendom the cave where you were born and the hill where you will die, to mention only the most important landmarks. Are these armies the crusades. That's right. And did they conquer what they wanted. No, but they slaughtered many people. What about the crusaders themselves. They lost just as many lives, if not more. And all this bloodshed in our name. They will go into battle crying, God wills it. And no doubt die crying, God willed it. Such a nice way to end one's life. The sacrifice isn't worth it. To save one's soul, My son, the body must be sacrificed. And you, Pastor, what do you say about these amazing events that lie ahead. No one in his right mind can possibly suggest that the devil was, is, or ever will be responsible for so much bloodshed and death, unless some villain brings up that wicked slander accusing me of having conceived the god who will oppose this one here. No, you are not to blame, and should anyone blame you, you need only reply that if the devil is false, he could not have created a true god. Who, then, will create this hostile god, asked Pastor. Jesus was at a loss for an answer, and God, who had been silent, remained silent, but a voice came down from the mist and said, Perhaps this God and the one to come are the same god. Jesus, God, and the devil pretended not to hear, but could not help looking at one another in alarm, mutual fear is like that, it readily unites enemies.

Time passed, the mist did not speak again, and Jesus asked, now with the voice of one who expects an affirmative reply, Nothing more. God hesitated, then in a tired voice said, There is still the Inquisition, but if you don't mind, we'll discuss that some other time. What is the Inquisition. The Inquisition is another long story. Tell me. It's best you don't know, you will only feel remorse today for what belongs to tomorrow. And You won't. God, being God, feels no remorse. Well, since I'm already bearing this burden of having to die for You, I can also endure the remorse that ought to be Yours. I wanted to protect you. You've done nothing else from the day I was born. Like most children, you're ungrateful. Let's stop all this posturing, tell me about the Inquisition. Also known as the Tribunal of the Holy Office, the Inquisition is a necessary evil, we will use this cruel instrument to combat the disease that persistently attacks the body of your church in the form of wicked heresies and their harmful consequences along with a number of physical and moral perversions, which, lumped together without regard for order of importance, will include Lutherans and Calvinists, Molinists and Judaizers, sodomites and sorcerers, some of these plagues belong to the future, others can be found in every age. And if the Inquisition is a necessary evil, as You say, how will it proceed to eliminate these heresies. The Inquisition is a police force, a tribunal, and will therefore pursue, judge, and sentence its enemies as would any police force. Sentence them to what. Prison, exile, the stake. Did You say the stake. Yes, in days to come, thousands upon thousands of men and women will be burned at the stake. You mentioned some of them earlier. They will be burned alive because they believe in you, others because they doubt you. Isn't it permitted to doubt me. No. Yet we're allowed to doubt that the Jupiter of the Romans is god. I am the one and only Lord God, and you are My son. You say thousands will die. Hundreds of thousands of men and women, and on earth there will be much sighing and weeping and cries of anguish, the smoke from charred corpses will blot out the sun, human flesh will sizzle over live coals, the stench will be nauseating. And all this is my fault. You are not to blame, your cause demands it. Father, take from me this cup. My power and your glory demand that you drink it to the last drop. I don't want the glory. But I want the power. The mist began to lift, and around the boat water could be seen, smooth, somber water undisturbed by a ripple of wind or the tremor of a passing fin. Then the devil interrupted, One has to be God to countenance so much blood.

The mist advanced again, something else was about to happen, some revelation, some new sorrow or new remorse. But it was Pastor who spoke, I have a proposal to make, he said, addressing God, and God, taken aback, replied, A proposal from you, and what proposal might that be. His tone, cynical and forbidding, would have reduced most to silence, but the devil was an old acquaintance. Pastor searched for the right words before explaining, I've been listening to all that has been said here in this boat, and although I myself have caught glimpses of the light and darkness ahead, I never realized that the light came from burning stakes and the darkness from great piles of bodies. Does this trouble you. It shouldn't trouble me, for I am the devil, and the devil profits from death even more than You do, it goes without saying that hell is more crowded than heaven. Then why do you complain. I'm not complaining, I'm making a proposal. Go ahead, but be quick, I cannot loiter here for all eternity. No one knows better than You that the devil too has a heart. Yes, but you make

330

poor use of it. Today I use it by acknowledging Your power and wishing that it spread to the ends of the earth without the need of so much death, and since You insist that whatever thwarts and denies You comes from the evil I represent and govern in this world, I propose that You receive me into Your heavenly kingdom, my past offenses redeemed by those I will not commit in future, that You accept my obedience as in those happy days when I was one of Your chosen angels, Lucifer You called me, bearer of light, before my ambition to become Your equal consumed my soul and made me rebel against You. And would you care to tell Me why I should pardon you and receive you into My kingdom. Because if You grant me that same pardon You will one day promise left and right, then evil will cease, Your son will not have to die, and Your kingdom will extend beyond the land of the Hebrews to embrace the whole globe, good will prevail everywhere, and I shall stand among the lowliest of the angels who have remained faithful, more faithful than all of them now that I have repented, and I shall sing Your praises, everything will end as if it had never been, everything will become what it should always have been. I always knew you had a talent for leading souls astray, but I never heard you speak with such conviction and eloquence, you almost won me over. So You won't accept or pardon me. No, I neither accept nor pardon you, I much prefer you as you are, and were it possible, I'd have you be even worse. But why. Because the good I represent cannot exist without the evil you represent, if you were to end, so would I, unless the devil is the devil, God cannot be God. Is that Your final word. My first and last, first because that was the first time I said it, last because I have no intention of repeating it. Pastor shrugged and said to Jesus, Never let it be said the devil didn't tempt God, and getting to his feet, he was about to pass one leg over the side of the boat, but stopped and said, In your pack there is something that belongs to

331

me. Jesus could not remember having taken the pack with him into the boat, but in fact there it was, rolled up at his feet, What thing, he asked, and on opening the pack he found nothing inside but the old black bowl he had brought from Nazareth. That's it, that's it, said the devil, picking up the bowl with both hands, One day this will be yours again, but you won't know you have it. He tucked the bowl inside his coarse shepherd's tunic and lowered himself into the water. Without looking at God, he said, as if addressing an invisible audience, Farewell forever, since that is what He has ordained. Jesus followed with his eyes as Pastor gradually swam off into the mist, from a distance he looked once more like a pig with pointed ears, and he was panting furiously, but anyone with a keen ear would have had no difficulty hearing the note of fear in it, fear not of drowning, what an idea, because the devil, as we have just learned, has no end, but of having to live forever. Pastor had disappeared behind the broken fringe of mist when God's voice suddenly rang out in farewell, I will send a man named John to help, but you will have to prove to him that you are who you are. Jesus looked around, but God was no longer there. Just then the mist lifted and vanished, leaving the lake clear and smooth from mountain to mountain, there was no sign of the devil in the water, no sign of God in the air.

On the shore from which he had come, Jesus could see a large crowd and, in the background, numerous tents, evidently an encampment for people who did not live there and who, having nowhere to sleep, had settled themselves as best they could. Curious, he lowered the oars into the water and rowed in that direction. Looking over his shoulder, he saw boats being pushed into the water, and taking a closer look, he saw Simon and Andrew, James and John in them, with others he did not know. Rowing hard, they were soon within speaking distance. Simon called out, Where have you been, obviously this was not what he wanted to know, but he had to begin somewhere, Here on the lake, replied Jesus, an answer as inane as the question, not a good start in this new chapter in the life of the son of God, Mary, and Joseph. Then Simon was clambering into Jesus' boat, and the incomprehensible and impossible was revealed, Do you know how long you've been out here in the mist, while we tried to launch our boats only to be pushed back by strong winds, asked Simon. All day, replied Jesus, then added, All day and night, seeing the intensity in Simon's face. Forty days, shouted Simon, then lowering his voice, You've been on the lake forty days, and all that time the mist never lifted, as if it were hiding something from us, what were you doing out here, we haven't caught a single fish in these waters for forty days. Jesus passed one of the oars to Simon, and both rowed and conversed in harmony, shoulder to shoulder, moving at a pace ideal for exchanging confidences, and Jesus said before any of the other boats could get closer, I've been with God, and I know what the future holds for me, how long I will live and the life that awaits me after this life. What is He like, I mean, what does God look like. God does not appear in only one form, He may be a cloud, a pillar of smoke, even a wealthy Jew, but once you hear His voice, you know Him. What did He say to you. He told me I am His son. Then the devil was right, during that business with the pigs. The devil too was here in the boat and heard everything, he seems to know as much about me as God does, sometimes I think he knows even more than God. And where, Where what, Where were they, The devil was on one side of the boat, between where you are now and the bench at the stern, which is where God sat. What did God say to you. That I am His son and will be crucified. If you're going to the mountains to fight on the rebel side, we'll come with you. You will come with me, but not to the mountains, we will not conquer Caesar with arms but make God triumph with words. With words alone. Also by giving a good example, and giving our lives if necessary. Are these your father's words. Henceforth all my words are His, and those who believe in Him must believe in me, for it is impossible to believe in the father without believing in the son, since the new path the father has chosen for Himself can begin only with me, His son. When you say we will come with you, who do you mean. First of all you, then Andrew your brother, the sons of Zebedee, James and John, which reminds me that God said He would send a man named John to assist me, but that cannot be the same John. We don't need anyone else, this isn't one of Herod's ceremonial processions. Others will come, perhaps some are already there waiting for God's sign, a sign He will manifest through me, that they may believe and follow. What will you tell the people. That they must repent of their sins and prepare themselves for God's new era, which is about to dawn, an era in which His flaming sword will humble those who have rejected and vilified His holy word. But you must tell them you're the son of God. I'll say that my father called me his son and I carried that word in my heart since the day I was born, but God Himself has now come to claim me as His son, one father does not make one forget the other, but the father giving orders today is God, so we must obey Him. Leave this to me, said Simon, dropping his oar and moving to the prow, and he called out in a loud voice, Hosanna, the son of God approaches, he who has spent forty days on the water speaking with his father and now returns to us so that we may repent and prepare ourselves. Don't mention that the devil was also there, Jesus quickly warned him, afraid of the difficulty he would have explaining this if it became public knowledge. Simon gave another cry, louder, causing great excitement among the crowd gathered on the shore, then he hurried back to his seat and told Jesus, I'll row, you stand on the prow, but say nothing, not a single word, until we reach the shore. And so they arrived, Jesus

334

standing on the prow of the boat in his worn tunic and with his empty pack over his shoulder, arms half raised as if wanting to greet someone or bestow a blessing but too shy, not confident enough. Among those waiting, three men were so impatient that they waded in up to their waists. Reaching the boat at last, they began pushing each other, one of them trying with his free hand to touch Jesus' tunic, not because he believed what Simon had said but because he was pulled by the mystery of this man who had been on the lake forty days, like searching for God in the desert, and who now returned from that mountain of cold mist, where he might or might not have seen God. Needless to say, in all the nearby villages people were speaking of nothing else, and the people gathered on the shore had come to see the meteorological phenomenon for themselves. When they heard there was a man lost in the mist, they muttered, Poor fellow.

The boat glided to its destination as if borne on the wings of angels. Simon helped Jesus step ashore, and in annoyance shook off the three men who had jumped into the water, Leave them alone, said Jesus, one day they will hear of my death and regret not having been there to bear my body, so let them accompany me while I'm still alive. Jesus climbed a rise and asked his companions, Where is Mary, and no sooner had he asked than he saw her. It was as if the very sound of her name had released her from a void, one moment she was nowhere to be seen, the next she was there, I'm here, Jesus. Come stand beside me, you too, Simon and Andrew, and James and John, sons of Zebedee, for you all believe me, you believed me when I was unable to tell you I was the son of God, the son summoned by God the father, spending forty days with Him on the lake before returning to tell you that the hour of the Lord has come and that you must repent before the devil gathers the rotting ears of corn fallen from the harvest God holds in His lap, for you are those rotting ears of corn if by sinning you fell from God's loving embrace. A murmur went through the crowd, passed over their heads like ripples on water, many of those present had heard of the miracles performed by this man, some had seen them with their own eyes or even been the beneficiaries of them, I ate that bread and fish, said one, I drank that wine, said another, I was the neighbor of that adulteress, said a third, but however wonderful these wonders were, they were eclipsed by the sublime moment when Jesus was proclaimed the son of God and therefore God Himself, a revelation as remote from those other miracles as the sky is from the earth, and to the best of our knowledge the distance between them has not been measured to this day. A voice came from the crowd, Prove that you're the son of God, and I will follow you. You would follow me forever if your heart were not locked inside your breast, you ask for the proof your senses can grasp, very well, I'll give you proof that will satisfy them but be denied by your mind until, torn between mind and senses, you'll have no choice but to come to me through your heart. Whatever that means, for I haven't understood a word, scoffed the man. What is your name, asked Jesus. Thomas. Come here, Thomas, come with me to the water's edge and watch me make birds of mud, see how easy it is, I mold the body and wings, the head and beak, set these tiny pebbles for the eyes, adjust the long feathers of the tail, balance the legs and claws, and once that is done, I make eleven more, look here, one, two, three, four, five, six, seven, eight, nine, ten, eleven, twelve birds, all of mud, just think, we could even give them names, this is Simon, this one James, this Andrew, this John, and this one, if you don't mind, will be called Thomas, as for the others we will wait until their names appear, names often get delayed along the way and arrive later, and now watch, I throw the net over my little birds to prevent them from escaping, for they will fly away if we're not careful. Are you trying to tell me that if

336

this net is lifted, the birds will fly away, Thomas asked. Yes, if the net is lifted, the birds will fly away. Is this the proof you think will convince me. Yes and no. What do you mean, yes and no. The best proof would be for you not to lift the net, believing the birds will escape if you lift it. But birds made of mud cannot possibly fly. Adam, our first father, was made of mud, and you are one of his descendants. It was God who gave Adam life. Doubt no more, Thomas, and lift the net, for I am the son of God. Well, if you say so, here goes, but I promise you these birds won't fly, and without further ado Thomas lifted the net, and the birds, freed, took flight. Twittering with excitement, they circled twice above the astonished crowd before disappearing into the sky. Jesus said, Look, Thomas, your bird has gone, to which Thomas replied, No, Lord, I'm the bird, kneeling here at your feet.

Some of the men in the crowd surged forward, and several women behind them did the same. They drew near and gave their names, I am Philip, and Jesus saw stones and a cross, I am Bartholomew, and Jesus saw a flayed torso, I am Matthew, and Jesus saw a corpse among barbarians, I am Simon, and Jesus saw the saw that would cut Simon's body, I am James son of Alphaeus, and Jesus saw him being stoned to death, I am Judas Thaddeus, and Jesus saw a club raised over the man's head, I am Judas Iscariot, and Jesus took pity on him, seeing him hang himself from a fig tree. Then Jesus called the others and said, Now that we are all here, the hour has come. And turning to Simon brother of Andrew, he told him, Because we have another Simon with us, you will be known as Peter. Turning their backs to the lake, the men started walking, followed by the women, most of whose names we never learned, not that it matters, for most of them are called Mary, and the rest will answer to that name, a man need only shout, Woman, or Mary, and they will look up and come to do his bidding.

337

JESUS AND HIS DISCIPLES TRAVELED FROM VILLAGE TO VIL-
lage, and God spoke through Jesus, and here is what He
said, Time has run full circle, and the kingdom of God is
at hand, repent and have faith in this good news. The local
inhabitants, hearing this, saw no difference between time's
running full circle and time's coming to an end, and so
believed the end of the world, which is where time is finally measured, must be fast approaching. They thanked
God for having mercifully sent them advance notice of their
fate through someone who claimed to be His son, a claim
that might even be true, seeing as he worked miracles
wherever he went, provided those seeking his help showed
genuine faith and conviction, as in the case of the leper
who pleaded, If you wish, you can make me clean, and
Jesus, taking pity on the poor wretch covered with fester-
ing sores, laid his hand on him and said, It is my wish that
you be clean, and no sooner were those words spoken than
the sores healed, the body was restored to health, and the
leper from whom everyone had fled in horror was now
free of all blemish. Another remarkable cure was that of

338

the paralytic. Such an enormous crowd had gathered around the door that the sick man had to be hoisted up, bed and all, then lowered through an opening in the roof of the house where Jesus was staying, which probably belonged to Simon, also known as Peter. Moved by the crowd's deep faith, Jesus told the sick man, My son, your sins are forgiven, but it happened that some distrustful scribes, eager to find cause for complaint and always ready to quote holy law, were present, and when they heard what Jesus said, they lost no time in protesting, How dare you say such things, this is blasphemy, only God can forgive, whereupon Jesus asked, Is it easier to say to one sick of the palsy, Your sins are forgiven, than to say, Arise, take up your bed, and walk, and without waiting for an answer, he continued, That you may know that the son of man has power on earth to forgive sins, I say unto you, and he turned to the paralytic, Arise, take up your bed, and go your way, and with these words the man miraculously got to his feet, his strength restored, and taking up the bed, he lifted it onto his shoulders and walked off, praising God.

Obviously we do not all go in search of miracles. In time we become used to our little aches and pains and learn to live with them, not thinking of importuning the divine powers. Sins, however, are quite a different matter, they get under our skin and torment us, sins, unlike a crippled leg, a paralyzed arm, or the ravages of leprosy, fester inside, and God knew what He was talking about when He told Jesus that every man has at least one sin, if not more, to repent. Now since this world is about to end and the kingdom of God is at hand, rather than enter it with our bodies restored by miraculous means we should pay attention to our souls, purify them by repentance, heal them by forgiveness. For if the paralytic from Capernaum spent most of his life on a bed, it was because he sinned, sickness as we all know is the result of sin, therefore we may safely conclude that the essential requirement for good health, not to mention immortality, can only be the utmost purity, a complete absence of sin, either through blessed ignorance or strenuous repudiation, both in thought and deed. Let no one think, however, that our Jesus journeyed through these lands squandering his power to heal and his authority to pardon sins, granted him by the Lord Himself. Though obviously he would have preferred, personally, to become a universal panacea than announce, for God, the end of time and urge men to repent. And in order that sinners not lose too much time wrestling with the difficult decision of confessing, I have sinned, the Lord put certain terrifying threats into Jesus' mouth, as follows, Verily I say unto you that some of you who are present here will not die before seeing the kingdom of God arrive in all its majesty. Imagine the devastating effect such words must have had on those who flocked from all directions to follow Jesus, hoping he would lead them straight to the new paradise the Lord would establish on earth, which would be different from Eden, enjoyed after atonement for Adam's sin by prayer, mortification, and repentance. Since most of these trusting souls were from the working class, artisans and road diggers, fishermen and women of lowly condition, Jesus ventured one day, when God allowed him a little more freedom, to improvise a speech that left its audience spellbound, tears of joy flowing at the prospect of salvation, Blessed are you poor, Jesus told them, for yours is the kingdom of heaven, blessed are you that hunger, for you will be filled, blessed are you that weep, for you will laugh, but then God became aware of what was happening, and although it was too late to retract what Jesus had said, He forced him to speak other words, which turned the tears of joy into grim foreboding, Blessed are you when men hate you, and separate you from their company, and reproach you, and cast out your name as evil, for the son of man's sake. When Jesus finished speaking, it was as if his soul had fallen to his feet, for in that instant all the torments and deaths God had foretold on the lake marched before him. Numb with fear, the crowd watched Jesus sink to his knees, prostrate himself, and pray in silence. No one there could have imagined that he was asking their forgiveness, he, the son of God, who was able to forgive the sins of others. That night, in the privacy of the tent he shared with Mary Magdalene, Jesus said, I am the shepherd who with the same crook leads to sacrifice both the innocent and the wicked, the saved and the lost, those born and those yet to be born, who will deliver me from this guilt, for I now see myself as I once saw my father, he had to answer for twenty lives while I must answer for twenty thousand. Mary Magdalene wept with Jesus and tried to console him, It wasn't your doing, she sobbed. That makes it all the worse, he insisted. And as if she had known all along what we have only come to understand little by little, she said, It is God who draws the paths of fate and decides who must walk them, He chose you to open a path among paths on His behalf, but you will not walk that path or build a temple, others will build it upon your blood and body, you may as well accept the fate He has chosen for you, your every gesture has been determined, the words you will utter wait for you in the places you will visit, there you will find the crippled to whom you will restore limbs, the blind to whom you will give sight, the deaf to whom you will give hearing, the dumb to whom you will give speech, the dead whom you will resurrect. But I have no power over death. You haven't tried. I did try, but the fig tree did not revive. You must wish what God wills, but He cannot deny you what you wish. That He should take from me this burden, that is all I ask. You ask the impossible, Jesus, for the one thing God cannot do is not love Himself. How do you know. Women see things differently, perhaps because our bodies are different, yes, that must be the explanation.

341

One day, because the earth is too big for the strength of one man, even in a place as small as Palestine, Jesus decided to send his disciples, in pairs, to announce throughout the cities, towns, and villages the coming of God's kingdom, and to teach and preach as he did everywhere they went. And so, finding himself alone with Mary Magdalene, for the other women had gone off with the men according to their tastes and preferences, it occurred to him that since they were traveling to Bethany, which is near Jerusalem, they might as well kill two birds with one stone, if you will pardon the expression, and visit Mary's brother and sister. It was time they made their peace and for the two brothers-in-law to get to know each other. Reunited, they could make the journey together to Jerusalem, for Jesus had arranged a meeting with all his disciples in Bethany in three months' time. There is little to tell about the works of the twelve apostles in the lands of Israel, first because notwithstanding a few details about their lives and the circumstances of their deaths we have not been called upon to narrate their story, secondly because they had not been given any mandate other than to repeat, albeit each in his own way, the precepts of their master, which means they taught just as he did, performing cures as best they could. A pity Jesus forbade them to follow the path of the Gentiles or to enter any city of the Samaritans, this surprising intolerance in one so well educated deprived them of the chance to reduce their future task, because given God's intention of extending the domain of His influence, sooner or later His message would not only reach the Samaritans but, above all, the Gentiles, both here and elsewhere. Jesus instructed his disciples to heal the sick and raise the dead, make lepers clean and drive out demons, but apart from one or two vague references there is no clear evidence that any such miracles were performed, which goes to show that God does not trust just anyone, however strongly recommended. Once they are reunited with

Jesus, the twelve disciples will undoubtedly have something to tell him about the results of their sermons on repentance, but probably little to report about healings, apart from the expelling of some fairly innocuous demons, who do not require much persuasion to pass from one soul to another. But the disciples will certainly tell Jesus how they themselves were often expelled, or given a hostile reception on roads where there were no Gentiles or in cities not populated by Samaritans, their only recourse being to shake the dust from their feet on leaving, as if the fault were that of the dust, which is trodden by everyone without ever complaining. But Jesus told them this was what they must do in such situations, as testimony against those who refused to listen, most regrettable, for this is the word of God Himself that is being rejected. Jesus told them, Don't worry about what to say, inspiration will come to you when you need it. But perhaps it doesn't work like that, after all, soundness of doctrine should come before personal delivery.

The perfume of freshly gathered roses hung in the air, the roads were clean and pleasant, as if angels were walking ahead and sprinkling dew as they went, then brushing the roads with laurel and myrtle. Jesus and Mary Magdalene avoided the caravansaries and the other travelers on the road, not wanting to be recognized, not that Jesus was shirking his duty, never easy under God's watchful eye, but it seemed that the Almighty had decided to grant him a breather, because no lepers came on the road to beg a cure, or possessed souls needing exorcism, and the villages they passed through were quietly rejoicing in the peace of the Lord, as if they had already made progress along the path of repentance. The couple slept wherever they happened to be, seeking no comfort other than each other's lap, sometimes with only the sky for a roof, God's enormous eye, black but speckled with lights, lingering reflections of eyes raised to heaven by generation after generation,

343

interrogating the silence and listening to the only answer silence ever gives. Later, when she is alone in the world, Mary Magdalene will try to recall those days and nights, but she will find it increasingly difficult to preserve her memories of sorrow and bitterness, as if trying in vain to protect an island of love from a tempestuous sea and its monsters. The hour is drawing near, but looking at heaven and earth, one sees no visible sign yet of its approach, just as a bird flies across an open sky without noticing the swift falcon drop like a stone, its claws ready. Jesus and Mary Magdalene, singing as they walk along, make an impression on other travelers, who think to themselves, Such a happy pair, and for the moment nothing could be truer. And thus they reached Jericho, and from there, because of the intense heat and lack of shade, they took two whole days to go up to Bethany. Mary Magdalene wondered how her brother and sister would receive her after all this time, especially since she left home to live as a prostitute, They may think I'm dead, she said, they may even want me dead. Jesus tried to dissuade her from dwelling on such thoughts, Time heals everything, he said, forgetting that the wound inflicted by his own family is still raw and bleeding. They entered Bethany, Mary half covering her face for fear one of the villagers might recognize her. Jesus gently rebuked her, Why are you hiding, your past is now behind you and exists no more. I'm not the person I was, it is true, but I am still bound to who I was by shame. You are now only who you are, and you are with me. Thanks be to God, but the day will come when He takes you from me. Dropping her mantle, Mary showed her face, but no one said, Look, there is Lazarus's sister, the one who went off to live as a prostitute.

This is the house, she said, but could not bring herself to knock or to announce her arrival. Jesus gave the unlocked gate a gentle push and called out, Anyone home, and a woman's voice answered, Who's there, and with those words she appeared in the doorway. This was Martha, the twin sister of Mary Magdalene, but now bearing little resemblance to her, for age had left its mark on Martha, or it could have been the hard life she had led, or purely a matter of temperament and outlook. The first thing she noticed were Jesus' eyes and expression, as if a dark cloud had lifted all at once, leaving his face luminous, but then she saw her sister and became wary, her frown showing displeasure, Who is this man with her, she must have thought, or perhaps, How can he be with her if he is what he seems, but pressed to explain herself, Martha would have been unable to say what he seemed to be. This is probably why, instead of asking her sister, How are you, or, What are you doing here, all she could say was, Who is this man you've brought with you. Jesus smiled, and his smile went straight to Martha's heart like an arrow and there it remained, making it ache with satisfaction, My name is Jesus of Nazareth, he told her, and I'm with your sister, the same words, mutatis mutandis, the Romans would say, as those he used when he took leave of his brother James by the lake, telling him, Her name is Mary Magdalene and she's with me. Pushing the door wide open, Martha said, Come in, make yourself at home, but it was not clear which of them she meant. Once inside the yard, Mary Magdalene took her sister by the arm and told her, I belong here as much as you do, and I belong to this man, who does not belong to you, I've been frank with both of you, so do not flaunt your virtue or condemn my wickedness, I come in peace and in peace I wish to be. Martha said, I will receive you as my sister, and I long for the day when I can welcome you with love, but it's too soon, and she was about to continue when a thought stopped her, she was not sure whether this man standing beside her sister knew about the life her sister had led and might still be leading, and she began to blush, hating the two of them and herself, until Jesus finally spoke so that Martha could learn what she needed to know, for it is not that difficult to tell what people are thinking, and he told her, God judges all of us and does so differently each day, according to what we are each day, now if God were to judge you at this moment, Martha, don't imagine you'd be any different in His eyes from Mary. Explain that more clearly, for I don't understand. There is no more to be said, but keep my words in your heart and repeat them to yourself whenever you look at your sister. Is she no longer. You mean am I no longer a whore, asked Mary Magdalene bluntly, despising her sister's delicacy. Martha flinched, raised her hands to her face, No, I don't want to know, Jesus' words are enough, and unable to restrain herself, she burst into tears. Mary went to her and embraced her, cradling her in her arms, while Martha kept saying between sobs, What a life, what a life, but one could not be certain whether she meant her own life or her sister's. Where is Lazarus, asked Mary. In the synagogue. How is he these days. He still suffers from those bouts of choking, but otherwise his health is not bad. She felt like adding resentfully that Mary was slow in showing concern, for during all those years of guilty absence, this prodigal sister, prodigal with both her time and her body, had not kept in touch with her family, had not once inquired after their brother, whose health had always been precarious. But turning to Jesus, who was observing the hostility between them, Martha told him, Our brother copies out books in the synagogue, it is as much as he can do in his poor state of health, and her tone was of one incapable of understanding how anyone could live without being engaged in some worthwhile task from morning till night. What ails Lazarus, asked Jesus. He chokes, as if his heart were about to stop beating, then he turns so pale, you'd think he was going to pass away. Martha paused before adding, He's younger than we are, she spoke without thinking, perhaps suddenly struck by Jesus' youth, and once again she felt perturbed, felt pangs of jealousy, which

346

brought words to her lips that sounded strange coming from Martha when Mary Magdalene, whose duty and privilege it was to say them, was standing there, You're tired, Martha said to Jesus, Sit down and let me wash your feet. Afterward, when Mary found herself alone with Jesus, she remarked half jokingly, It would seem that we two sisters were born to love you, and Jesus replied, Martha is sad that she has had so little pleasure in life. She's resentful, thinking there is no justice in heaven when a fallen woman gets the prize and a virtuous woman like her goes unrewarded. God will reward her in other ways. Perhaps, but God, having made the world, has no right to deprive women of any of the fruits of His creation. Such as carnal knowledge of men. Of course, just as you came to know woman, and what more could you wish for, being as you are, the son of God. He who lies with you is not the son of God but the son of Joseph. Frankly, ever since you came into my life, I never felt I was lying with the son of a god. You mean of God. If only you weren't.

Martha entrusted a neighbor's little boy with a message for Lazarus, informing him that Mary had returned home, but she did so only after much hesitation, for she was anxious that no one know that their disreputable sister was back in the village, because tongues would start wagging again after all this time. How would she face people on the street the next day, and worse still, how would she find the courage to walk out with her sister. It would be difficult to ignore her neighbors and friends, and she dreaded having to say to them, This is my sister Mary, do you remember her, she's come home, only to receive knowing looks and sly comments, Of course we remember, who doesn't remember Mary, let us hope these prosaic details do not offend our readers, because the story of God is not all divine. Martha was trying to suppress these uncharitable thoughts when Lazarus arrived, and embracing Mary, he said simply, Welcome home, sister, putting aside the

347

sorrow of all those years of separation and silent anxiety. Martha, feeling it was up to her to put a brave face on things, pointed to Jesus and told her brother, This is Jesus, our brother-in-law. The two men exchanged a friendly nod, then sat down to have a chat, while the women prepared a meal together as they had done so many times in the past. Now after they had eaten, Lazarus and Jesus went into the yard to enjoy the cool night air while the sisters remained inside to resolve the important question of how to arrange the sleeping mats, since they were now four instead of two. Jesus, gazing at length at the first stars to appear in the sky, which was still light, finally asked Lazarus, Do you suffer much pain, and Lazarus replied with surprising composure, Yes, I suffer all right. Your suffering will be over, said Jesus. No doubt, when I'm dead. No, I mean very soon. I didn't know you were a physician. Brother, if I were a physician, I wouldn't be able to cure you. Nor can you even if you're not. You are cured, Jesus murmured softly, taking him by the hand. And Lazarus felt the sickness drain from his body like murky water absorbed by the sun. His breathing became easier, his pulse stronger, and he asked nervously, puzzled by what was happening, What's going on, his voice hoarse with alarm, Who are you. A physician I am not, smiled Jesus. In the name of God, tell me who you are. Do not take the name of God in vain. But what am I to make of this. Call Mary, she'll tell you. There was no need to call anyone. Drawn by the sudden raising of voices, Martha and Mary appeared in the doorway, afraid the two men might be quarreling, but they saw at once they were mistaken, a blue light suffused the entire yard, from the sky, and a shaken Lazarus was pointing at Jesus, Who is this man, he asked, for he had only to touch me and say, You are cured, and the sickness left. Martha went to comfort her brother, how could he be cured when he was trembling from head to foot, but Lazarus pushed her away, saying, Mary, you brought him here, tell us who he is. Without stirring from the doorway, Mary Magdalene said, He is Jesus of Nazareth, the son of God. Now even though this region has been favored with prophetic revelations and apocalyptic signs since time immemorial, it would have been perfectly natural for Lazarus and Martha to express utter disbelief, it is one thing for you to acknowledge that you have been cured by miraculous means, and quite another to be told that the man who touched your hand is none other than the son of God himself. Faith and love, however, can achieve much, some even claim they do not have to go together to achieve what they achieve, as it happened Martha threw herself weeping into Jesus' arms, then, alarmed by her daring, she slumped to the ground, where she remained, her face completely transformed as she muttered to herself, And I washed your feet. Lazarus did not move, out of fear, and we might even suggest that if this sudden revelation did not kill him, it was because his sister's timely act of love had given him a new heart. Smiling, Jesus went to embrace him and said, Don't be surprised to find that the son of God is a son of man, frankly, God had no one else to choose, just as men choose their women and women their men. These final words were intended for Mary Magdalene, but Jesus forgot that they would only aggravate Martha's distress and desperate loneliness, this is the difference between God and His son, God does it on purpose, His son out of carelessness, which is all too human. Never mind, today there is rejoicing in this household, and Martha can go back to her sighing tomorrow, but she has one consolation she can be sure of, no one will dare gossip about her sister's past in the streets, squares, and marketplaces of Bethany once they learn, and Martha herself will make sure they are told, that the man with her cured Lazarus of his sickness without the use of potions or infusions of herbs. They were sitting at home enjoying one another's company when Lazarus remarked, There have been

349

rumors about a man from Galilee going around performing miracles, but it has never been suggested that he is the son of God. Some news travels faster than others, said Jesus. Are you that man. You have said it. Then Jesus told his story from the beginning, but not quite everything, he did not mention Pastor, and he said nothing about God except that He had appeared to him to announce, You are My son. Without those rumors of miracles, now turned into fact by the evidence of this latest miracle, and without the power of faith and love, it would have been difficult indeed for Jesus to convince Lazarus and Martha that the man who would shortly be sharing a mat with their sister was made of divine spirit. For it was with flesh and blood that Jesus embraced this woman who had embraced so many men without fear of God. And let us forgive Martha the spiritual pride that led her to mutter, under the sheet pulled over her head so she would not see or hear, I deserve him more than she does.

Next day the news spread like wildfire, people everywhere in Bethany praised and thanked the Lord, and even those dry souls who were doubtful to begin with, thinking the earth too small to hold such wonders, were forced to change their minds when confronted with a miraculously cured Lazarus, of whom it should never be said that he began selling good health to others, for he was so good-hearted that he would sooner have given it all away. Now people gathered around the door, curious to see with their own eyes this miracle-worker, whom they might even be allowed to touch, a last, definitive proof. The sick and infirm also came in droves, some on foot, others carried in litters or on the backs of relatives, until the narrow street where Lazarus and his sister lived was completely filled. When Jesus became aware of the situation, he sent word that he would address the crowd in the main square of the village, where they should go and he would join them shortly. But any man who holds a bird securely in his hand is not going to be foolish enough to let it escape. So understandably no one moved from his vantage point, and Jesus was obliged to show his face, leaving the house like anyone else, without fanfare, pomp, or ceremony, and without any tremors in heaven or on earth. Here I am, he said, trying to speak naturally, but his words were sufficient to make the inhabitants of an entire village fall to their knees and beg for mercy, Save us, cried some, Cure me, implored others. Jesus cured one man who, being mute, was unable to plead, but he sent the others away because they did not have enough faith. He told them to come back another day, but first they must repent of their sins, because as we know the kingdom of God is at hand and time is about to end. Are you the son of God, they asked, and Jesus answered enigmatically, If I were not, God would strike you dumb rather than permit such a question.

He began his stay in Bethany with these remarkable deeds, while waiting to be reunited with his disciples, who still journeyed through distant lands. Needless to say, people soon arrived from surrounding towns and villages when they heard that the man who worked miracles in the north was now in Bethany. There was no need for Jesus to leave Lazarus's house, because everyone flocked there as though to a place of pilgrimage, but he did not receive them, ordering them instead to gather on a hill outside the village, where he would preach repentance and heal the sick. The excitement and news quickly reached Jerusalem, which made the crowds even larger, until Jesus began asking himself if he should remain there at the risk of provoking riots, which are all too common when crowds get out of control. Humble folk were the first to come from Jerusalem in search of healing, but it was not long before people from every social class began arriving, including a number of Pharisees and scribes who could not believe that anyone in his right mind would have the courage, one might even say the suicidal courage, openly to declare himself the son of

351

God. They returned to Jerusalem irritated and puzzled, because Jesus never gave a straight answer when questioned. If pressed about his parentage, he said he was the son of man, and if he happened to say father when referring to God, it was clear he meant God as everyone's father and not just his own. There remained the troublesome question of these healing powers he exercised without recourse to trickery or magic. All he needed were a few simple words, Walk, Arise, Speak, See, Be clean, the leper's skin suddenly glowed like dew in the morning light when Jesus touched it with his fingertips, mutes and stammerers became inebriated with words, paralytics jumped out of bed and danced with joy, the blind could not believe their eyes could see again, the lame ran to their heart's content, then playfully pretended to be lame once more, so they could start running all over again. Repent, Jesus told them, Repent, and that was all he asked of them. But the high priests of the Temple, who knew better than anyone of the upheavals provoked in their time by prophets and soothsayers, decided that there should be no more religious, social, and political disturbances, and that from now on they should pay close attention to everything the Galilean did and said, and if it became necessary, to uproot and eliminate the evil, because, in the words of the high priest, This man does not deceive me, the son of man is the son of God. Jesus had not gone to sow in Jerusalem, but here in Bethany he was forging and honing the scythe with which he would be cut down.

Then the disciples began to arrive in Bethany, in pairs, two today, two tomorrow, or even four if they chanced to meet en route. Apart from a few minor details, they all had the same story to tell, about a man who came out of the desert and prophesied in the traditional manner, as if moving boulders with his voice and whole mountains with his arms, he spoke of the punishment in store for people and of the imminent arrival of the Messiah. The disciples never actually saw him, because he was constantly on the move, going from place to place, so their information was secondhand, they would have sought this prophet out, but their three months were nearly up and they didn't wish to miss their meeting. Jesus asked them if they knew the prophet's name, and they told him it was John. So he's here already, said Jesus. His friends did not know what he meant, except for Mary Magdalene, but then she knew everything. Jesus wanted to go look for John, who almost certainly was looking for him, but of the twelve apostles, Thomas and Judas Iscariot still had not arrived, and since they might have more information, their delay was all the more frustrating. The wait for them, however, proved to be justified, because the two latecomers had not only seen John but spoken to him. The others emerged from their tents, pitched outside Bethany, to hear what Thomas and Judas Iscariot had to tell, they sat in a circle in the yard of Lazarus's house, with Martha and Mary and the other women in attendance. Judas Iscariot and Thomas spoke in turn, explaining how John had been in the wilderness when he received the word of God, and went to the banks of the Jordan to baptize and preach penance for the remission of sins, but as the multitudes flocked to him to be baptized, he rebuked them with loud cries that frightened everyone out of their wits, O generation of vipers, who has warned you to flee from the wrath to come, bring forth therefore fruits meet for repentance, and think not to say within yourselves, We have Abraham for our father, for I say unto you that God is able from these stones to raise up children unto Abraham, leaving you despised, and now the ax is put to the root of the trees, therefore every tree that brings not forth good fruit is hewn down and cast into the fire. Terror-stricken, the multitudes asked him, What must we do, and John replied, Let the man who has two tunics share them with him who has none, and the man who has provisions do the same, and to the collectors of taxes John

353

said, Make no demands other than those established by law, and do not think the law is just because you call it the law, and to the soldiers who asked him, And what about us, what must we do, he replied, Use violence against no one, do not sentence anyone falsely, and content yourselves with your wages. Here Thomas, who had begun, fell silent, and Judas Iscariot took over. They asked John if he was the Messiah, and he told them, I baptize you with water unto repentance, but he who comes after me is mightier than I, whose shoes I am not worthy to bear, he will baptize you with the Holy Ghost and with fire, his fan is in his hand, and he will thoroughly purge his floor and gather his wheat into the granary, but the chaff he will burn with unquenchable fire. Judas Iscariot said nothing more, and everyone waited for Jesus to speak, but Jesus, with one finger tracing enigmatic lines on the ground, appeared to be waiting. Then Peter said, So you are the Messiah whose coming John prophesies, and Jesus replied, still scribbling in the dust, You have said it, not I, God only told me I was His son, he paused for a moment, then ended by saying, I will go look for John. We'll go with you, said the son of Zebedee who was also John, but Jesus slowly shook his head, I'll take only Thomas and Judas, because they've seen him, and turning to Judas, he asked, What does he look like. He's taller than you, said Judas, and heavier, he has a long beard as if made of bristles, and he wears nothing except a garment of camel's hair and a leather girdle around his waist, people say that in the wilderness he feeds on locusts and wild honey. He sounds more like the Messiah than I do, Jesus said, rising from the circle.

The three of them set out early the next morning, and knowing that John never stayed more than a few days in the same place and that they would most probably find him baptizing on the banks of the Jordan, they went down from Bethany to a place called Bethabara at the edge of the Dead Sea, intending to travel upriver as far as the Sea of

Galilee, and even farther north to the headwaters if necessary. But their journey was shorter than they imagined, for it was in Bethabara itself that they found John, alone, as if he was expecting them. They caught their first glimpse of the man from afar, a tiny figure seated on the riverbank, surrounded by somber crags resembling skulls and ravines that looked like open scars. To the right, beneath the sun and the white sky, was the sinister Dead Sea, its awesome surface agleam like molten copper. When they came within throwing distance, Jesus asked his companions, Is it he. Shading their eyes with their hands, the disciples took a careful look and replied, Either it is he or his twin. Wait here until I return, and come no closer, said Jesus, and without another word he began making his descent to the river. Thomas and Judas sat on the parched ground and watched Jesus walk away, appearing and disappearing as the land rose and fell, then when he reached the bank, they saw him approaching John, who had not stirred all this time. Let's hope we're not mistaken, said Thomas. We should have gone closer, said Judas Iscariot. But Jesus was certain the moment he saw him and had asked only for the sake of asking. Down below, John rose to his feet and looked at Jesus as he walked toward him. What will they have to say to each other, wondered Judas Iscariot. Perhaps Jesus will tell us, perhaps he won't, said Thomas. Now the two men in the distance were face-to-face and conversing excitedly, judging from the gestures they made with their staffs, and after a while they went to the water's edge, where they disappeared from view behind the jutting embankment, but Judas and Thomas knew what was happening there, because they too had been baptized by John. They had waded into the river until the water came up to their waists. John will scoop up water in his cupped hands, raise it to heaven, then let it fall on Jesus' head, reciting, I baptize you with this water, may it nourish your fire. When this is accomplished, John and Jesus will emerge from the river, retrieve their staffs, and bid each other farewell with an embrace, and John will start walking along the river in a northerly direction, while Jesus returns to us. Thomas and Judas Iscariot stand waiting for him, and he indeed appears, he passes in silence and leads the way to Bethany. Feeling somewhat slighted, his disciples walk behind him, their curiosity unsatisfied, until Thomas, unable to contain himself any longer and ignoring Judas's gesture, asked, Aren't you going to tell us what John said. In good time, replied Jesus. Did he tell you, at least, that you're the Messiah. In good time, said Jesus again, and his disciples wondered if he was telling them, by this repetition, that it was not yet time for the Messiah to appear.

Only Mary Magdalene learned what happened that day. Little was said, Jesus confided, no sooner did we meet than John wanted to know if I was he who has come or if we had to await another. And what did you tell him. I told him the blind regain their sight and the lame walk, the lepers are made clean and the deaf hear, and the poor have the gospel preached to them. And what did he say. The Messiah won't need to do much, so long as he does what is expected of him. Is that what he said. Yes, those were his very words. And what is expected of the Messiah. That's what I asked him, And what answer did he give you, He told me to find out for myself, And then what did he say. Nothing else, he took me to the river, baptized me, and walked away. What words did he use to baptize you. I baptize you with water, and may it nourish your fire. After this conversation with Mary Magdalene, Jesus did not speak for a week. He left Lazarus's house and went to join his disciples just outside Bethany, where he put up a tent away from the others and spent the entire day alone. Not even Mary Magdalene was allowed to enter the tent, and Jesus left it only at night to go into the mountains. Sometimes his disciples secretly followed him, on the pretext that they wanted to protect him from wild beasts, though there were no wild beasts in those parts. They found that he would choose a comfortable spot and sit there staring, not at the sky but straight ahead, as if waiting for someone to appear from the ominous shadow of a ravine or from around the slope of a hill. There was moonlight, so anyone who appeared would have been visible from afar, but no one appeared. At first light Jesus returned to the camp. He ate very little of the food John and Judas Iscariot brought him in turn, and he made no attempt to respond to their greetings. On one occasion he even dismissed Peter brusquely when Peter asked if all was well and if he had any orders to give. Peter was not completely mistaken, he had only spoken too soon, because after eight days Jesus emerged from the tent in broad daylight, rejoined his disciples, ate with them, and when he had finished, he told them, Tomorrow we go up to Jerusalem, to the Temple, there you will do as I do, because the time has come for the son of God to know what use is being made of his father's house, and for the Messiah to begin to do what is expected of him. The disciples wanted to know more, but apart from telling them, You won't have to wait much longer to find out, Jesus would say nothing. The disciples were not accustomed to being spoken to in this way or to seeing his face so severe, he was no longer the gentle, tranquil Jesus they knew, who went wherever God wished without a murmur of complaint. This change had been brought about by circumstances unknown, whatever had led him to separate himself from his disciples and to wander over hill and dale as if possessed by the demons of night, in search of who knows what. Peter, the oldest one there, thought it unfair that Jesus should order them to go up to Jerusalem just like that, as if they were servants and fit only to fetch and carry, to go back and forth with no explanation. So he protested, We recognize your authority and are prepared to obey you in word and deed, both as the son of God and as a man, but is it right that you treat us like irresponsible children or doddery old men, refusing to confide in us, giving orders without asking our opinion or allowing us to make our own decisions. Forgive me, all of you, said Jesus, for I myself do not know what calls me to Jerusalem, all I was told was that I must go, nothing more, you do not have to accompany me. Who told you you must go to Jerusalem. A voice in my head, it tells me what I must and must not do. You're much changed since your meeting with John. Yes, it made me realize that it isn't enough to bring peace, one must also carry a sword. If the kingdom of God is at hand, why carry a sword, asked Andrew. Because God has not revealed by what means His kingdom will come, we've tried peace, now let us try the sword, and God will choose, but I repeat, you do not have to accompany me. You know we will follow you wherever you go, John told him, and Jesus replied, Don't swear it, those of you who go with me will learn.

The next morning, Jesus went to Lazarus's house to say good-bye and also reassure Lazarus and Martha that he was again living with his disciples after his mysterious retreat into the wilderness. Martha told him that her brother had left for the synagogue. So Jesus and his disciples set off on the road to Jerusalem, Mary Magdalene and the other women accompanying them as far as the last houses of Bethany, where they stopped and waved, content to wave although the men did not look back even once. The sky is cloudy and threatens rain, perhaps this is why there are so few people on the road, those with no urgent business in Jerusalem have decided to stay at home and wait for a sign from the heavens. The thirteen men walk, and thick gray clouds rumble above the mountains, as if sky and earth were finally about to come together, the mold and the molded, male and female, concave and convex. They reached the city gates and found, though the road had been deserted, the usual crowd gathered there, and they resigned themselves to a long wait before reaching the Temple. But things turned out differently. The appearance of thirteen men, nearly all of them barefoot, with great staffs, flowing beards, and heavy, dark capes over tunics that had seen better days, caused the startled crowd to fall back and ask among themselves, Where can these men have come from, and who's the one in front. No one knew the answer until a man who had come down from Galilee said, He's Jesus of Nazareth, who claims to be the son of God and performs miracles. Where are they going, asked others, and since the only way of finding out was to follow them, many walked behind them, so that by the time they reached the entrance to the Temple, they were no longer thirteen but a thousand, and the people waited to see what would happen. Jesus walked on the side where the money changers were and said to his disciples, Here is what we have come to do, and with these words he began overturning the tables, berating those who were buying and selling, causing such an uproar that his words would not have been heard but for the fact that his natural voice rang out in stentorian tones, It is written that my house shall be called a house of prayer, but you have made it a den of thieves, and he continued to overturn the tables, scattering coins everywhere, which brought great joy to the horde that rushed to gather this manna. The disciples followed Jesus' example, and the tables of the dove sellers were also thrown to the ground, and the birds, released, flew over the Temple, circling wildly around the distant smoke from the altar, where they will not be burned now, for their savior has come. The Temple guards rushed to the scene, armed with batons to punish, capture, or expel the rioters, only to find themselves up against thirteen formidable Galileans with staffs in hand, who swept aside all who dared approach. Come, come, the lot of you, and feel God's might, they taunted, falling on the guards, destroying everything in sight, and putting a torch to the tents. Soon a second column of smoke was spiraling into the air, and a voice cried out, Call the Roman soldiers, but no one paid attention, for happen what might, the Romans were forbidden by law to enter the Temple. More guards rushed to the scene, this time with swords and lances, they were joined by a few money changers and dove sellers determined not to leave the protection of their property to strangers, so little by little the guards gained the upper hand, and if this struggle was as pleasing to God as the crusades to come, He did not appear to be doing much to help His side. This was the situation when the high priest appeared at the top of the steps accompanied by all the other priests, elders, and scribes who could be summoned in haste, and in a voice powerful enough to match that of Jesus he declared, Let him go this time, but if he shows his face here again, we will cut him down and discard him, as we do to tares that threaten to choke the wheat at harvesttime. Andrew said to Jesus, who had fought at his side, You weren't joking when you said you would bring the sword instead of peace, but staffs are useless as swords, to which Jesus replied, It all depends who is wielding the staff. What do we do now, asked Andrew. Let's return to Bethany, answered Jesus, it's not swords we need but determination. They withdrew in orderly fashion, their staffs pointed at the jeering crowd, who taunted them but went no further, and soon the disciples were safely out of Jerusalem and beating a hasty retreat, all of them exhausted, some even wounded.

When they reached Bethany, they noticed that that the people who appeared in their doorways looked at them with pity, but the disciples thought this only natural, given the lamentable state in which they had returned from battle. They learned the real reason for the gloom on everyone's face when they came to the street where Lazarus lived and sensed a tragedy had occurred. Jesus ran ahead of the others, entered the yard, the people gathered there stepped aside with mournful sighs to let him pass, and from within came the sound of weeping and lamentation, Oh my beloved brother, Martha could be heard sobbing, Oh my beloved brother, wailed the voice of Mary. Stretched out on the ground, on a pallet, Lazarus seemed to be sleeping, but he was not sleeping, he was dead. Nearly all his life he had suffered from a weak heart, then was cured, as everyone in Bethany could testify, and now was as composed as if carved from marble, as serene as if he had already passed into eternity, soon the first signs of putrefaction will appear, causing those around the corpse to feel even greater pain. Jesus, as if the strength had suddenly gone from his legs, fell to his knees, groaning and weeping, How did this happen, how did this happen, words that never fail to spring to our lips when we are confronted by something irremediable. We ask how it happened, a desperate, futile attempt to postpone the awful moment when we must accept the truth, we ask how it happened, as if we could replace death with life, exchange what is with what should be. From the depths of her grief Martha said to Jesus, Had you been here, my brother would not have died, but I know that everything you ask of God He will grant you, He granted you sight for the blind, healing for the lepers, speech for the mute, and all the other wonders that reside in your will and await your word. Jesus told her, Your brother will be raised from the dead, and Martha replied, I know he will rise to life on the day of resurrection. Jesus stood, an infinite strength took possession of him, in that moment he knew he could do anything, banish death from this body, restore it to life, give it speech, movement, laughter, even tears, but not of sorrow, and truly say, I am the resurrection and the life, he who believes in me, though he were dead, yet shall he live, and he asked Martha, Do you believe this, and she said, Yes, I believe you are the son of God who has come into this world. This being so, and with everything necessary in place, the power and the will to use that power, all Jesus has to do is stretch out his arms to that body abandoned by its soul, and say, Lazarus, arise, and Lazarus will rise from the dead, because it is the will of God, but at the very last moment Mary Magdalene placed a hand on Jesus' shoulder and said, No one has committed so much sin in his life that he deserves to die twice, and dropping his arms, Jesus went outside to weep.

LIKE AN ICY GUST OF WIND, THE DEATH OF LAZARUS EXTIN-
guished the zeal John had kindled in Jesus' heart, a zeal in
which serving God and serving the people had become one
and the same thing. After the first few days of mourning,
when the duties and habits of everyday life were gradually
resumed, Peter and Andrew went to speak to Jesus. They
questioned him about his plans, asked whether they should
go preach once more in the towns or instead return to Jerusalem for a fresh assault, the disciples were beginning to
feel restless, eager to be doing something, We didn't part
with our possessions, our work, and our families, they
complained, just to sit around all day. Jesus looked at them
as if in a blur and listened as if having difficulty recognizing their voices amid a chorus of discordant cries. After a
long silence he told them they must be patient, must wait
a little more, he still had some thinking to do, could sense
that something was about to happen which would decide
their fate once and for all. And he assured them he would
soon join them in the camp, which puzzled Peter and Andrew, for why should the two sisters remain alone when

the men still had not decided what to do, You don't need to come back for our sake, said Peter, who had no way of knowing that Jesus was torn between two duties, the first toward the men and women who had abandoned everything to follow him, the second here in this house, toward the sisters, duties similar yet opposed, like a face and a mirror. The ghost of Lazarus was present and refused to go away, he was in the harsh words spoken by Martha, who could not forgive Mary for having prevented their brother from being restored to life, nor could she forgive Jesus for not using his God-given power. Lazarus was present too in Mary's tears, for by delivering her brother from a second death she would have to live forever with the remorse of having failed to deliver him from his first. Like an enormous presence filling every space, Lazarus was also in Jesus' troubled soul, in which horses pulled in four directions, or four ropes coiled around winches were slowly tearing him apart, and the hands of God and the devil were amusing themselves, divinely and diabolically, with the remains.

The afflicted and diseased, hoping to be healed, came to the door of the house that had once belonged to Lazarus. Sometimes Martha would appear and drive them away, as if to say, There was no salvation for my brother, why should there be for you, but they would keep returning until they succeeded in reaching Jesus, who healed them and sent them away without once saying, Repent. To be healed is like being reborn without having died, for the newborn have no sins and therefore no need to repent. But these acts of physical rebirth, if I may call them that, although most merciful, left a sour feeling in Jesus' heart, for they were only a postponement of the inevitable, he who today leaves healthy and content will be back tomorrow with new woes that have no remedy. Jesus became so melancholy that one day Martha said, Don't you die on me, for that would be like losing Lazarus all over again, and Mary Magdalene, beneath the sheet they shared, whimpered like a wounded animal hiding in the dark, You need me now more than ever, but I cannot reach you if you lock yourself behind a door beyond human strength. Jesus answered Martha, saying, My death will embrace all the deaths of Lazarus, who will go on dying without ever being restored to life, and to Mary he said, Even if you cannot enter, do not abandon me, even if you cannot see me, stretch out your hand, otherwise I will forget life or it will forget me. A few days later he went to join his disciples, and Mary Magdalene went with him. I'll look at your shadow if you don't wish me to look at you, she told him, and he replied, I wish to be wherever my shadow is if that is where your eyes are. Loving each other, they exchanged these amorous phrases not only because they were beautiful and true, but because shadows were closing in, and it was time for the two to prepare themselves for the darkness of final absence.

News reached the camp that John the Baptist had been taken prisoner. Nothing was known except that he had been arrested and Herod himself ordered his imprisonment. Jesus and his followers were inclined to think that Herod had been provoked by John's prophecies about the coming of the Messiah, which he repeated everywhere between baptisms, He who comes after me will baptize you with fire, and between imprecations, O generation of vipers, who has warned you to flee from the wrath to come. Jesus told his disciples that they must be prepared for every manner of persecution, because rumors had been rife for some time that they were preaching the same message, it was only to be expected that Herod would put two and two together and pursue the carpenter's son, who claimed to be the son of God, and his followers, for this was the second and more powerful head of the dragon threatening to topple him from his throne. Bad news may not be preferable to no news, but it was received with equanimity by men who had been waiting and hoping for everything but lately had had to make do with nothing. They asked one another, and Jesus too, what they should now do, stand together and resist Herod's wickedness, scatter throughout the towns, or retreat into the wilderness, where they could eat wild honey and locusts, as John the Baptist had done before he left to herald the glory of Jesus and, by the looks of it, to meet a miserable end. Yet there was no sign of Herod's troops arriving in Bethany to slaughter more innocents, thus Jesus and his disciples were considering carefully the various alternatives when another report arrived, informing them that John had been beheaded and that his punishment had nothing to do with the coming of the Messiah or the kingdom of God, he had incurred Herod's wrath by speaking out against adultery, of which the king himself was guilty, having married Herodias, his niece and sister-in-law, while her husband still lived. The news of John's death brought tears to the eyes of men and women alike, and the entire camp mourned, but no one believed that he had been killed for the reason given. Judas Iscariot, whom, you may remember, John baptized, was beside himself with rage, he said that Herod's decision must have had a more serious motive, How can this be, he asked the company gathered there, including the women, John proclaims the Messiah is coming to redeem people, and they kill him for condemning an adulterous marriage between uncle and niece, when adultery has been common practice in that family since the time of the first Herod. How can this be, he railed, when God Himself ordered John to proclaim the coming of the Messiah, it must have been God, because nothing can happen without His willing it, so perhaps those of you who know God better than I can explain to me why He should allow His plan to go awry like this on earth, and before you tell me that God knows even if we don't, let me tell you that I insist on knowing what God knows.

A shiver passed through everyone listening, who feared the wrath of God would descend on this insolent fellow, and on themselves for not punishing such blasphemy at once. But since He was not present to deal with Judas, the challenge could only be taken up by Jesus, closest to the Supreme Being whose wisdom was called into question. Had this been another religion and the circumstances different, perhaps things would have gone no further than Jesus' enigmatic smile, which, however faint and fleeting, showed many things, surprise, benevolence, and curiosity, though the surprise was short-lived, the benevolence condescending, and the curiosity somewhat ironic. The smile, leaving, left behind a deathly pallor, a face that suddenly looked cadaverous, as if it had just beheld the image of its own fate. In a voice without expression Jesus finally said, Let the women withdraw, and Mary Magdalene was the first to rise to her feet. Then, after the silence had slowly formed walls and a ceiling to enclose them in the deepest cave on earth, Jesus said, Let John ask God why He allowed a man prophesying such good tidings to die for so paltry a reason. Judas Iscariot was about to speak, but Jesus raised his hand to silence him and said, I now see I must tell you what I learned from God, unless He Himself prevents me. Voices grew louder as the disciples began talking nervously among themselves, afraid of what they were about to hear. Judas alone maintained the attitude of defiance with which he had begun all this. Jesus told them, I know my future and yours, and that of generations to come, I know God's intention and design, and we will speak of these matters, for they concern all of us. Peter asked, Must we know what God has revealed to you, would it not be better to keep it to yourself. If He wished, God could silence me this instant. Then surely He doesn't care whether you remain silent or speak, it's all the same, and if He has spoken through you, He will continue to speak through you, even when you think you oppose His will,

as at present. Do you know, Peter, that I am to be crucified. Yes, you told me. But I didn't tell you that you too,
with Andrew and Philip here, will be crucified, and that
Bartholomew will be skinned alive, and that Matthew will
be butchered by barbarians, and that they will behead James
the son of Zebedee, and that another James, the son of
Alphaeus, will be stoned to death, and Thomas will be
killed with a lance, and Judas Thaddaeus will have his skull
crushed, and Simon will be sawed in half, these things you
didn't know, but I am telling all of you now. This was
received in silence, there is no further reason to fear the
future, once revealed, as if Jesus had finally told them, You
will die, and they replied in chorus, So what, we know
already. But John and Judas Iscariot have not heard what
will happen to them, so they ask, What about us, and Jesus
said, You, John, will live to a ripe old age and die of natural causes, as for you, Judas, keep away from fig trees,
because it won't be long before you hang yourself from
one. So we will die because of you, a voice asked, but no
one ever identified the person who spoke. Because of God,
answered Jesus. What does God want, asked John. He wants
a larger congregation than the one He has at present, He
wants the entire world for Himself. But if God is Lord of
the universe, how can the world belong to anyone but Him,
not just since yesterday or starting tomorrow but from the
beginning of time, asked Thomas. That I cannot tell you,
replied Jesus. But if you've kept all these things in your
heart for so long, why tell us now. Because Lazarus, whom
I healed, died, and John the Baptist, who prophesied my
coming, was killed, and now death has joined us. All creatures have to die, said Peter, and men like all the rest. Many
will die in future because of God and His will. If willed by
God, then it must be for some holy cause. They will die
because they were born neither before nor after. Will they
receive eternal life, asked Matthew. Yes, but the condition
should be less horrible. If the son of God has said what he

has said, he has denied himself, said Peter. You're mistaken, only the son of God is permitted to say these things, and what is blasphemy on your lips is the word of God on mine, replied Jesus. You speak as if we had to choose between you and God, said Peter. You will always have to choose between God and God, and like you and all other men, I am in the middle. So what do you want us to do. Help my death protect the lives of future generations. But you cannot oppose God's will. No, but I can at least try. You are safe because you are the son of God, but we will lose our souls. No, for if you obey me, you will still be obeying God. The edge of a red moon could be seen on the horizon of the distant wilderness. Speak, said Andrew, but Jesus waited until the entire moon, an enormous blood-red disk, had risen from the earth, and only then did he speak, telling them, The son of God must die on the cross so that the will of the father may be done, but if we replace him with an ordinary man, God will no longer be able to sacrifice His son. Do you wish one of us to take your place, asked Peter. No, I myself will take the son's place. For the love of God, explain yourself. An ordinary man, who has proclaimed himself king of the Jews to incite the people to depose Herod from his throne and expel the Romans from the land, and all I ask is that one of you go immediately to the Temple and say that I am this man, and if justice is swift, perhaps God's justice will not have time to stay man's, just as it did not stay the ax of the executioner who beheaded John. Everyone was struck dumb, but not for long, soon there was an outcry of indignation, protest, disbelief. If you are the son of God, then you must die as the son of God, a voice exclaimed, Having eaten your bread, how can I now denounce you, wailed another, Surely he who is destined to be king of the universe cannot wish to be king of the Jews, said one man, Death to anyone who dares stir from here to denounce you, threatened another. At that moment the voice of Judas Iscariot rang out above the din, I'll go. They seized him, were already drawing daggers from their tunics, when Jesus said, Leave him alone and do him no harm. He then rose and embraced Judas, kissing him on both cheeks, Go, my hour is yours. Without a word, Judas Iscariot threw the hem of his cape over one shoulder and vanished into the black night.

The Temple guards, accompanied by Herod's soldiers, came to arrest Jesus at first light. After surrounding the camp by stealth, a small detachment armed with swords and lances quickly advanced, and the soldier in command called out, Where is this man who claims to be king of the Jews. He called a second time, Let the man who claims to be king of the Jews come forward, whereupon Jesus emerged from his tent with a tearful Mary Magdalene and told them, I am king of the Jews. A soldier went up to him and tied his hands, whispering in his ear, Although now my prisoner, if you become my king, remember that I acted under orders from another, and should you ask me to arrest him, I'll obey you as I'm now obeying him. Jesus told him, A king does not arrest another king, a god does not kill another god, and that is why ordinary men were created, so that arrests and killings could be left to them. A rope was also tied around his feet to prevent him from running away, and Jesus said to himself, Too late, I have already fled. Then Mary Magdalene let out a cry as if her heart were breaking, and Jesus said, You will weep for me, and all you women will weep when such an hour be-falls your men or you yourselves, but know that for every tear you shed a thousand would have been shed in times to come had I not died thus. And turning to the soldier in command, he asked of him, Release these men with me, for I am king of the Jews, not they, and without further delay he stepped into the midst of the soldiers. The sun was up and hovering over the roofs of Bethany when the multitude, with Jesus in front, between two soldiers holding the ends of the rope tied around his wrists, began climbing the road to Jerusalem. Behind walked the disciples and their womenfolk, the men fuming, the women sobbing, but their anger and tears were of no avail. What are we to do, they asked themselves under their breath, should we throw ourselves on the soldiers and try to free Jesus, perhaps losing our lives in the struggle, or should we disperse before an order is also given for our arrest. On the horns of this dilemma, they did nothing, and continued following at a distance behind the retinue of soldiers. After a while they saw that the procession had come to a halt, and wondered if the order had been revoked, if now the ropes around Jesus' hands and feet would be untied, but one would have to be naïve to think any such thing. Another knot, however, has come untied, that of Judas Iscariot's life, there on a fig tree by the side of the road where Jesus will pass. Dangling from a branch is the disciple who carried out his master's last wish. The soldier leading the retinue ordered two soldiers to cut the cord and lower the body, He's still warm, observed one of them. Perhaps Judas Iscariot was sitting in the tree with the noose already around his neck, patiently waiting for Jesus to appear in the distance before letting go of the branch, finally at peace with himself now that he had done his duty. Jesus drew near, and the soldiers made no attempt to restrain him. He stood, staring at Judas's face twisted by sudden death. He's still warm, the soldier said a second time, and it occurred to Jesus that he could do for Judas what he had not done for Lazarus, bring him back to life, so that on some other day and in some other place the man might have his own death, remote and obscure, instead of being the haunting symbol of betrayal. But, as we know, only the son of God has the power to bring people back to life, not this king of the Jews who walks here, his spirit broken and his hands and feet bound. The soldier in command told his men, Leave the body there to be buried by the

371

people of Bethany, if the vultures don't eat it first, but check to see whether he is carrying anything of value. The soldiers searched but found nothing, Not a single coin, one of the soldiers said, and little wonder, for the disciple in charge of the community's funds is Matthew, who knows his job, having served as a tax collector in the days when he was called Levi. Didn't they pay him for his betrayal, asked Jesus, and Matthew, who overheard, replied, They wanted to, but he said he was in the habit of settling his accounts, and that's it, he has settled them. The procession continued, but some of the disciples lingered behind to stare in pity at the body, until John said, Let's leave it here, he was not one of us, but the other Judas, also called Thaddaeus, hastened to correct him, Whether we like it or not, he will always be one of us, we may not know what to do with him, but he will go on being one of us. Let's move on, said Peter, this is no place for us, here at the feet of Judas Iscariot. You're right, said Thomas, our place should be at Jesus' side, but that place is empty.

At last they entered Jerusalem, and Jesus was taken before the council of elders, high priests, and scribes. Delighted to see him there, the high priest said, I gave you fair warning, but you refused to listen, your pride won't save you now and your lies will damn you. What lies, asked Jesus. First, that you are king of the Jews. But I am king of the Jews. And second, that you are the son of God. Who told you that I claim to be the son of God. Everyone says so. Pay no heed to them, I am king of the Jews. So you admit you're not the son of God. How often do I have to tell you, I am king of the Jews. Be careful what you say, a statement like that is enough to have you sentenced. I stand by what I've said. Very well, you will appear before the Roman prefect, who is keen to meet the man who wishes to depose him and wrest these territories from Caesar's power. The soldiers escorted Jesus to Pilate's residence. The news had already spread that the man who claimed to be king of the Jews, the one who thrashed the money changers and set fire to their stalls, had been arrested, and people rushed to see what a king looked like when led through the streets for all to see, his hands tied like those of a common thief. And, as always happens, since not everyone is alike in this world, there were some who took pity on Jesus and some who did not, some said, Set the fellow free, he's mad, while some believed that punishing a crime serves as a warning to others, and there were as many of the latter as of the former. The disciples, mingling with the crowd, were distraught. You could easily recognize the women with them because of their tears, but one woman did not weep, she was Mary Magdalene, who grieved in silence.

The distance between the house of the high priest and the prefect's palace was not great, but Jesus thought he would never get there, not because of the hissing and jeering from the crowd, who thus expressed its disappointment with this sad figure of a king, but because he was anxious to keep his appointment with death, lest God look this way and say, What's going on, are you backing out of our agreement. At the palace gates, soldiers from Rome took charge of the prisoner, while Herod's soldiers and the Temple guards remained outside to await the verdict. Apart from a few priests no one was allowed to accompany Jesus into the palace. Seated on his throne, the prefect Pilate, for that was his name, inspected the man being led in, who looked like a beggar, with a heavy beard and bare feet, his tunic soiled with stains both old and new, the new from ripe fruit the gods created for eating rather than for showing hatred and leaving marks of shame. Standing before Pilate, the prisoner waited, his head erect, his eyes fixed on some point between himself and the prefect. Pilate knew only two kinds of culprit, the kind who lowered their eyes and the kind who stared in defiance, the first he despised, the second made him nervous, in either case he lost no time in passing sentence. But this man standing here seemed oblivious of his surroundings, and so self-assured that he might well have been a royal personage, in fact and in law, the victim of a lamentable misunderstanding who would soon have his crown, scepter, and mantle restored. Pilate finally decided the prisoner belonged in the second category, so he began the interrogation without delay, What is your name. I am Jesus son of Joseph and was born in Bethlehem of Judaea, but having lived in Nazareth of Galilee, I am known as Jesus of Nazareth. Who was your father. I just told you, his name was Joseph. What was his trade. Carpenter. Then would you care to explain how a carpenter named Joseph came to father a king. If a king can beget carpenters, why should a carpenter not beget a king. Hearing this, one of the priests intervened, Don't forget, Pilate, this man also claims to be the son of God. That isn't true, I am only the son of man, said Jesus, but the priest continued, Don't let him deceive you, Pilate, in our religion the son of man and of God are one and the same. Pilate waved his hand indifferently, If he had proclaimed himself the son of Jupiter, though he would not be the first, then this case would be of some interest, but whether he is or is not the son of your god is a matter of no importance. Then sentence him for claiming to be king of the Jews, and we'll leave satisfied. It remains to be seen if that will satisfy me, Pilate said sharply. Jesus waited patiently for this dialogue to end and the interrogation to resume. Who do you say you are, the prefect asked Jesus. I am who I am, king of the Jews. And as king of the Jews what do you hope to gain. All that a king can expect. For example. To govern and protect his people. Protect them from what. From whatever threatens them. And from whom. From whoever opposes them. If I understand you rightly, you would defend them against Rome. That is so. And in order to protect them, would you attack the Romans. There is no other way. And expel the Romans from

374

these lands. One thing follows from another. Then you are the enemy of Caesar. I am king of the Jews. Confess you are the enemy of Caesar. I am king of the Jews and will say no more. The high priest raised his hands to heaven in triumph, You see, Pilate, he confesses, and you cannot spare the life of one who publicly declares his hatred of you and Caesar. Sighing with exasperation, Pilate rebuked the priest, Be quiet, then turning to Jesus, asked him, Have you anything more to say. Nothing, said Jesus. Then I have no choice but to sentence you. Do as you must. How do you wish to die. I have already decided, How then, On the cross, Very well, you'll be crucified. Jesus' eyes sought and finally met those of Pilate, Can I ask a favor, he said. So long as it doesn't interfere with the sentence I've just passed. Would you have them put an inscription above my head which says who and what I am, for all to see. Nothing else. Nothing else. Pilate beckoned a secretary, who brought writing materials, and in his own hand Pilate wrote, Jesus of Nazareth, king of the Jews. Roused from his complacency, the high priest suddenly realized what was happening and protested, You mustn't write king of the Jews but Jesus of Nazareth who claimed to be king of the Jews. Annoyed with himself, Pilate regretted not having dismissed the prisoner with a warning, for even the most vigilant of judges could see that this fellow was no threat to anyone let alone to Caesar, and turning to the high priest, he told him dryly, Stop interfering, I have written what I have written. He signaled to the soldiers to remove the condemned man and requested water to wash his hands, as was his custom after passing sentence.

They led Jesus away and took him to a hill known as Golgotha. Despite his strong constitution, his legs soon weakened under the weight of the cross, and the centurion in charge ordered a man who had stopped to watch to relieve the prisoner of his burden. The crowd continued to jeer and shout insults, but now and then someone would utter words of compassion. As for the disciples, they walked in a daze. A woman stopped Peter and challenged him, You also were with Jesus of Galilee, but he denied it, I don't know what you're talking about, and tried to hide in the crowd, only to meet the same woman a second time, and once more she asked him, Were you not with Jesus, and again Peter denied it with an oath, I do not know the man. And since three is a number favored by God, Peter was challenged a third time, and for the third time he swore, saying, I do not know the man. The women went to Golgotha with Jesus, a few on either side, but Mary Magdalene, who stays closest of all, is not allowed to reach him, the soldiers push her away, just as they will make everyone keep their distance from the three crosses that have been put up, two already occupied by convicted men who howl with pain, the third now ready for occupation, standing tall and erect like a column that supports the sky. Ordering Jesus to lie down, the soldiers extend his arms on the crossbar. As they hammer in the first nail, piercing the flesh of his wrist between two bones, a sudden dizziness sends him back in time, he feels the pain as his father felt it before him, sees himself as he saw him on the cross at Sepphoris. Then they drove a nail through his other wrist, and he experienced that first tearing of flesh as the soldiers began to hoist the crossbar to the top of the cross, his entire weight suspended from fragile bones, and it was almost a relief when they pushed his legs upward and hammered another nail through his heels, now there is nothing more to be done but wait for death.

Jesus is dying slowly, life ebbing from him, ebbing, when suddenly the heavens overhead open wide and God appears in the same attire he wore in the boat, and His words resound throughout the earth, This is My beloved son, in whom I am well pleased. Jesus realized then that he had been tricked, as the lamb led to sacrifice is tricked, and that his life had been planned for death from the very

376

beginning. Remembering the river of blood and suffering that would flow from his side and flood the globe, he called out to the open sky, where God could be seen smiling, Men, forgive Him, for He knows not what He has done. Then he began expiring in the midst of a dream. He found himself back in Nazareth and saw his father shrugging his shoulders and smiling as he told him, Just as I cannot ask you all the questions, neither can you give me all the answers. There was still some life in him when he felt a sponge soaked in water and vinegar moisten his lips, and looking down, he saw a man walking away with a bucket, a staff over his shoulder. But what Jesus did not see, on the ground, was the black bowl into which his blood was dripping.